# Praise For Alexis Hall

"Hall is a dizzyingly talented writer, one likely to spur envy in anyone who's ever picked up a pen." —*Entertainment Weekly*

"Simply the best writer I've come across in years." —Laura Kinsale, *New York Times* bestselling author of *Flowers from the Storm*

# Rosaline Palmer Takes The Cake

"[Hall] crafts some of the most sparkling prose in contemporary romance...We give this fully baked concept our highest compliments." —*Entertainment Weekly*

"Hall does it again with this scrumptious, quietly subversive rom-com...Hilarious, heartwarming, and grounded, Rosaline's story proves that happy endings look different from person to person." —*Publishers Weekly*, Starred Review

"Hall seamlessly combines humor, romance, and drama to create a story that is intimately believable and at once cozy and sexy...The book combines sweet escapism and poignant cultural touchstones with well-crafted characters and hilariously familiar settings. Hall does it again with this culturally relevant, wonderfully escapist foray into the baking world. This is a must-buy for any library." —*Library Journal*, Starred Review

# A LADY FOR A DUKE

# A Lady
# for a Duke

## ALEXIS HALL

FOREVER

NEW YORK   BOSTON

Copyright © 2022 by Alexis Hall

Reading group guide copyright © 2022 by Alexis Hall and Hachette Book Group, Inc.

Cover design by Daniela Medina. Cover art by Judy York.
Cover images copyright © David Wagner Photography; Shutterstock
Cover copyright © 2022 by Hachette Book Group, Inc.

Forever
Hachette Book Group
1290 Avenue of the Americas, New York, NY 10104
read-forever.com
twitter.com/readforeverpub

First Edition: May 2022

Forever is an imprint of Grand Central Publishing. The Forever name and logo are trademarks of Hachette Book Group, Inc.

The publisher is not responsible for websites (or their content) that are not owned by the publisher.

The Hachette Speakers Bureau provides a wide range of authors for speaking events. To find out more, go to www.hachettespeakersbureau.com or call (866) 376-6591.

Library of Congress Cataloging-in-Publication Data

Names: Hall, Alexis J., author.
Title: A lady for a duke / Alexis Hall.
Description: First edition. | New York, NY : Forever, 2022. | Identifiers: LCCN 2021053687 | ISBN 9781538753750 (trade paperback) | ISBN 9781538753743 (ebook)
Subjects: LCGFT: Novels.
Classification: LCC PR6108.A453 L33 2022 | DDC 823/.92—dc23/eng/20211104

LC record available at https://lccn.loc.gov/2021053687

ISBNs: 978-1-5387-5375-0 (trade paperback); 978-1-5387-5374-3 (ebook)

Printed in the United States of America

LSC-C

Printing 1, 2022

# Content Guidance

Some characters who knew Viola before her transition refer to her deadname or use male pronouns when speaking about her in retrospect, but in keeping with the conventions of the period this is only in the form of surname and title.

Gracewood has a disability to which he and others will occasionally refer using ableist language. There are some references to his suicidal ideation, as well as references to drug and alcohol abuse.

Some language has been modernised for tone, voice and readability.

# A Lady for a Duke

Do not embrace me till each circumstance
Of place, time, fortune, do cohere and jump
That I am Viola

*Twelfth Night*

# CHAPTER 1

*1818, Devon*

I'm afraid that settles it." Having come to the end of the letter she had been reading, Lady Marleigh brandished it in a rather warlike fashion. "We shall have to intervene."

Her paid companion, Miss Viola Carroll, answered with a squawk. This had not been intentional. It was simply that she had driven her embroidery needle into the pad of her thumb.

"You do know," remarked Lady Marleigh dryly, "that contrary to popular belief needlepoint is not mandatory for our sex."

Viola shot her an amused look from beneath brows whose tilt, she knew, inclined to the devilish. "Well, forgive me for attempting to acquire some accomplishments."

"My dear, an accomplishment is inventing the hydraulic press or investigating the properties of nitrous oxide. It is not making a picture of a willow tree on cloth."

"Don't you think that's rather a matter of perspective?" Viola gazed upon her only mildly blood-spattered willow. "If putting pictures on cloth was the province of men, you may be quite sure it would be hailed as the miracle of the age."

That drew an appreciative chuckle from Lady Marleigh. "A fine point. And it is well taken."

"Unlike this fine point"—Viola put her needle aside—"which was very ill-taken indeed."

"To say nothing of ill-timed."

"I'm so sorry, Louise. I interrupted you with my self-impalement. What settles what? And in what must we intervene?"

Lady Marleigh, never one to have her thunder stolen without a fight, re-brandished the letter. "It's Miranda. I'm genuinely beginning to worry about her."

A long, helpless silence filled the blue drawing room, which was Lady Marleigh's preferred venue for drinking tea and brandishing correspondence. Viola's mother had usually spent her mornings in the garden room, but Louise felt strongly that the outdoors belonged outdoors and, truthfully, the difference was valuable. It reminded Viola that this was no longer her house. That her childhood belonged to someone she could no longer be. There was the past and the present and the bright, sharp line she had drawn between them.

"What's wrong?" she asked finally.

"She's turning into a gothic heroine. It really won't do."

Folding her hands in her lap, Viola attempted to still their trembling. "I... that is... I'm sure she's—"

"She's not. She's assuredly not." The paper crackled as it was, once again, waved in Viola's direction. "Listen to this: *My dearest Louise,* and so on and so forth, *hope this letter* and so on and so forth, *fondest affection for your family,* and so on and so forth, *we keep very quietly here, my brother preferring the company of silence and dark rooms to any that the human heart could afford him and having driven away, through infelicitous words, all but the most devoted servants and every neighbour within a radius of some two hundred miles.*"

"That does not seem like him," Viola murmured, in spite of herself. "His father, yes. But not him."

Lady Marleigh cast her an unreadable look before continuing, *"He still takes laudanum for the pain, and other spirits too, though I do not know what solace they are supposed to bring him. As for me, I find I am not discontented. After all, the country hereabouts, with its harsh skies and dark cliffs, is most picturesque."*

Viola winced.

"You see?" exclaimed Lady Marleigh. "No girl of…sixteen, is she now?"

"I believe seventeen."

"My point is, no young girl possessed of beauty, brains, and a dowry larger than the Prince Regent's backside should be reduced to taking an interest in the landscape."

"It's…it's a lovely part of the world."

"Viola"—Lady Marleigh's far-too-shrewd eyes pinned her in place—"I understand this can only be discomforting for you. But the de Veres are our friends and they need us."

"*Were* my friends. And they may need Lady Marleigh—they may even need someone I never was—but they do not need Viola Carroll."

A soft rustle as Lady Marleigh turned the letter to read the cross-hatching. *"I shall probably take up my watercolours again. I had a tutor, of course, as I had a tutor for nearly everything, but I never excelled. And now I may be grateful I have opportunity to practise. I do not think it will be as terrible as they say, to become an old maid. I am fortunate enough to have a portion of my own and I believe I will always have a home here. It is such a large house and I half fancy as the years pass my brother may entirely forget I share it with him."*

Viola put her head in her hands. "Very well. So Miranda is miserable. Why must you confront me with it?"

"Not to hurt you."

"I know that." Viola glanced up again, mustering the semblance of a smile. "You may be somewhat ruthless. But you have never been cruel."

To Viola's surprise, her sister-in-law actually blushed a little. "I'm grateful you recognise the distinction. I'm well aware that I'm not the easiest woman to like."

"I'd be lost without you. Asking for your hand in marriage is the only sensible decision my brother has ever made." It was an opinion in which Viola knew herself to be the minority. For all he was a second son, Badger's fortune was considerable, and his person accounted, by those better placed than Viola to judge, remarkable. Lady Marleigh, by contrast, was a small, unremarkable woman of peculiar habits and minimal wealth.

"Immodest though it may be to say it"—Lady Marleigh's lips twitched—"I agree."

Viola lifted a hand to her mouth to stifle a giggle that could only reflect poorly on her brother.

"I'm terribly fond of Badger," Lady Marleigh continued. "He's so biddable. And quite magnificent without his clothes on."

Retrieving her needlework, Viola tried to use her half-finished willow tree to distract herself from unwelcome images. "We are related. The former I knew. The latter I had no need to."

"Though it does rather make one worry for Little Bartholomew. We can only hope he's inherited my brains and his father's looks."

"And," asked Viola mischievously, "if it's the other way round?"

Lady Marleigh frowned. "Lord help us, I have no idea. I suppose we feed him to the nearest wolf and try again."

"If that's your solution for Bartholomew, I dread to think what you're proposing for Miranda."

"I propose we get her out of that dreadful old castle and into society."

"And then what?"

"Why"—Lady Marleigh gave Viola an *isn't it obvious* look—"a sensible marriage, of course."

"Could that not be simply exchanging one dreadful old castle for another?"

"It's a castle one chooses. And we women must cleave to our choices, Viola."

"Few know that so well as I." Viola's mouth curled irresistibly into a smile. "And cleave I shall, though, of course, I will never marry."

Lady Marleigh did not smile back. "Never have friends. Never marry. Is that really the life you want, Viola?"

"It is the life I must have. And still more to my liking than the one I was intended to live."

"You see the world too starkly, my dear."

"The world sees all things starkly," returned Viola, a little sharply. "That is rather the problem."

Fortunately, or unfortunately, Lady Marleigh was impervious to sharpness. "But you've already sacrificed so much. Title, lands, wealth, most of your rights, and the ability to be lauded for accomplishments other than needlepoint."

"I like needlepoint."

"Even so, with so much given up already, why give up things you could easily have?"

"Because I *can't* have them."

"Why not?"

"What do you mean, *why not*?" It was rare that Viola found herself lost for words. But her sister-in-law was renowned for achieving the unlikely. "Marriage is clearly out of the question. Even if I were to find a man who will see me as I am, the law and the church most certainly will not."

Lady Marleigh shrugged. "The church is a dumping ground for superfluous lordlings, what the law doesn't know won't hurt it, and men are more understanding than you think. After all, what is love but understanding?"

"And"—Viola lifted her brows into sardonic little arches—"Badger understands you, does he?"

"Well," admitted Lady Marleigh, with a smile, "not what I *say* much of the time. But he understands that I am the worst kind of arrogant, unsentimental, managing female, and he adores me."

"I'm not convinced our situations are comparable."

"Then you may well be a greater fool than your brother."

For a moment Viola was unsure whether to be offended— after all, Badger had once eaten an entire vase of silk peonies, and when questioned explained that he'd thought they were real— but then she laughed. "You do me too much credit."

"When it comes to measuring the folly of others, I am known for my magnanimity." If Viola had believed she had distracted Lady Marleigh from her purpose she should have remembered that Lady Marleigh on a mission was not easily diverted. She gave the letter its third brandishing of the day. "But *this*, Viola, this is a cri de coeur ineptly camouflaged as reassurance."

It was not something Viola could deny. "You should go to her."

"*We* should go to her."

"I was Gracewood's intimate, not hers. She will barely remember me."

There was the ominous pause of Lady Marleigh preparing to play her trump card. "It's not for her sake I'm asking you."

"Frankly, Louise, there's been a dearth of asking in this conversation."

"Well, I *am* your employer, so I'm not technically obliged to. But I'd far rather it was your choice."

Lady Marleigh had many qualities that seemed excellent when directed at others and quite the reverse when directed at Viola. "I'm not...I'm not ready," she said, wishing she sounded less pleading.

"It has been a year. I know this used to be...still is...your home. But you must leave it at some point."

Another of those ambiguous qualities as possessed by Lady Marleigh was a tendency to be right. Although in this case her being right did not make the prospect of moving beyond the small world Viola had built for herself any less terrifying. "True."

"And it will be easier," Lady Marleigh pressed on, "to go to Morgencald than London."

"And if I am recognised?"

"Then it will be by friends, in Gracewood's case, your closest friend, and far from idle tongues. Besides, it is unlikely that you will be. No-one will be looking for a dead soldier in a lady's companion." Lady Marleigh leaned forward conspiratorially. "The truth is, outside of sentimental novels, nobody looks at a lady's companion at all."

Viola could feel the beginnings of a headache gathering in her temples. This was too sudden and far, far too much. She had as good as forbidden herself to think of Gracewood for the past two years—for he belonged with the past she had surrendered to the only future she could bear. And what was it Miranda had said of him? That he had grown solitary? Careless? Perhaps even cruel?

Impossible.

That was not the man she knew. But then, he had not known her either.

"I think," she said, "I need some air."

And, gathering her skirts, she fled the room.

# CHAPTER 2

The Marleighs—who a less-documented part of their family history suggested may once upon a time have been wool merchants—had first risen to prominence during the sixteenth century, but it was not until the early eighteenth century that Viola's recently ennobled great-grandfather had acquired a piece of land in Devon and upon it the Stuart manor that would become Marleigh Court. It had taken some eighty years and two generations of Marleighs to transform that once modest family home into an enduring testament to Georgian taste: Palladian architecture, rococo interiors, and rolling acres of lushly landscaped parkland.

And this, too, Viola had abandoned. Rejected. Thrown away. Insofar as one could say that of a place one still inhabited. If someone had asked her yesterday, she would have said without hesitation that she did not regret it. Except today Lady Marleigh—however well-intentioned she might have been—had stirred up the past like it was Christmas punch, and now nothing seemed certain anymore.

Perhaps, Viola thought, as she made her way through the gardens and out into the park beyond, the paths as familiar to her as her own skin and bone, it was not the loss of her estate she mourned. Not exactly. It was what it represented. Legacy. Home. Family. Things she was, at last, liberated to want, but completely unable to have. There were times she could almost have laughed at how absurd it was. This endless dance of what was given and what was taken away, what felt like freedom, and what its cost had been. A children's game of barter: this piece of string for a marble, a sea-smoothed pebble for a peacock feather, your self for your future, your choices for the loss of them. After all, it was better to laugh than to weep.

Lost in her thoughts, she wandered further from the house than she intended. And it was not a good day for walking, being chill and blustery, without even the promise of brightness. The little woods that slanted down to the Plym were bare and bleak, just the squelch of decomposing leaves beneath her half-boots, and trees twisted in naked entreaty to an unremitting sky. But inclement weather did not deter Viola from her wanderings and nor, it seemed, did they deter Little Bartholomew, who was marching resolutely along the riverbank with the singular determination of aggrieved childhood.

Viola's immediate instinct was to run and catch him up in case he fell in and drowned, but that would have been contrary to Lady Marleigh's wishes. "A child who can't even make it past the age of seven without drowning itself in some brook or other," she would have said, "is likely to make a very annoying adult." And, to give Little Bartholomew due credit, he had managed to discharge his not-drowning duties thus far with admirable competence.

So instead of interfering with the course of nature, she made her way down to the riverside to see what the matter might be. Despite Louise's hopes, her son was showing little sign of inheriting his father's cheekbones, stature, or remarkable blue-purple eyes. In fact, he was taking strongly after his mother, being mousey in a number of areas. But also, from Viola's experience, in the realm of not being an unbelievable fluffhead.

"Hello, Bartholomew," she said. "Where are you going?"

Little Bartholomew continued to march. "I am running away."

He didn't seem to be running, more going for a strengthening stroll, but stubbornness was another trait that Little Bartholomew had inherited from his mother, and if he had resolved to run away, away he was liable to run. At least until something distracted him. "Why are you running away?"

"Because Mama is leaving and will not take me with her, and I think that very cruel."

"She is not leaving for very long," replied Viola, attempting what reassurance she could in pursuit of familial harmony.

"Where is she going?" asked Little Bartholomew.

"Northumberland."

"Why?"

That was complex. Too complex to explain to a child. Or perhaps that was an excuse. After all, she'd been similarly hesitant to explain who she was to Little Bartholomew, but Lady Marleigh had insisted. "Children are stronger than you think," she'd argued. "Besides, they haven't had years and years of silly people filling their heads with silly ideas about what you're meant to do or say or be." And she'd been right. He'd accepted Viola the same way he accepted that the sun rose or that audivi and auditum followed audio and audire.

Which was to say he'd asked *why* about sixteen times but ultimately been satisfied with "because that's the way it is."

"Your mother," she tried, "has had a letter from an old friend. You probably don't remember the Duke of Gracewood, do you?"

"No. But Mr. Dowling says the de Veres are an *illustrious connection for the family to possess.*"

Mr. Dowling was Little Bartholomew's tutor, and one of the dreariest men Viola had ever encountered. "He would. In any case your mother received a letter from the Duke's sister, Lady Miranda. And it seems…" Again Viola hesitated, wondering how best to explain so delicate a situation to Little Bartholomew without telling too many lies or too much truth. "I think," she went on carefully, "the Duke is very sad. And because he is sad, he is making his sister sad."

"Why is he doing that?" wondered Little Bartholomew aloud. "Is he a very wicked person?"

The question stung. No, not stung. Cut. For a moment Viola couldn't bear to answer. "No," she said at last. "No, he—I can think of no man less wicked. But I think perhaps I hurt him. A long time ago."

"Oh." For a moment Little Bartholomew seemed satisfied. Then he was immediately unsatisfied. "Are *you* a very wicked person?"

At this, she gave a half smile, for sometimes she thought she might be. "Dreadfully."

"That must be hard." Little Bartholomew looked grave. "Mr. Dowling tells me that terrible things happen to wicked people."

A chill came over Viola. A slow, sick chill that started below her stomach and ran up her back and over her shoulders. "I'm afraid that Mr. Dowling is wrong. Wicked people often prosper, and the good often suffer."

"Then should I be wicked?" asked Little Bartholomew. From the look in his eye, the idea held a certain appeal.

"It would make other people very sad," she warned him.

Little Bartholomew was briefly silent. Then he folded his

arms. "Well, other people are making *me* sad. That is why I'm running away."

Looking down, Viola did her best to strike an auntly tone. "One should not repay sadness with sadness."

Unfortunately, Little Bartholomew remained unconvinced. "Why? Would that not be equitable? Mr. Dowling says we should strive to be equitable."

Viola didn't quite have an answer for that. "Perhaps," she conceded. "But I suppose I believe that the world is always better with less sadness in it."

"And will Mama be very sad if I run away?" asked Little Bartholomew.

"She will."

Little Bartholomew stopped marching. "I should not like Mama to be sad. I should go to her and explain that I am safe and well, and tell her I am sorry for leaving."

If only, Viola reflected, it were that simple. But then it was, for a child. For a grown woman, with a lifetime of choices and regrets behind her, it was so much harder. "I think that's a good idea. Shall we return?"

Little Bartholomew nodded, and, still adrift in one too many pasts, Viola stooped in order to lift him into her arms. This, she quickly regretted. "You've grown," she told him as she set him back down. "A lot."

"I'm seven and a third," he replied. "Which is also seven and two-sixths, or seven and four-twelfths, which is the same as seven years and four months."

At least Mr. Dowling had taught him something. "Come on." She took his hand instead. "Let us not worry your parents more than we have to."

"When Mama goes to Northumberland"—Little Bartholomew pronounced the word very carefully, as if it were some distant country—"will you stay with me?"

It was wrong to be flattered by the affections of a seven-and-a-third-year-old. Viola was not, after all, his mother. Just his favourite aunt, although the competition for that title was somewhat limited, for she was also his only aunt. "I," she began, hardly knowing what words were going to come out of her mouth, "I don't think I can."

"Why not?" was Little Bartholomew's inevitable response.

And now they were back to complicated. "Because the Duke is my friend, and you help your friends if you can. Even if it is painful."

Little Bartholomew considered this. "See. I knew you were not wicked."

And now Viola considered *that*. "I hope I am not."

They made their way back to the house in thoughtful silence, Viola hand-in-hand with Little Bartholomew, who was now heir to the estate that would have gone to the son she would never have. He was a good boy, she thought, for all his occasional flirtations with wickedness. She expected he would grow up kind, like his mother and father. And she would be there to see it, for birthdays and Christmases and school holidays . A part of the family, if not at the heart of it. The spinster aunt in the guest bedroom. A small, solitary portrait in some dusty corner of the gallery for future generations to wonder about.

It was something. More than she could have hoped for. She had long told herself she could be content with that, imagining in turn a whole life for Gracewood—one where he grieved her and forgot her, and married and moved on. Became a better father than his own father had ever been to him. It would have been impossible, otherwise, to let him go.

But now there was the letter. And the letter was real. And it turned her imagined world into a thing of wisps and fragments. She did not know—could not know—what had become of Gracewood in their years apart. Only one thing was certain, the truth she had offered Little Bartholomew: that Gracewood was her friend, and she his, and that too was real.

Even before Waterloo, when everything else had been illusion.

# CHAPTER 3

The problem with long coach journeys—even putting aside the tedium and the discomfort—was that they gave one time to think. And the problem with thinking was that it furnished one with a comprehensive list of all the ways in which one's most recent decision was terrible.

"I think"—Viola lifted her head from where it lolled heavily against the squabs—"this was a terrible decision."

Lady Marleigh opened her eyes. "On the contrary, you've chosen to do as I suggested, which is always the best decision possible."

"Please don't make me do this."

"I'm not *making* you do anything."

"And how was I supposed to react when you told me that my oldest and dearest friend had sequestered himself in the country, lost to grief and laudanum."

"I think you'll find"—Lady Marleigh gave her a sharp look—"that what I said was *Miranda seems to have gone strange, she probably needs a season.* It was your mind that jumped straight to Gracewood."

"Perhaps," offered Viola, "he too needs a season."

It was a woeful attempt to be amusing, and Lady Marleigh denied it even the most cursory of smiles. "I understand this is difficult, but it's the right thing to do."

"How can it be? Miranda I barely know, and Gracewood I know too well."

"Too well for what?"

Twisting her gloved hands together in her lap, Viola wished for something to occupy them. Even a needle to drive into her palm. "Too well to be safe."

"Safe from his recognition?" asked Lady Marleigh, placidly. "Or his rejection?"

"Both. Either." Their separation had been a necessary wound; Viola was still waiting for it to feel like anything but a fresh one. "I cannot meet him as a stranger. But he has never known me as myself."

"Could this not be an opportunity for him to do so?"

"And if he does not wish to?"

"Then he's not worthy of it."

Viola made a noise she was not certain was ladylike. "That's the sort of thing it's easy to say. But much harder to live."

"Is it any harder than living in a world where your best friend thinks you're dead, and you have no idea what would happen were he to learn otherwise?"

"What do you imagine *could* happen?" The only thing worse, Viola realised, than being trapped in a small moving box was being trapped in a small moving box full of Lady Marleigh's opinions. "We cannot be friends as we once were. He could find me repulsive or absurd or simply incomprehensible. And, even if he does not, I may still have destroyed for both of us the memory of everything we used to be."

"Or"—to be well acquainted with Lady Marleigh was to understand that fortitude was not always a virtue—"he could simply be happy you're alive."

"And then what? Do we go riding? Do we wrestle and fence and shoot, and bathe naked together? Does he take me to brothels and gambling hells, and drink with me late into the night, while telling me of the women he woos?"

Lady Marleigh blinked. "I'm sure there must be other options."

"What other options? Men and women are permitted to interact in three ways: marriage, ruination, and polite indifference."

For a moment, Lady Marleigh was silent.

"Well?"

"Give me a minute. I'm just trying to think of counterexamples."

Viola gave her a minute.

"Oh dear," said Lady Marleigh finally, "that's a bit dreary, isn't it? And I suppose one and two are totally off the cards?"

"Entirely. And three would be intolerable." A pause, as Viola contemplated the possibility of such a life. "For both of us, I think. When we were young, Gracewood and I were closer than—as close as two people can possibly be. To be *aware* of one another but kept apart by station and society and…and all that goes with it. What will happen when he falls in love, when he marries? If I am *there*, watching from just over your shoulder as is proper for a lady's companion. If he *knows* that I am there? It would cast a shadow over his future happiness and it would—" Viola lost control of her voice, heard the tears in it, tasted them, salt-bitter, at the back of her throat. "Louise it would *break* me. I cannot countenance it, and I cannot risk it."

Lady Marleigh had that look she got when she had to deal with somebody having a lot of emotions at her. A sort of sincere expression of helpful bafflement, as one might wear if a Frenchman started asking one a series of complicated questions very fast in his native language. "I suppose you're right," she said, ever reluctant to admit another person could be.

This was about as close as Viola ever got to winning a conversation with Lady Marleigh. Not that conversation, strictly speaking, was a competitive sport and not that it felt, on this occasion at least, very much like winning at all.

Turning slightly, she let her gaze drift towards the window. The light was a fleet-foot creature in this part of the country, bold as the sun rose and set, and skittishly silver between. She had not expected so ephemeral a thing to bear such a weight of familiarity: as recognisable to her as the rough grey-green hills and the muddy swirl of the clouded sky, or the shimmer at the furthest edge of horizon that promised an ocean.

She had spent many summers here, and some winters too, images of the past crowding close around her like dreams too close to daybreak. She remembered the heaviness of stone. The dizzying swoop of vaulted ceilings. The edge of cold that never quite faded and the silence that layered the long halls, as thick as grave dust. She remembered the way the mist would roll in from the sea, smothering all in grey. How the vastness of the world blurred to nothing from the top of Morgencald's highest towers. And she remembered Gracewood, a severe angel even then, with eyes that saw only duty, and a mouth that none but she made smile.

It was full dark by the time they reached the gatehouse, deeper shadows sweeping through the carriage as they crossed between the two great towers and beneath the arch that spanned them.

"Good heavens," exclaimed Lady Marleigh, craning her neck as she peered out the window. "They don't make them like this anymore."

"Indeed no. Apparently it's never been taken, though many have tried, including Warwick the Kingmaker."

"I would not have thought you a historian, Viola."

At that, she laughed. "Nor has any person who has ever attempted to teach me history. But I can recall a little about Morgencald from Gracewood. He, of course, was required to know everything about it."

Lying on the banks of the Cam, the water made mirror-bright from the sun and softly greened by the reflection of the willow trees, he had told her once that his earliest memory was standing in the Faire Chamber before his father, reciting the names of his ancestors. He wasn't sure if it was on that occasion, or another, that he forgot Claudius de Vere (1575–1623). But he never forgot him again. Nor Tiberius de Vere (1100–1156), or Justin de Vere (1316–1371).

And neither had Viola, having seen when they had swum together the pale, upraised lines across Gracewood's shoulders: a price paid in pain for every name he missed. It took longer than Viola would have wished for the memory to wane. For the past to return her to the present, and to her present self.

"At any rate," Lady Marleigh was saying, as she disembarked, "let us hope a helmet does not drop on us."

Still a little intimidated by the potential for disaster offered by skirts and heels and carriage steps, Viola achieved a wobbly descent and joined her sister-in-law in the courtyard of Castle Morgencald. "You needn't worry. There's no sorcery here."

Just duty and silence, pride and loneliness.

Lady Marleigh paused for a moment, gazing around her at the grass and gravel and the endless stone. The keep itself was settled on a plinth like a monarch upon a throne, its walls some four feet thick, and its stonework mottled pink and grey and green through various restoration efforts down the years. Viola, of course, did not have to look. She already knew how it felt to stand here, to be insignificant among the centuries.

But, then, she had also stood on the battlements, spitting cherry pips into the clouds. Slid with Gracewood on stockinged feet the length of the King's Hall. Made him jump with her from the top of the highest cliff into the icy grey waves beneath. Far from his father's gaze, they had dared to laugh, and no-one had dared rebuke them.

Lady Marleigh, meanwhile, may not have had the advantage of Viola's irreverent memories to shield her against the weight of time, but the castle had not been built that could make her question her own significance. Succeeding where Warwick had failed, she straightened her bonnet and marched up the steps to the door—an iron-studded monstrosity wide enough, so it was claimed, to admit three riders abreast. Seizing the knocker, she beat it vigorously against the heavily scarred wood. And…

…received no answer.

Once, this place had housed an army. A quiet, vanishing army who served and waited and obeyed with the unnerving efficiency of automata. In a strange way, the stillness was worse. It reminded Viola of the shells she sometimes used to find on the beach below the castle, when you turned them over with your foot and discovered only a smooth hollow where once there had been *something*.

"Gracewood," remarked Lady Marleigh, "should fire his butler."

The narrow, arched windows that irregularly dotted the keep were mostly dark. "Recall Miranda's letter. Perhaps he already has."

At which point, with a growl like a beast ill-advisedly stirred from slumber, the door swung slowly inwards. On the threshold, candle in hand, was a servant, older than in Viola's memories, grey scattered through his hair, and his eyes dark with weariness.

"Janner?" she said, forgetting herself. "Why are you in the main house?"

He glanced from her to Lady Marleigh, in evident confusion. "Who are—how do you—"

"I am the Viscountess Marleigh"—being all of five foot had never stopped Lady Marleigh from looking down her nose when she wanted to—"and you are a terrible butler."

"That's because," Viola put in quickly, "he's a groom."

Janner's expression grew wary. "Have we met, Miss? And we weren't expecting company."

"That's not my problem." Before the poor groom could say another word, Lady Marleigh had not so much sailed as launched herself like an armada past him. "I wrote to your master several days ago."

Viola hurried after her into the entrance hall, which—with the fire little more than embers—was not much more welcoming than the courtyard. Not that this was so very different to her memories of the place. Morgencald had been built to withstand everything, including change.

If Lady Marleigh was at all concerned, she did not show it, although she did think better of removing her gloves. "My companion and I will require rooms to be made up for us," she said. "And I would like some tea."

Janner stared at her.

"Lady Miranda, I presume, is in bed. But see that the Duke is fetched. And do shut the door—you're letting in the, well, more cold."

Taking pity on the old groom, Viola put her weight behind the door and pushed it closed. The speck of light from Janner's candle suddenly seemed a firefly in the shadowy vastness of the hall.

"His Grace," said Janner slowly, "is not to be disturbed."

"He will be very disturbed indeed if he isn't here to greet me in"—Lady Marleigh flourished an imaginary timepiece—"approximately the next ten seconds."

"Lady Marleigh is an old friend of the family," Viola tried to explain.

Janner frowned. "Lady Marleigh? But the Viscount wasn't married."

"This," she said firmly, "is the wife of the *present* Viscount Marleigh."

A soft "oh" of understanding stirred Janner's candle flame. "If it's not speaking out of turn to say, we were all very fond of His Lordship. Fair broke His Grace's heart to come back from the war alone."

Viola's mouth had gone dry, but the need to give an appropriate answer was alleviated by Lady Marleigh, who simply said, "Thank you."

"Bit of a wild one, of course. Still, Cook's always said the master needs some wildness in his life."

The walls were leaning over Viola like jeering strangers.

"You're very kind," said Lady Marleigh briskly. "However, if I don't get some tea directly I will commit murder. I realise you're not an officially designated butling person, but do you think you could find someone capable of making me some and someone else capable of bringing it to me? And, in the meanwhile, I shall rustle up the Duke for myself."

A nervy shudder ran through Janner's whole body. "Please, m'lady. He's not fit for... he's not—"

"He's not *what*?"

"Not been the same," finished Janner, half-pleadingly.

Something—an instinct, perhaps a parting gift from her time with the 95th, or a sense of recognition, sunk heart-deep into her skin—made Viola glance towards the staircase. And there she saw him: indistinct among the shadows and the years, leaning heavily upon a cane, and in his hand—

Seizing Lady Marleigh's arm, she dragged them both to the ground the second before the gun discharged. The world became a tangle of noises: her sister-in-law's startled exclamation, the crack of the bullet—nowhere near them, Viola was relieved to note—its fading echo, rattling against stone, and Janner's muffled curse.

And Gracewood himself, his voice harsh from drink and slurred from narcotics: "Am I to have no peace?" His eyes seemed to both look at and through Viola. "Why won't you leave me alone?"

Then came the clatter of the gun against the floor. And he was gone.

"Correct me if I'm wrong," said Lady Marleigh after a moment or two, still crouched beneath Viola's protecting arm. "But did the Duke of Gracewood just try to shoot us?"

When Viola had read—or rather heard Lady Marleigh read— Miranda's letter, she had feared the worst but allowed herself to hope that it was at least in part the exaggerations of a young girl with a romantic spirit. But now it was clear that if anything the opposite had been true. "Well," she said carefully, "he more shot... *at* us."

"I'm not reassured." Lady Marleigh's tone was dry, although she was shaking very slightly.

"I do not think we were in danger."

"I'm not reassured," repeated Lady Marleigh. "What in God's name was he thinking?"

To that, Viola had no answer. She could not still quite believe it had been Gracewood. He had always felt the burden of his duty, certainly, but he had never been like this: haunted and lost, seeking refuge in violence like a cornered dog. "I must go to him."

"My dear, is that wise?"

It had not been wise to come in the first place. But she'd had no choice then—not truly, and not because of Lady Marleigh—and she had no choice now. For all she had said in the carriage, for all her fears and for all the risk of it, for all she stood to lose—for all they *both* stood to lose—Gracewood needed her. Their whole lives they had been there for one another, from the playing fields of Eton and Cambridge to the killing fields of Salamanca and Waterloo. She had left him only once, and only because the vicissitudes of war had torn her from him.

She could not abandon him again.

# CHAPTER 4

His head was full of mist. It used to comfort him. It used to soften the edges of the raw, empty places of his world, so he didn't cut himself bloody on them. It used to help him forget. But the memories were too strong, the good and the bad, running together like the blood and the mud in the rain at Waterloo.

"Too many ghosts," he told the figure that stood in the doorway.

Her mouth quirked upwards, eerily familiar as only phantoms could be, promising recognition and offering only heartbreak. "Perhaps if you took less laudanum, you would see fewer ghosts."

"Strange advice for a ghost to give."

"I'm not a ghost."

He lowered himself into a chair by the fire, pain clanging distantly from his leg. "You had better be. Otherwise I just shot a guest, and I'm not so lost to humanity as to think that's acceptable."

"In fairness, you shot . . . *at* a guest. Two guests, actually."

The spirit was resolving itself into the shape of a woman, tall and slender, dark haired and dark eyed. Her mouth a piece of laughter.

"*Two* guests?" he asked, with the easy curiosity of the inebriated.

"Yes, Lady Marleigh. And me."

"But you're not real. And there is no Lady Marleigh, because there is no Lord Marleigh. He died. Two and a half years ago. On the eighteenth of June." He scraped out a laugh, one that tasted as bitter as it sounded. "An easy date to remember."

"She's Bartholomew's wife. That makes her Lady Marleigh. Miranda stayed with them, remember, when... when you bought your commission."

He gritted his teeth against an anguish no opiate could soothe. "I was a damn fool."

"You were noble. And brave."

"No." When he shook his head, the room spun. And the ghost watched him through the eyes of the lost. "It was vanity. Not wanting to be like my father, leaving nothing behind but a name."

"You've always been more than that."

He had not seen her move but, glancing down, he found her kneeling by his chair. Her cheek felt warm against his fingertips. And the things she knew, the ghosts always knew. But on most nights they used that knowledge as he had once used a rifle: to maim and bloody and murder. "You're kind tonight. You're not usually so kind."

"Maybe tonight I'm telling you the truth."

"The truth isn't kind. Why do you think I...?" He gestured at the library, its guttering fire, and its chaos of bottles. "Why do you think I flinch so profoundly from the facing of it?"

"I think you blame yourself for something beyond your control."

"He would not have been there, if not for me."

And perhaps neither of them had truly left. Waterloo waited for him, behind his eyes, more vivid—more real—than anything he had seen since, the farmhouse and the sand-quarry, and the road where so many men had fallen that their bodies were nothing but a churn of blood and flesh beneath the artillery wheels.

"You are not responsible," she was saying, "for your friend's choices."

"I left him to die."

"You were injured." She raised a hand to her mouth, as though she had spoken unguardedly. Truly, she was a very polite ghost.

"I went back. I looked for him."

For hours, with the leg that they had insisted should be amputated burning like hellfire, surrounded by the groans of dying men and the bewildered torment of dying horses, most of the corpses already stripped of clothes, valuables, even their teeth. Rendered interchangeable: dirty skin and broken limbs, and Marleigh—that wicked boy, his laughing friend—unbearably among them. That was when he'd understood. All those bodies were someone's friend. Someone's brother. Someone's Marleigh. He'd not only lost, he'd taken. And ever since, when the dead clustered close about him, in their blue coats and bullet wounds, they always wore his Marleigh's face.

A tear landed on the back of his hand, as abstract as a raindrop. "I couldn't find him," he finished.

"I'm sorry," whispered the ghost. "I'm so sorry."

He blinked. Water in his eyes. Mist in his head. The thunder of the guns. This was . . . not how it was. Not how it was supposed to be. There was supposed to be anger, hatred, grief. He was a coward and a failure. He had sacrificed everything he most valued, all to spite a man who had never valued him. Everything for nothing. And devils laughing in the corners of his mind. Why would a ghost be sorry? And how was her skin so soft? He caught a lock of her hair, rough-smooth, like the wrong side of silk.

She turned her head away a moment, the glisten of moisture

on her cheeks. "Some things are beyond even a duke's control. But it does not follow they are without design."

"Design?"

"Reason then—even if we cannot see it."

"There is no design in war." He let out a strange sound—half laugh, half sob. "Nor reason. And no reason why a man like Marleigh should die, while I did not."

"Your friend would not want you to think so."

"I doubt he'd want to be a corpse either, rotting in some foreign field."

That made her shudder. "Not all are meant for the life they are given. Perhaps there could have been some mercy in what happened—beyond your understanding."

"My understanding? I knew him better than my own soul. He may well have been my soul, for what little I am worth without him." He paused, her hair still coiled about his fingers. The heat of her body was a soft constant against his leg. And, over the sourness of drink and the sickness of poppies, he thought he could catch the faintest scent of gardenias rising from her skin. "You, madam, are no ghost."

She pulled away a little—enough to make him abruptly and inappropriately, considering she was a stranger to him, miss her closeness. "There's no need to sound so upset about it. I did try to tell you."

"Oh God." He dropped his head into his hands for a moment, trying to banish at least some of the clouds of intoxication that still clung to him. "Who are you?"

"Viola Carroll. I'm...I'm Lady Marleigh's companion."

"What are you doing here?" Ordinary questions. A fragile

bulwark against what he was beginning to suspect might be an extraordinary situation.

"She was concerned about Lady Miranda."

"No." This was not right. None of this was right. If this woman was real, then this whole scene was thinkable. "What are you doing *here*? In this room? On your own with a crippled drunken madman? Who, unless I misremember, fired a gun at you?"

"You are truly inebriated beyond hope if you think your shot came anywhere near us."

The possibility of laughter twisted inside him like a blade. "Miss Carroll, you have nerves enough to shame a soldier."

"Let's not make too much of my courage. After all, you left your firearm behind."

"Yes," he agreed. "That does offer something of an obstacle to my shooting you again."

"And not to put too fine a point on it"—her lips curled teasingly upwards—"I'm not sure you have faculties enough to re-load it."

"I could have another."

Her head tilted enquiringly. "Do you?"

"No. I mean, yes. Armoury full of them. And swords. But, on my person, no."

"Good. I think the last thing your person needs right now is any kind of weapon."

He gazed at her, bewildered, lost, helplessly enthralled. Discourteous, of course, to stare. But that was the least of tonight's improprieties. And how could he not? When her mouth was made for laughing. And the darkness of her eyes was as restless as the sea at midnight. And down the side of her neck trailed a comet's tail of freckles. "Who are you?" he asked again. As if that knowledge could make sense of anything.

"Still Viola Carroll. Still not a ghost."

"You shouldn't be alone with me."

"We've already established you're in no position to do me any harm."

"Your reputation, Miss Carroll." He attempted a gesture and sent a glass spinning from the arm of his chair to the floor. Thankfully the rug ensured it did not shatter.

"I'm a paid companion of no fortune and little beauty. My virtue is not likely to be much endangered. Besides I was…" The slightest pause. "I was concerned for you."

"Most people in your position would have been concerned for themselves."

"Well, that's just a lack of imagination. I don't think we normally drink ourselves into stupors and greet our visitors at gunpoint to demonstrate our deep contentment with life."

"I wasn't trying to demonstrate anything," he murmured. "I wanted to be left alone."

"By guests or ghosts?"

"Both. I'm not fit for company."

"Are ghosts terribly discerning in that regard?"

Another laugh, this one catching painfully in his throat. "No. That's the problem. They're like great-aunts. Can't get rid of them, no matter what you try."

"Is that what you're hoping to accomplish?"

It was simplest to answer yes. Miss Carroll was, after all, not a ghost. And he was slowly becoming aware of the fact that it was only the alcohol in his system keeping utter mortification at bay. God, what had he said to her? He even thought he might have wept, like a schoolboy on the first night of term. He wouldn't—couldn't—compound that weakness by admitting why he had been on his way to the library that night, with one of a pair of duelling pistols in his hands and enough laudanum to drown what was left of his world.

"Perhaps then," she suggested, "if you cannot disperse the ghosts, you must find a way to live with them."

She made it sound so easy, as easy as it had once seemed with a companion at his side. "I don't know how to live. I never did."

"I think that might be nonsense." She gave him half a smile, then took it away again, as though she had crossed some line that Gracewood didn't understand and couldn't see.

"That's what he would have said. But it all came so effortlessly to him."

"What did?"

There was a note in her voice—some sharpness or sorrow—that might have checked him, had he been less shipwrecked upon laudanum's barren shores. "I'm not sure how to explain. There are so many forces that would shape us, or break us, or twist us, or re-make us: friends, family, 'what is done,' duty, history, expectation. And somehow Marleigh always found a way to be himself."

A stir of skirts as Miss Carroll spun abruptly away. "Perhaps we should not make assumptions about what does and does not cost other people effort."

"I've offended you."

She made a dismissive sound. "There is no use taking offence at drunkards."

"Nevertheless," he said, more out of politeness than because he understood her reaction, "I beg your pardon."

"It doesn't matter." She turned back, her cheeks a little flushed but her expression set. "Besides, if he meant so much to you, this

friend of yours, how do you think it would make h—" her words
faltered momentarily "—make him feel, to see you this way?"

"It is one of my few consolations that he cannot."

"But *if* he could?" she asked, something searching in her tone
and in her eyes. "Is this what Marleigh would want for you?"

It was not a conversation he could have with a stranger, at
least, not tonight, not when he was barely in his right mind. He
lifted a shoulder in something that might—had he been sober—
have been a shrug. "Non sum qualis eram."

"To hell with Horace."

There was a pause as he considered this. "You are familiar
with Latin, unafraid of guns, and unafraid of me. Are these usual
qualities in a lady's companion?"

The look she cast him at that was oddly defiant. "I am also
quite proficient at needlepoint."

"I wouldn't doubt your proficiency at anything."

"And"—a flush touched her cheeks—"I apologise for my language. It was not ladylike."

"I'm in no position to take you to task for it."

"Because you're too inebriated?"

"Because"—and here his tone grew rueful—"I've been far
from gentlemanly."

Her mouth quirked. "Oh, I'm not so sure. Is not running
around with guns and shouting the very essence of masculinity?"

"None I would aspire to."

"And yet…"

"Miss Carroll," he said softly, torn between the sting of mortification and something close to amusement, "you are unkind."

"You know I do not mean it."

And, to his surprise, he did.

"Besides," she went on, "I do not believe you're nearly as lost to yourself as you fear."

He wondered if she was teasing him again, but a glance at her face revealed only an unexpected sincerity. "What convinced you? The laudanum? The rambling? The inability to distinguish between what is real and what is imaginary?"

"The...the way you speak of your friend. Marleigh wouldn't have loved you had you not been worthy of it."

"Don't say that." Fresh tears made his eyes burn, but thankfully this time they did not fall. "I led him into hell, and left him there, and sometimes—God forgive me—I'm half-relieved I did, because what would he think of me now?"

There was a pause, heavy among the silence of unread books and empty bottles. Then Miss Carroll reached out a slightly unsteady hand and brushed a lock of hair back from his brow. He had meant to pull away, but there was something in her touch that stilled him. An instinct, trust perhaps, or familiarity—unearned but undeniable. "He'd think you need to drink less and sleep more. Be gentler with yourself. And, perhaps, take a bath?"

"Yes, that does sound like him."

"And no wonder you don't feel the way you might hope to. You look as though you've been living with wolves."

He felt the heat of a blush rise to his cheeks, and it was strange, this small new shame, amid the vastness of the old. "I wasn't expecting company."

"Lady Marleigh did write to say we were coming."

"I may have neglected my correspondence of late."

A rogue dimple, untwinned, glimmered at the edge of her mouth. "Oh, may you?"

"And my secretary, like the rest of my staff, is probably afraid of me."

"They're likely afraid *for* you. It's not the same thing."

"No, it's worse. I'm the head of this household. People are depending on me for their livelihoods, and I've abandoned them too."

"As far as I can see, the only person you've abandoned is you." She dropped to her knees again by the side of his chair, her eyes seeking his and holding his gaze so steadily, so surely, he could not look away. "You don't deserve your ghosts, Gracewood. Your place is with the living."

He brushed his fingertips over the shadows that sharpened the angles of her face. And for a moment he—

No. That was laudanum. That was madness. All he had seen tonight was his own guilt. "You should rest, Miss Carroll. It's late and I am not in command of my senses."

It almost seemed as though she would speak again. But she just nodded and stood, her hand rising self-consciously to touch the curve of her cheek and jaw where he'd touched her. And then she was gone, leaving only the faintest trace of gardenia behind to reassure him she hadn't been a phantasm after all.

# CHAPTER 5

Viola—tormented by her own ghosts—did not sleep well that night. She gave up on the attempt a little before dawn, enjoying the strange sense of respite that often accompanied such decisions. Weariness beat its batwings at the back of her skull, but lying in bed, full of fidgets and anxieties both nebulous and specific, was infinitely worse than being tired.

She dressed in dust-tarnished light in an unfamiliar room. Yesterday her footsteps had tried to take her to her old one, but thankfully she'd caught herself and put a stop to such foolishness. Bad enough that she'd spoken to Gracewood with such familiarity. She hardly knew what she had been thinking. But the truth was, there'd been no space for thought. She'd simply reacted with all the impulsiveness of love and dismay in finding her oldest, dearest friend so lost. And the things he'd said, unknowing, had ripped her apart like vultures.

He believed he'd left her to die. When, instead, it was she who'd left him to wander, in grief and guilt, a battlefield of corpses.

He believed he'd failed her. But how could he, when he'd never known who she was?

He believed he was a coward. And what, then, did that make her?

She'd never allowed herself to question whether the choices she'd made had been right. They'd simply been necessary, whatever their price. It was different, though, now that she understood that the cost was not just hers to bear. Not enough to make her doubt, but enough to make her hurt. After all, she had grieved for the same friendship. How could she ever have believed she would be doing so alone?

The strange room was starting to press upon her, struggling to find a place among her memories. And her mind would not quiet. Would not stop with its questions. Its unsalvable concerns. Its formless regrets. She performed enough of her toilette to make herself presentable, wrapped a shawl about her shoulders, and slipped out into the corridor.

Fresh silence settled over her, the shadows as thick as the stone. Perhaps, on the edge of hearing, she could catch the distant activity of whatever servants remained, or perhaps she only remembered it. She was not particularly conscious of her direction, but still she knew, somehow, where she was going. Where she wanted to go.

The climb to the top of the north tower was steeper and took longer than she remembered. Heels didn't help, nor skirts, nor—she suspected, somewhat ruefully—being older. But she made it, even though her legs ached, and her lungs burned, and there was a blister developing on the back of her heel. And it was exactly where she needed to be: open sky and fading stars, horizon all round, and the flat dark mirror of the sea gleaming up at her.

Resting her hands on the parapet, she was glad enough just to breathe. The air that swept in from the ocean was mercilessly cold, and sharp with salt, and she let it swirl through her, scouring away the past like rust from a neglected blade. How long she stood there, she wasn't sure. Long enough for the grey world to ignite anew and the waves to arch their gilded backs beneath the rising sun.

"Now you're king of the castle," said a voice behind her.

She spun, full of nameless dread. "What?"

"Well"—Gracewood gave her a crooked smile—"queen of the castle. My apologies...Miss Carroll isn't it? I've startled you."

"Oh...I...yes." He had meant nothing by it. Of course, he had meant nothing by it. Her hand went to her throat, where her pulse was still beating wildly, beneath the coral choker she had, at least, shown sense enough to put on before she left her room. What was it about this place that made her reckless? Normally she took such care with herself, and yet here she was in a dress chosen for comfort rather than art, with her hair unbound, and only a shawl to protect her.

If the duke found anything untoward in her appearance, he was too polite to show it. "You rather surprised me also. I've not climbed these towers for years."

He looked better than he had the night before—faint praise though that was—if somewhat taxed by the ascent. His grip was tight upon the handle of his cane as he limped forward, his sweat-speckled skin too pale, and his mouth tight with pain. But he had dressed with more care than she had and his eyes were clear. In fact, had it not been for the length of his hair and the wildness of his beard, she might almost have been able to pretend—

Pretend what? That the people they used to be stood upon this parapet?

She did not want that either.

And yet it was still terrifying to stand before him with nothing between them, no shadows nor candlelight nor laudanum dreams.

For a moment, she was caught in the silence, a fly struggling fruitlessly in the twisting web of it. *See me*, she wanted to tell him. *Show me how to be brave. Let me help you.* But his gaze was distant, nothing but civil. Lady Marleigh had been right again: She was a lady's companion now. Even to Gracewood—the man who had once been everything to her—she would never be more than that. "Should you be up here?" she asked.

His mouth turned up wryly. "I don't see why not. It's my castle."

"No, I meant..." Still too discomposed for lucidity, she gestured awkwardly to his leg.

And immediately wished she hadn't, as a look of mingled defiance and shame crossed his face. "Ah. Well. Had I consulted a medical professional, they would likely have advised me to sit quietly in a chair for the rest of my life. But I did not, and thus retained liberty of my own body."

"I'm sorry. That was a presumptuous question."

"No, I'm sorry." He braced his back against one of the merlons and stretched his leg cautiously. "I know you intended only kindness. And I've given you no reason to trust my judgement."

"That's true," she agreed.

Which had the desired effect of making him laugh, when it was no more her place to make him laugh than it was to ask him presumptuous questions. But perhaps it was something they could still do together. Perhaps it was the last thing she could give him.

"In point of fact," he went on, "I came rather to regret my stubbornness. But when one has made it to the halfway point of a spiral staircase, going on and going back become interchangeably unappealing."

"I experienced something very similar on my own journey.

Only in my case it was inspired by what I'm sure is a pitifully small blister."

He regarded her gravely. "There are few things in the world more misery-inducing than blisters."

"I understand grapeshot is also quite unpleasant."

"I would be glad enough never to encounter it again."

"Of course," Viola went on thoughtfully, "one tends to encounter grapeshot, and its consequences, when serving one's country. One tends to get blisters on account of preferring one's footwear to be prettier than it is functional."

"Could that, perhaps, be a foible of yours?"

"Me?" She shuffled her green satin slippers, with their embroidered cutaways and silver-blue ribbons, under the hem of her gown. "Never."

Gracewood's lips twitched. His smiles had always been rare; last night she had feared they might be lost forever. "They are lovely shoes, Miss Carroll. And in your position, I would have risked the blisters too."

And, just like that, she had no idea what to say. Worse, she was blushing. She just wasn't prepared to, well, to receive compliments from men, although she was, of course, aware in abstract that this was something that happened. In certain circumstances. From certain men. To certain women. Not her. And certainly not about something she had long regarded as a rather private pleasure, indulged for her own sake. It was, she reflected, slightly horrible to be so noticed. And also…wonderful. Except it wasn't her he was noticing. It was some other woman. A woman he'd never known, who'd never hurt him.

"I'm sure," she said faintly, "you didn't come all this way to talk about my…about my feet."

"To be honest, I'm still not entirely sure *what* I'm doing here." He eased himself upright, still clutching at his cane, and twisted to stare out across the sea. It was strange to see his movements so measured, all the effort of his motion bare before her—as if every gesture, every action, every shift and turn, had to be weighed in some invisible balance against necessity and the possibility of pain. "I used to come up all the time with Marleigh. We would race each other to the top, and whoever won was king of the castle and would get to decide how we spent the day."

Her heart tightened strangely, suspended somewhere between pleasure and grief. And she could not tell whether it was the pleasure or the grief that made her ask, "Who usually won?"

"He did. But, I think, sometimes I let him."

"Of course you did."

"Do you really think I'm too prideful to admit to having been outrun when I was a child?" Again that softening of his mouth, the promise of a smile. "My father died when I was seventeen years old. But even before that it was one of the first things I knew, one of the first things I understood about myself: that I would be duke one day. That all this, with its honours and its responsibilities and its legacy, would be mine. I suppose it sounds feeble, but it rather delighted me to be able to put a little of myself in someone else's hands. Just for a while."

"It"—her breath caught in her throat—"doesn't sound feeble to me."

"You're being kind again, Miss Carroll. Besides, Marleigh was always more imaginative than I. He invented better games."

Speaking with Gracewood like this was unfair on both of them. But what else could she do? He so plainly needed somebody, needed *her* to be somebody. And so she was forced to choose: Be a stranger in whom Gracewood could confide, who might bring him some measure of comfort in his loneliness. Or be the friend he thought dead, who had abandoned him and betrayed him and left him searching through corpses on the fields of Waterloo.

"What games did you play?" she asked, hoping that it was kindness, as Gracewood had claimed, but fearing it was cowardice.

"All sorts. Some of them very ordinary—tag, and hide and seek, building forts from the furniture, rummaging around for treasures in the attics and storerooms. I broke my wrist once, attempting to slide down the bannister of the main staircase on a tray we'd stolen from the kitchens."

"This friend of yours does not seem like a very good influence on you."

His eyes met hers. Memory had not done their blue justice, nor the warmth that lay beneath their beauty, like some undersea garden. "He was the joy of my life."

And what was Viola to say to that? It was simply too disorientating to have something—though far from the entangled totality—of her own feelings reflected back to her, all the while knowing it was only possible because he still did not see her. "He…I…I don't…"

"This was my world before I met him. And, heaven knows, I still hate this place—for all I should be grateful—but he taught me how to bear it."

She had no words, no comfort for either of them.

"Forgive me," he said. "I've imposed on you again."

"There's…there's"—she hid her trembling hands in the fall of her skirts—"nothing to forgive, Your Grace."

"I think we are past the point of titles, don't you?"

"I can hardly call you Gracewood."

"You did last night."

"Last night was…"

"Last night…" He gave an awkward cough. "Last night, I behaved inexcusably. I don't remember so very much of it, but of that I am all too aware. And I've been wondering how to beg your pardon ever since I came to my senses."

It should have been simple—a man caught in a moment of personal weakness apologising to a woman he believed he had shocked. And because it should, indeed, have been shocking Viola tried to pretend it was. That was the least she owed him. "My pardon is granted and gladly, no begging necessary."

"You are too generous." A pause, his hands restless on his cane. And then, in a rush of words, "Oh God, what must you think of me?"

She managed a shaky laugh, the wind—with unintended compassion—snatching away her tears. "I think that you've suffered. And that you are suffering. And that you have the truest heart. And…and aren't a very good shot."

"You know"—his tone struggled towards conversational—"I used to be. One of the few areas, in fact, where I surpassed Marleigh, though he was the better swordsman. It's why I remained in the quarry while he went back to help the Germans in that damn farmhouse. So, all in all, a skill I'm happy to let atrophy."

She remembered that day in fragments, that moment especially. The French had breached one of the garden walls. Without relief the Germans would have been done for. Of course, they were done for anyway, along with most of the 95th. Had she known everything that would follow she would have stopped—just long enough to pin the memory down, the colour of the sky, and the scent of the gunsmoke, and the look on Gracewood's face as she left him. She would have offered a proper good-bye. Instead, he'd wished her luck, as if he'd wanted to say something else, and she'd told him she didn't need it. That she always made her own.

"You can't truly believe it would have made a difference," she said aloud, "had your positions been reversed."

"Not truly, no. But I imagine it sometimes—to comfort, or torment myself, I'm not sure I can tell the difference anymore." Another of his studied, too-cautious movements, as he put his back to the sea and stood directly before her. "Miss Carroll, I really must thank you. You've been so very patient with me. I had not quite understood how badly I needed to speak of these things."

If only he knew—thank God he did not know—how little she deserved his gratitude. "It's no hardship."

His gaze drifted away from her again. And when he spoke, it was almost to himself. "We have so many ceremonies of loss for family, for public figures even. So few for friends."

"I . . . should have . . . I should have realised how lonely that would be."

They were of a height, so when he turned back to her there was no hiding from him, and she was afraid of what her words might have revealed. What she was revealing with every moment that passed.

"My dear lady," he murmured, "there's no need to weep for me."

"I-I'm not." It was not wholly a lie, for she wept for both of them.

"I would not be who I am without him. I have many regrets,

but knowing Marleigh—even if that meant losing him—could never be one of them."

There was an intimacy in facing him like this, one she had never before looked for, or recognised. Different to last night's closeness because he had chosen to share it with her, his mind unclouded by alcohol or opium. And different from the days of their youth because she knew he saw her—part of her at least—not some shell the world had created.

And for the first time in her life she allowed herself to look at him, truly look at him, as she had never dared before because it would have entangled her with a different set of possibilities—possibilities she had somehow always known weren't the answer she was seeking. She looked at him now as a woman to a man, claiming all the freedom of it.

The world might have tarnished him a little—darkened the bronze of his hair, left lines upon his face that hadn't been there before—but, to her, he was an angel still, a severe seraph, cast in shades of gold, whose presence at the gates of paradise would have done little to discourage sin. She had seen the set of his brow in the portrait gallery, the cast of his features, the cleft in his chin, yet never so generously united, as though eight hundred years of history had gathered like fairy godmothers round his cradle to bestow their best upon him.

And there he stood, all patrician hauteur and masculine symmetry, a testament to the splendour of his lineage, as unassailable as Morgencald itself. Except, that is, for his mouth, in whose austere curve she knew lurked whimsy and delight, and such gentleness. And his eyes, which were entirely his own—and would remain so, even when he took his place on canvas among his ancestors, since paint could never capture the light in them, the softness and the secrets of their lapis-lazuli blues.

He reached for her hand and, after the slightest of hesitations—relieved that carelessness had not extended to leaving her gloves behind—she let him take it. He had, after all, touched her often enough before, in play and affection, or comfort for some youthful setback. So she was expecting that it would be familiar. Except it was wholly different too: his fingers closing around hers in delicate possession, making her feel not fragile, precisely, but worthy of care. Even, perhaps, a little beautiful.

"It has been an unexpected pleasure, Miss Carroll." He pressed the swiftest of kisses to the back of her hand before releasing her. "But I've taken far too much of your time."

Her world was a piece of warmth in the shape of his mouth. "You haven't. You couldn't."

"I have duties, too many of them too long neglected—including providing a proper welcome to your mistress. Assuming, that is, I haven't terrified her out of her wits."

"Oh, please," she said, laughing. "It would take more than a stray gunshot to deter Louise."

"Well, at the very least I can make sure a proper breakfast is served."

"That would be wise. She's monstrous in the mornings." Viola paused. "That is to say, charming."

Another of those looks, suggesting mirth he had forgotten how to voice. "I appreciate the warning. May I ask one further consideration from you?"

"Of course."

"Will you forgive me the discourtesy if I don't accompany you down from the tower?" He suddenly seemed unable to meet her eyes, his downcast gaze settling on the flagstone beneath his cane. "It will be an ugly sight."

Words tangled in her throat, useless with urgency. "I'm agreeing because you're asking," she managed finally. "Not because I need to be protected from... from anything about you."

"Then allow me to protect myself. Weakness is hard enough to bear when it isn't the first thing everyone sees when they look at you. Besides"—his tone grew rueful—"you didn't hear the language I employed on my ascent."

"Were you very obscene?"

"Profoundly, Miss Carroll. You would have been appalled."

She did her best to suppress a smile—and did not succeed in the slightest. "I can't tell if you do me too much credit or too little."

"Perhaps for the best, then, that we do not find out." He offered her a slight bow. "After you, Miss Carroll."

"Actually, I think I'd like to stay a little longer."

"As you prefer."

He drew in a breath, seeming to gather himself, and then walked slowly past her, the resolute dignity of his bearing cast incongruously against the merry tip-tap of his cane upon the stone. Wanting to give him the privacy he'd requested, she crossed over to the parapet. The sun was higher now and cloud-smothered, its rays falling upon the rumpled sea in ribbons of silver.

She could still feel the impression of his kiss upon the back of her hand like sunlight on water, though when she peeled off her glove, nothing had changed. It was just her hand—a hand she did not always like—square-palmed and knotty-knuckled, flecked here and there by old scars and fading powder burns.

And yet…and yet…Her fingers traced the place he had touched her. The place he had touched Viola Carroll. And she thought of him, making his slow way down the endless spiral of the north tower, afraid that his suffering made him ugly.

Rushing back to the stairwell, she leaned into the gloom, and called after him. "You claimed that you would be swearing."

"Clearly," he returned, "I am not so lost to decency that I would swear within your earshot."

His voice already sounded strained. Pain-roughened. And, as she had last night, she knew she would do anything to ease it. "You need not hold back on my account."

Silence curled up from the staircase.

She shouldn't. She couldn't. She had to. "I'll go first. Culus."

There was a pause. Maybe he hadn't heard. Maybe he was shocked. Maybe he thought she was unhinged.

And then his voice floated back to her. "Verpa."

"Cunuus," she offered.

Another pause. And, finally, more hesitantly. "Testes?"

"Testes? Really? You chose testes?" Even though he couldn't see her, she curled her lip in playful scorn. "You promised I would be appalled."

"I sincerely apologise"—the echo caught his breathlessness and magnified it, but she could tell he was amused—"for having disappointed you with my inadequate obscenities."

"I suppose I shall have to forgive you yet again."

"Indeed. I am the worst of hosts. Can't shoot my guests. Can't swear at them properly."

Her laughter tumbled after him down the stairs.

"Please don't laugh, Miss Carroll. If you're laughing, you must be smiling, and I don't think I can climb back up to see it."

In truth, it was probably for the best he could not see her. He had made her blush again, and she felt absurd for being so affected by what was surely little more than idle gallantry. She had always known, in some vague way, that women liked Gracewood. That he was pleasing to them and pleased by them. But it was different to know something and *understand* it.

"My smile," she called out, "would not be worth such exertion."

"You are quite wrong."

"Even so, it is hardly an uncommon commodity."

"That does not lessen its value."

"Well"—and she *was* smiling, helplessly smiling—"perhaps it shall be yours again at breakfast."

"All the more reason for me to escape this tower."

"Coleos, by the way, was the word you needed."

"I am to be ever in your debt, Miss Carroll."

And with that, she thought it best to leave him to the descent. Pulling her shawl more tightly about her shoulders, she wedged herself against the battlements to wait. The wind grabbed at her hair with impatient fingers, tangling it into fresh knots. Had she really let Gracewood see her like this? Barely put together? Yet he had been so attentive, so courteous, even admiring. Not quite the man she had known. But not the ruin of him she had found last night. And in other ways—perhaps the deepest and most essential—still her oldest friend.

So who did that make her? Someone who took affection, trust, and loyalty and repaid them in hurt and loss and guilt. She should never have come here. She should never have listened to Louise. Because now she was trapped. Trapped between the lie her past had forced her to live and the lie that had made her future possible.

Except it wasn't a lie. Gracewood was right to mourn her. She had died two years ago on a battlefield in France.

She was Viola Carroll. She had always been Viola Carroll. And some part of her had always known it. There was only one thing she hadn't known. One truth that, locked in pursuit of her own, she hadn't grasped.

It was simply this: That love—that her love for Gracewood and his love for his friend—had not died with her.

Covering her face with her hands, she burst into tears.

# CHAPTER 6

It took Viola longer than she would have wished to compose herself, but sometimes—she was forced to concede—one simply had no choice but to be discomposed. And in such cases there were worse places for it to happen than at the top of a tower in a castle in Northumberland, with no one to see or hear or question you. Eventually, though, she returned to her room, where she cleaned her face, changed her dress, and spent a little while among her cosmetics, and by the time she was heading down to breakfast she was feeling much better.

Gracewood and Lady Marleigh were already at the table—he sitting rather stiffly and poking at a piece of honeycake; she ensconced behind a ham hock with a very black coffee at her elbow. It did not look like an entirely happy situation, but it could have been worse. Significantly worse.

"Ah, Viola." Lady Marleigh waved a fork at her. "There you are. Do be a wonder and get me a slice of that mutton pie, and some of the eggs, and maybe a kipper or two, and all of the bacon." She paused, apparently recalled to her better nature. "Well, any of the bacon you don't want."

Viola surveyed the various breakfast offerings. "I might just have toast."

"Your loss, dear."

Having re-arranged the dishes to Lady Marleigh's satisfaction,

Viola sat down next to her and helped herself to a cup of chocolate. She didn't quite dare look up, but she could feel Gracewood's eyes upon her—his attention as sweet as spring rain.

And suddenly she was nothing but questions, rushing about inside her like shoals of rainbow fish: Did he like the embroidery on her gloves, did he find the print of her morning dress becoming, did the curls she had left free from her chignon frame her face well, was any of this even the sort of thing gentlemen noticed? She always had, but that had been envy and longing and desperation. Oh God, this was a *torment*. Wanting so terribly to be seen, and terrified of what it might mean if she was.

"I hope," said Gracewood, his voice a little thick from exhaustion and the worsening after-effects of laudanum, "you slept well, Miss Carroll."

This earned an unladylike snort from Lady Marleigh. "Let's dispense with the courteous lying, shall we? Probably she slept dreadfully, as did I, because you were in no way prepared to receive guests. The room was dusty, I have no idea when the bed was last turned down, and I had to light my own fire. That is not a euphemism."

"I apologise"—Gracewood's tone was wry, but its sincerity was unmistakable—"for my poor hospitality. I will see chambers are properly prepared for you today."

"And don't think I've forgotten you tried to shoot me."

"Actually, I've been reliably informed that I rather more... shot *at* you."

Lady Marleigh, perhaps fairly, did not seem any more comforted by the distinction this morning than she had last night. "Oh, that's fine then."

"I was not myself."

That much, thought Viola, was obvious to anyone who knew him. He was, at least, sober now, but he was clearly in no fit state to face a morning of Lady Marleigh. The previous evening had caught up with him—laid shadows upon the shadows beneath his eyes, etched lines of weariness into his brow and about his mouth.

"For all our sakes," said Lady Marleigh, "I should hope not." There was a pause while she speared a piece of pie with the avidity of a committed hunter. "On the other hand, this is a very creditable breakfast."

The Duke inclined his head slightly. "Thank you. Though it is Miss Carroll who deserves your praise, not I."

"Yes, yes. *Obviously* this is Viola's doing. She knows how hard I find it to remain peeved in the vicinity of bacon."

"Bacon"—Viola pressed a hand to her bosom—"the way to every woman's heart."

Lady Marleigh nodded. "Exactly. Breakfast is the best meal of the day—as it should be, to console one for having to get out of bed. I don't like this current fashion for scraps of bread and watery tea. Frankly, I blame the French."

"Well," Viola pointed out, "we did kill some twenty-five thousand of them a couple of years ago, so they've probably learned their lesson."

"I'm sorry. That was insensitive of me." A touch of pink crept across Lady Marleigh's cheeks. "I'm not a very nice person in the morning. Wait, what am I saying? I'm never a very nice person."

"Your consistency, Louise, is part of your charm."

"And you must admit," Lady Marleigh went on briskly, "that as a nation we do have the oddest relationship with the French. We either want to murder them or be them, and we can't seem to make up our mind which."

"I think," Viola observed, "we're currently attempting both simultaneously."

"Do you mind if I ask"—Gracewood gave a soft cough—"and I'm aware this question is likely to compound your poor opinion of me, what are you doing here?"

Lady Marleigh subjected him to one of her most withering looks. "I'm eating breakfast."

"More broadly?"

"We came because of Miranda."

"Oh, Mira invited you?" He seemed at once bewildered and relieved. "She might have mentioned it."

"Well, she didn't invite us. Not as such."

"Not at all," Viola murmured.

"But," Lady Marleigh pressed on relentlessly, "her letters made it very clear that a visit of some kind was in order."

And now Gracewood just seemed bewildered. "Why? She's perfectly happy."

"Perfectly happy?" A slice of ham plunged from the tines of Lady Marleigh's fork and back onto her plate. "She's a seventeen-year-old girl. She should be in London, having love affairs with unsuitable young men in a controlled environment. Not stuck in a mouldering fortress miles from anywhere."

There was a long silence. It was oddly loud, and not at all comfortable. Viola had forgotten how easily Gracewood could become the man he was raised to be. Even in rumpled clothes, his eyes red-rimmed and his voice rough from drink and sleeplessness, the authority of eight centuries was its own armour: ice and pride and privilege, as unconquerable as his castle's walls.

"And she's told you this?" he inquired softly.

"Well"—the normally unflappable Lady Marleigh experienced a moment of something perilously close to flapping—"no. But—"

"But nothing, My Lady. I am inclined to believe that your actions are kindly meant, and in view of the friendship between our families, you are, indeed, welcome at my"—his tone grew, if anything, colder—"mouldering fortress. When it comes to my sister's happiness, however, I shall thank you for not presuming to know better than I what is best for her."

Lady Marleigh's eyes narrowed. "But what of her wishes?"

"Do you think I haven't talked to Mira myself?" One of Gracewood's eyebrows had lifted into the faintest suggestion of an arch. "Or did you prefer the idea that I was keeping her locked in a tower somewhere for obscurely sinister motives of my own? Good God, how many gothic novels have you read?"

"I'm sure," Viola put in anxiously, "there was no question of your being malicious."

His expression softened somewhat. "I see. Just negligent."

"It's not personal." Lady Marleigh waved a dismissive hand. "The world teaches men to listen only to what they want to hear and women to tell it to them."

Another pause, slightly less fraught than the last.

And finally Gracewood said, "I do see your point. But I assure you, of my many shortcomings, care of my sister is not one of them. When we have discussed her future, she has always told me she's perfectly content at Morgencald. And, you know, she is—"

Before he could finish, the door opened and Lady Miranda herself drifted into the room. The last time Viola had seen her, she had been twelve or thirteen, a prettyish child even then, but she had somehow grown into a fairy-tale princess with hair Rumpelstiltskin must have spun for her, and silver-blue eyes as bright as fallen stars.

The newcomer's gaze travelled dreamily over the breakfasters. "Oh, Justin, you're out of bed. And Auntie Lou. How lovely to see you."

"Mira, darling." Lady Marleigh offered her cheek for a kiss. "What in God's name are you wearing?"

For reasons not readily apparent to Viola, Lady Miranda was dressed in a gown from the last century—a vast-skirted creation, all ruffles and bows, with a waterfall of lace at the sleeves, and a petticoat of luridly embroidered roses. "This? I found it in the attic. I thought it was pretty."

"You look like a shepherdess in a pastoral."

Lady Miranda thought for a moment. "Thank you."

"Not a compliment," returned Lady Marleigh. "Now sit down. We're talking about your future."

"Are you? That's so kind of you. My ears weren't burning, though. Aren't your ears supposed to burn when somebody's talking about you? Or is that only if they're saying nasty things? So you must have been saying nice things."

"I only say nasty things to people's faces." Lady Marleigh smirked. "What's the point otherwise?"

Once again, Lady Miranda considered the matter. "Giving them sore ears?"

"Sometimes"—Lady Marleigh had apparently given up trying to find a direct response—"I worry you're a genius, Mira. And I've been remiss in not introducing my companion to you. Lady Miranda, this is Miss Viola Carroll. Viola, Lady Miranda."

It always left a sourness in the back of Viola's throat to be introduced to people she already knew. To say nothing of the seconds of predictable but uncontrollable terror that they might, somehow, recognise her. "It's a pleasure, Lady Miranda."

"Miss Carroll"—Lady Miranda offered her a shy smile—"I hope it's not too forward, but your gloves are beautiful. Did you make them yourself? I mean, not because you are too poor to afford gloves. Or perhaps you are. Which is fine. Or, not fine, because I imagine being too poor to afford gloves is rather wearisome. Not that it means one should be scorned, since it would hardly be your fault. Unless it was your fault and perhaps you gambled away a fortune at loo. Oh dear, I just thought your gloves were pretty."

"I'm not sure," said Gracewood sharply, "which of those possibilities is more or less insulting to Miss Carroll."

Lady Miranda's flush, not quite becoming on so porcelain a face, made Viola answer quickly, "None of them. Personally, I rather like the notion that I am some kind of glove-hunting adventuress. It is somewhat more exciting than the truth."

"I don't think being a companion is unexciting." That was Lady Miranda, looking much more at ease, and Viola was glad she'd spoken up. "Well, I'm sure it can also be drudgery. But it does imply you're good company. Whereas I suspect there are some people who would more likely pay me to go away."

Lady Marleigh rapped her knuckles on the tabletop. "Yes, Viola is an excellent companion. Yes, she made the gloves. Now can we please—"

"You did?" squeaked Lady Miranda. "That's wonderful of you. I've been practising so I am not completely terrible when I am drawing, but I cannot sew for the life of me. No matter what I design, everything I embroider ends up looking like the—wait, I cannot say that."

Unfortunately this only engaged Lady Marleigh's merciless curiosity. "Well, now I think you have to."

"I really can't. Not in front of Justin."

Gracewood's eyes widened. "What can't you speak of in front of me?"

"Oh. Oh dear." Lady Miranda glanced between him and Lady Marleigh. Then she put a hand to the side of her mouth, as if she could somehow stop him hearing by stopping him from seeing, and whispered, "My needlepoint. It always resembles... the male member."

"How," asked Gracewood sharply, "do you even know what the...what *that* looks like?"

His sister blinked at him. "Well, we live in the country. And there are farms. And also we have kennels and stables. Unless it looks different on humans than it does in dogs and bulls and horses. I hadn't thought of that. Does it look different?"

"I am not answering that question, Mira." He cleared his throat, looking, Viola had to admit, adorably flustered. "Now can you please tell Her Ladyship about our conversations regarding your future. She's under the impression you're pining for a season."

"What?" Lady Miranda's hands fluttered uncertainly. "Oh no. I never said that. You mustn't think I said that."

"You didn't," cut in Lady Marleigh. "But you're only human. You don't want to spend the rest of your life with your brother, do you?"

"N-not the rest of my life. But"—she took a deep breath—"for now I'm very happy where I am. After all, Morgencald is very beautiful and has a lot of...a lot of...nature. What more could I need?"

"Company? Diversion? Dresses that don't look like the fever dream of Marie Antoinette?"

Lady Miranda's eyes glimmered tragically. "I'm sure there will be plenty of time for such things in the future."

"There. You see." It was an abrupt conclusion to the conversation, but anyone could tell Gracewood had passed the limits of his endurance. Reaching for his cane, he pushed himself to his feet. "Her Ladyship had decided I was some kind of ogre, keeping you trapped here."

"That's not true," his sister protested, turning an imploring gaze on Lady Marleigh. "Justin would be a terrible ogre. He's far too polite. He would say things like, fee-fi-fo-fum, I smell the blood of an Englishman. Be he alive or be he dead, would you please forgive me the discourtesy were I to grind your bones to make my bread."

It did sound *exactly* like something Gracewood might say. Unable to help herself, Viola started to laugh. And was joined a second or two later by Lady Marleigh.

He gave them all a haughty look—which did nothing to quell their mirth and, from the amused curve of his mouth, was not intended to. "I think you'll find that the bone-grinding and breadmaking is generally left to giants. And now, if you'll excuse me, I have to…" He seemed momentarily at a loss, swaying slightly where he stood. "I must retire."

"Do try to sleep, Justin," Miranda told him. "And perhaps unaided? If possible?"

"When I sleep, Miranda"—now his manner was imperious in truth—"or how or where is none of your concern. And it's certainly none of our guests'."

And, with that, he was gone.

# CHAPTER 7

Later that morning, at Lady Marleigh's suggestion, they went for a walk in the walled garden, Lady Miranda still in her shepherdess dress, with her sketchbook under her arm. It was not one of Viola's favourite areas of the castle—the very notion of a walled garden felt unpleasant to her, and it had been built nearly a century ago, when the fashion had been for regimented geometries of gravel paths and enclosed beds. But then, given the width of Lady Miranda's skirts, perhaps it spoke more to necessity than aesthetics.

There was, of all things, a walled garden within the walled garden. It contained a white-painted gazebo and an ornate sundial, surrounded by yet more gravel and some rather ill-tended topiary, grown strange and knobbly.

Viola had as good as forgotten the existence of the place. The youthful adventures she had shared with Gracewood had taken them all over the castle and the estate, but they would hardly have chosen to sit in a bower together.

"This is one of my favourite spots," announced Lady Miranda, settling onto a nearby bench. "It's almost a kind of secret, isn't it?"

Lady Marleigh brushed some crinkled leaves away and claimed a spot of her own. "Secrets are things worth knowing. This is rocks crushed up small and some greenery."

"It was a present from...oh, one of the de Veres...Justin

will remember. Marcus, maybe, or Augustus. To his wife. And look"—lace flailed as Lady Miranda gestured—"he had the sundial made. It says *sine sole sileo*, which means *without sun I am silent*. Except the garden is too dark, so it doesn't work. Isn't that curiously unfortunate?"

"It's certainly...something," conceded Lady Marleigh.

"I sketched it once. Do you want to see?"

Lady Marleigh was clearly in no mood to indulge this girlish whimsy. "Not remotely."

Undeterred, Lady Miranda began turning over the pages of her book—and finally held it out to them. "I think I might call it *Audio*."

The drawing was far from the dainty watercolour Viola had been expecting and was under the impression well-bred young ladies were supposed to produce. Instead, it was a mesmerising shadowscape, the garden rendered in a haze of dark lines, with lighter strokes suggesting, perhaps, the figure of a woman, here seated upon the bench, or there half-lost beneath the looming walls, or even leaning over the sundial—its unchanging face as blank as the moon in the centre of the page.

"Had you run out of colours?" asked Lady Marleigh, visibly confused.

"Black's a colour," protested Lady Miranda. "As is grey."

"You mean it's deliberate?"

Her public role as paid companion offered Viola a degree of protection, allowing her to fade into the background with impunity whenever she wished. And, the truth was, she often wished. This, however, was showing every sign of being an occasion in which Viola fading was helping nobody. "Ignore her." She nudged her artistically disinclined sister-in-law. "It's very good, Lady Miranda."

Even this fairly generic praise earned a radiant smile. "Good? Do you think so? I was afraid it might be odd. Not that the two need be contradictory, of course. What do you think of this one? It's called *The Lovely Cruelty of Evanescence*."

Lady Marleigh just stared. "What is it?"

"I don't entirely know," admitted Lady Miranda. "It's sort of a feeling."

"Well, I'm sure that's very modern of you, Mira. But we really do need to have a proper talk about—"

"Oh yes." With a happy squeak, Lady Miranda bundled her sketchbook away. "We have so much to catch up on. How is Uncle Badger? Is it right that I still call you Auntie Lou and Uncle Badger? I'm old enough now to understand we're not properly related, even if it feels like we are. It would be such a shame to stop, though, wouldn't it? Except Uncle Badger is Lord Marleigh now. Which must be such a strange experience, sad and happy at the same time."

There was a long silence. Until, finally, Lady Marleigh observed, "You do know, don't you, that you don't have to utter every thought that enters your head?"

"Yes, I do know. I just don't see why not. And Janner always says better out than in." Lady Miranda paused, wrinkling her nose. "Although he was talking to a horse with indigestion at the time."

In other circumstances, Viola might have been inclined to giggle at this, but the fact that Lady Miranda was so starved for companionship that she was picking up stray phrases from stablehands was actually cause for concern. Concern that, to her credit, Lady Marleigh had shown from the beginning.

"Moving swiftly past the indisposed equine," she was saying, "you may call us whatever you please. We certainly still think of you as family. Which is why we want you to come and spend the season with us in London."

By way of response, Lady Miranda bounced off the bench in a flurry of satin and started circling the sundial. "It's not the right time."

"You're seventeen, absurdly beautiful, and have far too many peculiar ideas. They'll say you're an original. It's *exactly* the right time."

"Well, it's still no. You can't make me go to London, and have fabulous dresses, and attend balls and parties, and the opera, and see the fireworks at Vauxhall, and the carriages in Hyde Park, and maybe a dissection or two at the Royal Society." Seeming to remember herself, Lady Miranda stamped her foot. "No, Auntie Lou. You can't make me and I won't."

Lady Marleigh watched this small drama with a quizzical expression. "I'm not making you, Mira. I'm inviting you."

"That's . . . that's so wonderfully kind of you"—Lady Miranda's eyes filled up with tears, which, instead of making them red and swollen, just made them shimmer—"but I truly can't."

"Why not?"

"Because," Lady Miranda wailed, "because of Justin."

Oh God. Viola's stomach twisted like snakes. There was something inestimably cruel about the connectedness of lives. The way one's own suffering, and the things one did to relieve it, became so entwined with the suffering of others.

"You mean"—Lady Marleigh's voice grew ominous—"he *is* playing ogre?"

Her perfect eyes flying wide in horror, Lady Miranda uttered a little cry. "No, no. Of course not. He could never."

"Then what's the problem?"

"He's...he's so sad, Auntie Lou. I can't leave him."

Lady Marleigh contemplated this. "Given you've been with him since he returned from France and you're telling me he's still sad, it's hard to see what your presence is achieving. So you might as well come to London with us."

Covering her mouth with her hands, Lady Miranda gave a soft, muffled sob.

"What Louise means," said Viola hastily, "is that there's a limit on what we can do for others. And occasionally time is all that—"

"Don't try to tell me time is a healer. Because time also kills people."

Admittedly, Lady Miranda had a point. But Viola pushed on regardless, trying to fix the entire situation in a few desperate sentences. "He wouldn't want you sacrificing your happiness for his."

"You don't know how he's been. And, no, before you think all sorts of terrible things, he's never done anything to hurt me, and I don't believe he ever would. But sometimes it's like a completely different person came back from the war." Lady Miranda picked idly at a patch of lichen that had gathered beneath the gnomon of the sundial. "Of course, sometimes he's absolutely fine, and I wonder if my imagination is running away with me. I'm rather prone to that."

A brief pause, broken only by the scratch of fingernails against stone. Then Lady Marleigh threw up her hands. "I knew it. We should have come months ago."

"Why?" asked Lady Miranda, a trifle coolly. "What could you have done?"

"Honestly?" Lady Marleigh shrugged. "Very little. But at least you wouldn't have had to bear this alone."

"Oh, because it's bad for me to be alone, but perfectly acceptable for Justin to be?"

Lady Marleigh had the half-startled, half-rueful look of someone who, stepping into a puddle they believe to be an inch or so deep, is abruptly waist-deep in water. "I see what you're saying. So why don't we bring Gracewood with us?"

Fresh tears had sprung to Miranda's eyes. "But he'd hate it."

"Well," Lady Marleigh said ruthlessly, "it can't be any worse than living in a haze of narcotics."

"He doesn't. I mean, he didn't. I mean, it was only supposed to be for when it was bad. But—" Lady Miranda sighed. "It must be bad most of the time."

Viola couldn't look at anyone just then. She was thinking of Gracewood last night, shaking and shooting at ghosts. And then this morning, struggling to be an echo of the man he used to be. The man she knew he still was.

"I think," Lady Miranda went on, "some nights he might think he's there…you know…in France. Or rather, he knows he isn't—because I've asked him—but it feels the same? The strangest thing is, when he has those moments, he always says he has to go back. That they have to let him go back. Why would he want to go back?"

*To save me*, Viola could have said. But that wasn't her truth to share.

"London might well do him the world of good." Lady Marleigh was nothing if not persistent. "Can't really blame the fellow for being a few leaves short of a pineapple after what he's been through. And then the two of you being stuck in this ghastly old pile all alone."

"People do live in Northumberland."

"But are any of them here?"

"Well…no. Justin doesn't really like to see people anymore. Not"—and here Lady Miranda scowled—"because he's anything less than a fully functional and very hirsute pineapple. He's just a little, I suppose, self-conscious. Because of his leg."

"It's a war wound. He's a hero."

"And you think that will stop the pitying glances? The solicitous condescension?"

Lady Marleigh snorted. "He's a duke. The ton will see that before they see a limp."

"I'm not sure that's much better."

"You're being very stubborn."

"Yes. And?"

An already sad-looking topiary took the brunt of Lady Marleigh's frustration as she gave it a hearty kick. "Viola's right, you know. Your brother wouldn't want this. Are you really going to persevere in something so detrimental to both your interests?"

"What we want and what we need and what we think is best aren't always the same." Lady Miranda drew herself to her full height, the pride of the de Veres settling over her like a too-long cloak. "And I may be small and silly and seventeen, and maybe I can't go to war, or shoot people, or manage a great estate, but I can protect the people I love. And even though Justin won't listen to me or talk to me, and barely thinks of me, I'm going to look after him. And that's that. And I won't hear another word about it."

Viola stole a glance at Lady Marleigh. Her sister-in-law, who was rarely defeated in any context, looked bewildered but also lightly pleased, apparently just as glad to discover steel as she usually was to get her own way.

"Very well, Mira," Lady Marleigh said, with an air of conciliation that Viola immediately suspected. "It shall be as you wish."

Lady Miranda clapped her hands together. "Oh, I'm so glad. Arguing is such a bore. Why don't I show you both some more of the grounds? There's a tree—an apple tree maybe—where... Tiberius de Vere—I'm eighty percent sure it was Tiberius, but it might have been Claudius—hanged himself. Isn't that diverting?"

"Oh, it couldn't have been an apple tree. They only live for about forty years and they're neither tall nor strong enough to support a hanging." Given the subject matter, the authority in Lady Marleigh's tone was slightly disconcerting.

As, for that matter, was Lady Miranda's undimmed curiosity. "Is that so? What are the superior trees for hanging oneself? Well, let me show you this one and you can assess its merit as an instrument of self-destruction."

And so there was nothing for it but to follow Lady Miranda deeper into the gardens. As they went, Lady Marleigh maintained her part in a surprisingly detailed conversation about arboriculture, but Viola knew her too well to be deceived by it. She was scheming. She was surely scheming.

# CHAPTER 8

As it turned out, it took Lady Marleigh a mere handful of hours to devise a new strategy. Viola, meanwhile, had retired to one of the drawing rooms and was curled up in the window seat with her silks around her. The light was not kind, tending towards sallow in the late afternoon before it grew sunset wild, but Viola wanted quiet and the serenity of repetitive motion. She had started a new design—chrysanthemums, in shades of wine red and lion gold, their long petals unfurling like tongues. Bold had been her intent from the beginning. Sensuous had somehow crept in later. A memory of a hand touching hers. The warmth of a mouth against her glove. And what a thing to be dwelling on when there was so much else to preoccupy her.

She had thought she could live with the guilt. It had been something she had accepted along with the loss of her title and fortune, and a life that would have, in so many ways, been not just *easier* but about as blessed as a life could be. Except it would also have been a life of permanent imposture, closing around her like an iron maiden as the years passed. She was not sure how she would have borne it, but she would have had to, for she could never have done this had fate not intervened.

What, after all, would her choices have been otherwise? To walk away in the dead of night? That would have been too cruel, leaving too many questions for those who loved her, not to mention too dangerous, for the world was not kind to wandering women. Or perhaps she could simply have gone as herself to some ball or other, said to the world *I am the Viscountess Marleigh, and I defy you to say I am not.* They would have laughed. They would have thought her mad. And perhaps worst of all, they would, in their secret hearts, have said she was not.

But then Waterloo had come, and shot and shell had blown her old life to dust. By the time she had fully recovered from her injuries, everyone who had known her already thought her dead. They had mourned her, and they had moved on. At least, that was how it had been with Badger and with Lady Marleigh. And although they had welcomed her back when she had—after a year of searching and struggling with who she finally understood herself to be—built up the courage to go to them, she had never once felt that they *needed* her.

Perhaps she should have known that it would be different for Gracewood. They had been so close, after all. And God knew she had ached for him sometimes, yearned to be near him again, but she had taken that for her own weakness. Men, she had always been taught—and Gracewood had *certainly* been taught—took loss differently. They could grieve, of course; they could even weep in moderation, in private or among very select company. They did not *break*. A man returned from war with tales of valour, sometimes even with tales of terror, but he wore his scars like medals and his loss like ermine.

And so she had imagined him a hero, toasted by the ton for his gallantry and sometimes, perhaps, raising a glass to the memory of the childhood friend who had not come back with him. What she had found instead, when she returned at last to Morgencald, was darker than anything she could possibly have envisaged. Than anything that was discussed in the fine halls and smoky rooms where old soldiers gathered to speak of battle. Pain without honour, loss without pride, regret without end.

It should not have been possible. But then, she supposed, she should not have been possible either.

It was at this point that Lady Marleigh interrupted her, and Viola was more than glad for the distraction. Her mind kept taking her in circles through dark woods, and she was tired of catching herself on brambles.

"So," announced Lady Marleigh, sitting briefly on Viola's sewing basket and then relocating to the nearest chair, "new plan."

"Does the new plan have anything to do with minding our own business?"

"What do you think?"

"I think...hope springs eternal?"

"Viola, I mind my own business so consummately that minding other people's is all the joy I have left to me."

Viola squeezed her basket gently back into shape. "That's nonsense. Your life is full of joy, and you know it."

"Well, yes. But this is my hobby."

"I really do feel"—and here Viola had to acknowledge that hope wasn't so much springing eternal as trickling finite—"we should leave."

"Leave? We can't leave. Mira is already hovering perilously close to the line between charmingly unique and frankly peculiar."

That much was true, but Miranda was not Viola's only concern. Not even her chief concern. "And what of Gracewood? I cannot continue seeing him like this, letting *him* see *me* like this."

Sometimes, Viola wondered how much Lady Marleigh

exaggerated her naïveté when it came to emotional matters. Like now, for example, when she looked up quite innocently and said, "Whyever not?"

"Because it is *cruel*, Louise. He has...he thinks...he is...this is all for me. For the friend he thinks he lost."

"Rot."

That, Viola had to admit, was not the response she expected. "I beg your pardon?"

"Utter rot. You are not Gracewood's keeper. And it is no kindness to the man to claim a power over him you do not truly possess."

"You do not think we are able to hurt the ones we love?" This seemed a tenuous position to hold, even for Lady Marleigh.

"I think we cannot control the way that other people choose to behave. Gracewood thought you dead. So did Badger. So did I. Neither of us started abusing laudanum and neglecting our duties."

That made a flame catch in Viola's chest, a kind of nauseous anger. "You would not say such things if you knew."

"Knew what?"

"How it was, back then. In the war. With the guns and the shells and ever-present awareness that you were leading men to their deaths. It was..." She shut her eyes. Her memories of that time were not like Gracewood's. She had been trapped beyond hope of rescue long before they were pinned under fire in that damnable quarry. "It was such chaos that even a strong man, even a good man, might lose himself."

Lady Marleigh gave an inappropriate smile of a kind Viola knew well. It was her smile for logical traps, for when she'd made you admit the very thing you'd been telling her wasn't so. "You mean," she said, "that Gracewood's condition has as much to do with Waterloo as anything you may or may not have done in its aftermath? That Napoleon and Wellington are as responsible as you are?"

"Napoleon and Wellington didn't abandon him."

"And neither did you. I don't pretend to understand what the last two years have been like for you, Viola. Nor all the years before them, for that matter. But I know that when you thought Gracewood needed you, you went to him despite your fears. Until Miranda's letter, we none of us had any notion how things stood at Morgencald."

Viola took a deep breath, set her needle aside, and tried to be reassured. "I-I am beginning to think I should confess to him."

"If you truly think it is what you need to do, then I will not stop you. But it may not be wise."

"You were certain he would accept me," Viola reminded her a little sharply. "When we spoke at home, you were sure of it."

"And I still believe he would. Were he still the man we both remember. But for now, as good and kind as you believe him to be, the Duke of Gracewood is an unknown quantity. The shock of having you back—it might save him or undo him. There may come a time when that risk is worth it, but I do not believe that time is now."

Somehow, Viola had permitted her habitual suspicion of Lady Marleigh's ulterior motives to lapse. This had been a mistake. "You're about to tell me your new plan, aren't you?"

Lady Marleigh nodded. "We cannot let Miranda stay here purely for her brother's sake. Clearly, she'd love to come to London with us, but she feels she can't. Because blah-blah duty, blah-blah sacrifice."

"Those are admirable qualities."

"Not in excess, and not if they come at the cost of a young girl's happiness."

Viola opened her mouth, then closed it again, and finally said, "Let's say I agree with you. We still can't force Lady Miranda to accompany us. And don't even think about suggesting we kidnap her."

"As if I would ever suggest such a thing." Lady Marleigh looked quite affronted. "Kidnapping Mira would make her grumpy and mistrustful of us. Completely counterproductive."

"But you did consider it."

Shrugging dismissively, Lady Marleigh went on, "The ideal outcome for everyone involved is for Mira to inform Gracewood she wants a season entirely of her own volition. Which she will never do because she believes, quite rightly, that there is no telling what Gracewood will do if left to his own devices."

"He's certainly not...in the best state of mind." Viola smoothed her fingers over the patch of colour she had created, glad for an excuse not to meet Lady Marleigh's always too-shrewd gaze. "But he would be horrified if he knew how Lady Miranda feared for him." Or how she did.

There was the sort of coiled-tight silence that Viola associated with cats the second before they pounced. Lady Marleigh leaned forward in her chair, steepling her fingers meditatively. "Then isn't it up to us to stop her fearing for him?"

And all of a sudden, Viola knew exactly where this was going. "You're about to suggest I fix Gracewood, aren't you?"

"Who else?"

"*Anybody* else."

"Miranda has tried for two years and failed as, no doubt, has every servant in Morgencald. That means it is up to you, or up to me, and tell me honestly, Viola, am I the best person to gently soothe a fragile lordling back to health?"

She wasn't. There was probably nobody *less* suitable. "But I..."

"You know him, Viola, better than anybody. You know what he has suffered in a way few other living people do."

"Because I am the *cause* of thmmmf—"

Lady Marleigh had crossed the room and put her hand firmly across Viola's mouth. "Stop that. I will not hear it again. Arrogance does not suit you."

"Mm nff bmmng mmrmmrgrrrn."

"Yes, you are. Now, I'm only going to remove my hand if you promise to stop being silly."

"Mm mrrmfff."

Lady Marleigh removed her hand. "Good, now let's talk sensibly. I'm not asking for miracles. Just guide him gently away from his more self-destructive impulses. Get him to have a shave. That kind of thing."

"I'm not sure the beard is his biggest problem."

"I respectfully disagree." Lady Marleigh shuddered. "Can't abide beards. But either way all we need is for him to...to be a little more stable. So that Mira will feel safe leaving him."

"Leaving him alone with his grief, you mean?"

"Yes." It was a taut little affirmative, suggesting that, on this occasion, Lady Marleigh was less comfortable than her general confidence might lead one to assume. "If necessary, yes. I hope that you might—that is, that through you he might—the best possible outcome is that you truly bring him back to himself and all is well. But if you cannot, if he is truly lost...I am sorry, Viola, but while you and Gracewood were marching up and down

France fighting for King and country, Badger and I were caring for Mira, and so I fear that *she* is my priority, not her brother."

"That seems cold."

"Colder than letting Gracewood drag her down with him?"

No, that wouldn't have been right either. "And you want me to accomplish this while continuing to pose as a stranger to him."

"Until he comes to a state with more well-tied cravats and fewer loaded pistols, I think that may be best for all concerned."

Viola sighed. This was going to end badly for someone whatever happened—it was only a matter of scale. "One week," she said at last, "and then we go home. Even if nothing has changed."

"Agreed."

The swiftness of Lady Marleigh's answer confirmed the inevitable: that Viola had, once again, played straight into her sister-in-law's hands. But it was too late now. And there was a tiny, traitorous part of her that was...oh, not happy exactly. That would have been inappropriate in so many ways. Something else, then—a strange sweet hopefulness she knew she had no right to feel, but could not quell. Or maybe it was just her old friendship with Gracewood, which had waited for her as loyally as Odysseus's dog, lifting its weary head for one last acknowledgement before it let itself fade away. Except she knew it was not that either. It was another something else. The promise of something new. Soaring on impossible wings.

# Chapter 9

He was trying not to dwell on Miss Carroll, though when circumstances brought them together—usually at mealtimes—it was all he could do to behave with civility. He wanted to look at her like he wanted to breathe, like she *was* breath and he was drowning, and every moment of his not looking was a struggle towards the thing he most needed. Except once he looked, looking would not be enough. Then he would have to talk to her—draw the delicate spool of her thoughts from that smiling mouth, until he knew all the colours of her. Until he understood how a stranger could seem so familiar to him. How something in her could call to a part of him he had long thought dead. How it was possible she could feel like homecoming to a man who had never before had any sense of home.

It had to be loneliness. Or opium. Or some delirious combination of the two. And he was mortified, even vaguely remembering what he might have said to her that night in the library. Perhaps he had acquitted himself better on the tower, but that, too, was in danger of vanishing—not into a muddle of narcotics but into the husky warmth of her laughter, and the soft pressure of her hand in his. Was she beautiful? He was sure she must be, but it had been a long time since he had given consideration to such things.

His mind kept catching on odd details: the embroidery on her gloves, the vividness of coral against the pale skin of her throat, the freckles that trailed down her neck. She had such a compelling…he did not have the word for it. A *completeness* somehow, from the toes of her slippers to the curl of her hair. Had she been a man, he would have called her dandyish. Except that carried an implication of excess or absurdity, and she was neither.

He had never paid much attention to fashion before—in men or women—but now he was half-obsessed, lost in the mysteries of a piece of ribbon or the edge of a hem, the flicker of an earring that caught the pattern of a gown. It made him want to take her apart with the same exquisite carefulness she used to put herself together, find his way through all the depths and layers of her, like a pearl diver who barely knew how to dream the treasures he sought.

Which was why, lying in the dark, the need for alcohol or opium clawing at his innards, and Waterloo waiting just beyond breath, crouched in the spaces behind his eyes, he let himself think of her instead. And was shocked by the desire that suddenly pierced him. That, too, he hadn't thought of for a while. He hadn't particularly been aware of its fading, but his body had been first an instrument of death and then a site of pain. And he had left so much on the battlefield, so much that was good and true and vital, it made no sense to cling to sexual passion. Even now, it was strange—an impulse he wasn't sure belonged to him anymore. One he wasn't sure he deserved to feel.

But, God, the solace of it. A moment of remembering what it was like to be a different man. A man who chose his steps without a care. A man who could be pleased by a pretty woman without it being a betrayal of grief. A man whose flesh was not a graveyard for ghosts. The shame that came after, though, was worse for the respite, and left him shaken with its ugliness, and with his own.

Miss Carroll had shown him only kindness. And, in return, he had made her the unwitting subject of his basest nature. As transgressions went it was, perhaps, a minor one—after all, his thoughts were his, and she would never know them. But there was still a wrongness there, as if he was taking something that should more rightly be given.

By day, at any rate, he had plenty to occupy him. With guests in the house he would have been forced to maintain some semblance of composure even if he had felt indifferent towards them, and the effort of that was taxing. As for his nights, if they were inclined to seek for themselves a new torment, he was almost grateful for the novelty of it. Better, he thought, to be haunted by the living than the dead.

Though the disadvantage of Miss Carroll not belonging among his ghosts was that she did not leave with the dawn. She sat at breakfast, as neat as morning dew. Or wandered in the gardens, a pale figure glimpsed through narrow windows. Or took possession of rooms that had seen no use in years, leaving behind the occasional piece of silk, like the plumage of some fantastical bird, and a trace of gardenia upon the air.

And, sometimes, apparently sought him out in the depths of his father's study.

"Miss Carroll?" He glanced up from his papers, at once startled and delighted and guilty, and irritated at himself for all of it.

His voice startled her in return, and she gave an odd half jump, like a sparrow finding itself on the wrong side of the window glass. "Yes…no…I…"

She was usually more composed than this, even, he reflected wryly, when a madman was brandishing a firearm at her, and he could not help but feel responsible. His father had overheard him once—he could not remember the exact details, for his childhood was a patchwork of such incidents—hesitantly asking Janner for some small service and had beaten him for it. A duke does not ask, his father had said. A duke expects. Inferiors need to know their place. To treat them otherwise is to do them disservice, for it is the certainties of rank that hold society together.

That Gracewood had chosen to learn different lessons—caring less for the preservation of power than its obligations—did not absolve him of responsibility. Nobody needed a reminder of their position, their dependency on your largesse, financially or socially or politically, nor did they need your discomfort, your vulnerability, or your inner turmoil. They needed, simply, to be put at ease. It was the least you owed. A small price for a fluke of birth that gave you far too much of everything.

He'd been good at it once. But it had been easier then, with a friend—an equal—at his side, and a heart that had known little of fear, or loss, or the barbarous indifferences of war. All the same, he had to try, and keep trying. In the right light, to a kind eye, he might even pass for the Duke of Gracewood instead of this cracked vase of a man that everyone could see through.

"Can I help you with something?" he asked.

"You...your sister thinks you work too hard."

"Poor Miss Carroll." He offered her a consoling smile. "She should not have made you play messenger for her."

That made her laugh, if a little nervously. "Can you blame her when there exist actual aphorisms about the fates of messengers?"

"I'd reassure you that I'm unarmed today, but I suspect that would only encourage further commentary on my poor aim."

"It *might*," she admitted, with a wicked lift of her brows.

Could his trying—trying to be complete, to be stable, not to jump at shadows—could it truly be enough? It felt like such a nothing of an offering. Yet he was glad to see her poise returning, and with it the promise of her smile, for he hadn't exaggerated his pleasure in it when they'd met upon the north tower.

Some part of him knew he was allowing himself too much liberty. That he shouldn't be so drawn to her. That it wasn't fair on either of them. But this was also the closest he had come to feeling even a little bit real—as though the person he'd used to be wasn't some half-remembered dream. So he lied. He let himself lie about who he was or wasn't or couldn't be. Because he was lonely. Because she was pretty. Because she could laugh when he had close to forgotten how.

"Why don't you sit?" He gestured to a nearby chair. "I would appreciate the company."

She hesitated, her fingers, in yet another pair of beautifully embroidered gloves, twisting together. "I'm not interrupting?"

"Oh, you are, and I am so very *very* grateful."

Another smile—far brighter than his sally deserved—and she took a seat. She was dressed as charmingly as ever, in some sort of green striped muslin—simple, but he suspected deceptively so. She was tall for a woman, her figure too spare to be as fashion preferred, but there was a natural elegance to her and an enticing subtlety of form suggested by the fall of her gown. From beneath its hem, with its delicate lacework, he could just about catch a glimpse of dark green satin half-boots—a perfect match for the choker of malachite chips that encircled her throat.

None of which were details of a lady's attire he would have noticed before, but nor would he have wanted to. It was Miss Carroll he sought, in these pieces of her selfhood so carefully placed before the world, even if it reminded him how little attention he gave his own appearance these days. How little it seemed to matter.

"What were you embarked upon," she asked, "that made distraction so welcome?"

He indicated the papers strewn across his desk. "I was in the process of looking for a new butler."

"What happened to Frith?" Miss Carroll gave a little cough. "That is, I think I heard his name was Frith. I think I overheard a servant, perhaps. Yes. That must be it."

"He passed away while I was in France."

A look of real sadness passed across Miss Carroll's face. "I'm sorry."

"So am I." Absently, he picked up a letter opener—a heavy silver implement, with the family crest set into the handle—and put it back down. "I seem to have made rather a habit of absence. My father died when I was at school."

"That must have been hard as well."

"Will you think me terribly unfeeling if I tell you it was not?" And would she have told him if she did? He remained a duke after all, she a lady's companion. "I know I was apprehensive of the great responsibility that had so abruptly become mine. But when it came to the man? Relief was the strongest emotion I can recall." He gazed at her, scrutinising her features for any indication that this unfilial confession had made her despise him, but he saw only compassion.

"Perhaps," she suggested, "he deserved no better."

"I am certainly glad to have run out of opportunities to disappoint him. Frith, though, I wish I could have been here. I would have liked him to know how greatly he was"—he faltered, not quite daring to utter the word that seemed most apt—"valued."

"I'm sure he did."

Frith had been everything to Gracewood his father had not. He glanced away, hoping but not truly believing that she would take it for an idle gesture. "I...struggle with the idea of replacing him."

"Oh, Gracewood." Miss Carroll made a soft sound, mostly, he thought, consoling but tinged with an unexpected sorrow. "You are not replacing *him*."

"No. I know that. Rationally. And, regardless, Morgencald cannot run without a butler."

There was a moment of silence, broken finally by the stir of Miss Carroll's skirts as she sat forward in her chair. "I hope," she said, with a marked effort at lightness, "you are giving due consideration to the most important trait any butler must possess."

"Which is what?"

She made him wait, curious and tantalised for a second or two. "Why, an excellent name."

"Of course." What faculty did she possess, what gift, what magic that could conjure laughter from nothing. From dust and air. From places so full of tears. "After all, one can hardly say, we shall take tea in the green drawing room...Green."

Now he had made her laugh. Not, he knew, an uncommon accomplishment. But it still felt like one he would always celebrate, never tire of. "Or," she offered, "please show our guests upstairs, Carstairs."

"Is that someone at the door..." He was not as quick as she was and had to pause a second or two to arrange his reply. "Dorchester."

"If you please, my coat, Coates," returned Miss Carroll, without hesitation.

And he wanted very much to come back with something, something that would impress and delight her and show him to advantage for once—his spirit alive, for all the limitations of his body—but he was blank with mirth. Which was, in a way, its own reprieve: a few precious seconds where the world was a simple place again, and all he had to feel was simple too. Amusement. Appreciation. Companionship.

He pressed his fingers to his lips, not knowing what kind of noise was caught in the back of his throat, and almost frightened of it. Of what his own laughter had become in the years since it had last been natural to him. "What do you think would be the right sort of name for a butler, then?"

"Widdershins. What about you?"

"Oh. Well…" Again, he had to think. But, then, Marleigh had made him think too, and he had welcomed it—turning his mind from the tracks his father had laid out for him and into the unbound spaces of whimsy, absurdity, and mischief. "I am rather taken with the idea of having a butler called Swordfish."

She nodded gravely. "Yes, I like that. Stately yet enigmatic, with a hint of ferocity."

"And if I cannot find either a Widdershins or a Swordfish willing to move to Northumberland?"

"Perhaps Duckworth? Or Birtwhistle? Or you could do worse than Trickelbank."

"I could," he agreed, smiling.

"Or you could offer the position to a member of your current staff."

The thought had not occurred to him, though he saw immediately that it had merit. Those who had stayed with him through the last few years had already demonstrated their loyalty, and he

would at least know something of the person he was entrusting with his household, rather than having to rely on an agency
and references from a stranger. "I'm not certain anyone has the
experience."

"They would need guidance." She paused, regarding him with
a slight frown. "But I'm afraid I've spoken out of turn. This is
really none of my business."

"On the contrary, Miss Carroll. I was the one to raise the subject in the first place, and I respect your insight."

She was blushing now, and far too earnestly for it to flatter
her. "I'm just a lady's companion. I understand very little of estate
management."

"You have a quick mind, and a generous nature, neither of
which should be under-valued. The only reason I'm hesitating…"
And here he briefly lost his train of thought, unaccustomed
to being able to share such matters. "I find myself having to
resolve a peculiar calculus. I wish to disrupt the other servants
as little as possible, and I can't tell if that is best accomplished
by engaging an outsider with experience of the position but no
familiarity with Morgencald, who may very well decide after a
month of rain and isolation that the north is not for him, putting us back at square one. Or by promoting someone who lacks
direct experience of the role but understands the household—
risking the possibility of resentment among the rest of the
staff, or my appointment simply being unequal to the task before
him."

"I think," said Miss Carroll, "if you cannot reason your way to
the answer, you'll have to trust your instincts. And your heart."

"I'm not sure I was raised to set much store by either."

"How"—her voice trembled slightly—"how you were raised is not who you are. I know you'll make the right decision."

He folded his elbows on the desk, watching her across it, searching for something he barely understood how to look for. "Why is it that you have such faith in me? I have done nothing to earn it."

There was a momentary pause, Miss Carroll's eyes—which normally held his gaze so steadily—slipping away to linger, instead, upon the intricacies carved into the wood-panelled walls. Of course, he had embarrassed her. It had been too blunt a question.

"It is clear to me," she offered finally, "that you are a good man. Even if it is no longer clear to you."

"What a dangerous thing it is, Miss Carroll, to believe yourself good. In war we are all either meat or murderers." God, what was he saying? And without the defence of opium or alcohol. "But I'm... I'm glad you think well of me."

"In war, we do what we must. It is no sin to survive."

"I don't believe in sin any more. I'm not sure I ever did."

She tilted her head curiously. "You don't?"

"Does this seem an ordered universe to you? One designed with purpose and consistency, in accordance with some set of universal principles?"

"Not always," she admitted. "But there is beauty in it. And I sometimes feel, or at least dare to hope for, benevolence."

"Your world seems like it would be a fine place to live."

"And what is in yours? If not God?"

How long since he had just... talked to someone? He had taken it for granted with Marleigh. But how sweet it was, how wondrous, simply to share your thoughts in the surety of welcome, and to feel equal surety in your ability to offer the same. "I suppose," he said, "there's just... ourselves. The capacity in each of us to love more than we hate, do more good than we do ill, help more than we harm. Is such understanding really divine? Or is it simply human?"

"I was afraid you had grown cynical. But"—the dimple shimmered at the corner of her mouth—"perhaps you're an idealist, after all."

"I'm not sure I'm either. I think it's more that I wish to take responsibility for my actions. Those that I feel to be right, and those that I feel to be wrong."

Her eyes narrowed into sharp little blades, twisting his soul open as effortlessly as an oyster shell. "Are you implying that what you did in the war was wrong?"

"Of course it was wrong. How could it not be?"

"Préférez-vous parler français maintenant?"

"It's not that simple for me. What we did was necessary and just, perhaps even unavoidable. But all the pretty philosophies and worthy scholarship in the world can't change the fact that I have killed men who did not need to die. Men who were no better or worse than I. Who were doing nothing I would not have done myself."

"We were at war. It's not the same."

"I try to believe that, but it *feels* the same. And that is something I must live with."

He had to put a stop to this. It was a May Day dance, ceaseless and circular, ribbons of shame, guilt, regret, despair binding him ever more tightly. Worse, he had horrified Miss Carroll, for she was gazing at him with a terrible anguish in her eyes. And when she opened her mouth to speak, the sound seemed to catch in her throat, turning harsh and jagged. Then her gloved hands were shielding her face, and tears were spilling between her fingers.

"Oh God," she said. "Oh, Gracewood. My poor Gracewood. I...I...can't. I can't do this."

And before he could ask her why, or what she meant, or what "this" even was, she had fled.

# CHAPTER 10

Lady Marleigh was in the drawing room, deep in her correspondence, when Viola burst in.

"How are things progressing with—oh." It took her a moment, but Lady Marleigh saw the tears in Viola's eyes. "Has he hurt you? I shall be extremely stern with him if he has hurt you."

"If *he* has hurt me?" Viola found herself caught between laughing and sobbing. "Louise, this was *your* idea. I wanted to leave—I *should* have left. Seeing him like this, it's...more than I can bear."

"But he's getting better, isn't he?" asked Lady Marleigh. "Still has the beard, of course, and God knows if he's still drinking all night, but he's rising in the mornings and he's civil with the servants. A few more days of your ministrations and he might even be fit for company."

"I'm not ministrating. At best I'm...I'm *there*."

"Well then, you're improving him by your very presence."

That felt like an exaggeration. Certainly, Gracewood had been trying. Anyone could see he'd been trying. The thought that he had been trying for her was...gratifying and mortifying and impossible. "This isn't about the state of him. It's—it's the fact of him. Of me. Of us."

Realising the conversation might be significant, Lady Marleigh laid down her quill. "I don't follow."

"I don't know how to explain. How it *feels* to be with him again."

"Ah," offered Lady Marleigh sagely. "Feelings."

It was difficult to cry and subject one's sister-in-law to a withering look at the same time. Although, since Viola hated crying, she was relieved to be able to focus on the withering. "Yes, Louise, feelings. You have them too."

"Not disruptively in the midst of an otherwise successfully unfolding plan."

Viola managed a cool smile. "I apologise for the inconvenience."

"It is what it is." It was Lady Marleigh's reassuring voice. Then she paused. "Ah. No, *I* apologise."

The part of Viola she was sure was a sharp-tongued harridan—especially when she felt uncertain—was tempted to throw back "it is what it is." Except Louise would have found such a response genuinely hurtful. "It doesn't matter," she said instead. "I'm being a thousand kinds of foolish."

Lady Marleigh's brow creased thoughtfully. "You were the closest of companions for many years. It makes sense that seeing what Gracewood has become would be difficult for you."

"It is."

"But it is also"—this was already perilously close to turning into one of Lady Marleigh's encouraging conversations—"why you are best placed to help him now. And, through him, Mira."

"I know." It was acknowledgement and frustration both. And Viola wished she had her embroidery with her, simply so she had something to occupy her hands—not that she was calm enough to do anything other than make a mess of it. So she began to pace, her heels making anxious music upon the polished wooden floor.

It was not surprising that Louise had chosen this room out of the many available in Morgencald. The Faire Chamber it was called, being lighter in both the literal and decorative sense than almost anywhere else in the castle—one of the de Veres having had it renovated for some lady or another, with arched windows, gilt furniture, and a delicately carved mantel. Not the sort of place to hold much appeal to a young Gracewood and his friend, though truthfully Viola had always thought it pretty.

"Is it so very beyond managing," Lady Marleigh asked, "that you think well of each other still?"

Viola braced herself against the window frame, gazing down the smooth slope of the hill towards the village. "With him not knowing who I am? Or who he used to believe I was?"

"That may change. In time."

How could it? And, even if it could, in between there would still be conversations like today, where he would confide in her, and look at her, and laugh with her. Take comfort from her. Offer his thoughts to her. She would want to coax his smiles from him as she'd used to. She would want to share his life again. She would want—

She would want too much—of what it was not possible to have.

"It's different," she heard herself say.

A shuffling of paper from where Lady Marleigh was sitting. Like Viola, she was not at ease in idleness and, unable to continue her correspondence, had apparently chosen to organise it. "What is different?"

"With Gracewood."

"Well"—a touch of impatience coloured Lady Marleigh's tone—"he assumes you're a stranger."

"No. But...the way he talks to me. The things he says. It's different."

"Viola." Now Lady Marleigh spoke with more than a touch of impatience.

Viola let her fingertips skate lightly over the glass—patterns from the heat of her skin that faded as swiftly as dreams in daylight. "I thought I knew him. I *did* know him. We would have given our lives for each other. But this is the first time he has ever given me—"

Except she had no way to describe it. Some truth of himself, hidden before. *He was the joy of my life*, Gracewood had told her upon the north tower. Which was nothing he could have said when they had not been strangers. Oh, they had shared secrets, moments of vulnerability when in their cups or when some circumstance had cracked the shell of their youthful confidence. But mainly their closeness was built around common experiences of school and family, age, and position. He was her truest friend, and she had never seen him until now. She almost pitied the people they had once been, that they could be so dear and know so little of each other.

"Is this what men do?" Viola demanded, seeking refuge from her uncertainties in vexation. "Stumble to the nearest woman and pour out their hearts?"

"Well"—somehow Lady Marleigh's very tone contained a shrug—"a little bit. I mean, no. Not really. You were there for him at what—given that people do not generally roam their homes late at night with loaded guns because all is well—can only have been quite a dark moment. You have shown him understanding and compassion when he has probably felt alone for a long time. It is not so very surprising he trusts you."

A bitter laugh clawed its way out of Viola's throat. "I remind him of…me."

"Again," remarked Lady Marleigh with her usual well-intentioned pragmatism, "not so very surprising."

Viola sighed. "I am bad at dissembling, Louise. I have nearly betrayed myself repeatedly. He will recognise me. And then he will hate me. If not for who I am, then for the past two years. And it will be worse than anything I have imagined, because now I know...." Viola let the edge of her brow rest against the glass. It wasn't cooling, as she'd hoped, but a sick, sharp chill. "Now I know *this*."

"This?" It was an inescapably direct question, but delivered in Lady Marleigh's gentlest voice.

"Yes." Viola closed her eyes. Her own reflection, in that moment, hazy as it was, showed her too many flaws. "*This*. Knowing what it is to understand a little of his heart. What it is to have him look at me with...with a particular kind of admiration. To seek that admiration from me in return."

There was a kind of stillness in the room, that heavy sense of having said too much or perhaps too little.

Finally, Lady Marleigh spoke. "Is that what you want? From Gracewood? *With* Gracewood?" And, then, when Viola made no reply, for there was none she knew how to give: "Were you in love with him?"

Viola whirled round. She shouldn't have been startled—in fact, she had half expected Lady Marleigh might say something of the sort—but being uttered aloud had given the idea more substance than she had ever before allowed it. "*Louise*."

"It's not an unreasonable question."

"But it has no reasonable answer."

Ever supportive, Lady Marleigh considered this. "Yes seems reasonable," she suggested. A pause. "As does no."

Trying to be evasive with Lady Marleigh never worked. Although it wasn't really Lady Marleigh that, on this occasion, Viola was trying to evade. "It wasn't possible to love him. I could barely make sense of myself."

"And now?"

"Now?" repeated Viola, once again caught between laughter and tears. "Now it is even less possible. Every day I spend with Gracewood, I am trapped between who I am and who I was, always terrified that one will swallow the other."

Lady Marleigh winced.

"And I can't keep doing this." Despair was like stagnant water. It seeped through the cracks of her. And occasionally—as it did now, as it had in Gracewood's study—rose up to drown her in its bleak and brackish tides. "I can't keep offering some semblance of friendship to a man I—a man I must have always loved, in ways I had no hope of comprehending, and know that I am holding half of myself from him, and that I *must* for fear of breaking his heart for the second time."

Silence gathered like dust amid the gilt. Upon the inlaid writing desk, where Lady Marleigh sat with her letters. In the petals of the pink roses that ran along the frieze at the top of the walls.

"It appears"—Lady Marleigh was speaking very slowly—"that I have significantly underestimated the complexity of this situation. If you wish to go home, you may take the carriage. I will remain here and do what I can."

Viola should have been relieved. It was the reprieve she had been seeking. That she needed. But this abandonment felt calculated, in ways the first had not. It felt like defeat. "I do not think you will be well suited to the task."

"Neither do I." Lady Marleigh made a helpless gesture. "But

something must be done for Mira. And it was never my intent, in bringing you here, to cause you such hurt."

"And Gracewood?"

"Is already much improved. You've done more than enough."

For a wild moment, Viola imagined telling him, and damn the consequences. She imagined him seeing her—seeing *all* of her—and holding her to him and smiling and saying simply *of course* and *I understand* and *you are still the joy of my life*. She imagined his arms about her, his lips on hers, his hand on the nape of her neck as he drew her closer, whispering *Viola, Viola, my sweet Viola*. And then—then what? Would he lie with her? Marry her? Make her his duchess? A duke would need an heir, and that she could never give him. Even in this perfect world she had conjured for herself she could never be to him what she might, in her heart of hearts, wish to be.

Gracewood had thought her a ghost when he first saw her. Perhaps there had been more truth to that than either of them had realised. What was she, after all, but an echo, half a memory, a tale somebody once told about a girl who got lost on a battlefield? Whatever Lady Marleigh might have thought, it could never be her place to lead Gracewood back into the world. How could she when in the eyes of the world women like her did not, could not, exist?

If she had gone to him the moment she arrived in England, would it—could it—have been different? Could she have spared him some of his suffering? But she had come so far and changed so much and known so little of how to live in her new life that it had been all she could do to return to Marleigh Court and throw herself on the mercy of her brother and sister-in-law. And there she had made herself a prisoner, afraid to leave while she still walked stiffly, curtseyed awkwardly, held her hands and her head wrong. The more she had learned, the more she'd found she did not know and the more impossible it had seemed that she would ever show herself to society, to their friends. To the only friend who mattered.

And then...Miranda's letter. And the coach. And the gunshot. And the tower. And Gracewood, Gracewood, Gracewood. It was as though seeing him again had rewritten her story, made it strange and wonderful and terrifying, spun meaning where there had been none. And it was poison, to both of them.

Exhausted, her head a chaos of warring wants and fears, Viola sank into an armchair, hid her face in her hands, and, for the second time that day, wept.

# CHAPTER 11

It had been too late to leave the day before, so Viola had occupied herself with packing and spent a mostly sleepless night, waiting for light enough to travel safely by. She was doing the right thing. She wasn't doing the right thing. She was. She wasn't. Her mind was a pendulum, ceaseless and unresting. Motion without meaning. Because how could she know? How could she ever know? If she knew what she knew now, would she have acted differently in the past? Or was she Claudius in the throne room, full of remorse but unrepentant. Besides, he had killed his brother. She, only herself. And to have gone on as she was would have been its own death. The days would have bled her out. That was always the problem: Whatever you did, or did not do, whether it was just or the reverse, no matter how necessary it felt, life moved mercilessly forward.

Her possessions were sufficiently slight that she was able to carry her travelling trunk without assistance—though her journey with it down the corridors and staircases of Morgencald, doing her best not to trip on her skirts, was not particularly elegant. She had chosen not to seek assistance, partly because a lady's companion occupied an ill-defined space, neither servant nor family, but mainly out of cowardice, wanting to be gone before Gracewood noticed her absence. Not that she thought he would try to prevent her leaving. It was encountering him at all she hoped to avoid. And perhaps that made her selfish as well as cowardly, but she could not be both cause and cure, a stranger and a friend, his past and his future.

She should, she thought, be accustomed to impossible choices. If nothing else, her life ought to have taught her that. But it had not. And so here she was, fleeing from a house as familiar as her own, and the man she kept leaving behind—once at Waterloo, with no notion then that she would not return, and now certain that she could not.

There was light beneath the library door, a spill of dusty gold that made Viola flinch at the idea of Gracewood alone and sleepless in the shadows. But he was strong, for all he was lost, and for all he'd been hurt. And perhaps she'd helped a little? Perhaps in a few years' time he would be lying in some other woman's arms, his fingers idle in her hair, and think of a dark night and someone who might as well have been a ghost, and it would be nothing more than a chance encounter. A moment before he remembered how to seek his own happiness. Before he remembered he deserved to.

Oh, how she wanted that for him—even if she could not bear to imagine it.

Then came a crash from within, the discordant music of shattering glass. It could have meant nothing or very well been an accident, and she could have walked away—probably she should have—but she stopped. Truthfully, it felt inevitable she would. It was one thing to slip away, as irrelevant as she was always supposed to be. Quite another to turn from him when he was in need. Putting down her trunk, she let herself quietly into the library.

Gracewood, stripped to his shirtsleeves, was sitting at his

desk, gilt-edged in the candlelight. His head was in his hands, though he glanced up when she entered—seeming far from surprised to see her.

"Miss Carroll," he said. "You have an uncanny knack for finding me at my worst."

She had to admit, he did not look well. Perhaps even less so than on the night he had come upon them with a pistol in his hand. There was something almost feverish about him—his skin drawn tight across his bones, sallow-tinged and pricked with sweat. Though his eyes, at least, were clear. "I heard a noise."

"And you came to investigate dressed for travelling?"

"I…"

His lucidity should have been a relief—and it was. Except it left her nowhere to hide. "Are you leaving?" he asked.

"I think I must."

"Must you? I know I am poor company, but have I really driven you from my home?"

"It was not you. It was—" She broke off, not knowing how to finish and eventually settled on "Me." And, then to forestall, albeit only temporarily, further questions: "What happened? Did you break something?"

With a flicker of slightly trembling fingers, he gestured into the shadows beyond the circle of illumination offered by the candles. There was a dark stain upon the wall and, on the floor beneath, the glint of broken glass.

"What offended you?" Viola asked. "The wall or the bottle?"

"The bottle. I've been trying to reduce my use of laudanum. It is…" Gracewood grimaced. "More difficult than I expected."

"How so?"

He shook his head. "You do not wish to hear this."

"Of course I do."

But again, he demurred. "It's weakness, nothing more."

"Have you spoken to your doctor?" Viola suggested.

And was startled when he laughed—a grating, unpleasant kind of laugh. "Yes. He said that if I was suffering due to a lack of laudanum, I should alleviate myself with—"

"Laudanum?"

He mimed a bow, as best he was able when sitting. "Indeed."

"And you see no merit in this advice?" Hesitantly Viola stepped a little closer, conscious that she was once again alone with Gracewood at an unseemly hour, and this time—for all his inclinations ran to the smashing of glassware—he was fully in command of his senses.

"I am grown wary of a substance that seems to offer, in the same hand, both succor and pain."

It was easier, in that moment, to stare at a laudanum stain and some fragments of glass than meet his eyes. "That is wise, Your Grace."

"I had this fetched posthaste from London." The soft scuff of leather as he slid a book across the desk to her. "It was published over a century ago and yet remains in relative obscurity."

"I really should be—" Leaving. She should be leaving. He was well, or as well as could be hoped under the circumstances. But now she was curious. And being with Gracewood, for all the ways it was new, had an irresistible familiarity to it. Her life had changed beyond reckoning—as had she—but this *fit*. Like a groove worn into the passing years. "What is it?"

"*The Mysteries of Opium Reveal'd*. It claims to explain how its 'noxious principles' can be mitigated in order to render it safe for use."

Viola settled herself before the desk. "Noxious principles?"

"See here"—Gracewood tapped the page before them—"where it discusses the consequences of declination of use. And what it calls the 'seeming contradictions' in the effects of opium." He huffed out a breath. "How can it be that this supposed panacea induces both rest and wakefulness, perspiration and lack thereof, excites the spirits and quiets them, brings madness and composure both?"

"I believe you are right then," said Viola, "to discontinue its use. Though I am beginning to understand that it may be no easy matter to do so. Is there any aid regarding that?"

Gracewood's lips twitched. "For the nausea and related effects, it suggests the yolk of an egg. For fainting, a glass of wine. And for melancholy and heaviness of the spirit, I am to be exposed stark naked to the coldest air. There is only one of those solutions I am willing to contemplate, but I am also attempting to reduce my consumption of alcohol."

"You are in the right part of the country for the cold air." She offered a slightly uncertain smile—wanting him to laugh with her in adversity, as they had used to, and was gratified to see an answering gleam deep in his eyes.

"Given my staff already have to contend with me shouting at ghosts, shooting firearms, and breaking bottles, I feel it is my duty to ensure they do not also have to contend with me unclad."

"How considerate of you," she murmured, not needing the reminder that she had incidentally seen Gracewood unclad on many occasions. Not that she had ever dwelled upon it. And not, now that dwelling might have felt less bewildering, that her memory had retained much: just the glow of sunlight upon skin, an impression of strength, and the scars he did his best to hide. "Are the effects of reduced usage severe to experience?"

"Miss Carroll, please, I have some pride."

This, too, she had difficulty navigating. The balance of his confidences and withdrawals—of knowing there were some intimacies she did not deserve, and others he shared only with Miss Carroll. "What do you mean?"

"I would rather not encourage you to see me as infirm."

"And I don't." She had spoken, perhaps, too quickly, too surely. For she did not, but it was not the sort of thing that ladies lightly discussed with gentlemen.

Thankfully, other than a sharp look, he did not seem inclined to challenge her. "It is not," he went on slowly, "merely the physical effects with which one must struggle. There is a...I'm not sure how to describe it. The thought of laudanum is very...very *present*, in my mind."

She pondered this for a moment. "Well, I think that's natural, isn't it? If you know something will help what ails you?"

"But when you cut your hand, do you simply think you would benefit from a bandage, or do you crave one? Does your world feel diminished in the absence of a bandage? Do you learn to doubt your own capacity to resist a bandage if available?" He fell silent, his words fading into the surrounding darkness. "Forgive me. My thoughts are a little disordered. I should not be—"

"On the contrary"—she knew better than to cut over her social superiors, but on this occasion failed to prevent herself—"now I know why you smashed the bottle."

This surprised a laugh out of him—something younger, and truer, untainted by bitterness or despair. "Frankly, I did not think I could be trusted near it. But, with hindsight, I could just as well have poured it away."

"Had you done that, I would not have heard you and I..." Too used to speaking her mind to Gracewood, the words had already escaped. And there was nothing Viola could do to pull them back. "And I would be gone."

"Very true," returned Gracewood dryly. "And now *man suffering from laudanum declination* may join *man in the grip of loss and madness* among your treasured memories of Northumberland. But, Miss Carroll, I think we have been honest with each other, you and I. Will you not tell me what made you cry yesterday? Is it why you are leaving?"

Her heart was its own blade, twisting inside her. "If I told you I simply had a prior engagement I dare not miss? Or a friend waiting for me? Would you believe me?"

"I could believe you"—his voice grew soft as the shadows—"if that was what you wanted." And, when she did not know what to say, he went on. "How shall I think of this friend of yours? Let me guess: some acquaintance of Badger's, or Lord Marleigh as he would be now, perhaps the son of a nearby landowner?"

This felt like a game—one of their old games. Except there was an edge to it she did not understand. "I...I don't see why not."

"He met you at a card party. Or a dinner? Began to notice you upon his visits to the family. His smiles drew you in, his bright eyes, his easy companionship. When you dance with him, it feels like you are flying—"

And, again, she had to interrupt him, something that was not quite a laugh breaking on her lips. "Gracewood. What are you saying? And why are you saying it? There is no such person."

"Oh, but there so easily could be. Surely you do not believe your charms work only upon broken dukes?"

"I think they might," she replied. "And who is this imaginary man you are consigning me to?"

"He is a catch, Miss Carroll. Young, handsome, wealthy, pure of soul, sound of mind and body. Everything a man should be."

"Are you sure? He sounds conventional and, to be candid, not so very intelligent. I suspect he talks to me only of the weather and the health of our families."

"What would you have him talk to you about?"

"I…" Viola's head was already spinning. "I would have him talk to me as you do."

"I have given you an ideal suitor"—the words held a note of mockery, though perhaps not for her—"and you would subject him to war and grief, and the weight of his own failures?"

"No. I mean—why is this what you desire for me?"

He shrugged. "Is it so wrong, that I would prefer to think of you happy beyond the gates of Morgencald?"

"I want you to be happy also." Her voice was wavering. She took a second to steady it. "Perhaps we could promise each other?"

He lifted his brows. "Promise each other to be happy?"

"Promise each other to try," she finished desperately.

There was a long silence. She had not needed his sardonic look to recognise how flimsy, how absurd, an idea it had been.

"Miss Carroll," he said finally. "Are you—forgive my bluntness—an adventuress?"

Whatever she might have expected, this was not it. She spluttered. "What? No. Of course not. What made you—why would you—"

He held up a conciliatory hand. "I apologise. It was simply a thought that occurred to me."

She gazed at him, lost for any sort of response, and still more than a little horrified.

"You've been so very kind to me," he continued, now looking

rather abashed himself. "And I am so very drawn to you. But I do not understand why you should be kind, or why I should be drawn, nor why you fled me the last time we spoke."

"And so you thought it part of some…some twisted game I was playing?"

A faint blush swept the aristocratic arch of his cheekbones. "Now I have voiced the notion, it seems both presumptuous and implausible."

"And insulting," snapped Viola. Although it could almost have been amusing. All the time she had squandered, terrified he might recognise her, that she might drive him deeper into despair. And, instead, he had concluded she was some kind of…she hardly knew. Fortune huntress? Perhaps, in the end, that was better than the truth.

"Again," he said, "I apologise. I sincerely apologise."

Except…if this was better than the truth, why did it hurt her so badly? "Did you really believe I was trifling with you? That I would or could trifle with you?"

"Miss Carroll, I dream of dead men and shake for lack of laudanum. I have spent the past two years deep in my cups. And, honestly, before Waterloo I had little but youth and my name to recommend me. All of which is to say, I hardly know what I believe one moment to the next. You should not listen to me nor give any credence to my words."

She glared at him. "Is it so impossible that I might see good in you? Hope for better for you? That you would rather brand me a…a swindler than listen to me? Give credence to *my* words?"

"The fact is"—he met her fury, as he always had, without flinching—"I meant to tell you that it doesn't matter. I wondered if perhaps you'd had some change of heart or your conscience had made you second-guess yourself."

"Oh, so I am a *repentant* manipulatrix?"

Still, his gaze did not waver. There was something luminous in his conviction, more powerful even than his tired eyes or haggard complexion, and she allowed herself—for a few fleeting, stolen seconds—to find him beautiful. "Whatever the cause," he said, "your care has felt real. As have you. I am grateful, and I wish you would stay. If you can."

Restlessly, she rose. Then recalled that ladies were supposed to be restrained in action as well as speech and sat back down. Of course, neither standing nor sitting helped her make any more sense of herself. She was utterly storm-tossed, flung from regret to anger to hope and back again until she hardly knew what she wanted anymore, let alone what was the right thing to do. If the fact he had asked her to stay was absolution, or simply an excuse that allowed her to linger over the crumbs of their friendship when it was doing no good to either of them. "I shouldn't."

"Shouldn't is neither will not nor cannot."

"It's complicated," she tried. "You don't understand."

"Then help me." He leaned forward slightly, elbows on the desk, fingers loosely interwoven. "What happened yesterday? Perhaps I can be of use to you."

He looked so very earnest—and so very…not fragile, he could never be that. Precarious, perhaps? A man holding himself together with everything he had.

And as for her, she was trapped all over again. It was neither the time to speak nor the time to leave. So she chose what she hoped was the path of compromise—the path that did least harm—and told him the only truth she could.

# CHAPTER 12

Gracewood did not think he had really believed Miss Carroll was an adventuress, but it had not seemed entirely beyond the bounds of possibility. She was, after all, beautiful, mysterious, and—given she was working as a lady's companion—at least somewhat impoverished. And even if it did not, in any meaningful fashion, help him make sense of her, it at least offered some route to explaining him. How easy it was to talk to her. To trust her. The way his world felt complete again when he was with her. Had she been, somehow or other, practised in the arts of drawing people in, it would have soothed his pride a little.

Instead, there was only the truth, stark and unlovely though it was: that he was alone and she had been there, and it was easier to confide in her precisely *because* she did not know him. That it felt safer to offer the fragments of the man he had once been to a stranger than to anyone who might recognise how little of him remained.

"It's…" began Miss Carroll, before falling hopelessly silent again, her gloved hands twisting in her lap.

"Whatever 'it' is…I can assure you, I will not be angry or upset." It was an assurance Gracewood felt confident offering, given he was, at this point, curious more than anything.

She swallowed, a tense little click, and the sound was everywhere in the quiet room. "It's your sister. She…I don't know how to explain without—oh, to hell with it. Lady Miranda wants to go to London with us but doesn't want to leave you. And so Louise—"

"Miss Carroll, Mira has made it clear that she's not ready for a season." Normally Gracewood would have been more careful not to interrupt a lady, but this was nonsense.

"Yes," returned Miss Carroll with a kind of dogged patience, "she's doing something I understand to be fairly common when it comes to seventeen-year-olds and their guardians. She's lying to you."

Nonsense again, surely. His guardianship of Miranda had perhaps been a little neglectful, but Gracewood had given her no cause to lie to him. "Why would she do that?"

"She thinks she's protecting you."

"From what?" he asked, with a presentiment that he would mislike the answer.

"Most obviously yourself."

"Ah." He rose without hope of dignity, taking his weight on the back of his chair so he did not fall. "I was not aware she was harbouring such concern for me."

"You have not been paying attention."

Catching up his cane from where it rested against the desk, he limped heavily over to the window. There was very little to see outside, just a blink's worth of stone and sky, both grey with encroaching dawn. But it gave him the moment he needed for the wasp sting of fresh humiliation to fade into something he was used to. Something he could bear. "You're quite right, as always, Miss Carroll. But it does not explain"—and here he turned back to her—"what I did to make *you* so unhappy."

"It was not you," she said quickly. "Lady Marleigh had

encouraged me to try and raise your spirits. She thought if you seemed...better, then Mira would—"

"Accompany you to London."

She nodded wretchedly. "I think Louise felt you might be more inclined to listen to me than you would her."

"Well, she was correct. I trust you. And, despite the circumstances, I welcome your company."

"As I welcome yours."

It was such a mild expression of regard, barely more than an echo of his own, but, somehow, it felt like more. Or perhaps it was simply that she had given him exactly what he needed—the sense of being, even in such a small way, someone to someone else. He stepped back to the desk, lowering himself into his father's chair. "Thank you for telling me the truth, Miss Carroll."

She hung her head a little at that, her dark curls falling forward to momentarily obscure her face. Perhaps she was still distressed at her own role in what was a rather minor affair, and ultimately a well-intentioned one. "I," she said in a rather stifled voice. "I...have been a poor friend to you. And a poor agent to Lady Marleigh."

"How so?" he asked gently.

"Because I've failed in my task." Once again, her hands curled in her lap. "I was supposed to...help you. Not try to run away and then reveal the whole scheme in a fit of self-regard."

"And this scheme of Lady Marleigh's," he asked, "only works if I'm not party to it?"

The slightest of pauses. "What are you suggesting?"

"I'm suggesting"—he rested his elbows on the desk, before realising how familiar the gesture felt, how like the old duke it made him look—"that we continue as planned. If, that is, you have no objection."

"Continue as...?"

"Yes. You help me, however you were intending to. Mira concludes she is finally free to pursue her own happiness."

Miss Carroll raised her head at last. She had a most expressive way of thinking. It brought a brightness to her eyes. Made them shine like dark mirrors. "I confess," she said slowly, "I hadn't given much consideration as to how I, or you, or both of us would go about convincing Mira that you need not be a source of concern for her."

"A shame." He could not quite keep the dryness from his tone. "I was rather interested."

"Perhaps," she offered, "you could do as we have done, and simply talk to your sister honestly?"

He chuckled then, and the momentary liberty of it caused his elbow to knock against the cane that had been balanced beside him, sending it to the floor with a clunk. "Oh, Miss Carroll, you are indeed a poor conspirator. If I talk to Mira, then the whole of Lady Marleigh's plan unravels. I may even sow distrust between them."

Again one of her most fascinating looks—measuring and wicked. "So you want to play their game? But make it yours?"

"Ours." The word tasted like a kiss, like the heat of her mouth under his.

"I suppose," she said carefully, "that if I let Louise talk me into this in the first place, it is only fair that I allow you the same foolishness."

On her lips, the promise of *foolishness* sounded impossibly sweet. It reminded him of Marleigh and a world where laughter lived—where a little indignity was not to dishonour a legacy centuries in the making, and kindness need not be weakness.

Unfortunately, it was then that she chose to cross to the side of the desk in order to retrieve his cane.

And just like that, he felt entirely the wrong kind of fool again. "I would prefer you didn't treat me as an invalid, Miss Carroll."

He had expected to discomfort her—most people were discomforted when they noticed, or remembered, his injury, or when circumstance drew attention to it. And yet more so when he rejected the pity he knew it had become his duty to accept graciously.

Miss Carroll, though, simply re-settled his cane within easy reach and asked, "Why were the 95th sent to hold the sand-quarry?"

"Why were...?" The abrupt change of subject—and in such a specific direction—had caught him rather off guard. "Why were what?"

"Why were the 95th sent to hold the sand-quarry?"

"Well, because we were in position, and best suited to do it."

"I see. And did that reflect poorly upon the rest of the army?"

At this point, he wasn't sure how successfully he was concealing his bewilderment. "Of course not."

"I picked up your cane for you," she told him, "because I was in position, and best suited to do it."

He hardly knew if he wanted to concede her point or not—how to separate his pride from his shame, from his fear, from the need for her to think well of him. "That...that is not how other people would see it."

"Then that is their error." Her gaze held his, unflinching. "It need not be ours."

"Perhaps. But I do not relish the reminder."

"That you were wounded in service to your country?"

"That I am not…" His voice, in that moment, did not sound as a duke's voice should. "As I was."

Miss Carroll was still on his side of the desk. Lifting her hand, she let the tips of her fingers brush softly over his cheek, her gloves warm from her skin. And suddenly she felt like a stranger. And how odd for it to be this—this touch which was barely a touch at all—that seemed, at last, unfamiliar. "Nobody is as they were," she said. "That is what life *is*."

Perhaps. But, once upon a time, she could have been his. Of course, he would not have dreamed of seducing a respectable woman, and his father would never have permitted him to court a mere companion. They could have flirted, though, and shared secrets in the moonlight, and she might even have offered him a kiss or two from that smiling mouth. And then later, or so he hoped, thought back with pleasure on the time a duke had admired her.

Now what would she remember? A drunken, grieving, laudanum-addled cripple, shirking his responsibilities and neglecting his family.

He took her gently by the wrist, uncertain whether his intent was to prevent or prolong her closeness. "A generous sentiment. But not one, I think, that will fly in the face of Mira's—and I assume Lady Marleigh's—conviction that I am unstable and should not be left to my own devices."

"Is that what you want, though? To remain here by yourself?"

"Well, I'm a little old to make my debut."

"You know," she said, laughing, "that's not what I meant."

He shrugged. "Morgencald is mine. And I belong to Morgencald. It is who I am."

"You are not your name."

"All the same, I have a duty to it, which Mira does not. I would like her to…to be happy, Miss Carroll."

"Clearly that is something you wish for each other."

"Then"—he sat back in his chair—"you will help me?"

And very slowly, she nodded.

He hardly knew what he felt just then: relief, he thought, and the fretful pleasure of having something he knew he did not deserve. After all, he had no claim on Miss Carroll, or her time, and yet he coveted both. Still, she seemed willing enough to offer her company, and soon she would go back to London with her mistress. Was it really so wrong to have this now—whatever *this* was. The flicker of a shadow of a feeling like friendship.

"How do I restore Mira's faith in me?" he asked. "Or, at the very least, her faith in my mental competency?"

It was not a question a gentleman could pose to a lady and retain any semblance of pride, so he tried to make light of it. Unfortunately that just made him aware of what it might be like to be having a different conversation, one that was truly light, and how natural it would have felt, with her standing there, leaning delicately against the edge of the desk, the toes of her pretty green boots poking out from beneath the hem of her dress. But she had seen too much of what opium had done to him. What grief and war and weakness had done to him.

She gave him a sad smile, as one might give to a harmless elderly gentleman, long past his glory days. "I know the past couple of years have been difficult for you, but we can tell how hard you're working now. The changes you're trying to make."

All the *hard work* he had done so far was the work of putting down the bottle and facing the world with a clear head. But she was correct in that he was—if nothing else—trying. "Perhaps

Mira would feel encouraged if she knew I was to visit my ten-ants tomorrow. I've left the running of my estate to my steward for too long. I...that is. Do you like riding? Would you care to accompany me?"

At this, Miss Carroll positively glowed. Then she hesitated, looking down. He should not have accused her of being an adventuress; it had served only to remind her of the difference in their stations. "I *love* riding," she said at last, her voice a strange mix of pleased and plaintive. "That is to say—yes. Yes, I would be delighted."

"You would? That's wonderful. I'm sure Janner can find you a mount suitable for a la—"

Her mood seemed to shift again. "Wait. I'm sorry. I-I can't go with you."

He opened his mouth, then closed it again. Finally, he tried, "Miss Carroll, I am confused. What changed within the span of approximately five seconds that you would go from what seemed to be genuine enthusiasm to rejection?"

"I...I just...it's..." She sighed. "I had a somewhat, I suppose, irregular upbringing, and so I never learned to ride side-saddle."

"Oh, is that all? I know my nerves are a little strained, but I think I can bear the shock of witnessing a lady astride a horse."

"You might if you witnessed one astride a horse in a day dress."

This was moving rather rapidly into the complex, alien ter-ritory of female clothing. "I'm sure Mira has a riding habit you could borrow."

"They"—a hint of impatience crept into her voice—"are designed specifically for side-saddle. There is *draping*."

"Draping?" he repeated, inclined to be amused by her serious-ness, until he realised just how serious she was. Apparently one did not jest about draping to a lady. "I see. Draping. But, you know, we're far from anywhere of significance. You could wear breeches and none would look askance, or if they did, I would have them shot. Because I'm a duke."

She did not smile. "*I* would look askance."

It was a little curious, how she could be so bold in so many ways, yet it was here she would draw the line. He had not believed his suggestion to be entirely outlandish: Mira, who rode both side-saddle and astride, often wore breeches, and not just while on horseback. But then, again, Mira had been dressing rather oddly for a while. And no doubt there were improprieties that a duke's daughter could commit that a lady's companion could not. "My apologies. You could not have packed for this trip in the expectation of having to rehabilitate your host."

"You are doing that for yourself." Finally, her mouth softened. "And I will be happy to accompany you on some other errand."

She sounded wistful, and he felt suddenly guilty, wishing he had not issued an invitation that she was in no position to accept. And that was when a memory surfaced—a rainy afternoon, some distant summer, Marleigh's irrepressible curiosity taking Gracewood to parts of his own home that he had never thought to visit, let alone explore. "I might have an idea," he murmured, "if you would indulge me in a...a...small adventure."

# CHAPTER 13

He led Miss Carroll down half-remembered corridors and up staircases he hadn't climbed in years before finally reaching the door he was looking for—dark wood, and iron-riven, like all of Morgencald's doors. The room within was crimson silk and cloth of gold, from the floor coverings to the canopy of the ornately carved four-poster bed, to the wing chairs that waited by the fireplace that had been set into the stone itself. Across the walls, still un-faded, unfurled a hunting scene, a blur of people and animals, a wild-eyed stag, and a brightness of blood. Gracewood had never liked it much. Now it close to sickened him. The splendour and the dying hart. The cracked-open ribs of the vaulted ceiling.

"This is the King's Room," he said. "Henry the Eighth used to stay here."

Miss Carroll looked around. "It's, um, it's very...like the sort of room Henry the Eighth would appreciate."

Wanting to spend as little time here as possible, Gracewood limped over to the chest at the foot of the bed and flung back the lid. It was, as he had dimly recalled, full of clothes—he and Marleigh had spent that half-forgotten afternoon bedecking themselves in borrowed finery and laughing at the results. And yes. There it was. A little dusty, more than a little creased, but—

"Could you perhaps do something with this?" he asked.

"Possibly." She sounded uncertain, as though she expected some kind of trap. "If I knew what it was."

"Isn't it a riding habit?"

She frowned. "Haven't we had this conversation?"

"Not quite." He cast the garment—which was stark black and white, its sleeves extravagantly embroidered in a pattern of fleur-de-lys—across the bed. "See here, where the skirt splits? You would still have to wear breeches beneath, but I believe this was designed to allow a lady to ride astride."

Her eyes flicked from his face to the dress and back again.

"And there...there is draping?" He smoothed out the fabric, in an attempt to show how it would fall across a horse's back.

There was an unusual stillness to her. A wariness almost. "All this that I might go riding with you tomorrow?"

"So that you need not feel you couldn't."

After a moment or two, she came to join him, her fingers brushing almost idly over the skirt and bodice. "Why do you even have such a thing?"

"I possess many things"—his tone grew rueful—"and I don't know why I own them. I suspect that belonged to one of Henry's mistresses. They say Anne Boleyn was a superb hunter."

"When she was not the hunted."

He laughed, half-startled still by how easily laughter came to him when he was with her. "Can you make use of it?"

She fell silent, her face betraying such a strange admixture of emotions he could no longer tell whether he had delighted or devastated her. "I...Gracewood. You're being too kind to me."

"I'm being entirely selfish. I would like to ride with you."

"Lately," she said softly, "I am finding it harder and harder to tell where selfishness ends and altruism begins."

"Then you'll come?"

Another pause. And, at last, she nodded. "Yes. I'll come. Though, I fear I'll be quite the spectacle."

"I have no wish to make you uncomfortable, Miss Carroll."

"I shan't be. Choice is its own pleasure and this"—her gaze fell longingly upon the gown—"this is beautiful."

*She* was beautiful. Though he was not callow enough to say it.

"Just promise me," she went on, "that you will under no circumstances offer me some docile, half-dead creature. I want to *ride*. Not mince along demurely."

"You may have the pick of my stables." He would have given her anything. Everything. For nothing but the light in her velvet eyes. "Though you should know I'm not the horseman I used to be. I'm afraid you'll find me a poor companion."

"Oh, Gracewood"—she turned abruptly from the dress—"I cannot imagine a better one."

They were too close now, and it struck him how intimate it was, to stand with a woman in a bedroom, even the bedroom of a long-dead king. It certainly left his thoughts more inclined towards the carnal than the companiable. But he also desperately wanted to believe her, to be good for her, as he had once dared to be. In another life, when he had not been so lost or so alone. Or so incomplete.

His expression must have betrayed something of his thoughts because Miss Carroll looked up at him, her eyes wide and dark and searching. "What's wrong?" she asked. "Have I—I have said something amiss, I am sure."

What did she think she had said? What *could* she have said? "It isn't you. Or if it is, it is not your *fault* that it is you. You just... you make me wish I could be better. And I only knew how to be better when I was with Marleigh. The old Lord Marleigh, I mean. The one who…" He couldn't quite bring himself to finish the thought.

"The one you lost?"

*Lost* was a euphemism, of course. But Miss Carroll was far too kind to say *the one who died*. "Yes. He was—I could confide in him. Trust in him. And he saw me in ways nobody else did. When I imagine what he would think of me now, I—it shames me. It feels like a betrayal, like losing him twice over."

Miss Carroll let out a sob, her eyes brimming with the tears that Gracewood couldn't let himself shed. "You mustn't say such things. Mustn't think them."

She had too much compassion, and he wanted to comfort her. But he could scarcely comfort himself. "How can I not?"

"Because I—" Her hand came to rest against one of the bed-posts as though it was all that kept her from falling. "Forgive me. It is not my place to speak of such things."

Station. Always station, coming between him and the world. "Nonetheless I would have you speak of them."

"I—I have known you only a short while." For some reason this observation seemed to make her choke a moment, fresh tears drowning her thoughts. "But if what you say of your friend is true then…then I do not see how anyone, man or woman, with whom you had shared such a bond, could look on you now or ever with anything but…but love. And that is how your friend would think of you now were—were things other than they are. I am sure of it."

And to that, Gracewood had no idea what to say or how to say it. "Thank you." It seemed inadequate, but he had grown accus-tomed to inadequacy. "Not only for this, for everything you've done. For finding me when I most needed to be found. I still don't know how I came to merit the good fortune of...of *you*... but I swear by any God who gives a damn I will endeavour to deserve it."

She blinked away what might have been a sheen of fresh tears. "I think, perhaps, you are inclined to think too well of everyone, and not enough of yourself. You know"—her voice wavered—"you know your friend, for all you cared for him, and he for you, he was just a *person*. And I'm just a person."

"I was well aware of his faults, Miss Carroll. He was stubborn, and irreverent, more than a little arrogant, and rode like the very devil. Please don't think I put him on a pedestal. I saw him as well as he saw me. He just...helped me live, when nobody had let me before. And you are helping me remember."

Her hands came up, hovered a moment, and then settled lightly against his chest. "I believe you will live—as happily as you did before. M-more so. I believe you will thrive. You will be seen and be loved and...h-hardly think of Marleigh at all."

"I will never forget him. But"—he smiled at her, fingers brushing the back of one of her gloves—"I am beginning to realise I did not die with him."

She was trembling slightly—some sorrow of her own he wished he could share, in return for all the burdens she had borne for him. Perhaps she, too, had lost someone. He did not, however, think it was right or fair to ask her, no more than it was right or fair to simply draw her into his arms and hold her. So instead he tried to make her laugh.

"And now," he added, "all I have to do is convince my sister and a woman I'm barely acquainted with."

This had the desired effect of making her giggle, albeit in a tremulous, slightly watery way. "As far as I can tell, Louise mostly objects to your beard."

"Ah." He lifted a hand self-consciously to his face. "As it happens, I rather object to it as well. Unfortunately, my valet despaired of me some weeks ago, and I have not yet managed to replace him."

"So it's true what they say about gentlemen being lost without their valets."

She had meant it playfully, he knew that. It should not have stung. "I can shave myself," he told her. Except perhaps it would have been better to let her think he was a typically useless sort of aristocrat. At least then he could have spared both of them the truth. "The problem is, since I returned from France my...my hands. They shake. Not always, but without warning, sometimes when I'm anxious, sometimes for no reason as far as I can discern. I'm frankly afraid of cutting my throat."

"I'm so sorry." She made a gesture of frustration that seemed entirely aimed at herself. "I've never been able to govern my tongue. I always say the wrong thing. If it's not blasphemous, it's inappropriate, if it's not inappropriate, it's hurtful, and after all that, sometimes it's not even amusing."

He chuckled. He couldn't help himself. "I would rather your wrong than anyone else's right, Miss Carroll."

"Well, if it is neither blasphemous nor inappropriate nor hurtful, I could...I would...I would like to help."

"I appreciate that, of course. But unless you have a valet tucked in your reticule, I'm hard pressed to know how."

"I could assist you." She paused, uncertainly, and then began talking again, the words tumbling out of her. "I know how to shave a gentleman. Which, yes, is an unusual skill for a lady to possess, but I learned from my father, you see. He was somewhat infirm before he died. So I learned. And that's how I know. And it's really not so unusual."

He did not want her embarrassed for all the world—but, God help him, it was endearing. "Did your father also teach you to ride astride?"

"Actually...yes. Yes, he did."

"He sounds like a good man."

Her eyes softened. "He was."

"I would like to be such a father to my daughters. Should I be fortunate enough to have any."

"He loved me very much," she said. "And never knew me."

And there it was, again, that touch of sadness in her. It felt wrong to compare them—she was her own person, and still in many ways a mystery to him—but it echoed inside him nonetheless: this recognition of loss, shared and unshared at the same time. "I'm sure he would be proud of who you've become."

"I hope so." She shrugged. "And sometimes I am glad not to know—that way I get to keep my hope."

There was a moment of silence. And then a longer moment.

"So you see," Miss Carroll went on, awkwardly, "if you would like to shave, I am at your service. And the likelihood of my inadvertently murdering you is very low."

He gave a little cough. "I take comfort in knowing that when you murder me it will not be inadvertent."

She laughed at that. Still not quite without sorrow. "You should know I take your mocking me as a sign your spirits are recovering."

"As you should." For a moment, silence fell again. And then he said, "But I don't think I can ask this of you. It feels highly improper."

And all at once, she flinched. "I should not have offered."

"No, it was extraordinarily kind of you. But I am...you are... we have already...your reputation, Miss Carroll."

She was blushing, but at this her tone sharpened. "Ah, yes, because no man will want me if I am rumoured to have aided with the grooming of another."

"For what little it's worth, I would also prefer it wasn't common knowledge that the Duke of Gracewood has lost even the capacity to shave himself."

"Gracewood"—she reached out impulsively, their hands half colliding with the oddest sort of ease—"damn your pride, damn whatever is supposed to be proper. Let me help you. Please."

And with his fingers curled around hers, the press of her palm against his, the heat of skin reaching him even through the fabric of her gloves, it seemed blissfully simple—incontrovertibly right—to say yes.

# CHAPTER 14

Gracewood had not quite lost enough of his mind to invite an unmarried lady into his bedroom, nor to accompany her to hers, so they chose an empty chamber—one of the many—and Miss Carroll went in search of hot water while he fetched his shaving kit.

His leg was pulsing with a grey, dull pain—too many stairs, too many corridors—by the time he returned to Miss Carroll, which meant whatever qualms he might have felt were temporarily lost to relief as he settled into the chair she had already placed by the window for him. A little abashed, he handed her the leather wallet that contained his razors and his brushes and watched with a kind of helpless fascination as she laid everything out across the dressing table in swift, assured movements.

She'd shed her shawl, though not her gloves yet, and wound her long curls back into the heavy knot of her hair, exposing the elegant curve of her neck, with its treasure-path of freckles running beneath her necklace. Brushed by the early-morning light, she almost seemed to glow—her beauty as intricate and artful as an illuminated manuscript.

"I'm beginning to wonder," he said, giving abrupt expression to one set of thoughts in an effort to drown out another, "if I should not take Mira to London myself."

A pleasant splashing echoed in the room as Miss Carroll filled a bowl with water and began to soak a towel in it. "Oh?"

"I think I have allowed her to grow away from me. For us to grow away from each other."

"She's a young woman. Some of that is inevitable."

"Some of it, certainly. But you have made me realise just how little I know her." He extended his foot, trying to relieve the trapped, tight ache in his leg. "And if she has truly set her heart on a season, then I should be helping her to have one."

"It could be argued that by entrusting her to the care of her very protective, very enthusiastic pseudo-aunt, you *are* helping her."

"In the most detached way possible. I feel my duty towards her requires more of me than that."

"And what of your duty towards yourself?" she asked. "Will you be happy in London?"

"I begrudge what I know will be said of me. But neither my pride nor my fears are Mira's concern—however much I've already made them so."

She turned away from him in order to strip off her gloves and wring out the towel. "You know you can depend on Louise, whatever you decide."

"And what of you, Miss Carroll?"

"Me?" She offered one of the fleeting smiles he wished he could make linger. "I can be a little flighty and impulsive."

His lips twitched—her evasions were blatant, but they charmed him nonetheless. "If I did come to London, do you think we could continue our...our acquaintance?"

Her shoulders tensed. "I expect," she said, after the slightest of pauses, "you will be quite busy. And you may find yourself better received than you anticipate."

"Let us say that I do not. And let us also say that, while I'm thinking mostly of my sister, the possibility of seeing you goes some way to bridging the gap between what is best for her and what is best for me."

"You're too kind." Her footfalls were almost swallowed by the rug as she crossed to his side. "But you may very well find a lady's companion is quite a different proposition in town than she is in the country."

"Do you truly believe me so base?" It was a concern any woman would have, and it should not have wounded him.

"I believe we have known each other for less than a week."

It was probably a necessary reminder—and he was half-grateful, half-resentful for it. "I'm sorry. I'm asking too much of you."

"I'm afraid you might someday think the same of me." She gestured awkwardly. "You should…you may have to remove your…"

"Oh. Yes. Yes of course."

A tug or two was all it took to undo the knot of his cravat, and then he was unwinding the fabric, his eyes anywhere but Miss Carroll as hers were anywhere but him—except for the helpless handful of seconds when they'd been absolutely unable to look away, and her gaze had slid in honey-drop sweetness down to his mouth and then lower again to the strip of skin revealed by the opening of his collar.

He wasn't sure he'd ever felt quite this naked. But he'd also never wanted a woman's attention more. Or, conscious of his barely starched linen and unpolished boots, been less worthy of it.

Before he could apologise Miss Carroll wrapped a warm, damp towel about his face with the same facility she had shown in arranging his shaving tools. Deprived of sight, he was suddenly excruciatingly aware of her: the gentle pressure of her palms patting the cloth into place, the stir of air from her skirts as she moved, the heat of her breath when she leaned closer. And then there was the scent of her, just the clean nothingness of skin, and that familiar trace of gardenias, sweet and cool like a summer evening.

He thought it was probably best if he kept his eyes closed when she lifted the towel away. That way he could pretend she was his valet. Well, not that *she* was. But that what was about to happen—what was happening now—was a straightforward act of personal service, performed for him by a professional gentleman.

To whom he would have absolutely no attraction.

Miss Carroll's fingertips—soft, and slightly slippery—landed against his jaw, and he damn near jumped out of the chair. "This is something I happened to have," she said. "It's just some sandalwood and clove oil."

All he managed in return was a flustered noise.

"The clove is mildly numbing. The sandalwood...it helps with a smoother shave."

"You're"—he cleared his throat, his eyes still firmly closed, though his image of a middle-aged male servant, possibly balding, possibly called Cauliflower, was fading rapidly—"you're spoiling me. It's not necessary."

"So I should hack at your face like an amateur topiarist?" She let out an impatient huff and dropped another towel on him. "I refuse to do a bad job of this, Gracewood. My honour is at stake."

"Your honour?" he repeated, amused, if somewhat muffled.

"My vanity then. Which I set perhaps even greater store by."

She lifted the towel and he forgot to not look. And, oh God, she was close—he could have counted the shadows between her lashes, the tiny curls that clustered at her brow, the freckles across the bridge of her nose only half-concealed beneath a dusting of powder. It had never occurred to him to question beauty before. He'd always assumed it was obvious, fine eyes or a trim figure, rosebud lips or hair of whatever colour was currently fashionable. But it wasn't. It was *details*. The way you could wait forever for the dimple to appear beside someone's mouth, unable to imagine ever growing tired of seeing it.

He was probably blushing like a schoolboy. His face felt hot, but hopefully she would attribute that to the warm towels. And, in any case, she seemed to be entirely focused on his beard, frowning slightly as she dragged her fingers down his cheeks and up his throat, searching out the places where the grain of the hair changed direction. It was too considerate a touch to be clinical. It certainly wasn't sexual.

But the *care* in it.

His eyes closed. He could not have kept them open even if he'd wanted to. He was too lost. It felt too much like tenderness and left him almost as much relieved as longing when she finally stepped away. How did you bear something so wondrous? How did you live without it? Thank God she couldn't see—the flesh of his leg, as rough as stale meat and twisted like tree roots, or the scars on his back that were the tally of his failures. And thank God she didn't know. The blood and the mud and the rain and the guns. The indignity of dying. The banality of killing. Life measured in twenty-second intervals.

Bite. Pour. Ram. Shoot. Bite. Pour. Ram. Shoot. Bite. Pour. Ram. Shoot.

Then came the swish and scratch of his shaving brush against soap, the sound gradually softening as the lather rose. He focused on that. On the memory of Miss Carroll's fingers against his throat. The warmth she had left behind like gold leaf against his skin. He was here. At Morgencald. With her. Safe, in a way that—for perhaps the first time in years—was neither hollow, nor just another defeat.

"Are you ready?" she asked. "Can I start?"

He nodded, not quite trusting his voice.

She had deft hands, at once precise and thorough as she swirled the bristles of the brush in tight circles, her skill evident but surely not superior to anyone else's. All the same, he felt more. He felt…everything. Every hair, heat-softened and lifted into position beneath the lather. Every breath that slipped between his lips, as inevitable as a secret.

A rhythmic scraping: his razor, moving back and forth against the strop.

He curled his hands into loose fists, aware he was trembling and not wanting her to think he was afraid. Fear was familiar to him—it had come to him in many guises down the years, and was certainly not the edge of a straight razor. That, he would have thought nothing of, even wielded by someone he trusted less.

Yet, still, he found it difficult to hold still for her. Accept the placement of her fingers on his face, pulling the skin gently taut, and then the delicate rasp of the blade. It was the sense of exposure, perhaps. Physically, yes, but it cut deeper too. His father had raised him to be a duke. Marleigh had shown him how to be a friend. With Miss Carroll, he wanted…something else. Something that felt like the glide of steel against his throat, deadly and unerring and exquisite.

"Gracewood?" murmured Miss Carroll. "You…you're very tense."

"I am? My apologies."

It was only now she'd drawn attention to it, that he realised how rigidly he was holding himself—protection against his body betraying him, which was, he supposed, its own betrayal. So instead of fighting he...stopped. Surrendered. To the certainties of her touch. Its lulling cadence: stroke-stroke-pause, stroke-stroke-pause, as she cleaned the soap from the blade against the side of her wrist. And let the warmth and the lassitude take him. The hazy sweetness of being *cared for*.

He lost all track of time. And it didn't matter. And Miss Carroll seemed to be in no hurry either, which was, in its own way, oddly pleasing, for there was a subtle magic in having someone tend to you so meticulously. In the end, she did two more passes, across the grain and then against it, though the task was mostly complete at the second. The third did not even require a full lather—just Miss Carroll's fingers seeking out the few remaining rough patches at his jaw, and the cleft in his chin, which she remedied with a touch of oil and swift strokes of the razor.

Then she patted him clean with a towel and soothed his skin with a few splashes of cool water, and he opened his eyes to find her gazing at him, her expression a little shocked, a little wondering.

"Y-you...you're back," she said.

He lifted a hand to his face, feeling rather strange—revealed, and almost *awoken*, like Leontes's wife, stepping free from her prison of stone. Though, of course, any spell that held him he had cast upon himself. "I think I am."

There was a silence. And a heavy kind of awkwardness between them. Miss Carroll was flushed—on the verge of tears—and hesitant in ways she hadn't been only moments ago. Perhaps the potential impropriety of the situation had caught up with her. The vulnerability of being alone with a man.

"Do you think"—he offered her what he hoped was a reassuring smile—"I will pass muster with Lady Marleigh now?"

She swallowed. "I think you will pass muster with anyone."

"Thank you so much, Miss Carroll. You've done a quite extraordinary job."

A shaky laugh. "I should have thought to bring you a mirror."

"Well, I already know what I look like, and I can feel what you've done. I do believe you've given me the closest shave I've ever had."

"Oh I...I..." She turned to the dressing table and began to clean his razor and shaving brush.

Picking up his cane, he eased himself from the chair and joined her—though even this trivial closeness made her flinch slightly. "You don't have to do that."

"It needs doing."

"Then let me."

Their fingers tangled for a moment, and then Miss Carroll stepped away. "I should—I've already taken enough of your time today."

By which she surely meant he had taken too much of hers. "You will still ride with me tomorrow?" He was half-ashamed for asking, for how naked it sounded. But he also wondered if the shame was truly his. Or if it was just another ghost. An ideal of dukedom—of manhood—carved into him by somebody long dead.

The pause that followed seemed far too long, though it was probably only seconds. Finally, she nodded. "Yes. I meant what I said...I'd love to. Thank you for making it possible."

They parted ways soon after, and he wrapped up his shaving tools and took them back to his chambers. The face that was

waiting for him in his dressing room mirror was both familiar and unfamiliar—more like himself than the hollow man
whose reflection he'd spent so long turning from, but older and,
strangely, less like the portraits that filled the Long Gallery.

The lines of pain and grief that life had set beside his mouth,
and at the corners of his eyes, were somehow *his*, when the rest of
his features belonged to his lineage. It was not who he'd been, or
who he'd thought he would be, but it was who he was.

And, for the first time in a long time, he could almost bear it.

# CHAPTER 15

Viola had a dress to get ready. Which was why she absolutely couldn't dwell on Gracewood's throat beneath her hands. The trust he'd shown her. She just hadn't been prepared for the intimacy of it—the heat of breath and skin, how fascinatingly *responsive* a man could be. And in so many ways. It had made her want to feel the flicker of his eyelashes against her fingertips. The texture of his lips, with their valleys, and runnels, their hidden interior softness. He would, she knew, have tasted like Morgencald: of salt and strength, and something half-familiar, half-dreamed.

Though, honestly, it had been a shock to see him. With nothing to obscure the aristocratic lines of his features, or the hint of mischief in his mouth, or the crystalline blue of his eyes, she was confronted by the starkest sense of recognition. Of him, yes, but of her too. A collision of past and future.

It made her remember too vividly his friendship—*their* friendship—the bright summers and the long evenings, the ease of it, and she ached for everything they'd shared. Ached and missed and mourned for and would not have returned to for the world. Which was, she knew, its own betrayal. That she had promised to help him salved her conscience less than she might have hoped. It had become too muddled a gesture to pass for altruism—a jagged mix of guilt and hope and pleasure, of wanting to repair what she had damaged, when she knew she should not. Could not.

And then there were...different wants. New wants. Equally unsuitable and impossible. All because he looked at her the way she yearned to be looked at. Made her feel charming and clever and beautiful. As worth the attention of a handsome man as any other woman.

In any case, she wasn't thinking about *any* of that. She was making adjustments to a Tudor riding dress. Length, as ever, was the main issue, but the draping helped, and it was designed to be worn over breeches anyway. She wasn't sure why that made such a difference to her. Only that it did. She also wasn't sure why she couldn't just have worn the breeches in the first place. It wasn't as if clothes were magic, or indelibly part of who you were. Life wasn't a Shakespeare play where a crown could make you a king or a cassock a monk. But still. Even the idea terrified her.

Perhaps for what others might see. Yet more on her own behalf.

An old demon, mostly slumbering: the fear she would one day look carelessly into the mirror and lose herself.

Thankfully, this was not the day. The riding habit was, as she had suspected, rather theatrical. Current fashions were, honestly, something of a boon for...ladies of sparer figures. A décolletage could always be contrived, and with waists so high everyone's figure was, to some extent, a mere suggestion. The trend towards paler colours and soft patterns was not her favourite, but being older—practically a *spinster*, if she thought about it—allowed a little more freedom, hence her collection of mossy greens, dusty blues, and deep, burnished reds.

The riding habit, though, with its corsetry and its heavy velvet skirts, felt like armour. Even looked a little bit like armour, with the decorated sleeves, and the zig-zag pattern of exposed lacing down the bodice. And she loved it. On good days, she thought she could be quite elegant. On bad ones, well, best not to think of those. But dressed like this? She was sure she, too, could have snared the heart of a capricious monarch and...then been executed for treason when someone else did exactly the same thing?

So perhaps that was a bad example.

Nevertheless, she liked how she looked—how the garment shaped her, the way it seemed both soft and strong—and that was not a gift she took for granted. She pinned her hair loosely and secured it beneath a matching hat, shallow-brimmed and ornamented with a spill of ostrich feathers in the cavalier style. And, having already risked her reflection too much for a single morning, she hurried down to the courtyard.

Gracewood, still awaiting a valet from the shadow at his jaw, his unpolished boots, and the distinctly countrified cut of his coat, was already there, alongside Janner and two horses—a pretty dapple grey mare and a bay stallion, which, from its arched neck and short back, must have had some Arabian blood.

"Miss Carroll"—his voice recalled her to the presence of humans—"you look...you look quite magnificent."

She did. The riding habit was beautiful, and still too rich a gift for a lady's companion. Were things between them less... less as they were, she might have been able to enjoy the moment untainted by guilt and longing and old hurts. But she was here for Gracewood, and for him she buried those feelings and smiled. "You promised me that we would ride. And instead you bring me some...Well, I'm sure she's a lovely creature but I don't need a *suitable* mount. I need—"

"Gloaming is for me. And, yes, she is a lovely creature and, as you say, quite suitable for a number of riders, including gentlemen whose physical infirmities have made them cautious."

Oh God. She was awful. There was too much to navigate, that was the problem, too much lost, and too much gained, and no real way of knowing where the truth of you began and the shape of the world ended. Her fortune, her name, even much of her freedom, those had been easier to surrender; it had never felt much like freedom anyway. But she had missed riding—the indecorous liberty of a headlong gallop. Not enough, of course, to exchange her gowns and her needlework and a skin she could live in to get it back. But why—with such things as these—did one have to choose?

"I'm sorry," she said, blushing and utterly abashed. "I don't know what I was...I'm...I'm...I cannot..."

To her surprise, he seemed almost amused, his gaze reflecting a depth of understanding she could barely conjure for herself. "Think nothing of it. I am not here to deny your pleasures—indeed, I would not dream of it. But I am taking you at your word. Please don't take a tumble or break your neck. I'd probably never forgive myself, and I can't imagine you would enjoy it much either."

"Oh la"—she did her best attempt at a debutante flutter—"haven't you heard? Breaking your neck is *all the rage* this season."

To that, he returned only a stern look.

"I'm an excellent horsewoman."

"Well, this is Vainglory." Gracewood gestured towards the stallion. "He can be a little too spirited, but his heart is valiant."

He offered her a hand and, steadying herself against him, she climbed into the saddle. It was a little strange to be helped—she wasn't entirely certain she needed to be—but there was also something pleasing in it, a moment of closeness, his body offered briefly to her service. Vainglory danced a little, curious rather than wilful, as she settled, her skirts flowing over his flanks, and she calmed him with a touch and a few soothing words. She could already tell he was as eager as she was.

"We," she told him, "are going to be the best of friends, and have a wonderful time."

She urged him into motion, a walk, then a trot, circling the courtyard as they grew accustomed to each other—though mostly she was distracting herself from Gracewood, to whom she wanted to offer privacy as he mounted, with Janner's help, from a mounting block. She remembered how he had preferred not to accompany her down from the north tower—his choice to use one of the back staircases when he took her to the King's Room—and she was afraid of making him self-conscious. Especially because he had once been almost as fine a rider as she was, if not quite so neck or nothing.

"All right, all right." His voice, rough with pain, broke the silence. "That's enough. Get away from me, man."

She wheeled Vainglory round in time to see Gracewood sweating, seated on Gloaming, and shoving his cane at a rapidly retreating Janner. With a sharp gesture, he urged the horse into motion and was soon at her side.

"Let's go."

His face was ashy, his jaw set, pinpricks of sweat at his temple. So she just nodded and set an easy pace away from Morgencald. The countryside, once they descended from the castle, was fairly flat—a haze of green and gold and russet, over which the horizon hung heavy and silver-grey with the promise of hills.

Gracewood cleared his throat. "I'm sorry."

"You don't need to apologise to me."

"I will also apologise to Janner." He sighed. "It makes no sense does it? Every part of my life, from my house to my land to my ward-robe to the food I eat, requires the work of others. Yet whenever someone tries to help me…help me personally, I become monstrous."

"It must be hard, being reminded that there are aspects of yourself you can no longer take for granted."

"Nevertheless, I need to do better." He sighed. "I seem to per-sistently show you the worst of myself, Miss Carroll."

"And yet," she said, her heart whisked by the wind, soaring beneath that endless shining sky, "I persist in liking you."

"Y-you do?"

"Yes. You have found me a wonderful dress and taken me rid-ing. What more could I want?"

"Well, I can think of rather a lot of things, as it happens, but it clearly wouldn't be in my interests to suggest them."

As it happened there were a lot of things she could think of as well. But since she could have none of them, she just laughed, the air rich in her mouth with salt and the scent of frosted grass. "For now, this is all I need." The stallion had such an easy stride—a lightness in those strong legs that felt almost like floating and made her long to set him free to fly. "But, oh, Gracewood, if I don't gallop soon, I believe I shall die."

"Then," he said, with a kind of playful solemnity, "you had better gallop."

The lightest touch on the reins was all it took for Vainglory to break into a canter, and from there a gallop was but a breath away. As she had suspected, the horse was as impatient as she, making up for his smaller stature with stamina, agility, and a responsive-ness that thrilled her. They were strangers to one another, cer-tainly, but Gracewood had chosen for her a kindred soul, fearless and full of curiosity.

Thankfully, these paths and fields and little woods had retained their familiarity—more than that, even, they were still an instinct, a part of her, like the lines across her palms. She knew without having to think about it when it was safe to give her mount his head, when they needed to slow, which brooks could easily be forded, what hedges could be leapt. And all the while, Vainglory's hooves beat a rhythm as wild and joyous as her heart, and the world spun past in all its winter hues.

She thought the horse would have run himself to exhaustion, for the sheer joy of it, and part of her wanted that too, but he deserved better. And, for that matter, so did Gracewood, who was barely more than a pale speck, several fields back. Encouraging Vainglory into a trot, she circled back to meet him.

"Good God," he said, as she came within earshot. "You have as fine a seat as any man in England, Miss Carroll."

It was intended to be praise and meant nothing besides. But it still carried with it a sharp, sick, and private pain. "Thank you."

"Though you damn near stopped my heart when you took that jump at Fallow's Brook. I tried to follow Marleigh across it once—broke my wrist again."

"I'm sorry I gave you cause for concern."

"There's nothing to apologise for. Vainglory went over like a swallow. And you were…you are…"

"Whatever else I am," she interrupted, in case he struck her with another compliment she could not bear, "I have been a terrible companion. I didn't even think to ask where we were going before I went charging off."

"Well, I thought I'd like to go down to the village and then to visit some of my tenants. But there's no rush." He was gazing at her with a purity of admiration she found almost dizzying. "The way you ride, Miss Carroll. Even before my injury I could not have matched you."

No. He could not. He would never have admitted it before, though. "Vainglory deserves at least some of the credit. He's splendid." One of the horse's ears twitched with interest. "Yes, that's right. *Splendid*, you perfect creature."

"Have him," said Gracewood.

"P-pardon?"

"Vainglory. He's yours. Please."

Whatever she was feeling was enough to spook her steed— and it took her a moment to settle him. Which, in turn, gave her a few precious seconds to gather her thoughts. "Gracewood, you can't just...give people horses."

"I don't intend to give people horses. I'd like you to have Vainglory. He will be far happier with you than he could with me."

It wasn't really the horse, for all that the horse truly was an unacceptable gift. But for Gracewood's sake she feigned levity. "Oh fine. He can stay in the spare bedroom."

"The Marleighs keep a stable," he replied, as if this solved everything.

"And I am to tell them to pay for the care of my abruptly acquired new horse, am I?"

He opened his mouth, then closed it again. Then finally said, "I've been too impulsive. A gift should not be a burden."

"I could not have accepted, regardless. It's too much. I have my reputation to consider."

She wasn't sure if he would try to insist, but he must have known she spoke truly. A lady simply did not accept extravagant favours from gentlemen. "Of course. I understand. Vainglory will be at your service should you ever come to Morgencald again.

And I hope you didn't think I…" A blush rose to his cheeks. "That is…I had no expectation of—"

"It's fine. I know I'm not as young as I was, and that my prospects are not so very great, but I don't believe you intended me to sell myself for a horse."

He made a noise somewhere between shock and amusement. "He's a purebred Arabian. It would have been a very flattering offer."

"I cannot deny it," she agreed, forcing herself to laugh. "But it seems my virtue must remain intact on account of the logistics."

"I assume you mean the logistics of horse-keeping. Because the other matter I am fairly confident I could manage."

Oh God. He was…was he flirting? And in a way she knew— they both knew—was close to, if not over, the edge of inappropriate. It was not a situation that Viola was accustomed to, but it held an echo of something else. Of the old tangle of affections that had once drawn them together. That had made them spar with each other, challenge each other, push each other higher. And the feeling was still there—that tug that was not quite rivalry, and now carried with it something new. A *crackle* that danced across her veins like flint put to tinder.

A crackle that she was, unfortunately, utterly ill-equipped to deal with. What was she supposed to say? But she had waited too long, thought too much. And the silence was ashes from flames that had barely begun to burn. "I…I…that's good to, um, to know."

"Miss Carroll, I've gone too far." The speed and sincerity of his retreat only made her feel worse. "Forgive me."

"No. It's me. I'm not accustomed to…to talking this way."

"You are not accustomed to men offering a strategic circumnavigation of your virtue? That only reflects well on you."

"Or poorly, from another perspective. After all, it rather implies my virtue is not worth circumnavigating."

"That was—that is—I never—" He broke off. "You're laughing at me. That was a trap."

She nodded, still giggling. And for an unguarded moment she let herself forget everything that made their situation impossible and allowed herself simply to be with him. To relish talking to him, listening to him, letting him make her laugh in a way that wasn't quite the way he had in their youth.

But it was only a moment, because then he remarked, "How peculiar, the terms in which we speak of these things."

"Oh?" The sudden turn into seriousness at once surprised her and didn't—she had always liked his mind, its subtlety and suppleness, and its secret bent towards whimsicality. But the sheer familiarity of the shift brought all the context and complexity of what lay between them flooding back to her.

"Why is it virtue in women to preserve what it is virtue in men to pursue? And why do we even call it virtue? Surely that is a component of the spirit, not the body."

"Perhaps," she offered, "it is some combination of women, lacking property or much of material value, being required to have something of ourselves to sell, and men being terrified of the possibility that they could be raising someone else's child."

"Ah." Another pause. "I confess, I've never understood that fear."

"You would have no objection to your wife sleeping with other people?"

"Most men's wives *do* sleep with other people. Of course, I would prefer it if my own wife found sufficient satisfaction with me that she had no wish to seek it elsewhere, but I suspect that's arrogance and idealism on my part. I was actually thinking of the child."

Once again, he had intrigued her. And that, too, she realised was acquiring a...slow, sweet heat, like a mouthful of whiskey on a winter's day. She had always loved talking to him, swapping ideas and telling stories, but there was an openness to him now. Depths she had not known were there. A vulnerability he had either never shown her or she had never recognised. "What do you mean?"

"Well," he went on softly, "is a child of the body or...the heart? The mind? I am of my father's blood, and he did everything he could to shape me in his image, but I...I have never felt like his son. I have increasingly come to understand I would not wish to."

"You are by far the better man."

"Few would think so. But from you"—he cast her a smile, sunbright and heedless—"it is praise worth having."

They were pretty words, and doubtless came easily enough to Gracewood, who for all his high-minded ideas would still be married one day to a woman who could be everything a duchess was meant to be. He would be a fine husband, and a wonderful father. And perhaps...perhaps he would still feel warmly towards her, the lady's companion with whom he had passed a few short weeks one bleak January. Invite her to visit now and then with the Marleighs, so she could watch as the halls of Morgencald filled up with other people's joy.

# CHAPTER 16

They were not far from the village and so soon fell into companionable silence. Viola had a tangle of memories of the place, none of them specific enough to tie to a particular time. Just a blur of riding or running down cobbled streets. Acts of apple thievery that nobody dared rebuke them for. Pints of bitter from the local pub, slightly sweet, slightly woody, copper-gold like the end of a summer afternoon. She didn't think the place had changed—there, in fact, was the pub, and the church, and the smithy, and the farrier, and the shop, the houses with their thatched roofs—but there was a quietness now. A turned-in, closed-down, huddled quality to the homes and the people, the latter dutifully lining up to offer mumbled greetings to Gracewood as he rode by.

Things did not much improve from there. The farms they visited were ill-kept, the harvests poor, for it had been another cold, wet year. It felt like everywhere Viola looked she saw signs of neglect or disrepair, scrawny beasts listless in grey fields, surrounded by crumbling stone and rotting wood. Gracewood's tenants treated her much as they did him—with wary courtesy and empty eyes.

And as for Gracewood himself, he was mostly silent, his expression set into cold, unyielding lines. It was not an aspect of him she was used to seeing, and it reminded her—in ways she was not used to thinking about—that he was a man from an unbroken line of men for whom lordship was a birthright and power unquestioned.

The ride back to Morgencald was equally quiet. It was mid-afternoon, but the sun set early in this part of the country, and Viola could already see the glow behind the clouds as it began to sink towards the horizon. She wanted to say something, or ask something, but Gracewood's profile was a wall between them, and she did not know how to breach it. Or even if she should.

They arrived in the courtyard at about the same time the de Veres' steward had arrived. Viola did not know him personally, as he had worked for Gracewood's father, but she had passed him occasionally in a corridor or glimpsed him about the grounds. The intervening years had touched him surprisingly little: He remained a man as dour as he was dignified, iron-haired, his face a closed fist.

"Mr. Curwen." Gracewood lowered himself from Gloaming's back, only to stagger and right himself, clinging to the horse before Janner brought him his cane. "My estate is dying."

Curwen's back, if such a thing was even possible, pulled even straighter. "On the contrary, Your Grace. If you would care to examine the accounts, you will see the estate flourishes. Indeed, I am happy to report a five percent increase in profit from this time last year."

"Well, I should damn well expect to be profitable, considering I am as good as extorting my own tenants."

"That is a mischaracterisation, Your Grace. Rents have remained stable, bar annual inflationary increases."

"Stable?" Morgencald caught its master's voice. Turned it into echoes. "How does that help when we have had two years of bad harvests, and the Corn Laws keep the price of grain artificially high?"

Viola slid down from Vainglory, and—having no place in the middle of an altercation between a duke and his steward—began to pet him with a degree of concentration unnecessary for the task.

"I'm not a politician. And I would prefer"—here Curwen gave a tense little bow—"to have this conversation—"

"No conversation is needed, Mr. Curwen. Begin making repairs to all my properties immediately. Loans will be available to all in need upon a generous repayment schedule at no interest. And I want a doctor to visit every family. I heard an infant coughing and the mother mentioned fever—I will not be responsible for a typhus outbreak amongst my people."

There was a silence. Then, "This is…irregular. Advantage will be taken."

"I'm one of the richest men in England. I believe I can afford it. On the subject of which, there will be no further increase to the rents until the price of bread falls and the economy stabilises."

"Your Grace, your father—"

"I am not," said Gracewood, with a terrible kind of quietness, "my father. And you will do my bidding, or I will hire someone who will."

Viola wasn't sure what reaction she was expecting—anger, perhaps, or obsequiousness. But all she saw was something like hurt in Mr. Curwen's eyes. "I've been the steward of Morgencald for forty years. All I've ever done is my duty."

"I know." A gentler note crept into Gracewood's voice. "But understand that I am also trying to do my duty. I have no intention of bankrupting myself, and in the long term I have a number of plans to maintain the de Vere fortune. Right now, however, my tenants can barely afford to live, and if the people who work this land flee to the city, what will that leave of Morgencald?"

Another uncertain moment.

"I'm sure you think me naïve, Mr. Curwen, but I do not believe the good of the estate must come at the expense of those who live on it. Let us meet again tomorrow when you have had time to consider how my wishes are to be implemented."

Finally, the steward bowed, murmured a "Yes, Your Grace," and departed. Viola passed Vainglory's reins to Janner, and she and Gracewood were alone again. He was trembling very slightly, but also looked more himself than he had the whole ride back.

"Miss Carroll," he said, "I don't suppose you would care to walk to the beach with me? I don't feel like going inside, just yet."

"I'd be happy to."

"I'm afraid I can't offer you my arm—the way down is rather steep."

"We could jump off the cliff instead."

He laughed. "You jest, but I did once. With Marleigh. It was the middle of winter and the water was heart-stoppingly cold."

Too many memories, that was the problem. Kept like treasures, when they should have been only sea wrack. Oh, why had he not forgotten her? It would be better—for both of them—if he could. And yet part of her did not want him to. Had never wanted to forget him either. "That sounds like yet another occasion of your friend leading you astray."

"I certainly wouldn't have dared to do it without him. I was never led astray though—more shown paths I did not know were there." His mouth softened into a smile. "That's how I need to remember him. Through that feeling of freedom."

"I..." It felt strange to have given Gracewood something she had never possessed, but could it not be a fair exchange—her old affection, these recollections of happy days, for what she had taken? The pain she had caused? "He...he would have been proud of you today."

She had thought this might please him. That he might find comfort in talking of...of who he thought she'd been. Of happier times. But to her surprise, it was to her he turned. "And what of you, Miss Carroll? Do you think I'm doing the right thing?"

"Undoubtedly. I"—she was glad for the sharp edge of the wind, for it excused her too-bright eyes and too-pink cheeks—"I would have said I was proud of you too, but it seemed presumptuous."

"And now I feel I fished for your praise."

"Not at all—I wanted to tell you how...how I admire what you're doing. I just couldn't find the words."

It felt wrong to speak to him like this. To encourage him to—she hardly knew what. Seek her friendship. Rely upon her understanding. Trust her, as he once had. But it would have felt worse to abandon him when he needed so badly for somebody to reach out. And the last, terrible option, to burden him with the whole of her, with the reality of who she was and had been and could never be—that would be too cruel an intimacy.

"To tell you the truth," he said softly, "as much as I wish to honour my friend, he is gone. And it is your good opinion I would wish to earn."

This was...not flirting? But she was even less certain what to do with it. She could not dismiss it as mere gallantry. But nor was it some echo of old friendship, spilling from the walls of Morgencald and catching on the first person it struck. It was something new and strange and only for her. "Oh."

It was low tide, so the beach stretched before them like glass, the wave-smoothed sand banded silver and gold by the setting sun.

"When you said you liked me"—Gracewood had paused, and now he turned towards her, his eyes catching all the colours of the sky—"did you mean it?"

She should have said something frivolous. Something to make them both laugh. Something to break this moment. "Of course."

"Because I need to tell you, Miss Carroll, that I like you too. I like your quick mind and your kind heart and your bold spirit. You make me think as I had forgotten I could and laugh as I thought I never would again."

"I…I…" Oh God, what was she to do? She had to stop this. But she *couldn't*. She yearned for it too badly: so much she'd never dared want, now falling into her hands, as effortless as blossom in spring.

"I know," he went on hesitantly, "we have been acquainted for barely more than a week. But I would like to be the man you believe I can be."

"You already *are*." She could not tell, in that moment, if she was arguing with him or pleading with him. If only he could see himself as she saw him. If only she knew how to make him.

"I would like to be worthy of so remarkable a woman."

"Gracewood, I—"

"And I would like to kiss so beautiful a one."

He liked her. He thought she was—what was it—quick and kind and bold. He thought she was beautiful. And…he wanted to kiss her.

*He wanted to kiss her.*

The joy was too swift, too bright, and had burned itself to nothing in moments. There were a thousand reasons this couldn't be, because of who she was, and who she had been, and all the choices she had made in between. "Please"—the word tangled in her throat, full of edges it shouldn't have had—"please don't."

At this she saw something falter in him too, and then fade away. "I hope you can believe I would not wish...what was not welcome."

"You do not know me," she whispered. When what she really meant was...something else entirely. Something she had no idea how to say.

"Not as deeply as I would wish. But I believe I do, Miss Carroll. Somehow I believe I do." He drew back a little, a dull flush creeping up his cheeks. "All the same, I have been unforgivably impertinent. I suppose I thought if I could once jump off a cliff, I could today at least find the courage to tell a woman that I desired her. Except a cliff is not a person, and I am not insensible to the inequities of rank. You...you deserved better."

Let him think that. It was safer. She had come to Gracewood to help him find a future, not tie him to the past. Let him look back on her years from now as a woman of no family who had forgotten her station and tempted him to forget his. But oh, she was losing track of herself in deceit she had never intended, and she could not add another to that pile of needles. As if being wholly and relentlessly true when she was with him, she could compensate for the one truth that would have cost them both too much to share. "I shall never forget what you said. Or that, for a moment, you thought of me in this way."

His brows tightened. "Is that your fear? That my feelings are transitory?"

"I...I don't know."

"It has taken some time for me to remember the man I am capable of being, but I have never been fickle."

She smiled at him, the closest apology she could manage for his years of grief and guilt. "To a fault, perhaps."

"But"—and here he blushed again, even more deeply than before—"you do not believe me? Or"—and now he was almost laughing—"do you offer this indictment of my character as consolation for not...not wanting me?"

And she still could not give him the lie that would save them both. "You're a duke. I'm nobody. You can't—"

"Viola."

Stunned by the sound of her name—the way his deep voice wrapped around its vowels and lingered on its *l*—she fell silent.

"Viola," he said again, closing his fingers lightly around her wrist—not, she thought, to keep her but merely to hold some part of her as, in truth, she yearned to be held. "It is your wishes, and only your wishes, that hold sway here. Tell me you feel nothing for me, and I will honour it without question. But I will not yield to less."

The pulse that beat and thrummed and hungered beneath his touch felt like her whole heart: hot as a garnet and glowing beneath her gloves. "I suppose"—she strove for sharpness, found it impossible—"you think that because you are a great lord and I merely a lady's companion you can dally with me."

"Dally?" He didn't shout, but there was a pain in his voice, a real pain that Viola could never have expected. "I would marry you tomorrow if I thought you would have me."

In that moment she knew, starkly, that he meant every word, and it terrified her. "You...you're mad."

That made him laugh. "I know madness, and this is not it. A word from you, a glance, and I would lay all I have—all I am, or at the very least what's left of me—at your feet. And someday, when you are ready to hear me, and to trust me, I shall, and then you can have me, or not, as it pleases you."

"I could never marry you, Gracewood. The world—"

"Forgive my language, but"—his eyes were as steady on hers as the clasp upon her wrist, his mouth suddenly full of smiles— "fuck the world. I will change it for you if I have to."

It took her a moment to realise she was angry, and she hardly knew why. After all, had things been different—had she been born to the life she was meant for instead of the one she was given—she would never have met him in the first place. Or if she had, would they have known each other in the same way? But then, their friendship had never felt like this either. "You have... no idea what you're asking."

"I'm asking," he said gently, "to kiss you."

"Perhaps"—she was stalling, of course, when all she had to do to end this was tell him he was wrong and she wanted no part of it—"I have a fancy to be a duchess." There. Let him think she only sought his fortune.

But apparently, the thought was little deterrent. "If you like. But I think, right now, you might prefer to be kissed."

It was... a small thing, was it not? The tiniest corner of what he was offering—impossible though it was. Could she not have this? Just this? They would go to London. He would meet someone else. He would forget her. He'd had lovers before. She knew he had. It would be one kiss among many to him. Like swords in his armoury. Boots in his cupboard. And she had given up so much for so much. This was surely close to nothing. A fleeting part of someone she had loved, in one way or another, for most of her life.

But no. It was not hers to take. Not like this. Not in fragments and reflections in a place where the joy they shared still tasted of years-old grief. Not when there was still so much he didn't know. And she had no way to tell what that knowing might mean to him.

"I've never…" she began, and oh God, how did you talk to a man when he was so close and looking at you with such tenderness and desire? How could you convince him you didn't yearn for something you were only just learning you'd always yearned for? "I've never…before…"

He put an arm around her waist then and drew her even closer. And there was some magic inside her, as deep and inevitable as the sea, that made her body know exactly what to do—how to fit against him, where to nestle her hips against his, and anchor her shaking hands upon his shoulders. "Then, will you let me?"

"I cannot. It's…if you knew…"

His smile was its own horizon—one she could have followed, through sunrise and sunset, until the end of her days. "If I knew what? Are you already married? A French spy? Have you murdered someone?" He leaned in, his breath stirring the soft curls at her temples. "Do you need my help to hide the corpse?"

He should not have been able to make her laugh. Not when her world was as insubstantial as the tide at her feet. Not when her will was at war with her wanting and everything was collapsing down to this one instant of connection.

"Sometimes," he murmured, "and I can't believe I'm saying this, for I am usually the one who needs to be told to stop thinking, it is enough to live in one moment, and let the rest take care of themselves."

They were her words, of course, returned to her and made new by him. *She* was made new. And still she tried to find the strength to reject him.

A subtle motion, but certain too, changing the alignment of their pressed-together bodies just enough that the fresh places of their touching lit up like undreamed constellations. "So," he asked, "shall I kiss you?"

# CHAPTER 17

The silence beyond his question roared endlessly in her ears. Her heart beat nothing but *what now, what now, what now?* She thought perhaps she ought to shut her eyes. But she was frozen: hope and dread, and love and fear, the spun-sugar crackle of anticipation, and the hollow ache of allowing herself to want—even for this brief span of moments—what could not be hers.

"Viola," he said, his voice filled with promises he should not have been offering her. "Say yes, Viola."

And there was the magic again. More powerful even than that which he had wrought with his embrace. Her name on his lips. She was caught like a deer between the river and the hounds, her only choices to say no and drown or say yes and be torn apart. So instead she froze, half-enchanted in the circle of his arms, her words pinned upon her tongue.

Gracewood's cane landed softly on the sand. Bringing a hand to her cheek, his fingers—no steadier than hers—he traced a line down to her jaw. Some part of her was instinctively self-conscious. Had she been consulted on her own design, she would have liked more softness here, though one could compensate for much with powder and pencil. In his touch, though, there was only gentle wonder—and a pattern of warmth, like the glimmer of beach flow over rainbow seaweed.

He...he really did think she was beautiful.

Her attempt to put up her hair had not survived the ride and the loss of her hat, and the wind was making rather a game of it now, whipping the strands this way and that. The edge of Gracewood's thumb brushed her throat, catching the band of her tiger's eye choker, as he eased a heavy coil over her shoulder and out of her face, and she tilted her neck without really thinking about it, a little shocked by the way a caress so simple, and so incidental, could feel so intensely pleasurable. His lips quirked slightly— no mockery in it, just warmth—stroking her more deliberately this time, the sweep of his fingertips from pulse point to clavicle enough to make her shudder in shameless bliss.

What was happening to her? Her body felt at once more unfamiliar and more hers than it ever had. There was a hot greed unfurling inside her that almost frightened her. This restless, aching *need* for his hands and his mouth and his skin against hers. A bewildered carnality that had only the most half-formed ideas of what it wanted—his weight atop her, the animal heat of his passion, her nails down his back—but wanted nevertheless, making her breath catch and her heart race, and the blood rush through her veins, as sweet as summer wine.

At last, she found her voice, although—overwhelmed and overwrought—all she managed was a tumble of nonsense "Gracewood. You don't understand. You can't. I—"

"Your freckles," he murmured, half to himself.

He lifted his eyes to hers again—and there was something different there this time, a searching, a confusion, an increasing incredulity. And, then, worse than her worst imaginings: recognition.

And, with it, betrayal.

"You're..." He seemed too lost even for anger. "You're hi—"

She put a hand across his mouth before he could finish. "I'm not. I never was."

But it was too late. It was far, far too late.

"Marleigh?" His voice broke with such terrible relief. A muddle of laughter and tears. "Oh, Marleigh."

"Please. Don't. I—"

He pulled her into a tight embrace, almost knocking her off her feet. Not like before. Mere *moments* before. He touched her the way he had touched his friend. A rough-and-tumble affection that felt like a wound in her flesh. "You mad devil. Is this some kind of joke? God knows, I could damn near kill you myself for it. But I'm just so glad to see you."

"Stop. Stop it. Let me go." It was a wild and ragged cry. And she sounded—she had no idea. Not enough like herself. Like someone else was in her skin.

Hardly knowing what she was doing, she pushed against him—she had intended care, but it was all her strength—and he lost his balance, tumbling into the shallows, where he sprawled, staring up at her in dazed incomprehension.

"I am not a joke," she told him. "And I am not a mistake. I was born Lord Marleigh, but I am Viola Carroll. Do you understand? I am *Viola Carroll.*"

"I...I..." He pushed himself to a sitting position, staring at her in a way she had hoped he would never stare at her. And his silence was a bloody thing. "I don't understand."

"I don't know how to explain it. There are...It's not just...In France..." She paused and yet couldn't seem to catch her breath. "I met a husband and wife, they took me in after I was injured. He was like me. The world...the world saw him the wrong way."

"France?" he repeated, helplessly. "But you died."

"I never lived."

Another silence. The tide crept in. The shadows lengthened across the sky. The world turned as though it was not irretrievably broken.

The waves rippled around Gracewood, little bubbles playing about his boots, and yet—apparently oblivious to the wet and the cold—still he did not move. "There are molly houses where men who feel as you do can be with other—"

"No." She cut him off. "I am—I have always been—a woman. I feel as a woman. I desire as a woman. I…I could not bear being thought otherwise."

He blinked, his lashes damp. "But I…we…you've seen me naked. I took you to brothels. Good God, I took you to war."

"I *went* to war, Gracewood. And if I had not, I would never have learned how to…how to be myself."

"I thought"—his fingers brushed the surf and he glanced at them in faint surprise—"I thought you were dead."

"I was wounded. I might have died, but when the Barniers came to…to rifle through my pockets, they discovered I was still alive and took me in."

"For supposedly good people, they seemed willing enough to stoop to robbery."

"What use do the dead have for their possessions?"

"They deserve their dignity."

She shrugged. "The dead don't have much use for dignity either. And you have no idea what it was like for the farmers—their fields torn up, their crops and animals stolen, their families at the mercy of soldiers from both armies. It was desperation that drove many of them, not criminality."

For a long moment, he said nothing more. Stooping, she picked up his cane and offered him a hand—but he only stared at it. "I thought you were dead," he repeated.

"I was reported such. And by the time I'd recovered I...I don't know. My old life seemed like a prison. And for the first time, I saw an opportunity for freedom."

"You were the freest ma—person I'd ever met."

"I was blessed in many ways. I had wealth, a future, a loving family, a dear friend. And yet it was all a lie to me."

He rolled to one knee, and pushed himself upright with visible effort, hands scrabbling for purchase against the wet sand, before she passed him his cane. "And what of *your* lies, Viola? You let me believe you were dead. For two years."

"I know." Her voice was flat. For if she let herself be anything but cold in this moment she would break, and for this breaking there would be no remedy.

"And then you came back." He wasn't looking at her, and in some ways that hurt more than his words. "You came back and you stood in front of me, *saw* what had become of me without you, what I had suffered in losing you, and still you said nothing."

"I know," she repeated, for it was all she could manage.

"Have you no other reply?" She had been braced for his fury. Somehow, his bitterness struck her deeper.

"What other reply can I give you?" Speech spilled free, as useless as sand from a shattered hourglass. "That I am sorry? That I was too afraid—too afraid for both of us—to tell you. That I did not know how I had hurt you and that I feared to hurt you further?"

"Two years." At last his eyes fastened onto hers. She had lived this scene a thousand times over in the darkest places of her mind, terrified of his disgust, his hatred, his contempt, his cruelty. Except now she was here there was only pain—hers old and deep and aching, his new and whiplash raw, turned against her like the guns at Waterloo. "You were my closest friend. The best part of my life. The best part of me. You were...my joy, my hope, my faith in better things. All this time, I thought I'd left you. And it was you, who left me."

Tears were spilling down her cheeks, sticky with kohl and powder. "I didn't want to, Gracewood, please believe that. But I couldn't go on...I couldn't go on as I used to. It was destroying me."

"You could have told me."

"I could barely express what I felt to myself."

"After, then. When you came back. When you understood." He took a step or two towards her, a kind of anger lifting him from his sorrow. And for a moment he looked the image of his father. "Why didn't you come to me? If not when you returned, why not during your stay here? Have I shown you no kindness? Do you trust me so little? I would have—"

"You would have what?" She didn't know where the words came from—some splintered place inside her—but they gave her an unexpected conviction. "Understood? *Accepted* me? Would you have had me lay myself before you as some...some *thing* to be explained or excused, for you to find worthy or wanting as you saw fit? That choice was not yours to make. That is power no-one should hold above another."

"So you chose instead to break my heart?"

She had no answer to that, for there was none to be found.

"God damn you," he cried, the words scattering like cormorants into flight in the still evening air, "say something. Say anything."

Despair was spreading through her like gangrene. Numbing

and annihilating at the same time. "What would you have me say?"

"I don't know. Please...just...Help me. Tell me why you did this to me. Tell me what I did to deserve it."

Only that morning she had stood before her mirror in that magnificent riding habit and felt close to invulnerable. Yet now she might as well have been naked, flayed by wind and salt and sand, and the truths she had not known how to share. Truths that were not Gracewood's to judge. "It was not...it was not about you. If you understand nothing else, understand that."

"I nearly tore two countries apart to find your body. I brought all I had to bear in the search for you. My money, my status, my name...but there was no trace of you left. As if you'd never been. As if nothing good had ever been."

"Your good is yours. It always was."

He gazed at her, the sky in his eyes—grey and grey and grey forever. "You have been the only person to see it. The only person it mattered to. And you left me. Not, as I thought, taken from me in punishment for my foolishness or the happenstance of an indifferent cosmos. But because you made it so."

"Gracewood, please." Oh, where was her strength now? Where was her courage? How was she to bear his hurt, and her own? When, in this moment there was just a helpless ache to be understood, and the unspeakable humiliation of needing to? "That I am who I am is not something I made. It is simply what is. That I have done what I have done is—"

"Did I ever mean anything to you?" he demanded. "Say I didn't. Say it was easy. Say you didn't know...you didn't care... you saw so little in our friendship that you threw it aside and never looked back."

"I…"

His lips curled into a cracked porcelain smile. "Give me that at least."

It would have been easier. Perhaps, in a way, even honourable. Let him believe her faithless and live out his days contentedly despising her. And who knew—perhaps it would help her too, pretending that what she had done had not taken from her almost as much as it had given. "I can't. I wish I could."

"Then how could you do it?" His voice was raw, almost hoarse. "Was I not your friend?"

The question cut so deeply she could barely form the reply. "My dearest friend."

"And what of…what of everything else?" He sounded…not even angry anymore. Lost. Empty. A shadow come to swallow her. "How could we have lived as we did—at each other's sides—and it count for nothing with you?"

"You don't know what it was like," she told him. "There was so much good in my life, so much that brought me joy—and it still hurt. It hurt all the time."

He flinched then. She didn't know why, but it made her angry, perhaps at him, perhaps at herself, or perhaps at something abstract and impossible, and far beyond their capacity to confront.

"And it wasn't nothing." The words rushed through her like the waves at their feet. "Don't you dare believe it was nothing. I know what I did, and I know what it cost—I know what it cost us both, and I did it anyway." And all at once, the fury was gone, leaving her shipwrecked on the shores of her choices. Hardly knowing what she was doing, she pressed her hands against his chest. "You were everything to me, Gracewood. My oldest, closest, most beloved friend. Your happiness was my happiness. Where you led, I followed with all my heart. I would have died for you—and I nearly did—but I could not live for you."

Another silence, full of the restless silk of the sea as it swept back and forth across the sand. Her fingers curled into his waistcoat—clinging to him as a climber might, bloodying her nails against a cliff face. She felt the near-brush of his palms as his own hands lifted and then fell again.

"I did not know," he said at last.

She stepped away, her hands heavy and ugly in their too-tight gloves. "You could not have known."

"I wish to . . . I wish to now. I'm trying to understand." The way he was looking at her—confused and sincere and still so utterly betrayed. "But how am I to forgive you?"

It struck her like a shard of ice: a cold blade direct to her soul. And for the barest fraction of a moment, she despised him for the question. However she might have hurt him, he did not have the right to take who she was and make it a sin. "You're not. Because I will not ask for it. And I do not want it."

"Not even that," he murmured, with a soft and rueful laugh. "Not even my forgiveness is worth your seeking."

Even now, when he had seen her and condemned her and denied her, there was a part of Viola that wanted to comfort him. To tell him that he was not unworthy, as she would have when they were young. And worse, a quiet traitorous voice was telling her she *should*. This promise of absolution she would have hated herself for taking. It would have been so sweet and so simple to tell him she regretted her choices and let him say in return, *I understand, Viola. You did what you had to, Viola. I would have done the same.* Sweet and simple and a denial of everything she had fought to be.

"What do I say?" Gracewood's expression was an unreadable configuration of shadows in the last of the sunlight. But his voice was naked, raw, and pleading with her. "What do I do? Do I even know you? Did I ever?"

What could she tell him? *Yes* felt like a lie. But, then, so did *no*. "In some ways."

It was the only answer she could give him, and she knew it was not enough, the words themselves such frail, uncertain things that the wind snatched them from her lips and bore them away like scraps of paper.

But Gracewood heard them nonetheless, heard them and shuddered. "My God, Viola. Was it not enough to let me believe you dead? Why would you come back? How many times must I mourn you?"

A drop of water touched the corner of her lips, sharp as a wasp sting. "Once. You were...supposed to forget me. And live and... be happy."

"After I left you on the battlefield to die?" He laughed— though there was no mirth in it, no joy or pleasure. "Some creature you must have thought me."

"You should not have blamed yourself. I was—"

Another laugh, even harsher than the last. "And now you would reprimand me? For grieving you? For loving you in the first place? For beginning to love you again?"

"You loved a phantasm," she cried, with the sudden terror of a trapped animal. "Someone who wasn't there."

An endless, unbearable moment, his eyes on her eyes, frantically searching, and everything between them smeared to ash through the helpless wash of her tears.

Then Gracewood turned away from her, a shuffle of his injured leg and a clumsy pivot on his sand-spattered cane. "Perhaps you're right." His shoulders shifted. A crumbling wall, held together only by his pride. "Can you please just...go. Leave me alone as you intended."

Gathering up her sea-sodden skirts, Viola began walking up the beach. Did part of her hope he would call for her? Did part of her imagine running to him? Were her tears flowing freely now?

Yes. And yes. And yes again.

But she knew better than to look back.

# CHAPTER 18

Like Cinderella's ball gown, Viola's composure was in rags by the time she reached the house, the sobs ripping through her in great, uncontrollable gusts. Her tears were powder-thick, leaving pitchy streaks of kohl across her fingers when she tried to wipe them away. She was moving, as good as blind, on instinct alone, her feet tangling in her skirts and, finally, bringing her to her knees in the entrance hall—her weeping breaking into echoes, swallowed by stone.

"Viola?" Lady Marleigh came dashing from a drawing room. "What's the matter? What happened?"

"Oh, what do you think?" Even her words were ugly now. Clotted, knotted things. Toads falling from her mouth. "He realised. He was always going to realise."

A rustle of skirts. Lady Marleigh crouching beside her. "What did he say to you?"

"D-does it matter?"

"I suppose not. But I hoped better of him." Lady Marleigh was not one for unnecessary touching, but she seemed to feel now was the time to pat a shoulder. "I'm sorry."

"Sorry?" repeated Viola, wrenching herself away. "You may take your sorry and stick it straight up your meddlesome arse. This is your fault."

"Is it?"

No. Of course it was not. "Yes. I never intended to see him again. It wasn't...it wasn't...fair." A fresh storm of tears. "On *either* of us. But then you had to have another of your fucking ideas, didn't you?"

One of Lady Marleigh's thoughtful silences—which, in the moment, was worse than speech would have been.

And Viola, helpless in the face of a desolation that felt like rage, swept on, "Never taking no for an answer. Always thinking you can fix everything and everyone. So endlessly convinced you know best."

"But I usually *do* know best," offered Lady Marleigh in a small voice.

"You know nothing"—Viola's voice rose in a wild shriek— "you know nothing of me."

"I know...that you're family. And I know that I want you to be happy."

As Viola tried to stand, the heel of her riding boot snagged a seam, and she heard the velvet tear with a guttural cry like a dying beast. "Which was why you dragged me here? Without stopping for a moment to think what might happen. Or what it might be like for me, or for *him*."

"No, no," Lady Marleigh hastened to reassure her. "I absolutely did think about that."

"Yet still you disregarded us both. Insisted I should come. All so you could play saviour to Mira."

A little calmer now, Viola drew in a shuddering breath. It was not right to blame Louise. It was just easier.

And the more she argued with her sister-in-law, the less she had to think about...anything.

About Gracewood.

Who had twice given her his world. Who she had made to feel as though she thought nothing of him. And who had seen the truth of her, and everything that truth had cost, and called it a betrayal.

The way he had looked at her. With such passion and faith, and then such terrible loss.

Lady Marleigh sighed. "I thought it would be different."

"Did you really believe someone I've spent half my life with would not recognise me?"

"I thought"—Louise seemed oddly uncertain of her words—"you might recognise each other."

Viola had been about to cross to the staircase, but this brought her up short. Made her whirl round, salt water flying from the folds of her riding habit, leaving dark flecks upon the flagstones. "What do you mean?"

"Just that...if you saw him again, if you remembered how you trusted him once, and how much he cared for you, you might want to...tell him?"

The silence that followed these halting sentences had such a menacing quality that even the normally dauntless Lady Marleigh felt compelled to break it.

"So," she went on, "you could be friends again." And then, "Because you missed him, Viola. You know you did."

"You told me," said Viola softly, "this was for Mira."

Lady Marleigh, who was holding very still, as if Viola's fury might overlook her, nodded eagerly. "It was. It was. And for you."

"Are you trying to claim that you forced me into an impossible situation—one that could only bring heartbreak, misery, and betrayal to everyone involved—*for me?*"

"Yes."

Viola's laugh barely felt like hers, such was its harshness. "If this is your friendship, Louise, I quail from the prospect of your antipathy."

"Oh, nonsense," retorted Lady Marleigh. "I can see you're upset, so I won't take offence, but I'm a very good friend. And, besides, the notion that I forced you is ludicrous. You wouldn't have agreed to come if you hadn't secretly wanted to."

"You do not get to decide which of my wants—secret or otherwise—I act upon."

At this, Louise, who had evidently been as meek as she was capable of being for as long as she was capable of being it, rolled her eyes. "Well, obviously I don't. But"—her tone softened slightly—"despite my excellent friend qualities, the fact is I'm not an easy person to be friends with, and so I feel quite warmly towards those who succeed in putting up with me. Which means"—the softness fled, replaced by her typical briskness—"I can't for the life of me understand why you won't just admit you need Gracewood as much as he needs you."

Of course she needed him. But before coming to Morgencald that need had been a soft and distant thing. Now it was sharp and burning and immediate. "Must you interfere in *everything*?"

Lady Marleigh had many faults, but dishonesty was not one of them. "Yes."

For a moment, Viola had no answer beyond silence. Silence, and a thousand splinters in her chest. Here was a fragment of her pride, here a piece of shame, this a shard of longing, strewn across the battlefield of her heart. Mud and blood and edges and wounds, and how was she to put herself back together?

She burst into tears again, except she had already cried out her tears, and all that was left was the grief, bile-sour like retching, and without the relief of weeping. Lady Marleigh, whose moving she had been too lost to heed, turned her gently and drew her into an embrace. It took several long seconds, because even the idea of comfort felt alien in that moment, but finally, Viola crumpled, lowered her face to her sister-in-law's shoulder, and let Louise hold her. Take care of her. In a way that she could never have accepted before, because it wouldn't have been quite true.

"I don't deserve his friendship," she said, when she was calm enough to speak, though the words themselves were soft and ragged. "I threw it away."

Lady Marleigh's hand moved softly through her salt-roughened hair. "No, you didn't. You just had some difficult choices to make."

"And I chose myself. Over... everything. Everyone."

"Oh, Viola." Now a tug on her hair, and Viola lifted her head to find Louise peering up at her with sudden ferocity. "Sometimes it is the most vital thing in the world to be selfish."

Viola tried to smile. She did not think she succeeded. "Even you, dear sister, cannot make a virtue of selfishness."

"As far as I'm concerned"—Lady Marleigh shrugged, visibly unconcerned—"it is a necessity for happiness. I'm not trying to argue you should push over old ladies in the street for amusement, although some old ladies are very annoying, especially when they get together in groups and start talking about hats. Why are they always talking about hats?"

"Perhaps we'll find out when we are old ladies."

"My point," Lady Marleigh continued doggedly, "is that I don't see what use we can be to others if we must deny our own most fundamental selves. We all have the right to be recognised for who we are."

"But the cost—"

"Is an infelicity of circumstance." Lady Marleigh's fingers brushed lightly against Viola's cheek, where the skin felt tight, almost bruised from crying. "And should never have been yours to bear."

"I...truly had convinced myself I bore it alone. And now... now"—Viola hid her face again—"he will never want to see me again."

A pause.

Probably Lady Marleigh was trying not to point out that it had been Viola who, not so long ago, had been insisting she did not want to see Gracewood. The problem was, everything was different now. He had seen her, seen all of her, and she had seen him as she never had before and, more, seen herself *through* him as she had never imagined she could be seen.

*How many times must I mourn you?* he had asked her. But he hadn't stopped to think that she could well have asked him the same question. She had lived with the loss of her old friend, wrapped up the memories of him and put them carefully aside with the rest of her former life. The strangest thing was, she thought she'd known him then. And she had, she had. She'd known his father had hurt him. She'd known he hungered for adventure. She'd known he thought too much and laughed too little. She'd known he was a graceful dancer, a decent whip, an excellent shot.

But she hadn't known the way he looked at a woman he admired. She hadn't known the intricate vulnerabilities of his throat beneath her fingers. Hadn't tasted his breath upon her lips. Hadn't seen him gather up the dust of his heart and make an offering of it anyway. She hadn't known he would make her feel beautiful.

Beautiful, and understood, and still herself, and wholly herself.

Until he hadn't.

"I want to go home," she whispered. "I can't stay here. I won't."

For once in her life, Lady Marleigh didn't argue. Didn't have a better idea. "We'll leave at first light."

"Now."

"I'll pack my things." Louise gave her arm one last pat and turned towards the stairwell. Then paused, her small figure half-swallowed by Morgencald's ever-crowding shadows. "I'm so sorry, Viola. I always want to change things it is not my place, or perhaps within my power, to change. I went too far."

"You meant well."

"Is that ... enough?"

Viola hoped, for both their sakes, that it was, that good intentions could make up for bad outcomes. But, in her experience, they seldom did. Which meant all she could do now was wish that things had been different. That she had been stronger today. That she had contrived, somehow, to leave Gracewood behind before the truth of her had fallen so heavily upon him. That she had been kinder to Lady Marleigh, who, admittedly, was the person she knew least likely to be bothered by being yelled at. But still. Louise was not truly to blame.

Then again, nor was Viola, nor Gracewood, nor anybody. And perhaps that was the hardest truth of all.

The journey back from Northumberland was, in some ways, worse than the journey there: It was equally long, and they had made no reservations at any of the coaching inns they would need to stay at, and they were setting out at an ungodly hour. But while Viola had been assailed by the most impossible mingling of dread and hope and longing at the thought of Morgencald, she was straightforwardly glad to be leaving.

And with space and distance, months and years, she was sure she would…not forget. She could never forget. She owed Gracewood more than that. But the joys and sorrows of the past few days would blunt their teeth against the edge of time. They would sew themselves into the mismatched quilt of her life, and their colours would become her colours: a part of her, no more, no less, no worse, no better.

All she had to do was live through the pain. And she was nothing if not an expert at that. And Gracewood…what could she do but hope that he might do the same? She had seen him come out of the darkness once, and she had to keep faith that he would do so again. That he would do so without her.

It was to London, not Devon, that the carriage bore them. Viola would have preferred to return to the country, but Louise was right that she couldn't hide away forever and besides, Badger was expected at Parliament, for what little good it would do anybody. Which meant that it was an exhausted and on-edge Viola who greeted her brother in the hall, made a few minutes of polite conversation, and allowed Smithereen to help her out of her pelisse before making her way slowly upstairs and, like a fool, finding herself in the corridor outside her old room.

After a moment or so, she pushed open the door and went inside. It was much as she remembered it: a clean, rather neutral space, in shades of cream and dark green. Nothing really to reveal its occupant. But then, sharing Gracewood's antipathy for draughty mansions, she hadn't spent much time here.

Before the war had drawn them abroad, they'd taken lodgings of their own—a set of rooms not so very different to the ones they had shared at Cambridge, rather closer to the less reputable entertainments offered by the capital than its fashionable ones. She supposed they had both been searching in those days, neither one of them quite prepared to follow the path that had been set before them. Still, if they had not yet found purpose, for a little while at least pleasure had been a reasonable substitute.

And that had been a wild year indeed: drinking, dancing, fighting, gambling, and, in Gracewood's case, the occasional affair. He had, she thought, kept an opera dancer for a while, and there had been a widow, whose carnality he had declared quite the education. Occasionally he had teased her over what he saw as her lack of success in the romantic arena. Why would his friend, so bold in so much, be so hesitant with the fairer sex?

But how could Viola have been otherwise? She had felt no desire for women. Only a kind of dull terror, as if some bored-eyed prostitute was going to care whether she was paid for her body or her silence, especially when, as far as Viola could tell, most of them preferred to be paid for silence. Some of them had even asked her why—was she nervous, a virgin, a sodomite—and still others had tried to coax her into intimacy, promising her she would enjoy herself if only she tried. Such overtures had been kindly meant, she knew that, but they had never ceased to horrify her. As if her soul and her flesh were trying to peel themselves apart in some red velvet room.

She should have expected, perhaps, that returning to London

would bring back such memories, but it made them no easier to bear or to escape from. Sitting on the edge of her old bed, she let herself fall back among the covers. There was no dust—the staff were too careful for that—but there was a smell of...emptiness, somehow. Of absence. She had sometimes let herself wonder what Gracewood made of her reticence—if he had thought of her as the whores did. But it had not changed their friendship, so what had it mattered?

She had not been quite aware of it at the time, but, looking back, she was beginning to realise quite how deeply, and unquestioningly, she had accepted that desire was not for her. That it could never be a part of any world she inhabited. After all, such things were rooted in the body, and her body was too often misted glass—reflecting only the haziest impression of who she was supposed to be. When she could not always see her own truth, how could she trust that someone else would?

Except when Gracewood had looked at her—when he had touched her—she had felt not less like herself, but more. So many questions had lost their teeth in the heat of his eyes. So many fears had broken their backs upon the softness of his smile. And beneath his trembling fingertips: her skin, at last, uncaged. She lifted a hand to her neck and traced the line that he had traced, catching lightly upon the edge of her choker, as he had done— imagining the haphazard to-and-fro of the freckles that she knew were there. Of course, it was not the same. Her hand was not his hand. But the magic was upon her still, an echo of its hunger, as sweet as silver bells.

She had no right to cling to this. Not when she had caused such pain. Yet she could not let it go. Not his longing gaze, nor these small caresses, or his near-kiss. In posting houses, she had lain in dark rooms, on indifferent beds, and half dreamed of more—of mouth-on-mouth and a bloom of warmth like wild roses—and known herself a thief. Even now she felt it, a cat's tongue of fire licking into all her darkest, coldest corners, illuminating possibilities she had never dared imagine.

The door opened and she sat up with a start.

"Excuse me, miss." The maid on the threshold, unsure of Viola's status in the domestic hierarchy, gave an awkward bob. "You can't be in here. This is one of the family rooms."

Viola rose, blushing furiously. "Of course it is. I apologise. I'll...leave at once."

"Her Ladyship has had one of the guest rooms prepared. Your things have already been taken up."

"Thank you."

As soon as she was outside, the maid closed the door, turning the key in the lock with a soft, decisive click. It was probably for the best.

Only the past lay within, and there was nothing now for Viola there.

# CHAPTER 19

The last of the light had faded hours ago. Morgencald, ever-dauntless upon the rough rock of its outcropping, was a shadow at his back. The sky mostly clouds, as thick as soiled velvet. And Gracewood sat upon a piece of driftwood, just beyond reach of the tarnished silver tide, with the wreckage of his past, present, and future scattered amid the broken shells and tangled mermaid hair of the sea wrack at his feet.

Nothing made sense now. Or everything did. And to think he had half believed he might be losing his mind. Or falling in love. Because the way he had felt around Viola Carroll had seemed the closest to it he could imagine: hanging upon her words, longing for her laughter, dreaming of her kisses. That sense of belonging. As though the shattered edges of his soul could be made smooth again.

Which...Well. There were moments when he might almost have laughed at the absurdity of it. The absurdity and the impossibility. And the simplicity. *Of course* she was familiar. She was—

She was his oldest friend.

Who he had never truly known.

Two and a half years he had spent haunted by the ghosts of Waterloo. And yet had lived with one at his side far longer than that. Again, he came close to laughing, but his throat was full of salt and razor blades and would not allow any sound to pass. Had circumstances been other than what they were, Viola would surely have laughed with him. For it was she who had taught him how. To look for the ways the world was ridiculous and relish them.

Though maybe it was not laughing that struggled within him. Maybe he wanted to cry. The problem was, he needed alcohol for that. Viola's friend he may have been, but he was the old duke's son. And men did not shame their fathers by weeping or making fools of themselves over women.

Could she truly not have told him? If not before the war, then after? He would have offered the best of his understanding. The same love and faith and comradeship he always had. Except perhaps that was an illusion too. Perhaps it all was. The times they had drunk together deep into night. Neck-or-nothing rides through the wild forests of Morgencald. Deep play by guttering candlelight at some gambling hell and stumbling back to their rooms at dawn. None of these experiences could he have shared with Miss Viola Carroll.

Which meant he had, instead, lived half his life by the side of a man who never was.

He had lost not only his friend, but the memory of his friend too. Everything that had ever mattered to him. Everything that had not been given to him by the vagaries of birth or circumstance. The single thread in the inescapable tapestry of his life that was his, and his alone. That allowed him to believe he might be worth something on his own account. For Viola—lively, daring, quick-witted Viola—could have offered her friendship to anyone. And she had offered it to him: a sombre boy with a great legacy and his failure to live up to it etched into his very skin.

He wished he did not know. She should never have come back. But if she had not, he might well have been as dead as he'd believed his friend to be. It had not been a considered action—to avail himself of a gun that night—and perhaps some impulse of his own would have stayed his hand. Perhaps it would not have needed to, for he had trembled too much to steady it, nauseous on the chill of the metal, the scent of the powder. Yet he could not be certain.

At the time he would have given anything, done anything, for silence. For sleep as deep as it was eternal. To be relieved of duty, of grief, of a future as relentless as stone. The sheer relief of nothing. And then Viola had come and given him hope all over again. At first just hope for himself. And then hope for something else entirely.

The starless dark of her sharp eyes. Those devil's brows. Her wicked mouth, which he had so nearly kissed.

A woman who was willing to see him, flawed and unworthy and half-broken as he was. Who had let him see a little of her in return: her joys and her uncertainties and some of what had felt like her truths. A woman he could laugh with and talk to, call friend as well as lover. And damn her station and damn his own, and everything else his father had taught him. He would have jumped from the cliffs of Morgencald for Viola Carroll. Of course he would. He already had.

And she had saved him twice now. And ruined him nonetheless.

The dawn was breaking around him in shades of crimson and rust, the sun casting a bloody shadow across the charcoal sea. And it occurred to Gracewood he should return home—if for no reason other than the fact he would be missed. Potentially worried about. And that the life he had allowed Viola to recall him to was still waiting for him. Besides, her insufferable mistress… friend…sister-in-law…had likely been correct: Miranda needed a season. At least some good should come of this.

Exhaustion rolled over him as heavy as the passing hours. His leg had stiffened overnight. The cold had gnawed its way through him like a rat. But there was nobody to watch him sweat and stumble his way back from the beach. And Janner, who opened the door for him, had seen him in a far worse state.

"Miss Carroll," Gracewood asked, stripping off his coat. "I presume she returned safely?"

Janner accepted the garment as though there were nothing untoward in his master returning at such hour, his clothes salt-crusted from seawater. "Yes, Your Grace. But she's left again with her mistress."

For some reason, it had not occurred to Gracewood that she might. That she would. But of course she had. You could not speak to someone as he had spoken to Viola yesterday and expect them to desire further discourse with you. In all honesty, he was not entirely sure he wanted further discourse with her. It was too... Confusing? Uncomfortable? Heartbreaking?

Still, she was gone. And in her wake was emptiness all over again.

He knew the act of a sensible man—a man who was trying to do better—was to go at once to his room. But there was an especial torment in being sleepless in your own bed. Your covers too hot, too soft, too stifling, and every shadow a familiar monster. Besides, in the library...

In the library, behind *The History of the Decline and Fall of the Roman Empire, Volume V,* there was a brown-glass bottle. The very last of its fellows.

*Just in case*, he had told himself.

*What if you need it*, he had told himself.

*You can pour it away at any time. Or smash it as you did the other.*

*There's no harm in keeping it. It's only one. And only you need know it's there.*

The bottle in question turned out to contain less liquid than he had realised. Though that was almost a blessing. It meant he was preoccupied with disappointment—inclined to chastise himself for his former lack of consideration—and did not have to dwell on the fact he had as good as sworn he would give up laudanum entirely.

He had intended to. He had even believed he could, despite the physical consequences and the emotional torment. But this was not an act of desperation. It was not the need for opium over-whelming his reason and his will. It was the need not to feel. Not to think. Not to remember.

It was a choice.

Twisting the stopper free, Gracewood lifted the bottle to his lips and drank whatever remained within it. There was, in that moment, something almost comforting in the bitter familiarity of poppies. The way the world slowed. Detached itself. Peeled away at the corners and rolled up like an old carpet.

His leg was still in agony. A day's ride, a walk to the beach, a night outside, the walk back had been too much. But the pain was an echo from a deep, deep well, just like he was. A reflected man. A hollow man. And even that, the laudanum made soft. As insubstantial as dust motes in the morning.

At some point, Viola came to him, her beauty as cold as moonlight, and restless as the waves. He called out to her, but she didn't answer, and then he remembered she'd left hours ago. That she belonged now with the rest of his ghosts.

For she had never been anything else.

# CHAPTER 20

Gracewood returned to himself over the course of the afternoon. Stabbed by too much light into something like consciousness. He was sprawled upon the floor of the library, in yesterday's clothes, unwashed and unshaven, and sick to his very soul.

When he had turned back to the drug, he had told himself that he was making a choice, that it held no power over him he did not give it. But he was seeing that now for a lie. It had been dependency, barely disguised, and he had so easily given way before it. He even thought he had another bottle of laudanum—it was in the back of his bedside drawer.

A tightening and a twisting in his stomach flipped him onto his side, and he smothered a groan against his knuckles. His head throbbed and his body shook, and he could smell poppies—sour and sweet—upon his own sweat. It was repulsive and he was repulsive and God knew why Viola had nearly let him kiss her. How she could have gazed at him with such…such *wanting*.

Wanting and hope and fear.

And she had tried to tell him. How many times had she tried to tell him? Except—enmeshed in his own sense of betrayal—he had not stopped to wonder how it felt to live in a world that rendered such a telling necessary. The burden she had borne, not just these past few weeks for his benefit, but all her life. Her strength abashed him, as it always had. Her valour moved him. And it was in that moment that he at last understood the truth that grief and shock had previously obscured: Viola Carroll lived. She had always lived. And it was he who had not recognised her.

He pressed his face against his forearm. This was a different pain, a deeper one—the understanding of having failed so completely the only person who had never failed you—but he neither sought to deny it nor escape from it. That had been his answer too many times and for too many things, and this was where it had brought him. To loss entirely of his own making. When all he should have felt was relief and gratitude and joy. Two years of grief suddenly seemed the most irrelevant price to pay for Viola's return. For her chance to be who she was meant to be. And his, at last, to know her as she was meant to be known.

If only he had trusted her. And listened to his heart, instead of to his hurt.

What must it have cost her to come here? How much of herself had she risked? And yet she had, for him, and stayed for him, too, because he had needed her. In return, she had needed only understanding. And he had offered—what? His anger and his questions, his conviction that he had been forsaken and misused. And then his forgiveness? For choices she should never have had to make in the first place. Yes, those choices had hurt him. But what of her hurts? What did he truly know of those? And how unwilling had he been to consider them?

Gracewood had left so many certainties upon the fields of Waterloo. He had almost forgotten what it was like to know something, not just with his mind, but to the bone. And what he knew was this: Some impossible miracle had brought Viola to him. Until he had seen her on the beach, he had thought he had lost her to death and the cruelty of a meaningless universe.

Then he had accused her of leaving on her own account, of letting him suffer for her, in heedlessness or selfishness. But none of it mattered. What mattered was that he could—eventually—have found peace with either scenario had they been true.

What he would never find peace with was having driven her from him. For allowing his sense of being wronged to overwhelm his sense of her. A woman trying to navigate an impossible situation who was, and had always been, his truest friend. Perhaps it was already too late. Perhaps he had erred too grievously. And she would want none of him. He would not blame her for it. But even so. She had always come to him. It was time for him to go to her.

Though not like this. The empty laudanum bottle lay where he had let it fall, a few drops of viscous fluid clinging to the neck. He was close to being in command of his senses, and it dismayed him how easily he had slipped back into his old habits, the way opium had felt like a friend again, though he knew it to be an enemy. Of course some promises and few scant weeks of sobriety did not a new man make. But he had not realised how feeble his efforts had been, thwarted from the outset by the part of him that spoke in his father's voice and insisted it alone saw him clearly. Knew him truly. As the weak, worthless failure of a man he was, for whom any virtue was façade and any attempt at betterment was futile.

That voice had ruled him all his life, save when Viola was at his side. When he had let her words and her smiles and her sheer unending faith in him block out the shadows that haunted his other hours. But was that not a terrible responsibility to place on anybody? To make them and them alone the prop that held him steady? And what did it say of him if he could not be whole without her?

It was pitiable. It was wretched. And it would change. What Viola had helped him begin, he needed to finish alone. Not, this time, for necessity. Nor duty. Nor even love. He had to do it for himself.

Unsteadily, he rose to his feet. His head swam and his stomach churned, forcing him to sit again. But at least he could take comfort from the fact that he would not be spending all day in a drug-addled stupor on the library floor. Feeling a fool for revelling in so small a victory, he shut his eyes a moment.

The laudanum must have been lingering still in his system, for it was only when the door burst open that Gracewood became retrospectively aware that someone had been tapping upon it for quite some time and that his eyes had been shut long enough that it was growing dark again. It was, he reflected, a poor start to a new beginning.

"Justin," cried Miranda, rushing inside. "Oh, Justin."

He tried once more to stand and wished he hadn't, sinking immediately back down. "Whatever is the matter?"

"N-nothing. Just, Auntie Lou and Miss Carroll have gone, and you did not return all night, and you have been in your library all day and…and I thought you might be dead."

"Mira"—he put a hand to his temples—"that is nonsense."

She gave him an unexpectedly sharp look. "Is it nonsense?"

"The latter part most certainly."

There was a brief silence. Even the soft grey twilight felt like needles beneath Gracewood's eyelids.

"Why did you send Auntie Lou away?" asked Miranda, finally.

"I didn't send her away. She and her companion chose to leave."

"I see." Miranda twisted a lock of hair around one of her fingers. "I suppose there wasn't much to keep them here. We're so far from anywhere. But it was nice to have company."

This wasn't fair to Miranda or, for that matter, Lady Marleigh. But Gracewood's role in the abrupt departure of his guests was too complicated to explain. Not that he needed to explain himself. He might not have been able to master his thoughts, or his feelings, or the laudanum, but he could at least master his household. "I will be taking you to London soon."

"What? Why?"

"You need a season," he told her sternly. "And people around you."

"I don't need—" She broke off. Then darted forward, seizing the laudanum bottle from the floor. "Justin, what's this? You're only meant to take it at night."

He should have hidden the bottle. His habits were not his sister's business. "I did take it at night."

"Then you took too much." Her eyes, which in London would doubtless be the talk of the more poetic, less lascivious gentlemen of the ton, swept over him like limpid knives. "You are—look at—you are not well."

"I am perfectly well, and were I not, it would be none of your concern."

"None of my concern?" she repeated, more stridently than was appropriate for a younger sister. "You are my brother. How can you be none of my concern?"

Why didn't she understand? It was simple, all so simple. "Because our positions are such that I am responsible for your welfare. You are not responsible for mine."

"I can still care for you. I can still love you."

She had meant it as comfort, he was sure, but a man was not meant to need such things. Not from his sister. "Don't be so sentimental. I am the Duke of Gracewood. I have duties to attend to, and I do not need to be mollycoddled."

If he had pushed her too hard, Miranda showed no sign of it. But then perhaps their father's influence had shaped her as well. "That was cruel, Justin."

"As you observe, I am unwell. It is making me ill-tempered. Leave me be, and you shall not have to be burdened with my discourtesies."

Still she stood there, not defiant, exactly. He would have preferred defiance. To be defied, one had to be formidable. Instead she still looked at him with concern. Devotion. Pity. As if his injuries and his dependencies weren't emasculating enough, now he was being pitied by a child. "You could never be a burden to me," she half whispered. "And I would never be a burden to you."

"You are not a burden, but you are a duty, and one I have, to my shame, neglected."

"I don't want to be a duty." Her voice was rising now, not anger quite, but—hang it all, he could barely think. "I want to be your sister. Why won't you let me? What have I ever done except wait for you and stand by you and try to care for y—"

"That is not your place."

"How is it not my place? I only want to help. To be of some use to someone."

It was too much. It was all too much. "Then go. Tell the kitchen I shall be taking my meals in my room for the foreseeable future."

For a moment it looked as though Miranda might say more, but instead she nodded her understanding and turned to leave.

She just had her hand on the door when Gracewood called after her. "Mira?"

There was something in her eyes when she turned. A light almost. "Justin?"

"There is another bottle. In the back of my bedside drawer. I would be grateful if...Have the servants remove it."

The light faded. "Of course," she said.

And then she was gone.

Afterwards he feared that he had been monstrous to her. But the truth was worse: The truth was that he had been petty. Proud and cold and discourteous. Not even the picture of hauteur and arrogance he had been raised to be, but a cracked mosaic of it with most of the spite and none of the dignity. It was all he was, all he had ever been able to be except when Mar—except when Viola had been with him. When she had shown him who he could be, even if she had not been able to show him who she was.

And now he had lost her again. Let her leave him again. When he should have fought to stay beside her, in their youth and in the war and always.

There was so much in his past he could not undo. He could not unwind the years or unfire the guns that still echoed in his ears. But he could go back to Viola now. Find her. Fight for her.

For all that he was weary and broken, and less than a man, he could do that.

# CHAPTER 21

L ittle Bartholomew had caught a mouse.

"Look, Auntie Viola." He thrust the wriggling creature towards her. "I shall call him Arthur after Arthur Wellesley, and also after King Arthur."

They had been in London for some weeks, and Viola was slowly approaching a world where she could stop worrying constantly about Gracewood and start worrying constantly about everything else. Little Bartholomew was a welcome distraction. "That's a fine name for a mouse. But do you really think your mother and father will let you keep him?"

"I'm sure they shall. He is an exceptionally good mouse."

Not for the first time, nor the tenth, nor the hundredth, Viola felt a twinge in her stomach talking to Little Bartholomew. It was foolish, of course, to miss what she could never have. And ungrateful to feel that lack most keenly when presented with the nearest substitute. But feelings, in Viola's experience, came and went as they willed and cared little for how they reflected on the one who felt them. "How can you tell that?"

Little Bartholomew's face fell. "Is it not obvious? Do you *not* think he is an exceptionally good mouse?"

"I fear I am an ill judge of mice." An ill judge of many things. And, her mind slipping easily from thought to thought, Viola wondered what might have happened had she gone to

Gracewood, if not on her return from France, then when they had first arrived at Morgencald. *I am indeed a ghost*, she could have told him, *but not as you think*. And what then? Her imagination faltered, as it always did. Brought her instead, as it always did, to a beach, and bloody sunset, and the inevitability of two people who had loved and hurt each other beyond reckoning.

"Well," Little Bartholomew was insisting, "look at his face."

"Ah," she said, looking and trying to sound as if she truly had discerned a special nobility in the features of a rodent. "I see it now. Yes, he is a fine mouse indeed."

Little Bartholomew nodded with the blissful certainty of childhood. "I think he shall make a fine friend. He can teach me to wriggle through holes and eat cheese."

"Don't you know how to eat cheese already?"

"Not like a mouse does. I am sure mice eat cheese in special mouse ways."

That, Viola had to concede, was inarguable logic. "We are in London now. Will there not be other boys for you to be friends with?"

"I don't want to be friends with other boys. I want to be friends with a mouse."

"Very wise."

Deciding that standing up was altogether too much like hard work, Little Bartholomew sat on the floor, obliging Viola to sit next to him. "Were you friends with other girls when you were little?"

The question took Viola slightly by surprise. On the one hand, it pleased her that, in Little Bartholomew's mind, her upbringing would have been no different from any young lady's. On the other, she did not welcome that it hadn't been.

"No," she told him. "I was not friends with other girls. But I was very good friends with a boy."

"Oh." Little Bartholomew's nose wrinkled. So did Arthur's. "I didn't think girls could be friends with boys."

This, too, was a question without a simple answer. "We can't, as a general rule. But I was a very unusual girl and my friend was a...a very special boy."

"As special as Arthur?" Little Bartholomew held the mouse aloft.

"Almost. But it was hard sometimes. Because he didn't know I was a girl. And I had to pretend to be a boy because..." Because that was how it was. You wore these clothes, but not those; you learned some things, but not others; you behaved in certain ways and bore certain expectations—without truly understanding what they signified or what claims they made about you. That Viola chafed against them she had also assumed was universal. After all, she had chafed against bedtime too, and Latin grammar, much as Little Bartholomew did.

"Because otherwise you couldn't have been friends?" he asked.

"I suppose—there were other reasons, but yes, in part so that we could be friends. And in part because I did not know how to tell him. I think I scarcely knew how to tell myself."

"Didn't you already know?"

It was unexpectedly reassuring to speak so openly of who she was and the life she had lived. And she hesitated for a moment, uncertain whether it was selfish to do so, or if she was—in some nebulous way—imposing herself on someone else's child. But Louise was a great proponent of telling the truth to children, and, Viola reflected, had someone spoken of such matters to her when she was young, she might have been saved a lot of heart-ache. As might others.

"I knew in some ways," she admitted. "But it was hard to put into words. It took a long time. And when I went to Northumberland with your mother and saw my friend again I...I still couldn't tell him. But he found out anyway."

Little Bartholomew looked suitably upset. "Was he very cross?"

That almost made Viola laugh. "Yes. Yes, he was very cross and very hurt. He felt I'd—he thought I'd been a bad friend. And I think in some ways I had."

"Because you didn't tell him you were a girl?"

There was more to it than that. Far more. But Little Bartholomew was seven-and-a-third so could be forgiven for over-simplifying. She nodded. "I was too afraid to hurt him or to lose him. And in the end I did both."

"Then I think," declared Little Bartholomew, "that he has been a bad friend too. Friends should stand by each other no matter what. As I shall stand by Arthur, even though he is a mouse."

Arthur squeaked, and Viola took it for approval.

"Bartholomew!" Lady Marleigh's voice echoed from the corridor outside. "Bartholomew, will you please come back to your tutor *immediately*."

Viola looked down. "Bartholomew, are you meant to be with Mr. Dowling now?"

Little Bartholomew shook his head.

"Your mother seems to think you are."

"Mother doesn't know everything. Arthur says I am to play with him today, and I think I should listen to Arthur because he is a duke."

"There you are." For all her unyielding confidence, Lady Marleigh was seldom a burster-in to places. A barger and a poker-of-noses perhaps, but never a burster-in. "Viola, you *must* stop keeping Bartholomew away from his lessons."

"Viola wasn't keeping me away. Arthur was."

"Arthur is a mouse," explained Viola.

Lady Marleigh looked down at her son, hands resting on her hips. "Bartholomew. I would like to believe that your father and I have raised you better than to take educational advice from rodents."

"Arthur is a very sensible rodent, Mama."

"By rodentiary standards, he may be. But put him back where you found him. He's probably getting tired."

At this, Little Bartholomew looked wounded. "May I not keep him?"

"Where did he come from?" asked Lady Marleigh in a tone that Little Bartholomew was still too young to realise was a trap.

"The hall."

"Then he clearly lives in the house and we are already keeping him. Let him go, and if he wants to find you again, he will. Otherwise I am sure he has important mouse business to attend to."

For a moment Little Bartholomew looked like he was trying to marshal a reply to this faultless logic, but he failed and, bowing a polite farewell to both his mother and to Viola, went back to his tutor.

"You indulge him," said Lady Marleigh.

"Isn't that what aunts are for?"

A great believer in order, Lady Marleigh considered this. "Yes, I suppose they are. Carry on then. But I also wanted to ask if you could possibly do me the teensiest favour."

"The last teensy favour I did you ended poorly."

Lady Marleigh waved a dismissive hand. "Oh, pish, we did what was right, and circumstance conspired to produce an undesirable outcome. It is the fault of the world, not of you and certainly not of me. Besides, the favour I'm about to ask you is *much* teensier than the last one. You shan't even need to leave the house."

That eased some of Viola's trepidation, but far from all of it. "What's the favour, Louise?"

"Well, you see, I've had a visitor call upon me unexpectedly, and she's arrived just as Badger and I were about to...attend to some business, if you catch my meaning."

"I believe I do."

"My meaning is that we're going to have sex."

Viola nodded. "Yes, that was what I thought your meaning was."

"Quite a lot of sex. Probably for quite a long time. But apparently it's rude to leave a guest waiting while that happens, so since you're my companion and since neither of us want you to have sex with Badger for me—"

The mere thought made Viola choke. "Louise, he is my *brother*."

"Exactly, which is why we *don't* want that. Do try to keep up. But it occurred to me that you could, perhaps, stand in for me with Lady Lillimere instead."

And *that* thought caught Viola quite differently. Life in the country had been simple. She had been able to settle into her new life slowly and at her own pace. Even if it had sometimes seemed like every day revealed a new inadequacy, a new skill or expectation that her upbringing had denied her the chance to learn or embody. "I'm not ready."

"You are entirely ready."

"This isn't Devon, Louise, it's London. People expect a certain... refinement."

"Nonsense. In London people will put up with anything. You get all sorts. Lady Lillimere, for example, is a sort all to herself. Besides, you must be out in society at some point. You can't hide in your room forever."

"The last time I came out of my room I destroyed the remains of my oldest friendship."

"In which case"—Lady Marleigh beamed—"I scarcely see what you have to lose by leaving it again."

And like Little Bartholomew before her, Viola had no answer to this ironclad logic. So, she descended to the drawing room and prepared to attend to the business of her sister-in-law's guest, while her sister-in-law attended to the business of her husband.

After a minute or two Smithereen entered with the visitor. "Lady Lillimere, Miss Carroll."

As Smithereen faded away again, Viola rose in greeting. Wait, did ladies do that with each other? Never mind. Too late now. "My Lady." She bobbed a curtsey. "Please do come in. I'm afraid Lady Marleigh is... is..."

"Oh, fucking her husband, I suppose?" Lady Lillimere swept into the room and threw herself down on the sofa, as though it was her regular spot. "I should have guessed they'd still be at it. Sorry."

"N-no. It's"—Viola took a deep breath—"quite all right."

"Can't say I blame her though. Maybe if my husband had looked more like Badger and less like a potato, God rest his soul, I'd have found more joy in matrimony."

It was acceptable for Viola to sit too, wasn't it? The alternative was standing in the middle of the room, with her hands twitching in the folds of her dress. "Possibly?"

"Or maybe not. I see fellows who don't look like potatoes all the time, and I can't say they do much for me either." A pause, Lady Lillimere plonking her chin thoughtfully in her hand. "Is there any tea?"

"I'm so sorry." Recalled abruptly to her duties as...whatever she was in this context, Viola leapt to her feet and went to ring the bell. "I wasn't expecting—that is I'm not accustomed to—"

"It's just tea. There's no need to be missish."

"Missish?" repeated Viola, oddly delighted by the notion of being missish.

"Well"—a lazy shrug—"I don't really like to stand upon ceremony."

"So I gathered based on your immediate demand for refreshment."

At this, Lady Lillimere gave a delighted chuckle. "That's better. I was wondering what Lou wanted with a companion all of a sudden—but then I was imagining some kind of worthy, Christian creature with a face like a doorknob."

"Tea, please." That was to Smithereen, who had answered Viola's summons with his usual quiet efficiency. And then, to Lady Lillimere. "While I'm flattered my face has passed muster, why are you so quick to assume me a heathen?"

"I assume that of all the fun people. But you're very welcome to proselytise me any time the fancy catches you."

"I'm not convinced that word means what your tone suggests it does."

Lady Lillimere blinked at her. "Suggestive? Me?"

"I…" Flustered, and not quite certain how to answer, Viola

broke off. This was not how ladies spoke to gentlemen, but she wasn't sure it was how they spoke to other ladies either. And she had no idea if it was just Lady Lillimere having an unusual manner, or if she was responding to some signal of unusualness that Viola was unconsciously sending.

"I'm sorry." Lady Lillimere's tone softened. "I'm being a little beastly to you, aren't I? It's just you look so pretty when you're confused, I can't help myself."

Pretty? On the beach, before too many truths had destroyed them both a second time, Gracewood had said Viola was beautiful. She'd folded the word up inside her memories like a piece of old lace, but she'd been ashamed—felt vain—for making a keepsake of it. After all, he was still suffering the after-effects of abandoning laudanum, and she had lied to him. It was a bewildering moment, for both of them. He could not have meant it. But neither could Lady Lillimere, who was offering her praise as careless as showers in April.

"I have," Lady Lillimere went on, "what do you call it. Like Herrick. Delight in disorder."

It took Viola a moment to catch up. But only a moment. "Louise has the opposite of that. Satisfaction in organisation, I suppose."

Another easy laugh. "I can see why she likes you."

"You may change your mind when you see the dreadful mess I'm about to make of entertaining." Viola surveyed, with mounting despair, the necessaries for tea that Smithereen and a footman had just delivered to them. Most of her life she had been served things with such effortlessness on the part of those who served that she had never thought to pay attention. "How do you like your tea?"

"My tea? I don't give a damn, my dear."

"You're not helping."

Lady Lillimere shrugged. "What can I say? It's dried leaves in water. I have a hard time mustering an opinion."

"Very well then." Defiantly, Viola lifted the teapot and tilted it over one of the cups, only for the lid to fall off and chink into the saucer. "Bother."

"Were you raised by wolves?" asked Lady Lillimere, laughing.

"Yes. Yes, I was." Returning the lid to its proper place, Viola once again lifted the teapot, which was considerably heavier than it looked. "I'm a wild woman, found in the Forest of Arden and only partially re-civilised."

"How fortunate for me. I happen to prefer my women a little wild."

Viola was only half paying attention as she used one hand to hold the lid in place and the other, feeling the heat even through her gloves, to angle the teapot. An unprepossessing straw-coloured liquid sloshed forth, at first too slowly, and then far too fast, filling both the cup and the saucer.

"That," observed Lady Lillimere as Viola grimly handed her the cup, "looks like the contents of my chamber pot. I think it needed to stew a little longer."

"I thought you said you had no opinions."

"I did not anticipate the situation meriting one."

A pause. Viola could feel Lady Lillimere watching her, even though she stubbornly refused to look up herself, her eyes fixed on her hands, which were folded in her lap. She was too afraid of what her face might betray. She just knew she was embarrassed, and being embarrassed made her angry. At least until it made her cry.

"Do I owe you another apology, Miss Carroll?" asked Lady

Lillimere. "I sometimes think I'm teasing, but instead I'm being an arse."

Viola shook her head, striving for courtesy when she wanted to jump out the nearest window, dig a hole somewhere, and die in it. "No, no. I should apologise. I...I am not a good hostess."

"Your tea-related skills, I will not lie, are abysmal. But you're entertaining company and not too busy having sex to spend time with me, which right now puts you ahead of Louise."

"I think"—glancing up, Viola could not help a faint smile—"that is more about opportunity than principle."

"You little cat." There was, however, no rancour in Lady Lillimere's tone. And her eyes—which were a rather hard grey for all the ease of her smile—were amused. Then, putting aside the cup Viola had poured for her, she lifted the lid off the teapot and peered inside. "You know," she went on, replacing the lid before giving it a little swirl, "I rather envy you a life where you didn't spend your formative years learning how to do nonsense like this. Watch me. Aren't I disgustingly graceful?"

Moving with the precision of a fencer, she poured out two perfect cups, handing one to Viola with not a single drop spilled.

"I would have said intimidatingly," Viola murmured.

But Lady Lillimere shook her head. "Oh, don't. You have no idea how much I resent it. Every minute, every hour, I spent walking around with books on my head to correct my posture, learning how to curtsey to a duke or recite the family tree of Lord this-and-that, being taught how to smile—or not smile in my case, since you may have noticed it's not my best feature—and look pretty, though again not entirely within my natural purview."

It was true that Lady Lillimere—now some way past her thirtieth year—was not pretty, and it was hard to imagine she had ever been. Pretty suggested simplicity, and it was becoming clearer to Viola by the minute that her visitor was anything but. There was, however, a certain quality to her—something elusive and fascinating, like the dance of dust motes in a fall of light. "I like your smile."

"Thank you. Since I'm stuck with it, I thought I ought to learn to as well, though my parents felt otherwise. I spent quite a lot of my childhood with a metal *bandeau* ligated to my teeth."

Viola winced in sympathy, her own teeth full already of phantom aches. "That sounds horrible."

"And yet my—what did Chaucer call it?—coltes tooth, persisted. Perhaps that was what my parents feared—that I would turn out lewd like the Wife of Bath." Lady Lillimere widened her eyes. *"Imagine."*

"You could have done a lot worse."

"My family needed marriageable, and they meant well. So I'm glad to have obliged them."

Given how disparagingly Lady Lillimere had spoken of her marriage, Viola wasn't entirely sure this was true. "I understand," she said softly, "that the wedded state can sometimes be…a trial. Especially if one's husband is not—"

"My husband was the kindest, most honourable creature imaginable. He was just"—Lady Lillimere heaved a sigh— "awfully dull. And I felt grateful enough to him that I wanted to be a good wife. It's just…I am not, I think, suited for goodness of that kind, so it quickly became its own burden. One I believe I am in rebellion against, even now."

"How so?"

"Well, as you see, I say what I wish, do as I wish, and smile whenever I feel like smiling."

"I'm not sure being yourself really constitutes…rebellion?"

Lady Lillimere threw back her head and laughed. "Doesn't it? Then I envy you all over again, my dear. But, God, what a monster I am, to make a gift from the loss of a good man."

"You did not cause his demise—at least I hope not…"

"Thank you," said Lady Lillimere dryly, "for that brief suspicion of murder, but no. He died in Corunna nearly a decade ago now."

"And would it make you a better person if you continued to live in a way that made you unhappy?"

"I suppose not. But there is something awry in the world, is there not, that we women must give our everything to men in life, and they theirs to us in death?" Before Viola could answer her, Lady Lillimere slapped a hand to her brow and exclaimed, "Good God, my conversation is as dire as your tea. I blame your eyes—they draw one in. What would you say to a jaunt around the park in my curricle? Everyone else will be parading themselves. Why shouldn't we?"

There could be no harm in it, surely? Lady Lillimere was, after all, a friend of Lady Marleigh's—although, now Viola thought about it, that was not necessarily an endorsement. The criteria by which Louise selected her intimates was…quite specific to Louise. Except Viola was beginning to like Lady Lillimere too—her blunt speech and careless manners, the smile that rarely reached her eyes. There was a sense of stagecraft about her, somehow, guiding attention to the cards in her hand, rather than the ones up her sleeve. It made Viola feel oddly safe, this reminder that everyone lived their own illusions, chose their own truths, performed their own quiet magic before indifferent crowds.

"I'll get my pelisse," she said.

The pelisse got, they were about to make their departure when

Lady Marleigh—hastily attired in a pretty, cherry-print morning gown—came dashing down the stairs to catch them in the entrance hall. Badger followed at more temperate speed, for he did most things temperately, and the least said about his gold-trimmed purple dressing gown the better.

"Viola," cried Lady Marleigh. "Stevie. You had best not be trying to lure Miss Carroll into your curricle. If you are attempting to importune her, I will be quite extraordinarily cross with you."

A quite extraordinarily cross Louise was clearly something Lady Lillimere did not wish to contemplate. She bowed her head. "What if I importune her just a little bit?"

Closing the distance between them, Lady Marleigh stood before Lady Lillimere, hands on hips, glaring up at her. "What is wrong with you? I thought you were only coming for tea. You know it is not a requirement that you . . . you . . . solicit the favours of every lady you meet?"

"Not a requirement, no," Lady Lillimere conceded, sounding more subdued than Viola had hitherto heard her. "More a sort of ambition."

Lady Marleigh gave a little growl. "I swear you're the equal in selfishness of any man I've ever known."

"In my experience," came the cold reply, "we behave like men or we become for men."

"And I, who have stood by you all these years, merited no consideration at all?"

"Forgive me"—Lady Lillimere's whip was flicked restlessly against her boot—"but I was rather under the impression that Viola's favours were Viola's to bestow."

At this Viola thought it best to intervene. While she had not quite recognised that her favours were being solicited, and would have hastily demurred had she done so, she was not above being mildly flattered that somebody deemed them worth soliciting. "Lady Lillimere has done me no wrong. And while I appreciate your kindness, Louise, I don't want to be a burden to you. I believe I can take care of myself."

Before Lady Marleigh could reply to this there came a fresh ringing of the bell. And expecting some other friend of Louise's—or perhaps some accidental acquaintance of Badger's—Viola took the opportunity to excuse herself.

She had her foot upon the stairs when she heard Smithereen saying, "Good afternoon, Your Grace. It has been a long time, if I may say so."

And, surely, that could have been the sort of comment he could make to anyone. Well, anyone if they happened to be a duke or an archbishop. It didn't mean—

"Is the family at home?" came the reply.

Viola's hand tightened on the banister rail. She was bones, nothing but bones, sun-bleached and brittle, as empty as seashells cast upon some unmapped shore.

"Gracewood." Badger's greeting echoed distantly. "I'm confused. I thought you were in Northumberland."

"Yes," Lady Marleigh explained, "it seems he's left."

Badger made a sound of relief. "Oh, that makes *much* more sense."

"Viola?" Gracewood. Too familiar. His voice bearing too many memories. Too much joy. Too much pain. Too much. "I mean, Miss Carroll. I mean, Viola. I...I know I should not be here. I know I have no right, but...will you talk to me?"

"Well," drawled Lady Lillimere, "this is an interesting situation. And I should probably check on my horses. They'll be restless."

A faint moue of bewilderment from Louise. "But you said it was an interesting situation."

"Yes, my dear," returned Lady Lillimere, laughing. "That's why I'm leaving. I'm not normally one for politeness, but there's a fine line between irreverence and vulgarity."

"Really?" Lady Marleigh sounded heartbreakingly disappointed. "Badger, does that mean we have to leave as well?"

Whatever happened next was communicated without further need for words. It was followed by footsteps and the swish of Badger's dressing gown. Then silence.

And Viola could have fled. The opportunity was there. Part of her wanted to. Especially when the mere sound of Gracewood's voice brought back a rush of memories from Morgencald. His pain, yes, and hers, but above all else his anger. The way he had demanded that she explain herself, that he had asked her—not only wondered but asked her—how she could be forgiven. Forgiven for choosing freedom over a cage, life over death. Forgiven for being who and what she was.

And then, as if breaking in on her innermost thoughts, he said: "Viola, I beg you."

She turned slowly, in case she scattered into dried leaves and dust. And there he was, somehow like nothing she had imagined. He looked...he looked...better. Dressed for the town, instead of the country, his wild locks tamed, his face clean-shaven, though not—she could not help the thought—as closely as she had managed. One hand rested still upon a walking cane—more ornate than she had seen him use at Morgencald, its top tortoiseshell, with silver pique work.

She had forgotten—oh, how had she forgotten?—how polished he could be. How the refinements of wealth and power worked upon him. And how well he wore them. He was—had always been—an impossibility of a man, perfected in the crucible of centuries.

And she…who was she? A woman who had not known herself. Whose place and station gave her no means to resist or defy such a man. Who could do nothing but watch him choose, once again, to reject her.

"What…?" she asked, her voice a scratch of nothing in the house that was no longer hers. "What right do you have to expect anything from me?"

His eyes—clear now, all their blues released—sought hers as clumsily, as desperately, as an outstretched hand. "None. After how I treated you, the things I said to you, I know I have none. But, Viola, oh God, Viola, I cannot bear to lose you again."

# CHAPTER 22

She had lost all sense of her body beyond the wild stampede of her heart, the rush of her blood, hot and endless as the ocean. Sinking down onto the stairs, she hid her face behind her hands. "You never had me."

"My dear friend"—there was nothing but gentleness in Gracewood's voice, and it still left her ragged—"now is not the time to learn to lie."

"I am nothing but lies to you."

Silence, heavy as a battlefield.

"Will you look at me?" he asked.

It would have been unbelievably graceless to deny him. Slowly, she raised her head. Showed him her eyes, the kohl already beginning to streak. A face that felt naked and ugly, with its too-hard jaw, and its too-bold lines. He took a few steps towards her, his cane loud against the marble floor, and lowered himself, without even a pretence of ease, to one knee at the foot of the staircase.

"That I did not know how to see you," he told her, "is not your lie."

This should not have been harder to take than his anger. His sorrow and betrayal. It was more than she'd have dared hope for or dream of. And it was anguish all the same. Ruin in kindness. Or the other way round. "I could have . . . I should have told you . . . if not before, then—"

"You said you could not. And that hurts me, I cannot tell you how much it hurts me. But I believe you."

"I left you, Gracewood. When you needed me most, I left you. How"—the words filled up her throat, forcing themselves jaggedly into her mouth—"*how* can you forgive me?"

"You have not asked for my forgiveness."

"I . . . cannot."

"Nor do I wish you to. It is not what matters here."

She gazed at him helplessly, hating herself, and him a little too—half wanting him to turn from her again, and make it easy for them both. "What do you mean?"

"I said so many things upon the beach that I now regret. And you were right, Viola, then as now. Your life is yours, you did what you needed to live it, and it is not my place to forgive you for that."

"But the cost. Your grief. I—"

His fingertips brushed her lips. "Let us not speak of cost. Let us remember instead all you gave me. Your loyalty. Your trust. Your friendship. Hope, when I had none of my own. Joy, when I barely knew what it was."

"That wasn't me."

"Wasn't it?" And now he leaned forward, settling his hand lightly against her heart. "Did this change? Was this not true?"

Her breath snarled inside her. Became briars. Tore itself free in a sob as she knocked him away. "Don't."

"Last month, when we were together at Morgencald, those were the happiest days of my life."

"You just want your friend," she told him, shocked by her own bitterness, feeling the poison of it even to her fingertips. "He's gone, don't you understand? So you might as well mourn him, because he's never coming back."

To her surprise—her rising outrage—he laughed. "Oh, Viola, I never wanted to kiss my friend."

At that she could only stare. Of all the things he could have said to her, that was the one she had never contemplated.

"I miss my Marleigh." Gracewood's gaze did not waver. His eyes were pure water. Shadowless. "But if you think I came here for him, you are wrong. I am here for you. I am here for Viola Carroll."

"How," she asked, because it was easier—and safer—than to believe him. "How, when you do not know me?"

Slowly, he pushed himself upright and came to sit beside her on the stairs. "Do you sincerely believe that?"

Tucking her arms tightly around her knees, she nodded. Though, truthfully, not quite daring to drag the needle of her scrutiny down the rough seam between the life she used to live and the life she lived now, she was not sure what she believed anymore.

"Viola, we know one another." His shoulder was a ghost of warmth, not quite touching her own. "We have always known one another. When I was lost, you brought me back to myself. No-one could have done that but you. There is more between us than the rudiments of worldly expectation. My soul calls to yours and yours to mine, and that will never change."

She pressed her teeth against the interior of her lower lip—pressed until she tasted dirt and metal. "*I* have changed."

"And so have I. But I speak of what's eternal and immutable. I speak of you and me, and the best of ourselves."

The bitterness lingered in her still, turning her mouth into a sneer. "Where did you find these certainties?"

"In my heart."

"At Morgencald—"

"At Morgencald I was wrong. I let my grief speak for me when I should have listened."

"Oh, stop," she cried, shocking herself, but relieved, in some way, that she was not in tears. "This is *worse*."

Gracewood tensed beside her. "I'm sorry. What can I do? What do you need from me?"

"I need"—she was on her feet now—"you to stop pretending this is simple. With all your talk of hearts and souls. You don't know how it feels for me to live in a body that has never felt my own. You've not seen the days when I can barely stand myself. You think we can go back. That I can be your perfect, wonderful friend again and it will be exactly like it was. But—why are you laughing at me?"

"Because you have it so wrong, Viola." He was no longer laughing, but his mouth was still soft—soft, as it had only ever been for her, with its wealth of undared smiles. "Marleigh was a pain in the arse. I loved him dearly, but he was moody, reckless, impatient, short-tempered, notoriously sharp-tongued, merciless to those he thought foolish, and unforgiving of any who crossed him."

Viola swallowed. "That…that does sound like…" *Me?* She had no idea how to finish the sentence.

"I don't want to go back." Gracewood reached for his cane and struggled upright. "I want to go forward. And I'm not looking for perfect. Only for you."

Her voice was hoarse from pain, and from speaking of pain. "You can't mean that."

"Can't I? Viola, I am no great prize. I struggle with my dependencies. I still see ghosts, though you are no longer among them.

Some nights I hardly sleep or wake myself with screaming. I cannot ride like I once could, fight like I once could. I think even a country dance is beyond me now. Most would claim that I'm a broken man, and I'm not sure I would dispute them."

At this she closed the distance between them and put her hands upon his shoulders, drew his face to hers, and pressed their brows together. "I will not listen to you talk nonsense about yourself."

"I know it's not the same, but you weren't the only one with secrets. I never let Marleigh know how fearful I was. How unsuited I felt for the role cast upon me. How deeply I bore my father's scorn. But Viola Carroll saw—and found good in me, regardless."

Tears rose hot and heavy to her eyes. "Y-yes. Yes I did. And I always have."

"Viola. Oh, Viola."

His arm came round her then, and he drew her to him, where she wept against his chest, and felt the softness of his tears as they landed in her hair.

"Please don't leave me again," he whispered. "I think I could learn to live without you, but I have no wish to."

She curled her fingers into his coat, her head still lowered and resolutely tucked away. "I don't know how to do this."

"Do what?"

"Any of it. I don't know what we are to each other. If how you felt on the beach before you recognised me was real. If it can still be real when you…when you—"

Putting a hand beneath her chin, he turned her face to his. "It was real, Viola. It is real. As real as you are."

And then—before she could muster a denial—he kissed her.

It was as fragile as sunlight upon frost, a fresh-budding blossom not yet unfurled, just the press of his closed lips to hers, the taste of tears between them. But there was a surety to it too. A thousand promises of an impossible spring.

"Gracewood." She brought her fingers to her mouth, hating her gloves, wanting to touch where he had touched. Take the sweetness, and the lingering heat, make it a part of her forever, but knowing she could not. That what he offered was—had always been—could only be—a secret thing. A furtive, fugitive thing. The barest echo of what they both needed. "We can't," she told him, with all the resolution she could muster. "We shouldn't."

His eyes had been full of light, but now it faded. "Are you uncertain of me? Or uncertain of you?"

"Neither. Both. I'm…" She closed her eyes, ashamed. "I'm frightened. You think too little of yourself. You could have any woman you wanted. You need not choose one who is—"

"Who is what?"

"Complicated."

He shook his head with a kind of fragile melancholy that broke Viola's heart. "You know me better than anyone, Viola. Tell me, what would I do with an uncomplicated woman? What would an uncomplicated woman do with me?"

Marry him. Stand beside him in public. Give him children. But how could she say that to the man she had loved even before knowing what it meant that she did? The man who had just kissed her. How could she remind him of everything she could not offer him, when it was hard enough to face for herself everything she could not have? "We have only just returned to society," she said instead. "We have only just returned to each other."

His expression grew wry. "And I to myself?"

It felt too callous to say yes. And, besides, she would not have meant it as he did. Because Gracewood coming back to himself meant returning to wealth and power and all the splendour of his rank. It meant being someone who could never, under any circumstance, share a world with Viola Carroll. "You...you do look well."

"Thank you." He gave the slightest of shrugs. "I have a new valet. And I have touched neither alcohol nor laudanum for over a month. But how I felt on the beach hasn't changed. Nor has what I want."

"And what of what *I* want?"

That checked him, the doubts briefly as clear on his face as clouds before the sun. "I...if you did not—I am sorry, I thought that you...that you felt as I do." His hand came up and his fingers brushed almost questioningly against her mouth. "I've been presumptuous. Assuming—hoping—that you could see me as... a man. As well as a friend."

"It isn't a matter of feeling or not feeling, or seeing or not seeing. It is a matter of—of what is right. Waterloo shattered both of our worlds, and we are barely beginning to piece them together. What of a year from now? Ten years? How can either of us know what the shape of our lives will be? If we can ever fit together as once we did? Let alone be—" She did not know what word to give them—even the possibility of them—when all she had were words for things they were not and could never be.

"May we not at least try?" he asked, with a kind of flayed-bare simplicity.

Something that felt like anger flared inside her. It was safer if it was anger. Because it could so easily have been despair. "*You* may try. You are a duke and may do what you like with whom you like, and the ton will say nothing worse than *Well, he's a strange fellow, the Duke of Gracewood*. But me? I am a...I am a lady's companion, for now. Tomorrow I could be nothing at all. Or worse, I could be a scandal, a cautionary tale. Worse yet, a mystery, my very womanhood the subject of speculation in private salons and bets at White's. So no, Gracewood, we may not try."

"I would protect you. I would always protect you." He spoke with such gentleness, and yet with such strength—and in that moment she saw him as truly as she ever had. Not as the man he had been raised to be, or the man his title demanded, but the man she had always loved and believed in. Even though he could not love or believe in himself.

All the same, she could not live in his shadow. "I do not want your protection."

"My friendship then?" Now something a little desperate crept into his voice. "If we must be as we were, then so be it. There can be no scandal in our being friends."

Viola scoffed. "Are you friends with many lady servants?"

"I am friends with the Marleighs, and you are part of their household."

Even this, Viola feared, could easily become too dangerous an intimacy. But she couldn't keep rejecting him. Not even for his own sake. And certainly not against her own interests, her own desires, having lost him twice already—and nearly destroyed them both each time.

"That might, perhaps, be acceptable," she said. "Next time you call on Lord and Lady Marleigh, we can find opportunity to speak." Though no sooner were the words out than she saw them for the cage they were: the iron bars of a world that insisted there was only one way to be a man or a woman or a duke.

"If those are your terms," he said, "I shall content myself with them."

"Content?" exclaimed Louise, who had apparently retreated from sight but not from earshot. "How can you possibly be content with something so paltry."

Gracewood lifted a quizzical brow. "Your house has the strangest echo."

"It is not my house," Viola reminded him. "It's Badger's."

"Loubear," whispered Badger. "You have to be quiet when you're eavesdropping. Otherwise it's just a logistically difficult conversation."

"Or spirits perhaps?" suggested Gracewood, lowering himself back onto the steps.

"Oh God," said Lady Marleigh. "I forgot myself. Do you think they heard?"

A nearby potted plant rustled with an air of Badger. "Haven't a dashed clue. And, now I come to think of it, I haven't a dashed clue what an eave is either. And how do you drop them?"

Trying to retain a respectable distance, but not wishing to stand while Gracewood sat, Viola seated herself two steps further down, and then called to her brother and sister-in-law. "Badger, Louise. Do you think you're hiding?"

There was a long silence.

"No?" said Badger, in what he clearly believed to be a voice unlike his own.

"Just come out, will you?" Viola sighed. "And how long have you been listening?"

They emerged sheepishly, Badger with leaves in his hair, and Lady Marleigh endeavouring to explain. "Not the *whole* time."

"Not the whole time?" Viola repeated. "Well, thank goodness

for that. Because I find nothing objectionable in having my private conversations only *partially* snooped upon."

"You see?" Settling down on Viola's other side, Lady Marleigh cast a triumphant look at her husband. "I told you they wouldn't mind."

Badger made his eyes very big and very sorry. "We were worried, Vee."

"Do you think us," Gracewood asked mildly, "so incapable of managing our own affairs?"

"Loubear thinks everyone's incapable of managing their own affairs."

"Well, they *are*," put in Lady Marleigh. "You should have seen the terrible mess they made of things up in Northumberland. I have no reason to trust them to do any better now." She twisted round to look at Gracewood. "And what, may I ask, has finally compelled you to emerge from the bottle and join us in London?"

Badger cleared his throat. "Darling Loubear, saying *may I ask* doesn't always make something sound polite."

"It's a fair question," admitted Gracewood. "And the answer is Viola. But also Mira."

Fresh guilt from her time at Morgencald scraped across Viola's heart. "Oh God—Mira. We left so suddenly. What did you say to her?"

"Many things I should not have said." Gracewood glanced away, colour rising to his cheeks. "I was...not myself for some days after your departure."

"Is she with you?" asked Lady Marleigh, undistracted.

At this, Gracewood offered a conspiratorial half smile. "As little as I wish to encourage you, madam, for I suspect you are over-encouraged—"

"Oh no," Louise interrupted cheerfully. "I require very little encouragement to interfere in the lives of others."

"Nevertheless"—he bowed his head graciously—"you were quite correct. My sister deserves a season." His eyes darkened. "Though, currently, she does not seem to want one."

Lady Marleigh frowned. "That makes no sense. Had you not been an absolute wreck, she would have come with us, I am certain of it."

"Then," suggested Gracewood, "either your certainty was misplaced, or she has changed her mind. She is not at all pleased with me for bringing her to town."

A thought was occurring slowly to Viola—one that would not previously have crossed her mind, but came to her now through some peculiar combination of old knowledge and new perspective. "Gracewood, did you ask her?"

The look he gave her in response was both ducal and distant. "It was what she wanted and what I, as her guardian, deemed to be appropriate."

"Yes." She tried again. "But did you *ask* her?"

"Viola, she's my sister. I have charge of her affairs until she is married, and we all agree I have neglected my duties towards her for too long." Gracewood's voice. The old duke's words. It made Viola shiver to hear that cold echo. The oldest, and perhaps the strongest, of her friend's many ghosts.

"We do not, however," Lady Marleigh was saying, "agree she is chattel."

"I do not suggest she is," Gracewood returned, with quelling formality. "But she is a *child*. And, as such, reliant on my judgement until—"

Lady Marleigh glared up at him. "She is a young woman. And

your judgement, you must surely be the first to admit, far from sound."

There was a long silence. Gracewood's composure did not falter—his father had taught him too well for that—but Viola saw the flash of mortification in his eyes. The self-doubt that lurked in those exquisite blue depths, like the shadow of some private kraken. She wanted nothing more than to comfort him—to draw him back to himself—but she was not sure how to do that since so much had changed between them.

"Then what do you suggest?" Gracewood asked finally.

Of course, Louise did not hesitate. "Mira must come to us."

"Out of the question" came the equally implacable response.

"But," protested Lady Marleigh, "you clearly have no notion how to handle a young woman."

Gracewood's jaw tightened. "I have her best interests at heart. She will have to trust in that."

"How can she?" Say what you would about Louise, she was nothing if not fearless. "She hardly knows you. She has had no opportunity to know you."

"But don't you see?" At last, something of Gracewood broke through his icy demeanour, and he sounded lost. Half pleading now. "That is precisely why I cannot abandon her again. How can I send her forth into the world—into her own future—convinced she was as good as forgotten not just by her father, but her brother as well?"

Lady Marleigh looked somewhat mollified; above all else, she admired honesty. "You really do need to *tell* her some of this."

"I wouldn't know how to begin," Gracewood said. "I barely know how to look after her as it stands. And yet I must try. She is my sister. And...I am not insensible of her attempts to look after me, for all I was, at the time, incapable of gratitude."

Again, Viola caught that look of half-buried shame. She had not realised how difficult it was for him to allow himself to be cared for—at least when it was not partially concealed beneath the social rituals that had dominated their old friendship. And it abashed her, suddenly, to think back on the trust he had shown her at Morgencald. He had stripped the façade of his dukedom for her. Shown her the bloody places of his battered heart. And bared his throat beneath her hand.

"I have it," Lady Marleigh cried. "Take Viola. She can be Miranda's chaperone."

Viola made a startled noise. "I certainly cannot. I am not... qualified."

"What qualification do you expect to need?" Lady Marleigh gave a little laugh. "One can hardly read for a bachelor's of classics and chaperoning at Oxford."

"No, but—"

Lady Marleigh cut her off. "You are a respectable woman of good family and—if we must be candid—given your age and station, limited prospects. You are perfect for the role."

"And," added Gracewood softly, "whatever else is or is not, you are still my oldest friend." He turned to her then. And she didn't know what could have changed so immensely between them— within her—that the simple act of his looking at her should carry such velvet weight. Make her breathless. "The person I trust most in the world."

Viola's mind was a tumult of conflicting wants and fears. Being Miranda's chaperone—however ill-suited she suspected she was for the role—would mean being close to Gracewood. Perhaps as close as she could ever be. Except what, in reality, would that look like? A duke and a lady servant, who his sister would soon enough outgrow. The inevitability of her own irrelevance crept through her like slow poison and made her remember what she had tried to save them from in the first place. Surely the sharp agony of *nothing* would be less damaging than...whatever this was or would become. The shadowlands of fruitless love, where time took precious things and turned them into cockle shells and sea glass.

"I know—" Gracewood began, before stopping abruptly. And then, with a humility unbecoming of his station, he tried again. "I know I have no right to ask this of you, but...please, Viola. If not for my sake, then for Mira's."

For all her own survival and the vagaries of circumstance had pushed her to it once, it was simply not in Viola to turn from Gracewood. Not when he had been a solitary, cold-eyed boy whose great name the other boys had feared. Not when he had been an idealistic youth who had believed he would find his purpose on the battlefields of France. Not when he had been a grief-wracked ruin at the mercy of alcohol and laudanum.

And certainly not now that, in seeing her, in understanding who she was, he still called her friend. Still needed her and was asking, without pride or expectation, for her help.

So she told him yes.

Because it was the only answer she had. It was the only answer she would ever have.

# CHAPTER 23

Where Morgencald was ancient, its towers steeped in pride and honour and the crushing weight of centuries, Gracewood's London residence was a far newer acquisition. His father would not have approved of the purchase, but at the time, that had been its own satisfaction. All of twenty-three, the old duke long dead and buried, and his memory shedding its vividity year by year like a painting abandoned to the sun, what dazzling futures had he imagined here? The de Veres were an exalted but insular family, their power embedded in land and stone and the fortress none but they had ever held, but as a young man Gracewood had entertained other aspirations. He had cultivated a fast and fashionable set. Pursued witty, lively debutantes who would never have made the sort of duchess his name and responsibilities demanded. It had felt like freedom.

Now it felt like nonsense. And the town house, for all its light and airy rooms, its opulence and modernity, no more his home than Morgencald had ever been. Strangest of all, Gracewood found himself missing Northumberland. Not the isolation, nor the burden of his duties, nor memories of the grief that he had almost let destroy him, but the rigidity of his life there. Its expectations as set as the castle walls. Constricting, to the point of unbearable, and yet—in some way—safe.

London was loud and glaring, endlessly unpredictable. Full

of strangers who knew his name and assessed him with their eyes. The days scraped too harsh against his senses, and made him ache for the sweet dulling of laudanum. At Morgencald, he would have had to send for a bottle. Here, he could have purchased one from any shop, on any street, the promise of brown glass catching always at the corner of his eye, brighter than any jewel the world could offer.

"Your Grace?"

He glanced up from the mountain of his correspondence—invitations, mostly, on his own behalf and Mira's, and found the butler before him. "Yes?"

"Your visitor has arrived. I have shown the young lady into the yellow drawing room."

"Thank you, Frith." The word had fallen heedless from his lips. He nearly cursed aloud, then nearly apologised—neither of which was proper for a duke. "I mean—"

The man gave an impeccable bow. This household, at least, had run itself smoothly in his absence. "Jenkins, My Lord."

"Of course. Thank you, Jenkins."

The butler withdrew, closing the door neatly behind him, and Gracewood briefly put his head in his hands. To forget the name of a servant was not unseemly in itself—his father had prided himself on being unable to tell the lower orders apart—but to call him by the name of a dead man, a man who Gracewood had permitted himself to care for, that spoke to a private weakness.

A hand upon his cane, he rose. He had never, he thought, been a vain man, but nevertheless he paused a moment before his hazily reflected image in the library window—trying to see what the world would see. What Viola would see. A cripple, then. And an opium eater, irrevocably marked by his own mistakes and misdeeds. And to think, he had been handsome once. Worthy of her once. Or perhaps he never had been. What use had such a woman—a woman of spirit and courage beyond reckoning—for a weak man, even a rich and titled one.

In any case, it would not do to keep her waiting. As Gracewood turned from the window, he heard—in the far distance—the rattle of gunfire. Spinning back, sweat prickling beneath his hair and upon his palms, the breath turned glutinous in his throat, he discovered it was nothing but a horse, its hooves merry against the street below. Relief swept through him, relief and self-recrimination. He was in London. In Grosvenor Square. Far from any kind of warfare. Yet he could still taste the powder. The sour metal of too much blood and fear. And on this clear morning, he had neither grief nor opium to blame. Only the stark truth of the lives he had taken and the cost to his soul.

This was the part of himself he most feared would be exposed. This cowardice. He had come to London for Viola and for Miranda and because his pride demanded he put to rest the swirl of rumours that had arisen in his absence. Many said he was mad, others, merely unmanned. And the damnable thing was, they were right. If he could not exert better control over himself, the ever-ravenous jackals of the ton would rip him open and lick the blood from his bones.

As he made his way to the yellow drawing room, he tried to push away the battlefield. Two years and it still felt more real than quiet halls and strips of sunlight upon polished floors. Yet Viola had managed to leave those times behind. Why couldn't he?

"Your Grace." Viola rose as he entered, dropping into a curtsey.

Dressed in a gown of printed cotton, dark green leaves upon cream-coloured muslin, with a pattern of entwined flowers upon the embroidered hem, she was her own spring. And at once so familiar and so beautiful that—for a moment—the only past that mattered was the one they shared.

He took her gloved hand and brought it, with perhaps too much affection for their stations, to his lips. He had intended a polite greeting, but what he said instead was "Viola, will you not call me Gracewood again?"

Colour rose to her cheeks, her eyes darting swiftly to his. "I shouldn't. Especially not in public."

"And Justin, I assume, is out of the question?" He had not meant to press her, but *Your Grace* sounded too wrong for either of them to bear it.

At this, she smiled—her old smile, full of mischief and affection. "You know you could never be Justin to me."

Indeed, he realised, he could not. That was a name for relatives and for fleeting passions. *Gracewood* was for his intimates, few as they were. And it would always belong first to Viola.

The silence was stretching between them, not quite comfortable, and heavy with the weight of unsaid things.

"London suits you," she said, finally.

And, whether she offered the lie to be polite or to soothe him, the fact she lied at all was something else new between them. "You must see that it does not."

Something flickered in her eyes then—perhaps he had misinterpreted her and spoken too sharply. "I see the Duke of Gracewood, in possession of the house he bought, about to introduce his sister to society."

"Then perhaps I present myself better than I fear."

Again, she regarded him, a faint frown between those wicked, winged brows of hers. And then her hand landed lightly on his where it rested upon the cane. "They will not see this. They will only see you."

"You mean, they will see a fortune and a title and overlook the rest of me."

"Gracewood." His name came to Viola easily this time, although it contained within it a spark of her temper. "Please do not make me, of all people, reassure you that—while there may be those driven by mercenary concerns—there will be yet many more who admire you for yourself alone."

"That was not my intent," he said. Truthfully, the idea of any woman's admiration felt abstract and irrelevant. For it was Viola he wanted. Viola he had wanted even in the depths of an opium dream, believing her nothing more than a gentle ghost. And Viola he wanted still. Being with her like this, hearing her voice, catching the dark gleam of her eyes, remembering the shape of her mouth beneath his, she made anyone else impossible.

It was only when she pressed her palms against his chest that he realised how close they were standing. "You are a duke. You are young and handsome, and clever and kind, and—"

"And," he asked, unable to help himself, "you will not have me?"

She stepped so sharply away, he almost lost his footing. "You know I *cannot*. I am too…" A gesture that could have meant almost anything. "You are too…" Another gesture, this one half fury, half despair. "I came here for Miranda. Not for this. You are not…you are not being fair."

He was not, and he knew he was not. He was not being fair to either of them. So he offered a bow of contrition. "Forgive me, Viola. I promise, this was not why I sought your help."

"I know." There was something brittle, already half-broken in her voice.

"But I need you to understand"—he claimed her hand again, and she did not resist—"that this is no mere fancy. What we began at Morgencald only grows in truth and strength the longer I am with you."

"Whatever it is," she told him, her head turned away, her expression cast in shadow by the fall of her hair, "there is no place for it in the world."

If he allowed himself to think beyond the moment, beyond her closeness, and their entwined fingers, he would have known she was right. But he had no wish to think. "May we not at least try to make one?"

At this, however, she drew back, and with such certainty it was hard to believe he had touched her at all. "I will not enumerate for you, Gracewood, all the ways I am"—her lips twisted bitterly—"unsuitable. Unless that is, your intent is to seduce me, as a man of your rank may an unprotected woman?"

She had shocked him—but it should not have surprised him that she had, for she was always outspoken. It was one of the many qualities he had admired in her. Even envied the fearlessness and freedom of it. "I am no rake, Viola."

"Then stop this." Her voice had risen, with passion or frustration, or some combination of the two. But then she steadied herself and continued with a semblance of calm. "We must content ourselves with…with what is possible."

The fact she was, once again, correct did little to alleviate his regret. And the thought that perhaps he could or should seduce her, as she had suggested, uncoiled itself like a serpent. It would be something, and something was not nothing, and it offered… consolations. Consolations she possibly lacked the experience to consider. Except no. He could not do that to her, or to them. And how low had he fallen that consolation was all he had left to offer?

"But how do we bear it?" he asked, ashamed of the question, yet unable to leave it unspoken.

She had put her back to him, so all he had were the words, which were their own wall. "I don't know." And then, turning again, trembling with an effort at self-control, she went on, "Ring for Mira, Gracewood? Please?"

Leaving him with no choice but to obey.

# CHAPTER 24

When she finally—and given the silence between Viola and Gracewood, mercifully—made an appearance, Miranda was less outlandishly dressed than she had been in Northumberland, doubtless because there were fewer attics full of old clothes for her to dig into. But there was a melancholy to her that Viola hadn't expected, for all Gracewood's warning of discontent.

"Justin, Miss Carroll." Miranda made a polite little half curtsey. "You wished to see me?"

"I have good news, Mira." Gracewood was smiling, but Viola could see the strain in it, and Miranda probably could too. "I have spoken to Lady Marleigh, and she has consented to allow her companion to act as your chaperone."

Miranda blinked at him, then at Viola. "How is that good news?"

"We came to London to bring you out, Miranda. You must have a chaperone, and surely you would rather it be someone you know?"

"I would rather," Miranda said, with the same forcefulness she had once used in defence of her brother, "that you not farm me out to a stranger and expect that I be thankful for it."

"Viola is not a stranger." Again, there were shades of the old duke in Gracewood's voice. Miranda seemed to bring out the worst in him, but that was not so very surprising, given how he had been raised. "She is a friend of the family and will take good care of you."

Miranda did not seem at all quelled. "And you *are* my family. Why will you not take care of me?"

"I *am* taking care of you," Gracewood insisted, with far more hauteur than warmth. "This is how men take care of their sisters."

"It is how Father would have taken care of me, I daresay. I had hoped for better from you, Justin."

"Miranda..." Viola began, hoping to prevent anybody else from saying anything that they might regret.

But Gracewood cut over her. "I am your older brother, Miranda. More than that, I am the Duke. You will not speak to me that way."

"Sometimes"—Miranda's attempt to match her brother's pride was a little heartbreaking—"I believe you would rather I not speak to you at all."

"I only want you to be looked after."

"You want me *gone*. And I am happy to oblige you." Turning, she stormed out of the room. Her eyes had been dry as she left, but Viola, who knew much of tears, did not think that would last.

Gracewood took a step forward, but it proved too large or too sudden a step and he stopped short, cursing his injury. "Damn the girl."

Fearing to come too close, in case—following their earlier encounter—it invited further closeness, Viola hovered a hand's-breadth away from him. "You don't mean that."

The short, controlled breaths Gracewood was taking suggested that his real anger was for his leg, rather than for Miranda, and after a moment he seemed to come to the same conclusion. "You're right, I don't. But I wish I knew what she wanted from me."

"She just wants to be your sister."

"Then she's a very fortunate young woman, because she *is* my sister." Lowering himself into one of the gilt-edged chairs that accented the gilt-and-yellow décor of the yellow drawing room, Gracewood stretched out his leg in discomfort. "Unfortunately, I do not seem to have it in me to be a brother."

After a moment, Viola sat too. "Give her time."

"In this context," said Gracewood, ruefully, "I'm not sure what time is supposed to change."

"Then *you* change. Show her who you are."

He made a soft, half-pained sound as if even the idea was difficult to contemplate. "I don't know if I can do that. You were the only person with whom I dared be more than I was taught to be."

"And yet there was still so much of you I did not understand."

"How so?" His tone was wary.

"Oh, I always thought well of you. I thought you proud and dashing and brave and all that you should be. But I did not understand how much I meant to you or how deeply you felt your father's hurts. I did not understand your thoughtfulness or your gentleness or—"

Putting a hand on her wrist, he stilled her with his touch. "Viola, please. These are not admirable qualities in a man."

"Then they should be, Gracewood. For they are admirable in you."

"You may find that to be a unique perspective."

In this, she was almost certain he was wrong. But to have explained it to him would have meant explaining how it felt to have loved him in the confusion of not knowing who she was.

And how it felt now, to be herself and love him still, and live in the torment of that understanding.

"I don't mean," she said instead, "you don't possess those other qualities also."

With a soft laugh, he re-settled his cane against his leg. "I fear my dashing days are long since done."

"Dashing is about the spirit, not about the body."

"Perhaps"—he raised his brows at her—"it is in the eye of the beholder."

"All the more reason," she returned, "to allow people other than me to see you. The whole of you, not just your title, or who your father wanted you to be." It was the right thing to say. But it hurt too, for it was also a letting go.

Especially because there was a part of her that longed for him to speak as he had when she had first arrived—all wild promises and wild hopes, and his eyes alight with ardour—but she could not allow him to dwell in the past, among the remnants of a friendship that no longer was or seek a future with her that could never be.

"I will try," he murmured.

"Then perhaps"—it seemed safest to turn the subject—"put that trying into practice and go after your sister?"

The look he gave her, if not quite fearful, was more uncertain than she might have expected from the man who, unflinching, had once held the line with her amid the carnage of Waterloo. "Will you? In my stead? Miranda should have recovered her composure, and ideally her manners, by now."

"You heard her, Gracewood. It is you she needs."

"I doubt my welcome," he admitted. "And I...do not know how to talk to her at the moment. If I ever did."

There was no trace left of his former passion. He just looked weary. As remote as Morgencald itself. And Viola found herself half wondering if she'd imagined everything else: his trust and his truths, the way he had held her and touched her. Yesterday he had kissed her with that austerely carved mouth and it had offered nothing but warmth.

Hastily, she pushed the thought aside. It could do neither of them any good. "I will likely be no better received than you. Remember, she thinks me a stranger."

"No more than she thinks me."

There was more than a little regret in Gracewood's voice, and had things been otherwise, Viola might have pressed him to act upon his own behalf. But the situation had made cowards of them both, and in that moment, she suspected they were equally glad for an excuse to separate. To allow everything they were, and were not, to feel like something they could live with.

With a nod of acquiescence, she rose and went in search of Miranda.

A servant directed her upstairs, and the experience of pursuing Gracewood's sister to her bedchamber proved more alienating than Viola was quite prepared for. There was no impropriety to it, of course, but she had been raised her whole life to think otherwise, to believe that there were men's spaces and women's spaces and the boundary between them utterly impassable. And yet here she was. In the eyes of some, a thief, a rebel of a kind, but to herself, simply one lady visiting another in the course of a life no more extraordinary than anyone else's.

On reaching Miranda's door, she knocked and received no answer. So she knocked again, and then a third time.

"You may take my silence," said Miranda, unsilently, "as indication that you are not welcome."

"Can we talk?" asked Viola. She had no notion how this little vignette was going to play out and wished Lady Marleigh was with her, though what she thought Louise could protect her from she wasn't sure.

From within there came some vague noises—perhaps the sound a young lady might make turning moodily over upon her bed. "You may also take my statement that you are not welcome as indication that you are not welcome."

Viola stifled a sigh. What on earth was she supposed to do now? Miranda had asked to be left, and so the polite thing, surely, would be to leave her. But they had travelled to Northumberland with the express purpose of bringing Miranda out. And, right now, she was very much *in*. "You are being too hard on your brother."

This time, the sounds from the other side of the door had a determined quality. Perhaps a pillow being thrust aside or hurled to the floor? "You know nothing of my brother. And nothing of me."

"I..." Viola was about to protest that she knew them both far better than Miranda could possibly imagine, but two things checked her. The first was simply that she could not explain *how* she knew them without revealing herself to Miranda. And the second, more simply still, was that it would not have been true.

In all the long years she had been Gracewood's friend, all the times she had visited Morgencald, had she said as much as a thousand words to his sister? Had it ever crossed her mind she should?

"You're right," she said. "We are barely acquaintances. But I would like to change that."

For a moment there was no response, but then Viola heard the rustle of bedclothes and the sound of footsteps, and, at last, the door opened. Miranda had plainly been crying, but even that it seemed she did prettily, tears giving her eyes a kind of glow that all of Viola's paints and powders could not hope to replicate. "How convenient that you have developed an interest in me just as Justin chooses to foist me off on you."

"Surely"—Viola offered a hint of a smile—"that is preferable to the reverse?"

Miranda retreated into the room and sat down on the bed, and, after a moment of hesitation, Viola followed her.

"Well?" Mustering something of her brother's manner, Miranda cast her a cool, challenging look. "I thought you were to befriend me."

"I was going to *try*," Viola corrected her. "But it will be difficult without your cooperation."

Despite her clearly mixed feelings about the whole situation, breeding and—perhaps—kindness overtook Miranda's instincts, and her face softened. "I'm sorry, Miss Carroll. None of this is of your doing, and I am pleased to see you again." She patted a space on the bed next to her. "Won't you sit with me?"

Viola settled herself next to Miranda, relieved at the uneasy peace they had forged, but uncertain how to build on it. "Are you finding London pleasant?" she asked, finally.

"I think so," returned Miranda, her eyes a little drier now. "Although I have not been here long, and I have yet to—that is—I am given to understand that there will be balls."

"There will. A great many, I believe."

The expression on Miranda's face was not the look of rapt enthusiasm that Viola had been taught to expect from a young girl anticipating her first forays into society. She seemed rather more like a deer brought to bay by a hunting party. "Oh," she said. "Oh good."

"You have concerns?"

"Not *concerns*. Not truly. It's just I have spent so long on my own. What if people don't like me?"

"You are rich, titled, and beautiful," Viola pointed out. "Anybody who dislikes you will be required to do it from a safe distance." It was the sort of comment that, if nothing else, would have amused Gracewood. And sometimes, Viola knew from experience, it was easier to be amused than reassured.

Unfortunately, Miranda looked crestfallen. "But that won't do at all. I don't want *false* friends. Perhaps I should tell everybody that we have fallen on hard times—something to do with an entailment, perhaps, or that Justin lost all of our money gambling."

That couldn't help but draw a laugh from Viola. "I'm not sure entailments work quite the way you think they do, and while I understand that you are angry with Gracewood at the moment, perhaps you shouldn't put about that he is a degenerate gambler."

Miranda's lips grew thin and set. "I am *quite* angry with him."

"Even though he brought you down from Morgencald?"

"That was Auntie Lou's idea, not his."

Once again, this struck Viola as a little unfair. "You clearly *wanted* to come to London though."

"I wanted," retorted Miranda, with all the passion of a hurt seventeen-year-old, "not to be alone. I should not have cared where I went if I could just have—I don't know—*somebody*."

Once again, Viola was slightly at a loss. "It must have been hard these last two years."

"I wish it *were* only these last two years. But Justin has been leaving me for as long as I can remember." Miranda's hands fluttered restlessly. "He left me when we were children because Father wouldn't have his heir wasting his time with a girl. Then he left me for Eton, and when he came back in the holidays he left me for Marleigh. Then they both left me for Cambridge, then London, then the war. And finally he left me for laudanum and someone who isn't even here anymore."

And that was when Viola realised that Miranda wasn't angry. Not really. She was sad. Terribly, terribly sad. "Oh Mira. I'm so sorry."

"It isn't your fault."

It was a reflexive nicety, the kind of thing people said when you told them you were sorry about something beyond your control. But this was different. It was personal in ways Miranda had no way of recognising, because Viola had known Gracewood all those years and, looking back, she couldn't remember either of them sparing a thought for his sister—back at Morgencald with nothing, or worse, with the old duke, a damsel trapped in the castle of a cold and brooding dragon. "It was not your fault either," she tried.

Miranda gave a little shrug. "Perhaps. Or perhaps I am simply the sort of person other people leave behind."

The worst of it was, if Viola should have understood anything it was being alone. She should have understood it even when she'd been living a different life. She'd had Gracewood, of course, and that had made things bearable for a while, but she'd only had him because Miranda hadn't. Because an accident of birth had put one of them by his side and left the other with nobody.

"Miranda..." she began, not quite sure how she would continue. "You should...you should know that Gracewood is not leaving you with a stranger."

With a kind of terrible sincerity, Miranda patted Viola's hand. "I know. You are Lady Marleigh's companion and that makes you family, after a fashion. It was wrong of me to treat you like a servant."

"That isn't quite what I meant. I mean..." Viola swallowed. This was the right thing to do. Gracewood already knew, and it made sense to be open with the whole household rather than only part of it. Still, the words stuck in her throat, the awkward half-truth of them, the echoes of the lie she'd lived embedded so deep in the language that she could barely express herself. "I was—Gracewood and I have been friends for many years."

Miranda looked puzzled. "Really? He never mentioned you."

"He did. He would have mentioned me often."

Miranda looked even more puzzled. "I am sure he did not. He never spoke of any lady."

And here it was. The difficult part. Viola took a deep breath. "When we were friends, he...he did not see me as a lady."

After a while, Miranda came to the conclusion that, Viola suspected, most people would come to. "Did you disguise yourself as a man, like in a song? Were you trying to run away to war to be with your lover?"

"In a way. But it was a disguise I was given, not one I chose. I was—I was the Viscount Marleigh."

To her credit, Miranda did not look shocked. A little surprised, but not shocked. "Oh," she said. And then "oh" again. And, finally, "So it *was* your fault, in a way. That Justin had so little time for me."

Viola almost laughed at that—half relieved, but freshly guilty. There was the strangest comfort in learning that the ways you hurt people were yours and yours alone. "I can't tell if that reflects more poorly upon me or your brother."

"Perhaps it reflects poorly upon both of you."

The words were harsh, but the tone was not. And Viola offered a smile by way of acknowledgement. "Perhaps that is so. Though I am sorry, so very sorry, that we—that we were not there for you. In our defence, part of the blame lies with Napoleon."

"You did not have to join the army."

She had a point: They didn't. And perhaps it had been as much a desire to flee the lives they had been given as to serve their country that had driven them to France. "No. Except for that I cannot be sorry. It was not by design, but war let me live the truth of myself for the first time, and I will apologise for it to nobody."

Miranda was looking at her strangely. "Thank you for that. I am rather weary of false apologies and hollow promises. Justin keeps telling me things will be different, but here we are, and he has sent me away with—"

"With his best friend," Viola finished for her. "A young lady in society must have a lady to watch her, and your brother chose me. He loves you, Miranda. He just—he was raised not to show it."

As she fell back against her disordered covers, Miranda's hair spread about her like a peacock's tail of burnished gold. "I am not sure love unshown is really love at all. What good does caring for a person do if you're never there when they need you?"

When had the young developed their infuriating habit of asking impossible questions? And when, for that matter, had Viola reached so advanced an age that she thought of debutantes as *the young*? "He will do better. If you let him."

"I have been trying to let him do better for as long as I can remember."

Viola sighed and shut her eyes. She—*someone* should have reached out to Miranda years ago. Before she had given up reaching back. "I know," she said. "But the old duke would never even have thought to try."

This time Miranda laughed, and it was a rough laugh for a seventeen-year-old girl. "And this trying of Justin's? What reason have I to believe it will make any difference to anything?"

"Well..." Viola paused for a moment. It was important that she offer more than platitudes. "Because I will help him. And you will help him. And Louise will help him, whether he wishes it or not."

"That's true," agreed Miranda placidly.

"And also because"—Viola was obliged to pause again, this time to steady her voice—"I was sincere when I said I wished us to be friends."

There was something hopeful in Miranda's eyes, a soft light that made them shine even more than usual. "You are Justin's friend."

"I think I am permitted more than one friend."

"You never gave much indication of needing more."

"It was difficult," Viola said. Allowing the admission as much for herself as for Miranda. "Gracewood was—is—very special to me."

Miranda nodded. "You were his escape. I used to imagine sometimes what my Mar—what my *you* would be like. But it felt so impossible that it started to make me unhappy."

"What were they like? Your...me?"

"Oh." Colour rose prettily to Miranda's cheeks, like the first flush of dawn against pearly skies. "She was a little older than me, worldly and bold, and heedless in all the ways I don't dare to be. She wasn't afraid to say wicked things, and she made me laugh."

Somehow that was not what Viola had expected. In Miranda's place, she was sure she would have imagined a hero from a romantic novel. Someone like…Gracewood. "I fear I am not much of a substitute."

"You exist though," Miranda noted, with a solemnity that came perilously close to comical.

Viola hid a smile behind her hand. "That is an advantage I do possess."

"And…" Here Miranda faltered, though only briefly. "You really want to be my friend?"

"Yes."

A pause. Then Miranda's brows pulled into a frown. "You're only here because of Justin, aren't you? You'd do anything for him and he for you."

That was true. For her, he had offered to lay his title at the feet of a woman who society could never accept and who would doom him to be the last of his line. And for him, she had refused.

"Actually," Viola said, "my motives are largely selfish. You see, I've always yearned for female companionship. I knew I belonged at Gracewood's side, but I also wanted to belong in some… broader way. To feel right in myself and among others."

And it was a foolish yearning, perhaps, for a life and a society that she had seen only in glimpses: ladies and their maids, their sisters, their friends, a society like yet unlike the one of clubs and valets and late nights drinking brandy that she had shared, instead, with Gracewood.

And it was doubly foolish to want so badly a thing that so

scared her. For left to her own devices, she would have fled the company of other women, locked herself away in dark rooms in Devon where nobody could look at her and see all the ways in which she didn't fit.

Gently, Miranda squeezed Viola's fingers. It was a small gesture, but one that said she wanted to believe. That, like Viola, she wanted to belong. And that maybe they could belong together.

# CHAPTER 25

Bringing a young woman out, as Viola should probably have realised, was a *business*. In her former life she'd only seen the end of the process: the beautiful gowns and the debutantes gliding through ballrooms, flowers in their hair and pearls in their ears. And she had—furtively, barely allowing herself to complete the thought, telling herself it was mere curiosity such as anyone might experience—half wondered what it might be like to be among them.

And wasn't that strange and uncomfortable, yearning to be part of something that other women yearned to be free of? How many of those debutantes would have given all their silks and their pearls and their flowers to live instead the life that Viola had—one of travel and adventure and friendship?

But that time had passed. She had come into herself already an old maid, too old to be wooed even if her other complexities didn't make such a thing impossible in a hundred different ways. So she had long since accepted—welcomed—her role of spinster aunt, the watcher, the helpmeet. Her days subsumed in other people's days, assisting Lady Marleigh to shepherd—well, standing quietly back while Lady Marleigh shepherded—Miranda through a whirlwind of modistes and milliners and instructors. It was exhausting but, in so many ways, wonderful to be a part of it at last.

Viola took some—*pleasure* was the wrong word, entirely the wrong word—but some reassurance in the realisation that in certain respects Miranda's education had been as lacking as her own. Raised alone at Morgencald with a father who disdained her and a brother who...who spent too much time with his friends, Miranda's exposure to the feminine arts had been perfunctory at best. Fortunately she proved an apt pupil, and her natural grace and the softening effects of her wealth and status meant she was soon pouring tea and dancing the latest steps with an enthusiasm that more than made up for her lack of technical proficiency.

Still, the relative newness of both Miranda and her chaperone to the ton led Lady Marleigh to conclude that it would be best to begin their introduction to society with something small and intimate like a card party, organised by Louise herself.

As with most of Louise's ideas, it proved a good one. She curated a guest list of young people and amiable elders, along with a scattering of what she called "unthreateningly eligible gentlemen"—none of whom, it was something of a relief to discover, belonged to Viola and Gracewood's old set. But then they would have disdained a card party for debutantes, as for that matter would Viola and Gracewood.

"What will they be like?" Miranda asked, as her newly hired maid pinned up her curls. "The young ladies, I mean?"

Although Viola had been out of London life for years, the great advantage of the ton was that it never really changed. The same families shifting through the same set of scandals and intrigues, year on year, one generation eerily echoing the last. She met Miranda's eyes in the mirror and tried to contribute some semblance of useful information. "I know none of them personally, I'm afraid. I believe Miss Avon will be attending—her mother was accounted a great beauty in her day, and I understand she is likewise. And Louise mentioned that the Earl of Carden was sending his daughter. She...that is...her mother is not the lady to whom the Earl is married."

Miranda digested this information with only the mildest curiosity. "Who is she?"

"He met her in the West Indies. That's all I know. Miss Hanbury is his only daughter, and he dotes upon her. Other than that," Viola went on quickly, reluctant to contribute to the hum of speculation and innuendo that surrounded the Earl of Carden's daughter, "I believe Augustus St. Clair has promised to attend with his sister. She should be about your age by now."

"And will they—that is..." Miranda twisted awkwardly towards Viola, causing her maid to stick her with a pin. "Do you believe they will think well of me? All these ladies?"

"How could they not?" said Viola at once. Although in truth she had no way of knowing. She felt she *should* have known, but the minds of other women were so often opaque to her, which made her feel a fraud, for all that she told herself that nobody ever truly knew what was in another person's mind.

"In many ways," replied Miranda. "They might find me too haughty. Or too provincial. Or too haughty *and* too provincial."

"Hush." Viola hoped she had a reassuring tone. "They will love you. It will be impossible for them to do otherwise."

Besides, Louise had been right. There could be few safer environments than a card party hosted at home. Whatever anyone privately thought of any of them, they were unlikely to start spitting invective over Loo and Vingt-et-Un.

The gathering was held in the larger of the Marleighs' two

drawing rooms, with space for overspill if it became excessively crowded or the guests grew rambunctious. As Miranda's chaperone, it was Viola's task to stay not so much *by her side*, which would potentially have made it awkward for gentlemen to approach her, but within close enough distance that she could make approaching awkward at any moment if she had to.

Not that it seemed likely that she would have to. The gentlemen attending were mostly young and rather sweet, of good families rather than great families, wealthy enough that they would have no pressing need to marry for money, respectable enough that they would have no pressing need to marry for status, but not so wealthy or respectable that Miranda was quite a realistic match for any of them. It was, in a sense, a training party. One that offered all the delights of courtship with none of its dangers.

Miss Avon arrived at exactly the fashionable hour, neither too early nor too late, and Viola saw at once that she favoured her mother greatly, with the same chestnut curls and luminous hazel eyes. The Misses St. Clair and Hanbury she trailed behind her as a kind of entourage and seemed to accept as her due the small crowd of admirers that gathered about them as they arrived. All three of them were eligible and, in their own way, striking, although by Viola's estimation Miss Avon had chosen her friends specifically to show herself to best advantage.

Miss St. Clair had a fine figure, but her hair frizzed rather than curled, and possessed the kind of redness that reminded one of pumpkins and tangerines rather than wild flames and sunsets. As for Miss Hanbury she, too, favoured her mother, and although Viola thought she was quite beautiful, it was not the kind of beauty the ton was given to praise.

Eager to make what would be, Viola realised, her first friends, Miranda crossed the drawing room to meet them, with Viola following at a distance befitting her station.

"Lady Miranda." Miss Avon dropped a flawless curtsey. "It is an honour to meet you. I am Miss Avon. These are Miss Hanbury and Miss St. Clair." The other two misses curtsied with similar flawlessness.

"Oh, but the honour is all mine," Miranda exclaimed. "London is so new and so charming, and I am sure we shall all be the very best of friends."

"I'm sure we shall." The way Miss Avon smiled put Viola very much in mind of a man she once duelled in Spain, all calculation and thoughts of conquest. Then again, they'd made up their differences once the dust had settled, and he'd been a good companion until he caught a French bullet at San Marcial, so perhaps there was nothing to worry about.

A tallish gentleman with unruly hair cut across the introductions. "I say, would any of you ladies care to join my friend and me for whist?"

"Shall we?" Miss Avon extended an arm to Miranda in a manner that seemed to Viola at once pleasant and predatory.

Miranda nodded enthusiastically. "Oh yes, let's. But shall your companions not feel slighted?"

"We have grown accustomed over long acquaintance," said Miss Hanbury, her lips quirking into a half smile. "Come, gentlemen, the eligible ones have gone, who will speak for the rest? I *am* still an earl's daughter, and I assure you I can be quite diverting."

Miss Hanbury's connection to earldom and Miss St. Clair's magnificent bosom—not that it was any place of Viola's to be making such observations—saw them accompanied soon enough, and

Viola was about to retreat to the side and watch when somebody *ahem*ed behind her.

The irrational part of her that hoped every man would be Gracewood hoped it would be Gracewood, but he was not an *ahem*er. Turning, she saw Sir Reginald Thurlow, a dull but harmless man in his mid-fifties. "Sir R—" she began, before reminding herself that she had not been introduced and had no especial reason to know his name. "Sir!" she tried instead. "You startled me."

"Terribly sorry. Just thought that since the young ones had sorted themselves out, you might like to make up the numbers at my table."

There was, in truth, little she would have liked less. But there was no plausible way to refuse, and so she found herself for the best part of the next hour seated opposite the tedious Sir Reginald, trying to keep an eye on Miranda without forgetting which suit was trumps.

"—ss Carroll," Sir Reginald was saying.

"I'm sorry, I was distracted a moment."

"You are a fine card player, Miss Carroll," he repeated.

She ought to have been, for she had learned among soldiers and in gambling hells—not that a lady was permitted to publicly own her capabilities. "All luck, I assure you. I scarcely recall how many tricks have been played most of the time."

Sir Reginald was just in the process of telling her that she was too modest when there was a sudden uproar from the direction of Miranda's table.

"Good Lord," the tousle-haired young man was saying, "do it again."

Miranda squared up the deck of cards and asked for a little space. "I shall endeavour to, although it is a taxing feat."

Fearing that her charge was about to make a spectacle of herself, Viola made her apologies and crossed the room to join the crowd. Half the party, it seemed, had gathered to watch, and that fraction was growing rapidly.

"Observe," Miranda said, shuffling the cards overhand while turning her face theatrically away from the table, "that I shuffle the cards quite without looking at them." This she did. Then, still turning her face away, she continued. "Now will somebody—I don't mind who—take the pack from me."

A short man with reddish hair—Mr. Philips, Viola thought. One of the Mr. Philipses, at any rate, for there were several—took the deck as instructed.

"Now please examine the bottom card and commit it to memory. And show it to everybody else that they might also remember it but do not"—here Miranda covered her eyes with her hand—"I beg of you do not permit *me* to see it or you shall ruin the whole enterprise."

Mr. Philips did as he was bid, revealing the nine of hearts to the assembly.

"Is it done?" asked Miranda.

"Yes," replied Mr. Philips, "it was th—"

"Don't tell me. It is vital that you not tell me. But please shuffle the cards as thoroughly as you might manage, and hand them back to me."

The ever-obedient Mr. Philips did as instructed. And Miranda, removing her hand from her eyes, lifted the deck to her forehead and made an expression of intense concentration.

"Let me see," she said. "I think it would help me greatly if you were all to visualise the card in question as clearly as you are able." She paused while the assembled guests did their best to comply with her instructions. Or at least, most of them did. Miss Avon was doing her best not to glare, and her best was proving inadequate to the task.

"...becoming clearer now," Miranda was saying. "I believe it might be—that is—yes, I think, could it possibly be the nine of hearts?"

The room erupted into applause, applause to which Miss Avon contributed exactly three slow claps. "Why, Lady Miranda," she purred. "How accomplished you are."

Miranda gave her a slightly bewildered look. "Oh, it's nothing really."

"And to think"—Miss Avon's smile had become positively serpentine—"the rest of us have been squandering ourselves on deportment and the pianoforte."

"Well, our piano at Morgencald hasn't been tuned in ten years. But I did find this splendid book in the library by a man named Reginald Scot, and it has all sorts of clever things in it."

Miss Avon gave a cold laugh. "And here I am mistaking you for a gentlewoman when you are apparently a conjurer."

Unworldly as she might have been, this was a clear enough insult that even Miranda took it in the spirit it was intended. She looked to Miss Hanbury and Miss St. Clair for support, but to Viola's complete lack of surprise, found that both ladies had become intimately fascinated with some other part of the room.

It was at this moment that Lady Lillimere, who had been among the watchers, gave a polite cough. "Miss Avon," she said. "May I make the tiniest of suggestions?"

"I suspect you shall anyway," Miss Avon replied, not quite willing to test the balance of power between a desirable debutante and a wealthy widow.

"I shall. My recommendation is that you give *serious* consideration to heading down to the Thames and drowning your head in a bucket of eels."

There was a stunned pause, in which Miss St. Clair stifled a sound that most certainly was not a laugh.

"Well," said a well-groomed, young man, "I for one think you are a marvel, Lady Miranda." It took Viola a second or two to place him as Viscount Stirling—and what was he doing here? He outranked every other gentleman in the room save Gracewood and surely had better things to do with his time than to attend quiet card parties for ladies. "What other wonders can you show us?"

Still a little flustered, Miranda seemed relieved at the distraction. "I...I am sure I can think of something. Would you, perchance, have two shillings?"

"You aren't going to make them disappear, are you?" asked the Viscount teasingly.

"I shall return them, I promise."

The Viscount produced two shillings. "I cannot help but feel I am being swindled."

"Now"—Miranda put one shilling in each hand, and then stretched her arms out to either side—"I shall wager that I am able to move both of these shillings from being in opposite hands to being in a single hand, without moving my arms from this position or bending my elbows."

"Now I *definitely* feel I am being swindled. But go on..." The Viscount laughed. "What do you wager?"

This made Miranda stumble a little. "I—I don't know."

"I'd ask for a kiss," the Viscount said, "but I fear that would be improper."

"It most certainly would," agreed Viola. This was exactly the kind of talk it was her place to put a stop to, even if it did come from a viscount.

"And a kiss against two shillings," added Miss Hanbury, who had just been drifting away from the crowd when the shilling drama had begun to unfold, "seems to set a very low price on her virtue."

"Not if she knows she'll win," observed Miss St. Clair. "Then it's just two shillings for nothing."

Concerned that this was straying from harmlessly flirtatious to genuinely inappropriate, Viola decided to settle matters. "What if she wagers a simple turn about the room? That is surely worth at least two shillings, even to a viscount."

"Oh, undoubtedly," declared Viscount Stirling. "Very well then, I shall lay my two shillings against a turn about the room that you cannot contrive to bring those two shillings into one hand without moving or bending your arms."

The wager agreed, Miranda stood, turned her body so that one hand lay over the card table and set the first coin upon it. Then, keeping both arms stretched straight out like a scarecrow, she rotated her whole body a hundred and eighty degrees, tilted over to bring her other hand down, and scooped up the shilling with her fingers. "There." She smiled triumphantly at the Viscount. "And my arms remained in position, and my elbows did not bend."

A laugh rippled through the crowd.

"Won fair and square," he conceded. "But I wonder, despite your victory, might you take a turn about the room with me anyway?"

Miranda shot Viola a nervous glance, and Viola nodded her

approval. After all, this was exactly what Lady Marleigh's card party was for—to allow Miranda to meet gentlemen and to interact with them in controlled circumstances. So about the room they went, and it was a seemly enough arrangement that Viola felt little need to follow them closely. Stirling was a man of good reputation and fine family, despite his late father having been a bit of a scoundrel.

Now she was free to take her eyes off her charge a moment, Viola found them wandering naturally towards Gracewood, who had been sitting quietly at the side of the room for much of the evening, since constantly standing and moving between tables was bad for his leg and, as a duke, he could readily expect people to come to him rather than the reverse.

He was there now, sat just where he had been. And Miss Avon was sat with him. Because of course she was. What young, beautiful woman would miss the opportunity to approach a duke while every other eye in the room was distracted? Then, as Viola watched, she saw him laughing—a polite laugh, she thought, but a laugh nonetheless—at something Miss Avon was saying to him. And her heart clenched and her stomach churned and she was seized all at once by the need for air.

Strictly speaking, it was a dereliction of her duties to abandon Miranda at a card party. But since said party was taking place under the auspices of Lady Marleigh, there was no real danger. Besides, nobody would dare trifle with the Duke of Gracewood's sister under his very nose.

And that was who Viola saw when she looked across the room at Gracewood. Not the friend she had known all these years, or the—the whatever they had become to each other during her last fateful visit to Morgencald. She saw a man rich, titled, and—for all his protestations—both young and handsome. How could he fail to draw the eye of every unmarried woman in the room? And for that matter, several of the married ones, and one or two of the gentlemen.

At first it had been almost flattering to watch him, because for a while she had been able to believe that he still had eyes for nobody but her. But to see Miss Avon by his side—young and well bred, of marriageable age, and beautiful in ways that Viola could sometimes imitate or aspire to but never felt she truly attained... It was too much. For the moment at least, it was too much.

Trying not to sigh too deeply or too audibly, she slipped away to the garden. And there she found Little Bartholomew picking up rocks.

"Looking for spiders, Bartholomew?" she asked.

"Gold," he explained, and went on rummaging.

"Do you think it very likely that there will be gold in the garden?"

Setting down his most recent rock, Little Bartholomew sat on the ground, looking up at Viola quizzically. "I don't see why there shouldn't be. Pirates might have buried it."

"Were there many pirates in London?"

"No." He gave her a look as if he could not believe how foolish she was being. "Which is why it would be an excellent place for them to hide their treasure. Nobody would think to look in the back garden of a London town house for a treasure stolen on the Spanish main."

Sometimes, Viola thought, Little Bartholomew took after his mother a great deal. "How right you are. Carry on then."

"Will you look with me? It will go faster with two. And when we find the gold I will share it with you, although I should take the larger portion since this is my expedition."

Kneeling in a garden and digging for imaginary gold with a child would ruin both her dress and her gloves, but in that moment there was little Viola wanted to do more. She settled herself beside Little Bartholomew and began surveying the ground. "I think perhaps there might be something by that tree."

Obedient to his curiosity if not Viola's authority, Little Bartholomew hurried over to the tree in question and began scrabbling through the long grass. Viola came over to join him, although she did not search with quite such eagerness, partly because it was not ladylike, partly because she knew there would be nothing to find, and partly because on the off chance that they *did* stumble across something—Badger was forever losing things and could easily have dropped the odd guinea in the garden somewhere—it struck her as better that Little Bartholomew be the stumbler.

"What about this?" asked Little Bartholomew, holding up a small, slightly unusually shaped pebble. "It isn't gold, but it may be some variety of precious stone."

"I think it's just a stone."

"Were I a pirate," Little Bartholomew observed, "I should make all of my precious stones look like ordinary stones. That way nobody would steal them from me, and I should be the richest pirate on the seven seas."

"But if all of your precious stones looked like ordinary stone,"—Viola had the sneaking suspicion she was walking into another of Little Bartholomew's traps—"nobody would buy them from you, so your wealth would bring you nothing."

Little Bartholomew shrugged. "But *I* would know that I had

it. And I think if I knew that I shouldn't much care what other people said."

There was, Viola had to concede, a solipsistic wisdom to that.

"Why may I not go to the party?" Little Bartholomew asked, clearly growing tired of the topic of piracy.

"I don't think it's the kind of party you'd enjoy." It seemed like the answer Little Bartholomew would be most likely to accept, and it also had the virtue of being true.

Never one to take another person's word for it, Little Bartholomew persisted. "How can I know, if I am not permitted to attend?"

"That's a reasonable objection. But if it helps, the event contains disappointingly few pirates."

Little Bartholomew looked disapproving but unsurprised. "Not even one?"

"Not unless they are very well disguised." The moment she'd said it, Viola knew it was the wrong thing to say. Dangling the prospect of disguised pirates before Little Bartholomew was not a way to discourage him.

And sure enough, he brightened significantly. "They may be. Disguise is a common strategy in piracy. When I am a pirate, I shall disguise myself as a merchantman and take other merchantmen unawares."

"Won't that be rather unsporting?"

"When I am a pirate, I shall say sportsmanship is for landlubbers."

"Might you not say that now?"

Little Bartholomew considered this for a long moment. He had, Viola was relieved to note, at least been distracted from the thought of going inside. "Well, I might," he said, "but I think I would get into trouble with Mama and Mr. Dowling, so I don't think it's worth the effort."

Viola was not certain that *be virtuous, because vice is too much bother* was quite the lesson a young gentleman was meant to be learning in these days of reason and enlightenment, but she let it go. "Come on," she told him. "I think I saw something gleaming by that patch of long grass."

She should have gone back inside. But Little Bartholomew was not the only one who would have preferred the party to have more pirates. More pirates and fewer debutantes making eyes at the Duke of Gracewood.

# CHAPTER 26

The evening was going well—which was to say, Miranda seemed to be enjoying herself, even if her turn for conjuring had taken Gracewood somewhat by surprise. Probably he would need to have a word with her later about talents it was appropriate for a young lady to display in public, but it was not a conversation he could foresee either party relishing. Especially in the wake of the fragile peace only recently established between them. If, that is, by "peace" one meant "strained courtesy." It should have been preferable to the alternative—sulks and complaints and outbursts—but somehow it was worse. As if, after years of hovering on the outskirts of his life, Miranda had slipped away entirely. As if she had, at last, given up on him.

Both Lady Marleigh and Viola had made it clear that he needed to talk to her. That it was not enough simply to protect her and provide for her and expect her to trust his judgement and obey his commands. But he had been raised to govern people, not share himself with them. And certainly not his doubts, his mistakes, the things he was most ashamed of. Viola had always been the only person to see him. The only person he'd let see him. For all that he'd never seen her.

He saw her now, though. Saw her, yearned for her, suspected he was falling in love with her. As he had been at Morgencald, possibly even all his life. So many years he had wasted searching for meaning beyond his legacy, for the freedom to be the man he could be, rather than the man his father demanded. He had tried scholarship, he had tried debauchery, he had even tried war. But he was as trapped and as helpless as he'd ever been, unable to make his sister feel cared for, unable to be with the woman he loved.

It was fortunate he had not been required to make a fourth at any of the tables, for he could think of nothing but Viola and could barely keep his eyes from searching for her. She was in blue tonight, some enigmatic shade he could not name, touched here by grey, there by purple, as glossy and restless as the winter sea. This new world of hers, with its patterns and prints, and silks and sarsnets, was still rather a mystery to him, but now he understood how it spoke her truths, it bewitched him more than ever. Her gown was of the simple, flowing style he was starting to recognise she favoured, the hem embroidered with some Grecian geometries to match her gloves. At her throat, a delicate choker of blue topaz and pearls, softly shadowed by the fall of her hair.

For the early part of the evening, she had kept mostly to herself as if she somehow believed she could be overlooked. And then, Sir Reginald Thurlow—visibly taken with her—had claimed her for whist. He was a perfectly respectable fellow but, in that moment, Gracewood quite despised him. The fact he could so easily speak to Viola, laugh with her, take her arm to lead her to her seat. No doubt he was flattering her, telling her she was an excellent player. Damn right she was.

*She will fleece you, old man.*

"Forgive my forwardness"—a lady was standing before him, her cheeks caressed by a pretty blush—"but I think, perhaps, you don't remember me?"

He did not, in fact, remember her.

"We *have* been introduced," she assured him, apparently eager to clarify that her forwardness extended as far as reminding a gentleman of a former connection but not so far as approaching a strange duke.

"Of course I remember you, Miss—"

"Avon," she finished, neatly preserving the mutually beneficial fiction that he knew who she was.

As it happened, the name was familiar—albeit only vaguely. He thought she might have made her debut when he and Viola had first come to London, and made quite a stir with her beauty. Strange that she should not yet have made the brilliant match predicted for her. "A pleasure to meet you again, Miss Avon." Grasping his cane, he rose to greet her properly. It had been a long day, escorting Miranda here and there as a brother must, and so the movement was—

It was not elegant.

And Miss Avon, for all she struggled valiantly to hide it, flinched as she took his hand. "Renewed acquaintance is practically friendship. We need not st—" Then she flinched again. "That is—I mean...Insist. We need not insist upon ceremony."

This was what he had expected. Revulsion disguised as pity turned into uncertainty. And yet it was not nearly so excoriating as he had feared. Perhaps he had grown accustomed over weeks of hastily averted eyes and unnecessary solicitousness. Perhaps it was simply that his mind was distracted. Or perhaps the idea of the man he used to be was beginning to feel less like something he had lost than something he had moved beyond.

"That is not the phrase, Miss Avon," he said, as she began to fidget in the silence, "and well you know it."

"Your Grace?" Miss Avon did not quite bat her eyes, but she blinked in a way that conveyed, as if it needed to be conveyed, that she understood what he meant but would on no account admit to understanding it.

"The phrase is not *to insist upon ceremony*." There was, Gracewood realised, a cold power in this. In turning one's own weakness into a kind of weapon. "It is to *stand* upon ceremony. You seem to have avoided the word *stand* because I, as everybody in this room is doubtless aware, have difficulty standing. Whether you do this for my comfort or your own, I cannot say. But I should tell you that if you intend it as kindness, you have chosen a poor strategy."

Her flush deepened, although whether it was from anger or embarrassment, Gracewood couldn't tell. "I certainly did not intend to be unkind, Your Grace."

"No, you intended to coddle my infirmity. But that is just unkindness of a different sort." It was a sharp reply—too sharp, perhaps. But Gracewood was growing increasingly convinced that he did not wish to be speaking with Miss Avon. Not that there was any particular deficiency in the lady herself. But the woman who presently occupied his time was not the one who occupied his thoughts.

"I have given offence." Miss Avon bowed her head, the sudden performance of contrition abruptly reminding Gracewood that, for all she had irked him, he remained a duke and she a young woman, whose means were moderate and her future less assured than it had been four years ago.

"As have I," Gracewood admitted. And, because his interest had been a commodity once in the marketplace of politics, intrigue, and influence that was life among the beau monde, he gestured to a nearby chair. "If you are not engaged for a game, would you care to sit with me a while?"

Miss Avon offered a smile that drifted across her face like petals upon the surface of a pool. "Thank you, Your Grace. I would be honoured." Settling herself as indicated, she arranged her skirts around her and contrived not to be looking at him as he sat down beside her. "How are you enjoying the season?" she went on smoothly.

"I am mostly here for my sister's sake."

"You mean"—a delicate, sideways glance—"there is nothing in town that might capture your attention?"

He had lost the trick of these games. Once the blade dance of flirtation would have intrigued him. Now all he wanted was a quiet room with an old friend, and only honest words between them. Nevertheless, he offered a polite laugh. "Did you have something in mind?"

"I'm sure," she said, visibly encouraged, "I could show you the sights. It has been some while, I think, since you left Northumberland?"

"Again, it is for Miranda's sake that I did."

"Of course. But..." And here her eyes slid to his again. "There is your own life to think of too. Your own... needs."

"My needs," he repeated, with a lift of a brow.

She nodded. "Yes. A duke has responsibilities to his estate and his line and his place in society. He needs—"

"A wife?"

"Support," she concluded.

There was a brief silence. Gracewood scanned the crowd, looking for Viola, but she was nowhere to be seen. "You do not wish to marry me, Miss Avon," he said.

He felt her tense beside him. "I am not aware of having been asked."

"No, but you do not strike me as a woman who acts without purpose."

"You flatter me, Your Grace."

And such was the determination in her voice, to be flattered, whatever his actual intention, that he almost smiled. Almost liked her, for the calculation in her eyes, the poise she wore like armour, and the moments when something human, and uncertain, shone through the chinks of it. "I am not for you," he told her. "You've disliked nearly everything I've said to you, and my presence—by which, of course I mean my leg—makes you uncomfortable."

Her fingers tightened in the folds of her gown. "One is always a little uncomfortable with strangers."

"But Miss Avon"—he could not resist—"I thought renewed acquaintance was practically friendship."

A pause. For a moment, he hoped she might laugh. The look she turned on him, however, suggested the very opposite of amusement. "So the rumours are true. You have changed."

He smiled at that. "In more ways than you could possibly imagine, Miss Avon." Rising, with the help of his cane, he gave the briefest of bows. "Now if you'll excuse me, there's someone I need to speak to."

Except he could not find Viola among the guests, and his circuit round the room was making him feel more than usually like a spectacle. In the end it was Lady Marleigh, sitting watchfully close to Miranda, while she demonstrated another of her card tricks to a visibly infatuated young man, who directed him to the garden.

He walked—he did not quite want to think he hobbled—outside. And there he saw her, kneeling beside Little Bartholomew, scrabbling beneath a tree for some imagined treasure.

"When I am a pirate," Little Bartholomew was explaining, "I shall say sportsmanship is for landlubbers."

"Might you not say that now?" Viola replied.

"Well, I might," he said, "but I think I would get into trouble with Mama and Mr. Dowling, so I don't think it's worth the effort."

"Come on," Viola told him. "I think I saw something gleaming by that patch of long grass."

Then, turning, she saw him. And the look in her eyes was—what? Not shock exactly, but she clearly knew she had been observed, and some instinct made her shrink from it. He had not, he thought, been watching her for that long. Not *improperly* long, certainly. Just a stolen moment to admire how quickly, how instinctively she responded to young Bartholomew. To recognise the ease with which she took his childish fancies and the grace with which she indulged them. And to feel with fresh keenness the wounds his absence had left in his sister's life.

Walking forward carefully, for the ground was a little uneven and his gait still a little unsteady, he approached to see what Little Bartholomew would find in the long grass.

For a while, Little Bartholomew rummaged contentedly, then all at once sprang up triumphant. He had found a penny, which he declared confidently must once have belonged to the great Bartholomew Roberts. "He," the child added with the sort of certainty that Gracewood almost envied, "was the best pirate."

"Why was he the best pirate?" asked Viola, smiling and glancing conspiratorially up at Gracewood.

Little Bartholomew looked solemn, as if this were a weighty matter and deserving of serious consideration. "Because he had the best name. Also because he wrote the pirates' code, which is a very good set of rules that I think we should have in this house. Then every man would have a vote in the affairs of the moment and have equal title to the fresh provisions or strong liquors at any time. Which means I could have whatever I wanted from the kitchens and Cook couldn't stop me and neither could Mama or Papa."

"Under the pirate's code," Viola pointed out—and Gracewood recalled she had gone through her own phase of being enamoured with Defoe as a child, "no women or little boys would be allowed in the house at all."

"Then I should run away to sea," he said, "and be a pirate."

There was, Gracewood was certain, a flaw in Little Bartholomew's logic, but it did not seem prudent to articulate it. "Perhaps it would be simplest all told if the rules of the household remained as they are."

The door to the garden opened once more and the Viscount Marleigh—and it was becoming easier, now that Gracewood had seen Viola for herself, to use that name for her brother—emerged looking flustered. "I say, you haven't seen Bartholomew, have you? The one who isn't me, I mean?"

"He's here, Badger." Viola rose, her gown shifting around her like a waterfall of silk and muslin. "I'm sorry, I should have brought him back immediately."

Apparently having no wish to admonish his sister, the Viscount Marleigh leaned over his son and wagged his finger like a Gillray caricature of a stern parent. "Now, now, Little Bartholomew, you have been a very naughty boy. Your mama sent you to bed an hour ago."

"By the pirate's code," young Bartholomew explained, "candles are put out at eight, but men may drink on deck as late as they please."

"As we have established"—Gracewood hoped he was striking the right tone between firm and affectionate, but how would he know?—"you are too young to be a pirate."

Standing, young Bartholomew pulled himself up to his full height, which was about level with Gracewood's hip. "I shall have you know, sir, that I am a man of three-and-twenty."

Viola laughed her free, beautiful laugh. "And very bold you look, but I think you may need to wait a few years before people will believe you on that count."

"Come now, Bartholomew." Viscount Marleigh was holding out his hand. "Say good-bye to Viola and Gracewood. But you should know that because you've been bad, I'm afraid I'm sending you to bed without any supper."

With innocent perplexity, young Bartholomew gazed at his father. "But I've already had supper."

"Then I shall have Cook make some more supper, in order that you may be sent to bed without it."

Young Bartholomew seemed to accept that this was a just and fair punishment and, after bidding a round of goodnights to Viola and Gracewood, allowed himself to be taken back to bed by his father.

"Did you know he was meant to be asleep?" asked Gracewood, when the Bartholomews had departed.

Viola looked a little abashed. "I—I think I should probably have surmised."

"Yet you elected not to?"

"Well." She smiled at him, and he lingered in it a moment. "I do try to avoid surmising wherever possible. But yes, I think I—I am probably too lenient with him."

"Perhaps, but he plainly adores you."

"As the shark adores the herring?"

"As a boy adores his aunt."

That made her sigh a little. "I find I am well suited to be an aunt. It means that there will always be a mother around to make up for my deficiencies."

"I did not say you were deficient," said Gracewood hurriedly, hoping he hadn't offended or, worse, hurt her.

"Oh, but I am. I let him miss lessons and stay up past his bedtime. I fear I would be a terrible mother."

It occurred to Gracewood that they were now alone, and although the garden was plainly visible from the house, it could damage Viola's reputation if he were to stand as close as he wished. Speak as intimately as he wished. These were the new rules they lived by, and it was harder than he had anticipated to be confronted by them. Perhaps Little Bartholomew had been correct and they should adopt the pirate's code. "Terrible is too strong a word. You might be a little . . . lax in some departments?"

She giggled. "*Not terrible, merely lax.* Next time I need a reference as to my character, I shall be certain to call for you."

"I'm sorry. I think I'm . . . I think I must still be learning how to talk to you. When there is so much I want to say." And wasn't that absurd? The most desired, the most eligible women in London could approach him with all their arts and courtesies, and he could trade words with the calm surety of a lifetime's practice. But this one woman—his oldest, dearest friend in the world—left him tongue-tied. "If it helps," he went on, "I believe I would also be a terrible father."

And at that, she did not giggle, but shut her eyes and looked down. "You will be a wonderful father, Gracewood."

"I had no example."

"But you have you. And you have always done what you know to be right."

Unbidden, his thoughts drifted back to Waterloo. "I have always *tried* to do what I *believed* was right. That is not the same thing."

"It is close enough to make no difference, much of the time."

He wished he believed that. But the pain in his leg and the shadows in his dreams and the way he had hurt and been hurt by the one person who meant the most to him was proof that it was false. "Perhaps between us our faults would balance out. You would shower our children in love and joy and turn them into tiny terrors, and then the little reprobates would be able to break through my cold, ducal façade to find the caring man within."

It had been meant as a joke, but Viola wasn't laughing. She didn't even smile.

"Oh God. I did not mean to—"

Raising a hand, she waved him away. "I know. But it is hard to speak of something I know we can never have."

"I'm sorry." How many times would he blurt out something requiring apology in a single conversation? But it was so easy, sometimes, to let his mind run towards fantasy. She made it easy. "I would—I would give that to you if I could."

"You can't. You are a powerful man, but you are still a man, not a miracle worker."

There was nothing of rebuke in her voice. Just a kind of resignation that was somehow worse. "You are far from the only woman who cannot bear children."

"And how happy are such women? How marriageable?"

To the first question, Gracewood could not speak, and to the second he did not wish to. "I daresay many are happy. Not everybody wishes for that kind of family."

"But I do."

And he wanted her to have whatever she wanted. But she was right. He was, when all was said and done, just a man. And an incomplete one, whatever kind words she said to him, however pretty fortune-hunters flattered him.

Of course to many women an incomplete duke was worth any number of whole untitled men—especially since any woman he married would, he was sure, seek wholeness elsewhere. But the truth was he did not *want* to marry any woman. Speaking to Miss Avon had proven that. She was everything he should have desired. Everything his father would have approved. And she had made it very clear she was willing if not to overlook his shorcomings then at least to tolerate them.

Indeed he would be, in so many ways, a fool *not* to marry Miss Avon.

But did love not make a man foolish?

And standing here, now, in this tiny London garden with its one tree and its ornamental rockery, was there anybody he wished to be with, wished to be near, wished to bare his soul and give his heart to, save Viola Carroll?

"I . . ." he began at last. "I am not a miracle worker, but—"

"Gracewood, stop." The pleading in her eyes was too much to endure, but the charade they had been living the last few weeks, pretending to be strangers to one another, to be little better than master and servant, was still worse.

"I cannot."

"You can, and you shall. We have an arrangement, and it functions." Viola was shaking, just slightly, and it took all Gracewood's strength not to go to her.

"It does *not* function. It is unbearable. For me, at least, it is unbearable. Perhaps you feel differently." His tone was becoming harsh. He had not intended it to, but passion sometimes led him back to old lessons. To pride and command and a private capacity for cruelty.

"I am not like you, Gracewood. I do not have the luxury of feeling whatever I will. I have lived my whole life within constraints that I did not choose and did not create, and I have learned to content myself with them."

Ever since he had recognised its effect on his father, Gracewood had tried to resist anger, but it was growing harder. "You cannot possibly be content with this. Not when you could have—"

"Could have *what*, Gracewood? I will not be a…a sacrifice you make."

"Is that what you think you would be?"

She was close now, improperly close, and he took a step back for fear of her reputation and his composure. "Look me in the eyes," she said, "and tell me you wish to be the last of your line. The last de Vere at Morgencald."

"Miranda will marry."

"She may, but even if she does, her children will not have your name."

He wanted to say that it didn't matter, that if there was one thing he had learned from his father, it was that a name and a bloodline didn't make you a worthy heir, or even a worthy man.

But he couldn't. Not quite. And the realisation that he couldn't chilled him. The weight of his legacy and his duty pressed down on him like old stone, and he froze.

"You see?"

She knew him too well to brook denial. "And is that all there is for us?" he asked. "Marriage or...or nothing?"

"You are a duke. What else could there be?"

"Dukes take lovers." He knew the moment he said it that it was a mistake.

She whirled away from him with such ferocity that he was terrified somebody from the card party would see the commotion. "I am to be your mistress, then? You told me that you were no rake, Gracewood."

Having started down this road, he saw no choice but to continue along it. "I am not—I was not suggesting...It would be a compromise, of sorts. The closest we could come to the life we—the life you want."

"I will not be a sacrifice, and I will not be a compromise. It would feel wrong."

If he was honest, it would feel wrong to Gracewood too. He had kept mistresses before—treated them well, and enjoyed the time they had shared—but what he felt for Viola was something else entirely. "Then...then may we not be friends? As we used to be?"

"No."

"Why not?"

"Are any of your *other* friends women?"

He tried to laugh at that, but he was still too raw. "Viola, you know I *have* no other friends."

"We do not live in a world where a man and a woman can simply—can simply be together as we once were."

Not long ago, that would have defeated him. Because she was right, in a way. But what good was wealth or title, what good all that he had fought for—at Waterloo and afterwards—if he could not fight for this. "Damn the world. The world told you that you had to live the life it shaped for you, and you defied it. The world told me that I had to be as my father was, and I defied it, or am trying to. We can make our own world, Viola, with our own rules."

At last she faced him again. "You make it sound simple. And…and a little wonderful."

"Only a little?" He hoped that he sounded charming, perhaps even roguish, instead of achingly afraid she would refuse him.

"How would we…?"

Gracewood tried to look nonchalant, as if he knew well how everything would fall out. "We would be discreet. Which we know we can do, for we have had years of practice, sneaking around at school and at home, evading our various masters. And we would talk, as we once did. Sit up late in the library. Drink brandy together and—unless, unless you would feel that I was merely…I want to know you as once I did, but I do not want…I am not only attempting to recapture…"

For a moment he thought he had ruined it, that he had convinced her that it was his friend he wanted, not the woman who stood before him. "It would still be a compromise," she said.

It would. And he would have been lying to himself and to her if he pretended it would satisfy him forever. "Our current arrangement is a compromise. This would be no worse, and it would be on our terms, not society's."

For a long while he was worried she would say no, that she would think it a trick, or a denial of herself. But at last she smiled. "Then I shall see you in the library?"

Gracewood offered her his arm. "I should like that very much. Now, if you will, we have been absent too long. And I should not like people to talk."

Trying not to think too much of the closeness of her, the heat of her, he took Viola back to the drawing room. It was not enough, of course, not nearly enough. But it was more than either of them had that morning. And beyond that he would not let himself speculate. Small acts of defiance, he well knew, could become great acts of rebellion, and little intimacies could become alliances or passions that shaped lives and worlds. But for now Viola had agreed to meet with him, on occasion, in the library at his home.

If that was all that they could ever have, he would strive to be content with it. And if it was not—well. It did no good to run ahead of himself. They were both still learning, in so many ways. Having spent so many years dwelling on yesterday, it would be the height of folly to dwell instead on tomorrow, when there was so much joy to find in today.

# CHAPTER 27

Gracewood's invitation hovered like a butterfly on the edges of Viola's conscious mind. But she did not, for several days, take him up on it. Partly she was busy, organising Miranda's coming-out ball with Lady Marleigh and accompanying Miranda on several rather bizarre sight-seeing trips around the capital. And partly it was cowardice.

Of course she wanted to join him—as she would once have done without a second thought—but nothing felt the same any more. Even being with Gracewood was a puzzle box of the past and the present, easier in some ways, more difficult in others. Easier, at least, to give the name to everything he was to her. More difficult to bear the weight of it. For all it had ever been part of her.

She dreamed of him, sometimes. And of summer at Morgencald, when sunlight buttered the grey stone and glittered upon the iron waves of the North Sea. Of some half-other world where everything had always been as it was meant to be, and a restless girl and a lost boy could always have been friends. Where she would have made him smile and he would have kissed her in the rose garden, and someday their children would fill all those cold halls with their laughter.

They were good dreams, though she sometimes wept for them when she woke. Except every now and then, they'd catch her in the early hours, when the night was still stretched ahead of her and the business of the day little more than a dream itself, and then they'd cling to her like devils, refusing to depart.

It was one such occasion that—despite an exhausting and, to Miranda's mind, disappointing trip to the Tower of London— had Viola sitting up in bed, wiping her eyes, and trying to tell from the colour of the darkness if it was before midnight, or after midnight. Not that it made much difference: She would not sleep.

Suddenly the guest room, the very nice guest room she had been given close to the family, seemed a chill and transient place. Her future a string of transient places. And the sense of being alone that could be side-stepped, pushed aside, disregarded, and distracted from in daylight crashed over her with suffocating force.

She was not, she knew, truly alone—not nearly alone as she could have been, for she had Louise and Badger, and Little Bartholomew. She even, in a way, still had Gracewood. And she had new friends like Miranda and Lady Lillimere. But there was a larger loneliness, one that came from inhabiting a space she'd had no choice but to build for herself, only to find that nobody could inhabit it with her.

Would Gracewood still be awake? For his sake, she hoped not. For her own—oh God, she wanted him to be. Because even when everything else in her life had felt wrong, he had always felt right. And, whatever else could or could not be between them, she still needed her friend. Besides, it was the middle of the night. He would likely have retired by now. There could be no harm, surely, in going down to the library. If he wasn't there— which he wouldn't be—she could occupy herself with a book. If he was…

Well, if he was, it would be happenstance. The purest serendipity.

Rising, she lit a candle and drew a wrapper over her nightrail. And because she was not sure it was late enough to guarantee she would not encounter a servant, she paused at her washbasin to tidy her appearance. Then, having tied a ribbon around her throat and pulled on a plain pair of gloves, she crept out of her room and made her way to the library. The glow of light from beneath the door suggested occupation, but it could also have been the remains of a fire lit earlier in the evening. And was not, on its own, reason enough to either press forward or turn back.

With something that was nearly a knock—though she would never have knocked before—she went inside. And found Gracewood, in his shirtsleeves, sprawled in a chair by the fire. At first, and this was not a thought whose primacy she relished, she feared he might have succumbed afresh to laudanum. But on her entrance, he came as suddenly to his feet as his leg permitted, a book tumbling to the floor.

Reading. He had only been reading. And she was furious at herself for doubting him.

"Viola." His smile was a golden thing in the firelight. "You came."

"I could not sleep," she admitted, abruptly recalled to her bare feet and her unbound hair.

"I'm sorry for that. But I'm so very glad to see you." He gestured to a second chair. "Will you join me?"

She nodded and sat, stiffly at first, but then realising how ridiculous it was to insist upon propriety when you were in your night clothes, curling up with her legs tucked beneath her.

This was a very different library to the one at Morgencald. Creamcoloured panelling took the place of oak, age, and ostentation. The collection was less expansive, but the volumes it offered were more modern, and while the desk was a mahogany monstrosity that must have come from Northumberland, the room was mostly dominated by its large square windows. By day, it would be suffused with light. At night, its modest proportions meant that even a fading fire could keep the shadows at bay and offered a warm, bright circle for the two scroll-backed chairs set before it. Cosy. It felt cosy. A place for a reserved gentleman to conduct his business and, later, take his ease with a close friend.

"What is this?" Viola asked, retrieving the fallen book.

Gracewood looked slightly abashed. "Something Miranda wanted. I had thought I had better read it to ensure it was suitable."

"And is it?" The title page proclaimed the work the third volume of *Frankenstein; or, The Modern Prometheus.*

"Probably not. But"—and here he shrugged—"I shall give it to her anyway, in a shameless bid to make her hate me less."

"She does not hate you, Gracewood."

"I have failed her so completely. All these years I have spent, fearful of failing my father, then obsessed with defying him. And I never spared a thought for Miranda."

"You were not raised to," she pointed out.

His gaze drifted to the fire. Viola tried not to notice the way the flames licked up the column of his throat or brushed the crests of his cheekbones. "I named her, you know."

"I did not know."

"The old duke wanted a second son, for he was not a man to leave anything to chance. I think he almost believed it was done to thwart him—I mean, that my mother died, and Miranda was a girl." Gracewood smiled then, and while there was a touch of self-mockery in it, there was something else there too: pride. "Not a day old, and she was already braver than I had been for my entire life."

"You were twelve," said Viola. "How many opportunities for bravery should a twelve-year-old encounter?"

Gracewood's eyes flicked back to hers, their brightest blues lost to the firelight. "You do not know—that is. My father..."

"I know how he treated you." The worst of it was, she had known for years. And this was the first time they had been able to speak of it, even indirectly. "That was always a reflection on his inadequacy as a father, never yours as a son." Impulsively she reached a hand across the space between them, and he immediately clasped it. "Or a man."

He gave an odd, bitter laugh. "That night he told me he wished I didn't look like him. Because he would have preferred to imagine my mother played him false than face the truth that any son of his should be..." He faltered momentarily. "Like me. As weak as me, and as worthless."

"If he was not already dead," Viola said softly, "I would wish him so."

"My sweetest friend." His fingers tightened around hers. "When we are next at Morgencald we shall spit on his grave together."

The *when* was its own private pain. What did Gracewood really think would happen to them—to Viola—when Miranda's season was done? But it was not the time to confront him with that. Nor to force herself to confront it. "I do not believe he deserves even that consideration. You are here, and he is not, and your life is yours to live."

"Of course, you're right. And I would rather do what I can for the wrongs that I have committed than dwell on any that may have been done to me."

She followed the rough line of his knuckles with the pad of her thumb, wishing she dared shed her gloves and put her skin to his. "Miranda will come to see that not every wrong was of your making."

"I am *trying*, Viola." He swallowed. "It is against everything I was taught to believe I should be, but I am trying. I hope she will come to see that at least." There was a pause, the taut lines fading from Gracewood's expression as a touch of mischief curled his lips. "And in the meantime, I shall arrange for her to see dissections and buy her books about monsters."

Viola's eyes widened. "Books about what?"

"This *Frankenstein* of hers." Gracewood waved the volume in question. "It's the story of a man who discovers how to impart life to non-living matter. He animates a being so hideous he immediately abandons it in terror and disgust, though we later learn his creation is intelligent, sensitive, and capable of love. However, its appearance makes it impossible for it to find acceptance within human society." Again, his mouth softened with the quiet mirth that he seemed to share only with her. "I am concerned Miranda feels some sense of connection."

"She is no monster," Viola said, laughing. "Quite the contrary."

"No, but she was created by a man who cared nothing for her and then thrown into a world of bewildering cruelty. Besides, I think there are few of us who do not occasionally feel like monsters."

"Or," she added, "helpless against the context that created us."

There was a moment of silence. Then Gracewood said, "I am being the worst of hosts. I have talked about nothing but myself, and I haven't even offered you brandy."

Viola risked a smile. "As we agreed, in this room you are only my friend."

"I have an 1811 cognac."

"Should…should we be drinking?"

"Do you mean, should *I* be drinking?" That self-mocking note had crept once more into his voice. But it was gentle mockery this time. "I have a rule I try to keep: I may occasionally take a glass, though only a glass, and only in company. As for the laudanum, that is its own demon."

"It troubles you still?" she asked.

He glanced away, a flicker of shame in his eyes. "Sometimes." A single word, heavy with its own cost. "But," he went on, "I will fight it. And keep fighting—for the rest of my life if that is what is needed."

"I know you will." She released his hand and—with her fingers light against his jaw—turned his face back to hers. A few days, maybe even a few minutes, ago she wouldn't have dared. "Even if you falter, I know you will still fight."

The faintest of tremors ran through him in response, but he did not draw away. Just let her look at him, the way she wanted, his breath pooling in the palm of her glove. There was something half-surrendered in it, how still he held for her, like the wild hart come in all its savage, fragile glory to lay its head in her lap.

Then he startled away from her. "Let me get you that drink."

She should have helped, for he had to carry the two glasses separately once he had poured them, but she did not trust herself to stand. If she'd tried, she would have come apart entirely, turned into a thousand feathered things and swirled away beneath the stars simply for knowing, even for the barest scattering of seconds, how it felt to touch Gracewood as if he were hers.

"We should make a toast." He had reclaimed his seat, his cane propped beside him. Two glasses of cognac rested on the table between them.

Thoughtfully, she lifted her glass. "To compromise?"

"Viola"—he gave a chiding look—"I will not drink to that."

"Then what would you prefer?"

"To friendship?" he suggested.

But she could not drink to that either. It would have been too much like a lie. "To . . . our own terms."

"To our own terms," he echoed.

The cognac was butter rich and summer warm, sliding down her throat in a deep, velvet caress. It made her almost dizzy, the way the evening felt at once like every other evening they'd ever shared and yet nothing like them. As if some hitherto unheeded door had opened for her, offering glimpses of an unknowable future.

# CHAPTER 28

The day of Mira's coming-out ball was—like the days preceding it—mostly carnage. Gracewood had valiantly mustered opinions on ices, on soup, on violinists, on flowers, and Lady Marleigh had disregarded all of them. Which was something he had chosen not to take personally, given Lady Marleigh's general wariness towards opinions that were not her own.

She had settled, in the end, on a simple spring theme, filling the ballroom with rambling roses, lavender, and wisteria—gentle sunset colours that pearlesced dreamily in the candlelight and would, no doubt, show his sister to fine advantage. While their heavy scents would, more practically, go some way to alleviating the inevitable consequence of crushing too many people into a hot room.

Miranda, of course, had been delighted with everything—at least delighted with Lady Marleigh, and Viola. With Gracewood she was distant still, neither of them quite sure how to navigate the bloody shingle of seventeen years' neglect.

"You look beautiful, Mira," he told her in her dressing room, just as the ball was about to begin.

"I do?" She regarded her own reflection quizzically. "Thank you, Justin. That is kind of you. I sometimes thought I might be a little pretty. But it's different hearing it from someone else. In your own head, it's quite a dull idea."

"You're going to dazzle the world."

And he meant it. Her ball gown had been of Viola's orchestration, his sister's taste being—as Viola had put it lately—unorthodox. It was embossed gauze over an under-dress of deep sunshine gold, against which her skin shone with a pristine lustre. They shared the same fair colouring, as did most scions of the de Vere line, but Gracewood's hair was darker, his eyes less lucent in their blues—as if the elements that were tarnished in him had achieved their rightful purity in his sister.

"I brought you something," he added, putting a rosewood box down on the table in front of her. "They belonged to Mother."

That seemed to rouse her slightly. She gave a little gasp when she saw the pearls lying upon their bed of dark velvet. "She's wearing these in her portrait."

"She would have wanted you to have them."

"How do you know?" The glance she cast him was sharper than she had lately allowed herself to be with him. "She's dead."

It was an old grief and should have been a faded one. But it had never quite lost its poisoned edge. "You are right. I don't know. And I can't know. But I believe what I said: that she would have wanted you to have her jewellery. Would you prefer something else? Most of the grander pieces are held at the bank, but I—"

"No, no. These are…these are…" Miranda's voice trailed away, as she lifted the necklace, letting the light create its private rainbows across the surface of the pearls. "Justin, would she like me?"

"She would love you."

"That's not what I asked."

"I'm not quite sure," he said finally, "of the distinction."

Instead of answering, Miranda swept her curls away from her neck. "Will you help me with this?"

"Of course."

The task, however, proved more involved than perhaps either of them had realised. Gracewood's days of draping jewellery effortlessly upon ladies were long behind him, the clasp was old and small, and his hands could not find the steadiness they needed, even for so slight a span of time that they would have needed it. In the end, with her brother reduced to simply holding the necklace in place, Mira managed to fasten it herself.

"Will you tell me about her?" she asked.

"Mother?" It was a tragically facile question. But Gracewood needed the moment that uttering it gave him.

And, to her credit, Mira only nodded.

"I'm afraid I didn't spend much time with her. His Grace didn't allow it."

His sister's eyes were an endless, aching question. "You must know something."

"She liked poetry. And riding—she had a cream-coloured mare, I think. She always rode past the schoolroom window. The Duke thought she was too soft with the servants." What more could he say? That had she not died in childbirth, her joy would have soaked like old blood into the stones of Morgencald until she was just as cold and hard as everything else there? "She was supposed to be a great beauty."

"I discerned *that* from her portrait."

"I'm sorry."

She shrugged. And then, with an effort at a lighter tone. "Thank you anyway."

"Why are you thinking about this now?"

"What do you mean?" Bewilderment crept into Miranda's tone. "I think about it all the time."

What answer he could have given he had no idea, but he was released from the obligation of doing so by a knock at the door.

"It's me" came Viola's voice. "Do you need any help?"

Mira was on her feet so quickly she nearly knocked her chair over. "Not at all. Please come in."

Viola was in blue again. Mazarine blue, as deep as a summer evening. He had known she would be, because he had watched her buy the fabric, but he hadn't been prepared for its shimmer and her starkness. The way it would turn her skin to starlight. Her eyes to midnight. Her mouth to some velvet flower. The dress itself was unadorned, unembroidered, just a fall of silk down the subtly implied curves of her. In that moment, the memory of holding her upon the beach at Morgencald felt almost impossible. As though he had become a man in a fable: lain with the wild ocean and woken, salt-stricken, forever changed, upon an unfamiliar shore.

"I'm going downstairs," announced Mira into what, Gracewood belatedly realised, had become quite a long silence.

Which became an even longer silence after her departure.

Viola was looking at him in mild concern. "Are you all right?"

"Clearly not. I'm still barely able to talk to Miranda without hurting or failing her somehow."

"You'll find a way. You have the rest of your lives to learn to be brother and sister."

It seemed, at that moment, scant reassurance. "It may *take* the rest of our lives."

"Then you will wait. And you will be patient and you will be strong. You are a good man, Gracewood, and if Miranda can forgive me for leading you astray in your youth, she will eventually forgive you for being led."

He hoped so, and when Viola said it he almost believed it had to be true. Because she made everything real in ways nobody else could. "Before we go down, there's something...something I'd like you to have."

Her expression grew curious. "What is it?"

"A gift." He withdrew a second box from the interior of his coat and offered it to her. "For tonight."

"Why would you...?" Her voice trailed away as she saw what he had bought for her. A mesh of diamonds tipped with sapphires, all fragments of light and impossible blues. Furthest skies and deepest seas, the colours of an ever-shifting moment. The best match for her gown—for her—that he could find. "Good God. You know I can't accept this."

"Why not?"

"You know why." She cast him a glance far sharper than Miranda had managed. "At least I hope you do."

"Because," he said quickly, "an unmarried woman should not receive gifts from gentlemen. But what about from a dear old family friend?"

She gave an unseemly snort. "Gracewood, please. You're hardly some doddering uncle dispensing harmless trinkets to his nieces."

"Do you...do you like it, though?"

"You know I do." There was a note of resignation in her voice. "It's stunning. But you still shouldn't have bought it."

"You recall I am quite offensively wealthy."

"These are jewels for a duchess."

"Not at all." He paused, smiling at her. "That would surely involve a tiara of some kind."

To his delight, relief, she smiled back, though her tone

remained grave. "Even so, what would a lady's companion be doing with a piece like this?"

"Perhaps everyone will think you're a jewel thief."

"If I were a jewel thief," she retorted, "I like to think I'd have the good sense not to wear my stolen property in front of my victims."

"Say they're paste then," he offered.

"That is not a conversation I envision having." She cast her eyes down, abashed and perhaps a little nervous. "I doubt anyone will pay me the slightest heed."

She was wrong. She would shine like a star in a room full of shadows. "If that is the case, what does it matter what you wear?"

"Don't be logical at me, Gracewood." Her brows dipped into a glare that fell somewhere between playful and sincere. "I have never enjoyed it."

He hung his head, his gift suddenly outlandish in her hands. "I'm sorry. I should not have presumed. It was selfish of me, but I wanted to... I want to give you something beautiful."

"It *is* beautiful." With a cool touch of gloved fingers beneath his chin, she made him look at her again. "*You* are beautiful."

The words were so surprising, so utterly unexpected, that he actually laughed. "What nonsense, Viola."

She looked at him with such honesty that he could scarcely bear it. "You don't believe me?"

"Well..." He had no idea what to say, for ugliness had lived in him long before the war had ruined his body. "I know you would not lie to me."

"Then how do you think I see you?"

He gave what he hoped was a mollifying smile, although her tone did not suggest she was likely to be easily mollified. "Through kind eyes."

It was not the correct answer. "And is that," she demanded, "how you see me? *Kindly?*"

"God no. Of course not."

"Oh, oh." She gazed at him with an expression of mock incredulity. "So you are capable of perfect clarity, whereas I am partial and compromised?"

"What? No. That's not what I—"

She gave him the lightest of pushes. "Where is your logic now?"

"At your feet, clearly. As I am."

There was a long silence, Gracewood wondering quite how badly he had handled this whole situation. And then she smiled, one of her wildest, brightest, most reckless smiles. "I'll wear your damn jewels."

"Are you sure? I have no wish to—"

"I want to. I'm not afraid. Nor"—her eyes were still upon his—"will I let myself be ashamed for desiring beautiful things."

Taking his hand, she brought it to her lips and pressed a swift, hard kiss to the underside of his wrist. And when he glanced down, he saw upon the skin between his cuff and his glove a mark in the shape of her mouth, red-pink, and softly shining from the rose-coloured salve she favoured.

It made him feel claimed. Promised. Reassured. Seen—in ways he still could not see himself—as someone better than he had ever believed he could be.

# CHAPTER 29

The ball, needless to say, was a great success. Or at least it was shockingly well attended, though whether that was support or vulgar curiosity at the Duke of Gracewood's sudden return from Northumberland—and whether it mattered—Viola wasn't sure. Mira, despite some visible nerves at the beginning of the evening, soon seemed to be genuinely enjoying herself, her dance card filling up in a matter of minutes. That she was rich everyone already knew. That she was beautiful they recognised immediately. That she was declared an *original* could have been a consequence of the first two, but Viola was inclined to doubt it.

"Half the men dancing with her look like they don't know which way's up," observed Lady Lillimere, resplendent in maroon velvet. "Can't say I blame them."

Viola gave her a sharp look. "What's that supposed to mean?"

"I'm rather offended you think I'd seduce a child, so I'm attributing it to your wild jealousy that I made a positive comment about another woman."

The notion that she should, or could, be jealous rather rankled Viola. But then it was supposed to. "She's not a child. And have you not made a point of claiming for yourself all the vices usually reserved for men?"

"Yes, but I have some standards." Lady Lillimere's lip curled. "I've no idea what could possibly produce a creature like Miranda—"

"A grand and a noble family?" asked Viola, earning a snort of laughter.

"More like six wild unicorns, a rose that blooms only at midnight, and three barrels of skydust. My point is, she's...who she is, and I have absolutely no wish to ruin her."

Since their meeting, Viola had learned a lot more about Lady Lillimere. Or at least, her reputation, and her reputation with women in particular. It made her growing closeness with Miranda complicated in ways any chaperone ought to be conscious of. "And yet you spend such a lot of time together."

"Christ, woman. Because Louise asked it of me. She said I was to show her the sights, keep her from getting bored, that kind of thing."

Viola blinked. "L-Lady Marleigh did?"

"Yes. She trusts me. And"—Lady Lillimere scowled, as she was wont to do when forced into sincerity—"she's my best friend. I would sooner pluck out my eyes than lose her good opinion."

It was a sentiment Viola shared. "I...I'm sorry for—"

"Oh, hush." Lady Lillimere waved a weary hand. "Apologies bore me almost as much as declarations of love."

Before Viola had a chance to answer, they were interrupted by Lady Marleigh herself. She had the dark-eyed, frantic look of someone who has spent several weeks organising a ball. "This is an outrage" were the first words out of her mouth. "Absolutely unacceptable. Hello, by the way."

"What's the matter?" asked Viola, somewhat alarmed.

"Amberglass is here. Amberglass. *Here.* How *dare* he."

Lady Lillimere looked askance. "You didn't invite him?"

"Of course I didn't invite him," retorted Lady Marleigh. "I'm not a goosewit. He came with his stupid friend who is stupid for being friends with him."

"Viscount Stirling?"

"Yes. He's been taken with Mira since my little card party. And he's a good suitor for her."

"A good suitor?" Lady Lillimere's heavy-lidded eyes bestirred themselves to widen. "He's so boring."

"Some women value that. Especially in a husband."

"Well, you would know, darling."

Lady Marleigh gave a shocked little gasp. "No, I wouldn't. Badger's the most amusing person I've ever met. But my husband isn't the issue. Amberglass is the issue. The nerve of the fellow. I should have him thrown to the dogs."

"We don't have any dogs," Viola pointed out.

"If I'd known he'd inveigle his way in here, I'd have taken the precaution of acquiring some."

Viola glanced between Louise and Lady Lillimere—the former was practically vibrating with fury and the latter looked uncharacteristically grave. "What...who...is this Amberglass?"

"The Duke of Amberglass," Lady Lillimere explained. "Mira is dancing with him as we speak."

There was nothing, as far as Viola could tell, particularly exceptional about Miranda's current partner. He dressed well, moved with grace, and—if Mira's smiles were anything to go by—was pleasant company.

"Is he a rake, then?" she asked. "Or a fortune hunter?"

"Yes. No. Well...sort of?" Lady Marleigh wrung her hands. "I don't know how to...He..."

In the end it was Lady Lillimere who finished the thought: "He is a beast who destroys for neither necessity nor pleasure."

"While still being received almost everywhere," added Lady

Marleigh bitterly, "because he has a lot of money and a title, and that makes him a matrimonial prize."

Viola's eyes flicked anxiously to the dancers—but, once again, there was nothing to see except a perfectly ordinary couple interacting in perfectly ordinary ways. "Even though his behaviour is so very beyond the pale?"

"That's the thing with men like Amberglass." The set of Lady Marleigh's mouth was grim. "Their behaviour is never your concern. Until it is."

"You sound"—Viola tried to keep the question delicate—"as though you speak from experience."

Lady Marleigh shrugged. "I suppose we were...friends? Once upon a time. Before Badger, naturally."

Whatever Viola had been expecting, this was not it. "You were friends?"

"Well...he has a way about him. He can make you feel understood, when he cares to. Or perhaps he just likes to give you what you need so he can take it away again."

"For what it's worth," offered Lady Lillimere, with unusual gentleness, "I always thought he cared for you. As much as someone like that can."

"Perhaps. Perhaps not." Lady Marleigh sighed. "Though he very nearly put me off marriage entirely. I had no notion why any woman with options to the contrary would voluntarily enter a state in which, you know, *that* was a regular duty."

A steel claw of rage scraped the length of Viola's spine. "Did he hurt you?"

"No. I mean, no more than could be expected, given my inexperience and uncertain arousal. It was how he looked at me while we were...engaged. There was this blankness in his eyes, as though I disgusted him."

Lady Lillimere threw an arm out so violently, she nearly toppled a passing dowager. "Men. Only men. They complain if you aren't fucking them. They complain if you are. And in his case particularly it makes no bloody sense. Fellow's a libertine. A notorious seducer."

"Well, maybe it was me?" said Lady Marleigh in a small voice. "I didn't know what I was doing and I'm not...not very pretty, really? Except to Badger. I remember being quite surprised, even at the time, he wanted to seduce someone like me at all. Amberglass, I mean. Not Badger. I'm very clear on the subject when it comes to Badger."

"Do you think he did it to...to shame you?" Viola wondered. "Or dishonour your family?"

"I honestly have no idea. I told him afterwards it was terrible and I never wanted to do anything like that again."

"I can see why that might have compromised your friendship."

But Lady Marleigh shook her head. "That's the thing, he laughed. And asked me to marry him. Though, of course, by then I didn't want to do that with him either. Thankfully"—and here she brightened—"I later met Badger, who changed my mind on a number of important matters."

Lady Lillimere pressed a hand to her heart. "I do love a happy ending. But"—her tone grew sharp again—"what about Mira? I don't like the idea of a man like that getting his hooks into her. For all you deemed him worthy of your friendship once, Louise, he displays little merit these days."

"I'm still not sure we can have him thrown out." Viola's gaze collided with Lady Lillimere's as they searched the ballroom for

Miranda—her gown its own gleam among the candles. "It would cause quite the scene."

Lady Lillimere nodded. "And probably play right into his hands. It's been more years than I care to remember since I was Mira's age, but I do know how much I liked things simply because my parents didn't." She paused. "And I haven't shaken the habit, if I'm honest."

Before they had a chance to devise a plan of action, the music ceased, bringing the dance to its end.

"If he tries to take her onto the terrace," muttered Lady Marleigh, glaring across the ballroom, "he will wish we had dogs."

Lady Lillimere raised her brows. "Cry havoc indeed."

Though as it happened, the Duke of Amberglass tried nothing of the sort, choosing instead to lead his partner back to her guardians quite properly. Viola was relieved to note that Miranda looked much as she usually did—neither conspicuously wounded nor enamoured. And, as for Amberglass, she rather resented her own curiosity there. It felt as if she was granting him power he did not deserve to possess.

But Lady Marleigh was right. He possessed *something*, some quality of his own, that seemed too elusive for beauty, too edged for charm, and, occasionally, seemed like nothing at all. For he had also mastered the art of making himself unremarkable. Just a slight, grey-eyed man, with a ducal signet upon his finger.

"I have too grieved a heart," he murmured, bowing politely over Mira's hand, "to take a tedious leave."

Perhaps it was Viola's imagination, but she thought she caught the flash of his gaze. Except then he was turning. About to vanish into the crowds.

"Thus losers part," said Miranda.

He paused at that, glancing back. "Pardon?"

"It's…it's the next line. Isn't it?"

"Ah. So it is." The pale blade of his mouth twisted upwards slightly. "Be careful who you follow, madam. You might not like where you're led. Thank you again for the dance."

And then he really was gone, leaving Miranda somewhat perplexed and Lady Marleigh holding the pieces of the fan she'd just snapped. "Auntie Lou!" cried Miranda, "Are you all right? What happened to your fan?"

"I…" Lady Marleigh blinked down at the wooden wreckage in her hands. "It's nothing. I'm fine."

This did not seem to convince Miranda. "I can only speak for myself, but I do not, in general, break things when I'm fine."

"She doesn't like Amberglass," put in Lady Lillimere, "and she's worried telling you will make you like him more."

Miranda tilted her head in visible confusion. "Why would she believe I'd think well of someone on that basis?"

"Novels." Somehow Lady Marleigh contrived to make the word sound deeply ominous. "They teach us to make heroes from villains."

"Is the Duke of Amberglass a villain then?" asked Mira, with far too much interest. "I've never met a villain before. But I suppose that's because I've barely met anyone."

Louise unleashed a despairing sigh. "You see? Now I've gone and made him all intriguing. I wish you hadn't agreed to dance with him."

"Oh, I didn't. I was supposed to be dancing with Viscount Stirling again, but His Grace…sort of…I don't know…interceded somehow."

"And the Viscount just let another man usurp him like that?" demanded Lady Marleigh.

"It was a little odd," Mira conceded. "But I don't think it was entirely the Viscount's fault. The Duke was so very...he was laughing, but neither of us quite knew how to cross him. Oh! Is this why he's a villain?"

"He's a villain"—that was Lady Lillimere—"because I cannot think of a single person involved with him who has not been damaged by the experience. He cares for nothing but his own appetites, whatever they may be."

"An appetite for claiming dances that aren't his?" suggested Viola.

This raised a small, and perhaps needed, laugh.

But Lady Marleigh remained uncharacteristically anxious. "You won't encourage him, will you, Mira? I know it's wrong of me to ask, and if you really like him, I don't think I can stop you, but—"

"I neither liked nor disliked him." Miranda took one of Louise's hands gently between her own. "But I am certainly disinclined to pursue acquaintance with someone who makes you so uncomfortable."

"He can be very charming. Probably he will make you feel quite special."

"I already feel quite special. You brought me to London, didn't you? And made Justin hold this ball for me."

"Yes, but"—Lady Marleigh's eyes darted nervously to the ceiling and back to Mira—"he will make you feel special in a very specific way that ladies commonly experience in the company of gentlemen."

Another of Miranda's interested head tilts. "What does that mean?"

"With his eyes," explained Lady Marleigh, perhaps less coherently than she imagined. "And the shape of his lips. And your stomach will fizz like you drank an entire glass of champagne without stopping. Alongside some other effects I can't talk about in public."

There was a pause.

"Oh." Mira blinked rapidly. "And that is...commonly experienced in the company of gentlemen?"

And Viola saw Lady Lillimere open her mouth, then close it again.

"In any case," Mira continued, "I don't think I am particularly interested in the Duke of Amberglass, even if he is a villain."

It looked like Lady Marleigh was going to fret the remains of her fan to splinters, so Viola took it away from her, giving the pieces to a passing footman, and did her best to turn the conversation down less fraught channels. "Are you enjoying your evening, Mira?"

"Yes indeed." She nodded vigorously. "Very much. Only..."

"Only?"

"Only...well. Perhaps I'm being foolish, but I feel I've met such a lot of gentlemen. How does one get introduced to ladies?"

That—rather than her fanless hands—claimed Lady Marleigh's attention. "What about Miss Avon? You met her at the card party. I'm sure you could seek out her company."

Miranda's head drooped like a frost-struck snowdrop. "I think I must have offended her."

"Really? I thought she was perfectly civil when we spoke earlier this evening."

"She said my gown was a bold choice."

"Well"—Lady Marleigh gave a little shrug—"it is rather. But you didn't want white or pink. And there is no power on earth that would have made me agree to red."

"I know. But it was the way she said it. And when I turned away, she whispered something to her friends and they all started laughing."

It was at this juncture that Gracewood joined them, which at the very least saved the group from a bleak conversation about the cruelties of the ton.

He was accompanied by another gentleman—a rather stately young man with a long, serious face—and a lady of about Miranda's age who Viola quickly recognised as Miss St. Clair, which meant the man was probably her brother, Augustus St. Clair. She would have placed them both more quickly, but truthfully, there had been a moment, perhaps more than a moment, when all she could see was Gracewood.

He had been so many people to her down the years. From childhood friend to comrade-in-arms to whatever they were to each other now. She had seen him made foolish on wine stolen from his father's cellar, laughing as they rode together along the beaches of Morgencald, rain-soaked and ragged and grey as they marched from Quatre-Bras.

But he was still the Duke of Gracewood, bearer of an ancient name, with wealth enough to fulfil the dreams of kings, and never more so than among his peers. It was who he had been created to be, fashioned by centuries and cruelty, and not even the cane in his hand, or the slight ungainliness of his gait, could diminish it. He was a man of gold and shadows in his eveningwear, as refined as the power he wielded. Beautiful and impossible and...he wanted her. Viola Carroll. A woman who was quite literally nobody.

Nobody but herself.

"Miranda," Gracewood said, "may I introduce Augustus St. Clair to you?"

She considered this. "I don't know? Can you?"

"I would very much like to." Gracewood's lips were twitching. "St. Clair, this is my sister, Lady Miranda."

Mr. St. Clair executed a very proper bow. "It is my pleasure, Lady Miranda. And may I in turn present my own sister, who I believe was not formally introduced at your recent event."

"I'm Lydia," said the young woman at his side, a little flatly.

Her brother seemed to be unaware that he was squeezing the bridge of his nose despairingly. "Lydia, please, this is the Duke of Gracewood's sister. Be civil."

"I *am* being civil." She turned large and imploring eyes on her brother. "I just—these matters are complicated."

"Because you're friends with Miss Avon?" asked Miranda, a little hurt.

Miss St. Clair nodded. "There are rules, you see. And one must pick sides."

"Don't talk rot, Lydia," said Augustus St. Clair. "You're alienating the duke's sister."

Lady Lillimere gave him a withering look. "Sadly, she isn't talking *rot* at all. You gentlemen are a prized commodity, and competition for you is cutthroat. Miss Avon might be an odious little social climber, but that's because odious social climbing is rather her job."

"Am I expected to odiously social climb?" asked Miranda, somewhat aghast.

"As a duke's sister," explained Lady Lillimere, "you have nowhere *to* climb unless you fancy seducing the Prince Regent. No, my dear, I'm afraid your purpose is odious social *maintenance*. It is your sacred duty to make certain that the Miss Avons of the world die in gutters for looking above themselves."

Clapping her hands to her mouth in a gesture that Viola thought a little melodramatic, Miranda gasped. "I have no wish to see Miss Avon suffer at all."

Lady Lillimere gave a louche shrug. "But the world does, and it will make you its instrument whether you will it or no."

"Oh, that's ghastly." Miranda's eyes were wide with shock.

"It's a ghastly world," replied Lady Lillimere.

Miss St. Clair looked down. "So you can see why we can't quite be friends. It would be simply unnavigable."

Miranda seemed crestfallen. "Yes, yes, I suppose so."

"Might I suggest," offered Lady Lillimere, "that in order to avoid creating an impossible situation for everybody, Miss St. Clair acknowledges right now that Miranda is a perfectly pleasant young lady once you get to know her, and then she scurries back to Miss Avon to gossip about what a terrible provincial scrot she is, and nobody will be any the wiser."

Lydia gave a small skip, curls and bosoms bouncing. "Yes, that sounds like an excellent idea."

"And you really shan't think so unkindly of me?" asked Miranda, plaintively.

"Oh no." Miss St. Clair beamed. "In another world, I think we could be quite good friends."

"I should like that very much. But if you will excuse me, I think I am engaged to dance with"—a quick check of her card—"Lord...dear me...that could say anything. Lord Wankerbunk?"

"Winterbank," murmured Gracewood, with a valiant attempt at solemnity.

"I can at least," said Miss St. Clair, "escort you to find the gentleman. Then I can tell Miss Avon how awful you were on the way back."

They were gone without another word, a ripple of sunshine yellow and strawberry pink, skimming across the surface of every mirror they passed.

"I am not sure," said Augustus St. Clair, "if I need to thank you or apologise."

Gracewood put a reassuring hand on his shoulder. "Neither. But if you would like to avail yourself of the brandy in my library, you would be most welcome."

"I…" For a split second, the young man looked tempted. "No. But thank you. I should not stoop to spirits. I am trying to set an example for Lydia."

"Do you really think that's wise?" asked Lady Marleigh.

Augustus frowned. "I believe it is usual. I am, after all, the elder sibling and thus responsible for my sister's moral education."

There was the sort of silence that usually ensued when Lady Marleigh wanted to say something but was trying very hard not to. She was just opening her mouth when Gracewood said, somewhat hastily, "How is Lady Beatrice?"

"In good health, I thank you," returned the other gentleman.

"I am sorry she was not able to come tonight."

"Oh w-well." A dark flush travelled down Augustus's neck. "She felt it might not be appropriate. A coming-out ball, and Lady Miranda the daughter of a duke."

"Lady Beatrice is also the daughter of a duke."

Now Augustus's cravat seemed to be throttling him. "Yes, but…"

"Please assure her"—Gracewood's eyes were frost—"that she is always welcome in my home."

"Of course." Augustus sketched a shaky bow.

"And now, if you will forgive me, I must ensure my sister has found Lord Winterbank." The gentlemen took their leave, and Viola tried to remember if London had always felt this way—a world of mercurial tides and hidden currents. Probably it had, but she had been too lost within her own secrets to care.

"I don't think I have the slightest understanding of what just transpired," she admitted. "Who is Lady Beatrice to Mr. St. Clair?"

"His mistress. His wife is"—Lady Lillimere gestured with a discreet motion of her fan—"dancing with her lover."

"As are several wives. And several husbands."

Lady Lillimere nodded. "Indeed. But the St. Clairs are more open in their alliances than most. And Lady Beatrice is not herself married. I don't quite know the history. Jilted, I think. Though who would jilt a duke's daughter?"

"Loubear?" Badger was determinedly pushing his way through the crowds to join them. "I saw you'd taken against your fan, so I brought you another." He handed her a new one with a proud flourish. "And I was wondering if I could tempt you into something a little unseemly."

Lady Marleigh looked a little startled. "At a ball?"

"Not *that* unseemly," he clarified quickly. "I was wondering if you'd like to dance with me."

"Oh, Badger"—Louise paused to control her laughter—"what are you talking about? Nobody dances with their spouse."

"Yes, but nobody else is married to you."

"Well. No. Because that would be bigamy, which is a crime. Also why would I want to be married to more than one person? I'm quite happy as we are."

He gazed at her, with none of his usual vagueness. Just those absurd blue-purple eyes and the smile he smiled only for his wife. "Then dance with me, Loubear. I refuse to spend another moment in the company of people I like less than you."

"Oh, very well then." Visibly flustered, and more than a little pleased, Lady Marleigh slid her hand into the crook of Badger's arm. And then they, too, departed—moving among the dancers to take their place in the next quadrille.

"Woe is you," murmured Lady Lillimere to Viola. "Abandoned in the company of a renowned defiler of innocents."

"Then"—Viola gave her what she hoped was an arch look—"I am quite safe, for I am no innocent."

Lady Lillimere just gave an indulgent, too-knowing chuckle. "So you wish."

And for all she tried to come up with a sharp retort, Viola was caught by a blush.

"Will you come to supper with me?" asked Lady Lillimere instead.

It was a mercy as undeserved as it was, in that moment, necessary. And Viola smiled and nodded and tried not to think of everything she yearned for and yet feared to know. "I would love to."

# CHAPTER 30

The ball passed, much as Viola had expected it to, with strange timelessness, hours turned fluid as mercury in the candle gleam. The last guests, the most stubbornly lingering, departed just before sunrise. Mira, incoherent with exhaustion and swaying slightly on her feet, had retired, at Gracewood's insistence, somewhat earlier. As for Lady Marleigh, Badger had discovered her fast asleep behind a curtain and carried her away to bed.

Which left Viola and Gracewood in the petal-strewn ballroom, caught between the remains of the evening and the beginning of the day. The dawn was not gentle to Gracewood, his eyes shadowed by lack of sleep, the pain lines at their edges scored knife-point deep.

"You should rest too," Viola told him.

"I know." His knuckles were white upon his cane. His arm shaking slightly. His shoulders too tense with the effort of keeping his back straight.

Tentatively, she put a hand upon his wrist, not sure if her intent was to support or to soothe, or merely to touch. "Are you all right, Gracewood?"

"Tonight was…" His jaw tightened, as if he wanted to hold back his words. And then he finished anyway. "Difficult."

"Good Lord, it was *exhausting*."

He gave a brief nod, but his gaze was distracted, travelling around the ballroom as if he barely recognised it. In profile, he was pure de Vere, all stark lines and autocracy. "We often used to attend events like these."

"When we could not avoid it, certainly."

"I do not remember them being quite so..." His voice faded away.

"You had a personal stake in this one," Viola offered. "This is your house. Miranda is your sister. It is not so very surprising that it felt different."

"Yes, but..." Yet again, he seemed to stop himself. Though, for all his weariness, there was something a little frantic in his eyes when he looked back at her. "I think I must simply have grown unaccustomed to crowds."

"There was an impressive turnout. Everyone wanted to admire Miranda."

His mouth curled up wryly. "And find out what became of her brother."

"You both acquitted yourselves well."

Plucking her hand from where it still rested upon his wrist, he brought it to his lips. "Someday," he said softly, "they will see through my semblance. And several times I thought it might be tonight."

"You are no semblance, Gracewood."

"Am I not? What would the world call a man who sees a red dress and half imagines it a soldier's coat? A man who feels the brush of a stranger's shoulder and half believes himself back in the gun line? A man who cannot distinguish the press of a crowd from the press of battle?"

"I don't care what the world would call such a man," she told him fiercely. "I would call him my friend. And I would say he has faced terrible things without looking away."

"Oh, Viola." He drew her in then, and she let herself be drawn. "I have never deserved you."

She could have kissed him with the barest of movements. But she didn't. In that moment it was enough simply to look at him, his eyes level with hers, and so close she could see the striations, as intricate as lace, in the pristine blue of his irises. "I'm not sure I like the idea of being deserved. But I have only ever seen your strength, Gracewood. I watched for years as you fought to be the man you knew you should be. And that gave me courage when it was time for me to fight for myself."

He smiled at that, although it was a sad smile, a regretful one. "Some strength it is," he said half-rueful, "when I come to a ball and cannot even dance. Not even with the woman I would dance with until the end of time if she would let me."

And Viola tried to smile back, through the quiet ripple of her own sadness. For she too would likely never dance again. Even if an occasion arose on which a lady's companion might be required to make a set by standing up with a respectable gentleman, she doubted she would have been able to. While she had, in private, practised the appropriate part, she did not know she could perform it correctly. Certainly not with a stranger, who might begin to wonder things she would not have him wonder and ask questions she would not have him ask.

"You are my everything," she said. "You know I do not need you to dance with me."

"No, but God help me, I want to." Again, his eyes closed, but not before she saw the yearning in them, a shadow of pain as blue as the jewels in her choker. "And I must be losing my mind because I never cared much for dancing."

"I remember. I think you called it pleasantries put to music."

His mouth twisted in a self-mocking smile. "I did. And yet now my heart is as good as breaking because I cannot do it with you. Even if the ton would stand it, my leg will not."

"Strange," she said, trying to make him laugh, "that you would want to share with me something you don't enjoy."

"And yet all I could think of, all these damnable hours, was being able to take you in my arms and whirl you away." Lifting his free hand, he curved his palm beneath her jaw, and for once her own blunt angles did not trouble her because she fit him perfectly. "You are always so beautiful in motion. As wild as the sky in winter."

She made an uncertain sound, pleased and abashed, and slightly overwhelmed. Embarrassed to be so susceptible to what was surely little more than courtesy. Except then she saw again how tired he was. How full of pain. And she realised this was not flattery. No polished seduction. Just words, peeled from his heart, offered to her because he believed them.

"It is absolutely impossible?" she asked. "Your leg..."

"Will barely support my own weight. I could not trust myself with both of us."

Turning slightly, she kissed his hand. "Can you trust me?"

"With my life."

"Just with a dance," she told him, smiling.

His answering smile was still not particularly happy. "Viola, there is no need to indulge me."

"It's not a matter of need. It's a matter of...of...pleasure."

"Of pleasure?" The question hung there between them, half-quizzical, half-hopeful.

"Yes. Mine. Is it not my prerogative to indulge you? If I wish?"

"I'm sure there is something I should say, but I doubt I have sufficient faculties to debate this."

She lifted her brows wickedly at him. "You said you wanted to dance. You didn't say anything about debating with me."

"And if we end up in a heap on the floor?"

"Then we will be in a heap on the floor together."

Very slowly he released his cane, which fell with a clatter. He staggered a moment and then clutched at her. Immediately she slid an arm around his waist, steadying them both, and he let out a rough breath that was almost a gasp.

"So far," she said, "no heap."

He laughed, though that too was a little shaky. Sweat gleamed at his temples. "I'm sorry I'm such a coward."

"I'm attributing that nonsense to your temporary lack of faculties. Here..." She took his hand and drew it into a better position. "How's that?"

"I...I don't want to hurt you."

"Gracewood"—she could not help the sharpness of her tone—"we used to wrestle and fight with swords. You think because I'm a woman I am suddenly weak?"

"God. Never."

She lifted her other arm and his came up to join hers, clasped hands meeting gracefully above their heads. They were closer than perhaps would have been proper, even for a waltz, but what did it matter? There was only the two of them to see. And Viola welcomed the intimacy of it, the way they held each other, though she bore some of Gracewood's weight. He was lighter than she remembered, thinner beneath his beautifully tailored eveningwear—not enough to make her anxious for him, but enough to remind her that time had passed. That they were neither of them entirely who they used to be. And that, while he would always be her friend, Viola Carroll's Gracewood was a man more beautiful, more vulnerable, and more complicated than she could have known before.

"Do you think you can move with me?" she asked him.

His mouth quirked with amusement. "As long as you don't expect me to jeté."

"Slow waltz only." And, in that moment, it did not feel like any sort of compromise. It felt like something at once old and new, strong and tender. It felt like a beginning.

Slow, as it turned out, was accurate. Waltz was...less so. But still, they continued. Turning together through the silence and the flower petals, upon the floor, which had long since lost its polish. While in the endless horizon of the ballroom mirrors Viola would occasionally catch glimpses of a handsome man and a woman in a blue dress.

And it was strange because it could have been anyone. Any couple reflected there. But it wasn't.

It was the Duke of Gracewood and Viola Carroll.

And they were dancing.

# CHAPTER 31

She had danced with Gracewood last night.

And yes, neither of them had been as young as once they were, and yes, he had not moved with the grace he had once been capable of, but for a moment, for that private, frozen eternity in the ballroom, she had let herself live in a dream. In a world where a lady's companion could dance with a duke, could be loved by a duke, could even, perhaps, marry a duke.

The dawn had done its best to chase away such girlish fancies, but throughout the day Viola had been waltzing through life like a princess in a fairy tale. She had been so distracted that Miranda had been concerned she might be ill.

"No, no, I'm quite well," she said, sitting down and taking up her needlepoint. Not that she had quite the wherewithal to begin working on it. "It's just—I danced with your brother last night."

Miranda gave a little gasp. "Oh, Viola, was it—did you—was it wonderful?"

Yes. Yes, it was wonderful. It was so wonderful that not knowing if it would happen again was almost more than Viola could bear. "It was...it was very nice."

"Oh." Miranda looked away. "And is Justin—that is, do you think he is happy when he is with you?"

"I don't know." And this much was true. She thought so, but her private fears would never quite let her believe it. "I think he is happy in general, now. He has come to London. He is—he is spending more time with you."

"I am not sure that makes him happy."

"It does. I know it does." She wished there was more that she could say, but she continued to hold out hope that all Gracewood and Miranda needed was time.

Before either Miranda or Viola could say more, a footman entered, announcing that Miss Avon, Miss St. Clair, and Miss Hanbury had arrived to visit Lady Miranda. The two women exchanged puzzled glances, neither entirely sure what the complicated Miss Avon and her still more complicated friends might want, calling on Miranda so soon after spurning her at the ball.

Still, Miranda asked that they be sent up, and the footman dutifully showed them through to the yellow drawing room. There they stood beside one another like a very demure chorus line.

"Lady Miranda." Miss Avon bobbed a curtsey. "I have come to apologise."

Viola eyed Miss Avon suspiciously, but Miranda smiled warmly and said, "That is very kind of you."

"I am truly sorry," Miss Avon said in the polished tones of one who had been raised to treat social niceties as being every bit as important as food and water, "for having behaved so shabbily towards you on our last two meetings. Will you think very ill of me if I confess to having found you a trifle intimidating?"

"Me?" Miranda looked shocked and perhaps a little flattered.

"Come, Lady Miranda." There was something about Miss Avon's smile that Viola disliked, but perhaps it was just her instinct to protect Gracewood's sister coming into play. "You are *so* pretty, and so very remarkable in your accomplishments, I quite despaired of keeping pace with you."

"It's true," added Miss Hanbury. "She's fearfully lacking in the realm of accomplishments. Plays the pianoforte hardly at all, and sings very ill indeed."

"Even so," Miss Avon continued smoothly, "I misjudged you and behaved poorly to you. I hope that you can forgive me, and I hope that we shall be friends."

If there was a magical incantation designed to make Miranda giddy with joy, it was the phrase *I hope we shall be friends*. And Viola couldn't begrudge her, for what would she have given at Miranda's age to be so accepted? What would she have been if not for Gracewood?

"Then it is settled." Miranda rose to her feet and went forward to take the hands of her guests. "We are friends from this day forth."

"And we shall have such fun," agreed Miss Avon. "I shall show you all the sights of London."

"The interesting ones, at least," added Miss Hanbury.

"I've seen some of the interesting ones," Miranda said before Viola could check her. "Only I found the Tower of London very disappointing, and I was so disheartened not to see Mr. Davy's new lamp."

For the briefest of moments, a wolfish look flashed across Miss Avon's face, but then it was gone. "How sad for you," she said with unimpeachable sincerity. "But I'm sure we will find some diversions you have yet to experience."

"That is likely," agreed Miranda. "I've seen very little of the city. Why, I have yet even to visit Vauxhall Gardens."

"Then we shall take you." The confidence in Miss Avon's voice was a thing to hear, and Viola quite envied it. "And you must call on me as soon as you are able in order that I may return your kind hospitality."

"Oh!" Miranda seemed suddenly aghast. "But I have been quite remiss in that regard. Please do sit, and I shall send for tea at once."

So they sat and tea was sent for, and—feeling only a slight twinge of resentment—Viola found herself not exiled, exactly, but obliged by social necessity to retreat to a discreet corner and observe silently.

Miranda, whose education had been lacking but not nearly as lacking as Viola's, poured tea with adequate grace and engaged her new friends in polite conversation about the ball. It skewed, as conversation among young ladies often did, in the direction of the gentlemen they had danced with and their various merits and disadvantages.

"Oh, yes," asked Miss St. Clair with what, from Viola's limited perspective, seemed genuine curiosity, "how was Lord Wankerbunk?"

"Lord Winterbank was very…" Miranda paused, searching for the right word. "Attentive."

Miss Hanbury winced. "Ooh, the *attentive* ones can be awful. Which parts of you was he attentive to in particular?"

This seemed to throw Miranda. "All of me, I suppose. I just mean he was very solicitous of my welfare."

"Ah," said Miss St. Clair. "That's not the kind of attentiveness I usually get. I usually get gentlemen paying very close attention to my bosoms."

Miss Avon took a sip of tea. "In my experience, Lord Winterbank is very kind but very dull."

"But very attentive," agreed Miranda.

"Oh yes." With a little clatter, Miss Avon set her teacup down. "Are you certain you are well, Miss Avon? Are you *quite* certain,

Miss Avon? If your feet are growing tired, Miss Avon, we can sit, Miss Avon."

Miranda giggled at that, and the atmosphere in the room relaxed noticeably.

"What of the Viscount Stirling?" asked Miss Hanbury. "He seemed very taken with you last night and at the card party."

"And he's very dashing," added Miss St. Clair. "In a stern sort of way. I could see him being quite the suitor if you find that sort of thing attractive."

This left Miranda looking confused. "I'm not quite sure yet *what* sort of thing I find attractive."

"Oh, it's very simple," explained Miss St. Clair. "There really aren't that many types of gentlemen to choose from. You have dour ones, dandyish ones, rakes, soldiers, and everybody else."

"And you avoid rakes and soldiers," added Miss Avon, "because neither will marry you save for your fortune. Which is quite the wrong sort of arrangement to be in."

Miss Hanbury nodded. "It's like Mr. Johnson said about writing: no woman but a blockhead ever married except for money."

They all laughed at that, although Miranda's laughter was perhaps a little behind the rest.

"And are gentlemen," she asked, "the only possibility?"

An expression of exaggerated shock crossed Miss Avon's face. "Oh, but Lady Miranda, you must not say such wicked things. You shall wind up like Lady Lillimere."

"Lady Lillimere has been very kind to me," replied Miranda, a little defensively. "And I do not see she has so very bad a life."

"I'm sure her life is very pleasant." Miss Avon took another sip of tea. "But pleasant is not the same as respectable."

"Not," added Miss Hanbury, "that one always has to be *entirely* respectable."

Miss St. Clair put a hand to her significant bosom. "I believe if I had Lady Lillimere's money, I would cheerfully tell respectability to go hang."

They continued to chatter in this vein for a little while, and after a decorous amount of time had passed, the visitors departed, making promises of future intimacy. Miss St. Clair, Viola noted, was strangely quiet during the farewells. But then it must be difficult to speak up when Miss Avon was present, for she was clearly a force to be reckoned with and would be a formidable figure in society one day. Provided, of course, Lady Lillimere's predictions about Miranda causing her destruction proved unfounded.

On another day, in another time, or in another world, Viola might have been envious of these girls, with their talk of marriage and of the right and wrong sort of gentlemen. They would have reminded her too strongly of the life she knew was meant for her. The life she knew also she could never have. But last night, when the world had belonged only to the two of them, Viola Carroll had danced with the Duke of Gracewood. She had danced with the Duke of Gracewood, and now everything was different. After all, a lady who could dance with a duke might do anything.

# CHAPTER 32

A nd so I hope," concluded Viscount Stirling, who had been talking long enough it had hoarsened his voice, "you will look favourably upon my suit."

Gracewood tried not to think of his ledgers and the stack of correspondence requiring his attention. (Or of Viola, who would probably be curled in some corner with her embroidery.) "If you will forgive the question, how many times have you actually met my sister?"

"Four. Oh wait. Five. Yes, five, Your Grace."

The weeks after the ball had been a constant stream of visitors and tributes—including some turtle doves in a silver cage who had escaped and made the most tremendous mess of the green drawing room. So Gracewood probably should have anticipated...if not this exactly, something like it. "Five?" he repeated.

"Yes, My Lord. Once at the card party at Lady Marleigh's, once at her coming-out ball, again the next morning when I came to call, once in Hyde Park when she was with Lady Lillimere. And once at the opera."

"So, by *met* you, for the most part, mean...seen?"

"We have discoursed, My Lord."

"Oh good." Gracewood paused, wondering how to continue. "And these discourses have led you to the conclusion that you wish to spend your life with Mira?"

Viscount Stirling seemed—not that Gracewood accounted himself any sort of judge—a decent enough kind of man. Handsome, in a squarely symmetrical sort of way. Right now he was nodding sincerely. "She is a very charming young lady."

"And..." It was a shame this wasn't the sort of task Gracewood could delegate to Lady Marleigh. She would have known exactly how to handle it and would have had far more insight than he did into whether wanting to marry someone after barely meeting them five times was the sort of thing Mira might be inclined to do. He thought not. But she was far from the most predictable of creatures. "And Mira? She looks favourably upon...upon this?"

There was an unpleasant pause.

"I like to think," said the Viscount, somewhat stiffly, "I am too much of a gentleman to encroach upon a female without her guardian's consent."

"And yet I hope you would also secure the, ah, female's consent?"

Viscount Stirling flushed, seeming to feel he was being toyed with. "If it please Your Grace, what is this in aid of? Do you mean to tell me you will not give your blessing?"

"It's not—"

"Might I know upon what grounds? I am of good family with extensive holdings in Hertfordshire. Moreover, I am no libertine and will treat your sister with the respect she deserves. I fully intend to be the best of husbands, Your Grace."

God. Had Gracewood ever been so young? So impetuous and so tender? "I'm in no doubt you would," he said mildly. "But I am trying to..." Be a better brother? He could not say that aloud. "I have lately been reminded that ladies have preferences in these matters also."

"Nevertheless"—Viscount Stirling leaned forward intently—"she would be guided by you."

At this, Gracewood almost laughed aloud. "I take it you have no siblings?"

"I'm afraid I don't see how it's relevant."

"Only because, if you did, you would know for yourself that there are few things a sister desires less than an elder brother's guidance."

There was a pause. Viscount Stirling was looking at him with an expression of faint consternation. Gracewood could almost see the thought scrolling behind his eyes: *So they were right. He did run mad after the war.*

"You mean," he said finally, "you will not accept my suit."

"I will—"

The Viscount's eyes brightened.

"But only at Mira's behest." Gracewood offered what he hoped was an encouraging smile. "I'm afraid, if you wish to marry my sister, you will need to do something a little unusual and...ask her."

This idea seemed to enter the Viscount's mind but find no purchase there. "So I have your permission?"

Gracewood gave in. "Yes. Fine. You have my permission."

"Thank you, Your Grace. Thank you." And what relief there was in the Viscount's voice as he stood and made his farewells. Perhaps he had truly fallen in love with Miranda.

Perhaps she had fallen in love with him in return, though it was hard to imagine why she might. Then again, Gracewood did not wish to dwell too much on the qualities that drew women to men.

Viola was not mercenary enough to set much store by his title, his houses, his wealth. Which left him with what exactly to offer her? Scars and shaking hands. Sleepless nights. The spectre of opium that haunted him still. His friendship—for all that it had wavered once—would always be hers. And his heart was a caged bird that had never learned to fly.

His leg was already beginning to stiffen. London did not agree with it. Nor him, though neither did Morgencald, with its salt-toothed winds and ice-pick nights. But then it was not built to be a home—it was power, it was status, it was duty, and he should have felt no need for anything else.

Grasping his cane, he pushed himself upright and moved absently to the window. He was just in time to see the Viscount leaving, a spring in his step that Gracewood personally considered unwarranted.

Perhaps he should…warn Mira. He wasn't certain she was ready to receive spontaneous marriage proposals. Or perhaps she was? Perhaps she would see his concern as interference. Resting his head against the glass, he allowed himself a private sigh. How absurd it was—his utter bewilderment when it came to his own sister.

On the street below, the Viscount had fallen into company with the same gentleman who had come—uninvited—to the ball. Years ago, when Gracewood had been keeping company with Lady Beatrice, she had occasionally spoken of the Duke of Amberglass, though only ever obliquely for her profession did not reward indiscretion.

As a general rule Gracewood had little time for gossip, nor was it in his nature to condemn someone on the basis of idle speculation, but he trusted Bea and the rumours that swirled around Amberglass were grimy indeed. Thankfully, for all that the duke had danced with Mira, he had paid little heed to her, and Gracewood had not seen her display any especial interest in return.

The men themselves had long since gone. But Gracewood's misgivings—baseless though they likely were—remained with him for the rest of the afternoon. And might have for longer, but he was obliged to accompany Miranda to Vauxhall that evening and the general clamour of leaving the house with a large party drove most other thoughts from his head.

They made what he believed might be termed a lively gathering: Miranda, her new friends, Lady Marleigh, Lady Lillimere, and Viola too—in an evening gown of green silk net that glistened as she moved. And things only grew livelier as the night progressed, their box overspilling as they were joined by what felt like a ceaseless flood of their mutual acquaintances.

Still, it was better than the ball, because people came and went, rather than pressing upon him constantly, like walls within walls, and the noise of the throng was softened beneath the open sky and the surrounding greenery. Of course, opium would have softened it still further, but Gracewood discarded the thought as he might a rat that had crept beneath the wainscotting.

It was rather the nature of Vauxhall to encourage high spirits and certain informalities, something about the outdoor setting and the lanterns twinkling in the trees like multi-coloured stars. Gracewood was mostly just relieved to have a chair and for a chance to slip into relative irrelevancy—not an opportunity offered often to a duke. He was not completely safe from introductions or the occasional broad hint that some young lady's mother would enjoy it were he to accompany the young lady on a walk. But he always politely demurred. Let them think what they liked of him.

After all, they would anyway.

It must have been close to ten by the time they left their supper box, Miranda having expressed a desire to see the Cascade. The paths were busy—many of the guests apparently drawn to the same spectacle—and Gracewood slightly jostled, but they reached the wooded area near the Centre Cross Walk without incident. Or at the very least without him sprawling into the dirt from having put his cane upon a piece of uneven ground or tripped over a stranger's foot.

The Cascade itself, which included an illuminated scene of a waterfall and bridge, across which a variety coaches and figures passed, was well received.

"What a wonder," cried Miss St. Clair. "How is it managed, do you think?"

"By a series of mechanisms far too dull to trouble a lady with." This was Viscount Stirling, who had joined their company some time ago, though without his friend, Gracewood was relieved to note.

Miss St. Clair gave him a somewhat exasperated look. "If I was in danger of thinking it dull, I wouldn't have mentioned it."

"Is it not better," enquired the Viscount, "to allow beauty her power to enchant us? Rather than strip away her mysteries?"

"Hmm." The curtain had closed again across the Cascade, but it was only now that Miranda stepped back from it. "I believe it eminently possible to find some things beautiful even when we understand them."

"I am inclined to agree." Miss St. Clair's gaze grew somewhat challenging. "So explain it to us, if you please, My Lord?"

"Well." The Viscount gave a little cough. "It's all done with pipes and mirrors. And a pump, isn't it?"

There was a thoughtful pause.

"Where are the mirrors?" asked Miss St. Clair.

The Viscount tugged at his cravat. "There's always mirrors with these flummeries."

Another pause.

Miss Hanbury, who had so far been watching the conversation with an amused expression, folded her arms. "How would mirrors help?"

"They'd...reflect. Things that weren't there."

Yet another pause.

"How can a mirror reflect what isn't there?" asked Miss St. Clair, innocently.

Gracewood was about to put the young man out of his misery when Miranda spoke up. "I don't think it can be mirrors exactly." She glanced again at the curtain, her eyes narrowed. "But I think the effect could be achieved with...I'm not sure, I think perhaps tin sheets attached to a series of wheels?"

"Wheels?" repeated the Viscount. "What nonsense."

"Yes, wheels." Miranda nodded emphatically. "If perhaps a small amount of water were to come in at the top and then some men behind the scenes were to turn the wheels, then because the tin shines it would look like there's lots of water cascading down like a waterfall. When really it's just...wet metal."

The Viscount gave an indulgent laugh. "What a wonderful imagination you have, Lady Miranda."

And, once again, Gracewood would have said something, but Miss St. Clair was already talking. "It's amazing, isn't it? How easily things we thought might be interesting turn out to be just wet metal. Let's go back to the Orchestra."

"Yes, do let's," said Miss Avon, reaching out to take Miranda by the hand. And perhaps it was Gracewood's imagination but he thought he saw something pass between them as she did. A square of paper, folded small.

Still cautious of the ground, he moved over to where Viola was walking, her eyes very properly on the girls at all times.

"Did you see that?" he asked.

"Tin sheets, apparently," replied Viola with a smile.

He allowed himself to smile back, but not too much. This was a potentially serious situation. "No, I mean did you see what just happened between Miranda and Miss Avon?"

"I did not. But did she, perchance, slip her a piece of paper?"

Gracewood's eyes narrowed. "Do you mean to tell me you knew of this?"

"I suspect it has been going on some while."

"And you permitted it to continue?" For all his affection, Gracewood could not help but wonder if Viola had been the right choice of chaperone—she had always been the kind to encourage adventures rather than to curtail them. "What were you thinking?"

"That young people pass notes. We did it in school all the time."

Gracewood struck his cane down with a force that divoted the earth. "That was different."

"Was it?"

"This could compromise her," Gracewood insisted. The only role Miranda permitted him in her life was that of an abstract guardian. And even there he was failing her.

"She is beautiful and rich; a little compromise will do her no harm. Besides, for all her whimsies, she is a sensible girl. She does not write back. That *would* be scandalous. And in the event that she does run off with this nameless suitor—"

"You think it's a suitor?"

"Well, it's that or she's spying for the French. Honestly I suspect it's the Viscount Stirling. His attentions have been quite marked, and he looks like the kind of man who would express himself better in writing. Besides, the wonder of notes is that if there are any…complications, we will have a complete record of their correspondence."

"You don't think she's destroying the notes after she reads them?"

Viola laughed. "Miranda is an unusual girl, but not quite *that* unusual. I don't think she would ever destroy a love note. I kept every letter you ever sent me."

"I'm not sure I recall sending you any."

"You seldom had to. We were together most of the time." She gave a little shrug. "But there were occasions when I would be at Marleigh Court and you would be in Northumberland, and you would write me then, though you were always a rather terse correspondent."

It struck oddly against Gracewood's heart, this image of his old friend, sitting alone in her room, reading letters whose significance only she understood. "I did not realise."

"You did not realise," she asked with a lift of a brow, "that you were a terse correspondent?"

"I did not realise what our friendship must have cost you."

Just for a moment she reached out and laid her hand on his arm. "Oh, Gracewood, our friendship was the only part of my life that made sense. And I understood too little of myself to understand my feelings for you." Before Gracewood could reply, she looked ahead. "The other ladies are outpacing us, I fear I may have to run after them. Will you be all right?"

Gracewood nodded. "Go. Be a chaperone."

And so she went on, leaving Gracewood alone to navigate the rough ground and the darkness. And while he would have preferred not to be worrying about the possibility his sister might want to marry someone like Viscount Stirling, it did offer him a distraction from worrying about the ache in his leg and whether he was about to make a spectacle of himself in the middle of Vauxhall Gardens.

He was just allowing himself to conclude that he wasn't about to make a spectacle of himself in the middle of Vauxhall Gardens when he heard—

Guns.

He heard the guns.

Their deep, unmistakable rumble, like he was trapped in the belly of some great metal beast. And then the crackle of bullets like its own storm.

His breath snarled wire-sharp in his throat. Then tore out of him, filling his mouth with something sour and copper-tinged.

He was dreaming. He had to be dreaming. But he was awake.

And the sky was the colour of blood. Not real blood. Which clotted into mud and rust. But crimson and scarlet and cherry slick like someone had ripped open the heart of the world.

And made it shine hellfire bright.

Not dreaming. Dying. He had to be dying.

Or dead already, broken bones and ashes, in some mass grave on a ruined field in France.

No. No. He was—

At Vauxhall Gardens. Breathless. Shaking. The sweat running in torrents down his back.

And any moment now someone was going to see.

Everyone was going to see.

And know. They would all know.

The way fear festered inside him still. How the acts that made other men heroes had left his soul in tatters.

That he was broken. A coward. Unworthy of the name he bore.

The sky was yellow-gold and bilious. Dead men's eyes. And the guns. Came again. And again. And wouldn't stop. And he couldn't wake and couldn't die.

And—

"Gracewood." It was Viola's voice. From another life.

Her body was suddenly pressed to his.

As they had sheltered once in that wretched rain at Waterloo. He remembered the heat of her. A bridge from past to present.

"Please forgive me." Her voice came louder. Not meant for him this time. "But I've always been deathly afraid of fireworks. I...I think I feel a little faint."

Other voices. Impossible to hear across the gulf of time.

He pushed his face desperately against her hair. For a moment catching the scent of gardenia. Before it was lost to the acrid burn of powder in his nostrils. And the rotting-meat reek of the dying.

"Louise, you'll take care of Mira, won't you? Gracewood's kindly offered to take me home." She swayed. And, instinctively, he clutched at her. But her arm was already around him. Bearing the weight of them both.

Another memory. Churned from the charnel house of his mind.

A man and a woman dancing in a silent ballroom. Flowers on the ground and in her hair. Night-sky eyes on his. As familiar as his own reflection.

And he thought...he tried to believe...

That had once been real too.

# Chapter 33

The sky was still the colour of perdition. And the guns would never stop. But he could feel tree bark against his back. And Viola's hands—gloveless—against his face.

"Gracewood," she said. "You're...I...whatever you think is happening isn't happening."

"I..." His mouth hurt. He pressed his fingers to his lips, expecting blood and found none. "What...? Where...?"

"I don't know. It was the fireworks."

"No. No. I...I heard the guns."

She gazed at him, her expression calm but searching.

"Can't you?" he asked, horrified by the way his voice shook. Because which was worse? That she could, and they were back in France? Or that she couldn't, and he was truly mad?

"Gracewood." So soft. She sounded so impossibly soft in her certainty. "There are no guns. Only fireworks."

She would not lie to him. She had never lied to him. "Oh God. Oh God."

"It's all right. Please. I'm...I'm here. Whatever you feel, I'm here with you."

His whole body wrenched with nausea. Pushing her away, he landed heavily on hands and knees, and vomited up a thin stream of bile. It burned through him like acid. Made his eyes flood with tears. Not since the opium had left his system had he felt quite

this physically abject. As mentally ravaged and spiritually deso-
lated. "Oh God."

He could feel her palm against his back only by the weight of
it. All temperature, all texture, was lost in the sweat-sodden layers of his clothing.

"Don't look at me," he sobbed.

"It's nothing I haven't seen before. You were sick on my boots
once."

"Yes, but I didn't know then."

"Know what?"

"Who you were. How I felt about you."

"Gracewood. My dearest Gracewood." She knelt beside him,
producing a handkerchief from one of her many prettily embroidered reticules. "There is no vomit in the universe that could
drive me from your side."

He almost laughed. But did not dare. Was afraid how laughter might sound in the mouth of the deranged. "Viola, what is
wrong with me?"

"I...I don't know." And there was a sorrow in her voice that
almost sounded like fear.

"I heard them. I could smell it...the battlefield. I could
feel—" He stared down at his hands, curled helplessly into the
grass. Vauxhall's lamps had dappled them pink and yellow and
blue like stained glass. Except there were no cuts. No powder
burns. "I t-thought I was there," he finished. "Please believe me.
I was there."

"Of course I believe you." She helped him into a sitting position. "But you also know you're not there, don't you?"

He was starting to. The world had a peculiar thinness, like
the pages of a book stuck together, the text from one bleeding

into the next. Images of furrowed fields and heaped-up corpses still floated before him. But beyond them he could just about see Vauxhall again. A dimly lit grove that Viola had brought him to. Where she now knelt beside him. "I am unsound."

"You are not."

Now he did laugh. And it burst from him, just as rough and wild and maddened as he had feared. "Then explain *this*." He made an expansive gesture, trying to encompass not only his body but his whole being. "What is this if it is not the sign of a man who has lost his mind."

"I do not think it is a sign you have lost your mind," she said slowly. "I think it is a sign that you suffer."

"I served my country. I lived when many did not." He pressed knuckles over his mouth to contain another attack of that dreadful laughter. "I'm a fucking murderer. What right have I to suffer?"

She took his hands and kissed them, her mouth as insubstantial as moonlight against his skin. "Suffering isn't something we earn, Gracewood. It's something we bear."

In that moment, he would have given anything to believe her. To accept the benediction of her regard. But he would always feel the truth between them, like a bayonet through his spine. "It is my own cowardice I bear."

And still she did not pull away from him in revulsion. "Have you forgotten I fought at your side? You are no coward."

"Yet I am reduced to this. By...by"—for a moment, he thought the shame would not even let him say it—"*fireworks*. It must mean something."

"Why?"

"What do you mean, why?" His voice rose slightly. But he was too hollowed out for anger to be more than the faintest sputter of long-dowsed embers. "Viola, my hands shake. I wake myself some nights with screaming. And now this—which is not the first time I've experienced something like it, though it is the strongest and the most public. I have always been weak. We have always known it."

Her eyes flared like the deepest heart of a flame. "How dare you. I have *never* known it. And I will *never* believe it. Strength is not the capacity to hurt. Or the capacity to remain unhurt. It is…what we let ourselves feel. And how truly we love."

He had run out of words. Out of everything. Or maybe he had simply stopped fighting for…or against…something he should never have been fighting for in the first place. Pressing his face against her neck, he released a few very quiet, very shuddery tears. And she held him until all the artificial rainbows had faded from the sky, and all the fireworks fell silent.

"You aren't like this," he said, when they finally separated.

"No." She sat back on her heels. "But I never meant to make you feel it was easy for me. I…I do think about the war. Dream about it sometimes."

"It doesn't…it hasn't…" He swallowed. "Damaged you, though."

"I think it probably has. I mean…" And here she broke off, her laugh strained and self-conscious. "It was bloody awful. Bloody, bloody awful."

It was terrible to hear her say. Knowing she had experienced it, too, with him and because of him. But there was a strange mercy in it, something almost like relief. "It was."

"Gracewood?" she asked, after the smallest of pause. "Do you think me callous?"

"Why would I?"

"Because I do not feel what happened…what we did…as you do."

"Of course not."

"Then I think you must accept that your own feelings are no reflection on your character either."

This made him laugh again—but it was a true laugh this time, warm with mirth. "I've had a very difficult evening. It is unfair of you to try and use logic against me."

"There is nothing I will not stoop to when it comes to your happiness." She smiled at him, all wickedness and the sly flash of a dimple. But then grew serious again. "We both went to war. And we returned bearing different wounds." Her hand came to rest very lightly against the knee of his injured leg—she was too careful to cause him pain, but he felt exposed and sensitive regardless. "Not all of yours may be visible. But none of them make you any less the man that you are."

He opened his mouth to—what? Thank her inadequately? Start weeping again? But thankfully she didn't seem to need an answer. And perhaps it was better that he not try to provide one.

When her words had been her gift.

To wear like the jewels he had given her.

# CHAPTER 34

Their departure from Vauxhall drew very little attention, a dishevelled gentleman and his companion leaving one of the secluded groves being an occurrence so commonplace as to barely be gossip worthy. They encountered no-one but the Duke of Amberglass, who stepped from the shadows as they emerged onto the Grand Walk.

"Fireworks," he murmured, "can take such a toll on one's nerves."

Viola, feeling Gracewood's forearm tense beneath her hand, simply offered her blandest smile and said, "Indeed. Though likely there are some who would laugh at me for it."

"On the contrary, madam." Here Amberglass sketched a bow. "I'm sure your delicacy does you credit."

She dropped an equally indifferent curtsey. "Forgive me. I am still a little unwell."

He detained them no further, and Viola did not look back, though she was half-convinced he was watching them, his attention a coiled and lurking thing that made her stomach twist.

"I'm sorry," said Gracewood, the moment they were in the carriage. "You should not have to counterfeit weakness to cover mine."

It was very much the least of Viola's concerns. "The Duke of Amberglass may think of me as he pleases. It is nothing to me."

"But you aren't some wilting blossom to be overthrown by a few loud noises."

"And what if I were? Would you think less of me?"

Leaning his head against the squabs, Gracewood regarded her with weary eyes. "I hope I should not be so hypocritical."

"You needed my help," she told him. "And I needed to get you somewhere private. It was all I could think of at the time."

"I'm infinitely grateful. I am not sure how I could have borne it had any more of... of *that* been public."

She shrugged. "That the world expects weakness from women is an inequity that we can sometimes twist to our favour."

"It was still wrong of me to suggest that an admission of distress would be to your—or any woman's—discredit."

They fell silent then, Gracewood's eyes drifting closed, and Viola feather-soft inside for his pain, his courage, his unconquerable desire to be a better man.

When he was already the best man she knew.

The house was quiet upon their return. Normally Gracewood would have invited her to join him in the library or she would have gone to seek him there. But tonight—and it was not quite clear who led whom—they went upstairs together.

She had been in a bedroom with him before. As friends, they had thought nothing of wandering in and out of each other's chambers. But, of course, it felt different now. He was neater than she remembered—because he was older, perhaps, or had a better valet. Still, she thought she might have recognised the room was his simply from the details: the haphazard pile of books on the floor beside the bed, the precision with which his brushes and shaving things were laid out upon the dressing table, the jacquard silk banyan, with its pattern of pearl-grey flowers, that lay cast over a chair.

The sight of that alone was enough to make her smile. For a man whose tastes normally ran to the restrained, Gracewood had always harboured a secret weakness for extravagant dressing gowns. She could remember teasing him mercilessly over one with gold and burgundy stripes.

It was also, she realised, not the master bedroom that he had chosen to occupy, but one of the guest rooms. It had been re-decorated in a more contemporary style than some of the others in shades of blue and cream. The four-poster bed, which was set into its own alcove, had neither curtains nor canopy—just some artfully gathered muslin to soften the edges of its wooden frame. And Viola knew at once why he preferred to sleep here. It was the room of someone who loved light. Who feared to be trapped.

As soon as they were inside, Gracewood stripped off his coat, and without really thinking about it, she removed her gloves. She wasn't sure when she had lost her self-consciousness about her hands around him—there was no way to date it from a single touch, or a single moment, but something had been changing, something that was about her, and no-one else.

Gracewood crossed to a nearby table, poured himself some water from an ewer, and performed some brisk ablutions over a basin. Again, it was nothing Viola had not witnessed before, nor done herself in his company. Yet she looked away, abashed by the intimacy of it. The whisper of cloth-on-cloth, however, caught her attention, and glancing back, she discovered he had put down his toothbrush and was unwinding his cravat. And while she probably should once more have averted her eyes at the sight that followed—Gracewood dragging his shirt over his head—she... she didn't.

Couldn't?

Because there he was, half-naked in the candlelight, running a damp cloth over his body. And, oh God, did he have any notion how beautiful he looked? The way the shadows spilled down the groove of his spine. How the water upon his skin made him shine like a spider's web in the morning. He still had the scars, but they had faded over time to a series of silver lines—frail mementos of long-vanquished cruelties.

He turned, started, and snatched up his shirt, holding it against his chest. "I'm so sorry. I...forgot myself. You have seen so much of my frailty this evening that I lost sight of propriety."

"No." She made an impatient, greedy motion. "I want to look at you. If...if you will consent to be looked at."

Now he was actually blushing. His hair damp and copper-dark. "Viola, I should warn you I am no portrait."

Her arms prickled, as if the blood in her veins had turned to lightning. She had no idea what she was feeling, only that it was there—hot, but not anger, too sharp for joy, but close enough to make her bold and bright and reckless. "I have seen portraits. They are cold and flat, and their eyes are dead. You are—you are here, and you are alive, and you are more to me than the world and you are beautiful, Gracewood. You have always been beautiful."

"That is courteous," he said, "but false. My life has granted me many blessings, Viola, but beauty is not one of them."

"There are other kinds of beauty. And you possess so many of them in abundance."

He looked at her, unconvinced. But not, at least, withdrawing from the closeness of her. "That still sounds like courtesy. The way one might say that an elderly dowager possesses beauty of spirit, or a plain girl past marrying age has a beautiful temper."

"And both are true." She let her lips curl into a half-mocking smile. "You *do* have a beautiful spirit, although your temper, I fear, leaves much to be desired."

"Viola." He was reaching for sternness but fell short and found only amusement.

"But you are also *beautiful*, Gracewood. As any man might be beautiful." She reached out and touched him, letting her fingertips follow the line of his bare arm. "You are not just a title, or an estate, nor even a set of fine virtues. You are a man that any woman might..." Her hand crossed his shoulder, tracing droplets of water from his collarbone. "Might desire."

"Viola, you—" Gracewood's voice caught in his throat. "You have been kind to me this evening. But there is no need to—"

She placed a finger over his lips. "This is not about kindness. This is not about duty. This is about wanting. This is about— we have come so far together, Gracewood. From Cambridge to Waterloo to Northumberland to London. We have sat together long into the night. You have held me and we have danced and I..." She thought again of how it had felt that night, to embrace him in the empty ballroom, and to live for a moment in a world of their own making. "I am tired of denying myself, of fearing what others will think or say or see. I do not know if we...if there... what a future can look like between us. But I know that I want to be with you, Gracewood. And not as friends, not as your sister's chaperone, but as...as myself. As a woman. As the woman you—who you could...could want to be with in return."

His shirt dropped, and she gazed with helpless longing at everything he'd exposed for her. The stark geometries of collarbone and clavicle. The gold-leaf brush of the curls across his pectorals and down his stomach. New scars too—still rough, as arbitrary as the war that had caused them.

"I have wanted you since Morgencald," he said simply. "In every way it possible for a man to want. But you deserve better than to be a mistress."

He was right. Still, she tried to laugh. "To be a duke's mistress is no mean thing."

"Viola, you—"

Again, she held back his words with a fingertip. "Let us speak no more of deserving, Gracewood. Who deserves anything in life, good or ill? And I will no longer tarnish what can be with what cannot."

That his chest rose and fell a little more quickly than usual was the only sign that he felt his own nakedness. "Tell me again that you're certain. Because I don't think I have the strength to keep resisting."

"I'm certain." The steadiness of her own voice surprised her. Surprised and reassured her both. "I would not have offered myself otherwise. Though if you keep resisting me, I believe I shall take it quite amiss."

He smiled at that, but only a little. "I am trying to do what is right. Before my own desires run away with me."

"Then listen to what I am telling you. Which is that I wish to be run away withed, not resisted."

For a terrible moment, she thought he might reject her still— because he felt it was the right thing to do or, worse, because now that it came to it, he did not truly desire her. "Lovely Viola," he said, "I possess neither the power nor the wish to deny you." He reached out and began removing the pins from her hair, with far more patience than she ever allowed herself. "Whatever you would have of me is yours. As I am yours."

Except now that she was here, she hesitated. It was not that she had spoken falsely. She wanted this—wanted him—more completely and more surely than she could remember wanting anything, save freedom. But the reality of it, the close, intimate, *complex* reality of it filled her heart and her throat with a hundred questions she could not answer. "Gracewood." She could barely speak past her knotted tongue and clotted nerves. "You should know I've never—that is I don't—what is the—I mean, is it—are we—even possible?"

He let her finish, incoherent though she was, and while she spoke, he continued to undo her hair, the movement of his hands among the strands almost hypnotic, until at last it tumbled free down her back. The unrestricted weight of it was at once a relief and a burden.

"Of course *we* and *it* are possible," he told her gently. "Why would we not?"

"I don't know. Just—" She broke off, her fears only magnified by the fact she could not express them. "I don't *know.*"

Gracewood kissed her lightly on her forehead before taking up his cane and limping over to the bed. She had rarely seen him move with such visible difficulty; the evening must have taken quite a toll on him. Or it was another offering of trust—of truth—like his scars and his bare skin. It shamed her a little, that he would share so much, simply because she had asked him to, and in return she had pulled away.

Sitting down, he reached a hand towards her. "Come. Be with me."

So she came. Hesitant and wary and shaking though she was, she went to him. As she had gone to him that first night in Northumberland: believing in his friendship and his character, the goodness not even his father could take from him. "Gracewood.

You can't have—I mean have you? Lain with…with…I thought you only desired women."

"I do. Though I would consider it neither sin nor shame if my tastes ran otherwise."

"Then have you"—oh God, she sounded so pathetic, half-ready to beg him for a reassurance she wasn't even sure he could offer—"ever lain with a woman like me?"

"I have not." If the question surprised him, or if he took exception to it in any way, he gave no sign. His answer was soft and plain, a simple fact offered without judgement or comment.

"What if you don't like it?"

"Why wouldn't I like it?" His mouth tried to entice a smile from her. "Do you want to do something depraved with me?"

"You aren't concerned this might be depraved already?"

"As far as I'm concerned, depravity applies only to acts committed without consent or without care."

She ached to believe him. To give herself what he offered. "I'm not sure many people would agree with you."

"That does not mean I'm not correct." And there he was—the Duke of Gracewood, before whom the world would bend if only he chose to make it. "Why are you laughing at me? I'm in earnest."

"I'm laughing because…because"—and suddenly she felt capable of courage again—"I love you. I love you when you're arrogant. And I love you when you're kind. And I love you when you're both at the same time."

"You…" He swallowed. "You love me?"

There was something almost comical in his surprise. "You know I do," she told him.

He swallowed again, blinking what could have been the glitter of tears from his eyes. "I'm not certain I do know. Have known, I mean. Hoped for, perhaps. But love is not the sort of thing I was raised to—to seek or to need. But I...I cannot be ashamed to have sought it from you."

"Gracewood..." She turned her body towards his where they sat together on the bed. Then put her hand to his jaw and made him look at her. "I have always loved you. And it has brought me nothing but strength. Even now when I...I am so full of wanting and yet so afraid."

He leaned in and gently pressed his brow to hers. "Please do not fear to be with me."

"I can't help it." She tried to breathe through the scratchy tangle of lungs. "I worry you will only be able to see the ways I am... I am like you. When another woman might not be."

"Viola." He drew back then, gazing at her with an expression of the gentlest mockery. "Forgive me for what may be an exaggerated sense of self. But I believe who I am resides in some element of me that is immaterial and immortal. Not my body."

"You say that, but you aren't engaging yourself in carnal acts."

"Not right now," he agreed mildly. "But I have certainly engaged myself in several."

She sighed—and tried not to be distracted by what Gracewood might do when alone. "Now you think I'm ridiculous."

"Never. But I don't wholly think it's me you doubt."

"I know." Burying her hands in her hair, she curled them tightly and used the pain in her scalp to sharpen her own edges. To remind herself she was real. "I am not very carnal. I mean...I seek release. When I have to. But I...I always worry I might find reason not to like...what I find."

He was silent then, watching her steadily. Letting her keep the silence.

"I should though, shouldn't I?" she said at last, her tone soft, the words full of uncertain wonder. "I should trust me."

Gracewood offered her the faintest of smiles. "I would trust you with my life."

"I betrayed you once, though."

"It was not a betrayal of me for you to do what you needed to save yourself."

The words lingered a moment in the quiet room, heavy with the truths they carried. For she had, indeed, hurt Gracewood more deeply than she would have believed either of them had the strength to bear. And yet they had lived through it and beyond it, tumbling together into the impossible future that had brought them to tonight. Because that was the truth of trust. It was neither weak nor fleeting. It was steel and fire. And would endure as long as you let it.

"Oh, Gracewood," she said. "I am done being afraid of myself." Standing again, she reached behind her to the buttons of her gown and began, with not entirely steady fingers, to unfasten them. "I am who I am, and my body is what it is."

"You are who you are." His eyes did not stray from hers.

"I'm not going to apologise." She pulled her loosened dress from her shoulders and pushed it to the floor, followed by the silk under-dress. "Or treat any part of me as though it is some kind of mistake." Now she yanked at her stays, undoing the cunningly designed corset that gave her the suggestion of curves. "Or feel any shame at all." Off came the corset, leaving her in just her chemise, the thin material clinging to her, concealing nothing. "This body can fight. And ride. And sew. And play the pianoforte badly. It is mine. It deserves any carnal acts I want to indulge with it. And if you want to find it beautiful, Gracewood, I will let you. Because I don't see why it can't be."

"Come here." His voice was so low she almost felt it vibrate in her bones.

So she shed her chemise, pulled off her shoes and stockings, and went to him. Into his outstretched arms, kneeling over him so she could keep her weight from his leg, gazing down into the face of her best friend. Her lover. Her Gracewood.

"Next time," he said, "leave the shoes. You always wear such pretty shoes."

She wasn't sure what thrilled her more—the fact he spoke so readily of *next time* or that he still noticed her shoes. "That does not sound like a spontaneous thought."

"What do you want to hear? That I've imagined it? Countless times? You beneath me, with your legs around me, wearing nothing but your pretty shoes?"

It was an erotic portrait of herself that, even an hour ago, would have been impossible to imagine. Now it was almost easy and that was almost frightening. But mainly it was exhilarating—all the things they might do together, so many possibilities, as abundant as pomegranate seeds.

His hands settled on her hips, as if they belonged there. "I am very happy to discuss your shoes. Also, if you wish, your embroidered stockings. But I need to tell you something first. Tell you properly, whether you already know it or not, before passion overthrows me entirely and now I am no longer lost as I was at Vauxhall."

"Oh?"

"Yes." His face was serious, but there was a smile too, sweet upon the curve of his mouth. "I need to tell you I love you, Viola. Not only *that* I do but *how* I do."

"You don't have—" she started. But she fell silent beneath the brush of his lips across hers. Besides, he had been right. It felt different to hear it.

"I would say"—he shaped the words close to her mouth, as if each of them was its own kiss, a private prayer—"I love you as a man loves a woman, but we both know that love is not bound by such narrow terms. So instead let me simply tell you that I love you. I love you with the unfading flame of my friendship. With every drop of ardour in my blood. I love you with my soul, as some reserve their faith for absent gods. I love you as I believe in what is right and hope for what is good. I love you with everything I am and ever was—and if you will only let me, with every day that comes, and every self that I could ever be."

She was silent. For a while it seemed the only possible answer. Then she smiled. A smile that felt like no other smile she had ever smiled. "Good. Now give me all the pleasure."

# CHAPTER 35

He was laughing as he kissed her, his mouth tasting faintly of tooth powder, and then just of him. And it felt different to kiss—to be kissed—when you were naked. The press of skin to skin and the beat of heart to heart. The way his hands curled into her, half-rough, half-entreating, as if he could not bear even a moment's distance. And then there was, oh, she had not been prepared for the *detail* of bodies. No longer just the texture of his lips or the slide of his tongue to hers. But the silk of his chest hair and the heat of his groin and the clench of his stomach muscles as his breath grew harsh.

"All the pleasure," he repeated, when they finally broke apart again.

She was panting softly. Acutely aware of the flush rushing down her neck. The sweat beneath her hair. The stir of arousal in her flesh. "What do we do?"

"Whatever we want."

"I need specifics, Gracewood."

Laughing again, he gathered up her hair and drew it over one shoulder. "May I touch you?"

"You're doing that already."

"Yes, but I want to touch you everywhere." He trailed a fingertip over her knee where it rested beside him on the bed and Viola stared down in bewilderment. Shocked that a touch so light to a place so banal could feel…like anything at all. "Everywhere."

"A-again," she told him.

His palm this time, circling in some impossible fashion that fell halfway between soothing and maddening.

"Oh." She heard herself gasp. "Oh. More."

"Where?"

Her eyes, which she had barely noticed closing, opened. It was a little strange, looking down at herself. She half expected to find she had changed in some way, become wild and magical, vined in Gracewood's caresses like a forest nymph. But no. She was skin and bone, blood and sinew, just like always.

"Here?" She brushed the exterior of her thigh.

He followed her hand with his own, a languorous sweep along the length of the muscle that drew a sound from the back of her throat. Pure, lazy satisfaction.

"Now where?" he asked.

"As you choose."

A spot above her hip. A line of freckles that arced like a serpent's tail. She almost forgot how to breathe, knowing she would never think of that piece of skin the same way again. It would forever be the part of her that Gracewood chose.

"I die for your freckles," he murmured.

She would have insisted that was nonsense, but then he touched her again, the tip of his thumb drawing a line from her chin to her stomach. And all she did was sigh and arch her spine, her head feeling as heavy as a chrysanthemum in full bloom.

"God." Gracewood's voice was slipping again into its deepest register. "You are so beautiful in pleasure."

She unleashed another sound of her own, letting it coil through her like smoke and out into the world. "I feel it."

He embraced her again, the heat of his hands shocking on her bare back. She leaned into him, tightening the muscles of her shoulders so they pressed against his palms, and let him bear the weight of her upper body. Her hair was its own dark wave falling behind her, tips brushing the floor.

She had never let herself be so naked. Nor so fearless.

Gracewood pressed forward and put his mouth to the notch between her collarbones. He only breathed, but the warmth of it spread through her in tendrils until she half imagined her fingertips glowing.

"Like this?" He kissed his way down the curve of her body.

"Yes."

"Here?" His lips brushed her nipples.

It was enough to make her shiver, but it was a spring day kind of sweetness. Not a summer storm. She shifted uncertainly and he drew her upright again.

"No?"

"I...I liked it," she told him. "But I don't know. I think I expected to more than like it. Is there something wrong with me?"

His eyes were the darkest blue she'd ever seen them. A secret blue, just for her, waiting on the other side of midnight. "Not in the slightest. We are all sensitive in different ways."

She was silent. She was, in so many ways, an expert in her own body. She knew how to dress, how to move, how to speak. And yet—naked with Gracewood—she still felt so full of mysteries. But perhaps that was true for everyone. Perhaps there were things you could only learn about yourself when you shared them with someone else.

"You respond to this." His hand returned to her leg. And—perhaps it was because she had always liked her legs, how strong they were, how fast and sure they made her—she moaned outright as he dragged the blunt edges of his nails up her inner thigh. "And this." The sweep of his thumbs from the crease of her groin and over her hips.

"Yes." Catching his wrists, she drew him up to her throat, letting him caress her there too—even the places she normally covered with her chokers. "And this. But"—she met his eyes—"what about you?"

"What about me?" He seemed almost amused.

"I want to know the same about you."

There was, she knew, very little finesse in her touch—just the span of her palms across his chest—but it made him gasp nonetheless. "Viola..."

She laughed, startled and delighted by how good it felt. The way his response rippled through her until it was only by looking that she remembered whose hands were upon whom. Slowly, she followed the contours of his pectoral muscles, lost in the way his breathing changed, the minute variations of texture as she moved through hair and across the occasional scar to the blood-warm rough-smooth planes that were simply his skin.

It was accident rather than design that brought her to his nipples, but just the possibility of her fingers made him tilt his head back and groan. "Viola..."

"Oh." She hardly recognised her own voice in that moment—the power in it, and the joy. "*You're* sensitive here."

"Yes, but—"

Whatever he had been about to tell her was lost in the shudder that overcame him as she bent her head and pressed a kiss, first to one nipple, then the other.

"Viola," he protested, as her mouth lingered, "you will unman me."

She glanced up, smirking. "I thought you said your manhood resided in some immaterial and immortal part of you."

"Then you will *un-person* me, and I will spend like I have no control over myself whatsoever."

"Is control something either of us needs to strive towards under the current circumstances?" she asked, because she had always loved teasing Gracewood, and teasing him like this was its own magic.

His laugh was already a half-broken thing. "You have no idea how long it's been since someone has touched me."

"How long?"

"Before the war."

It was still a shorter time than *never*. But Viola wasn't sure if it was worse, somehow, knowing about...this. All this. And then not having it.

"It doesn't matter," Gracewood went on. "Nothing matters but what's between us tonight."

She kissed him again. She didn't share Gracewood's certainty in souls, but she could have believed then. In something that bound them, transcended them, and softly mingled in the joining of their mouths. "What do people...? How would someone like me and someone like you...? What can we do?"

"Anything, Viola." He looked a little dazed, hazy-eyed from her kisses, his hair wayward and his cheeks flushed. "Bodies are made to fit. To give each other pleasure. Whatever shape they take."

She hardly knew how to tell him what she wanted. Not an act, specifically—but to claim something she had half convinced herself belonged to others. "Can we be...one flesh?"

"All love-making is becoming one flesh. Whether it's with mouths or hands or any other parts we wish to share. But if you mean, can I take you inside me, or you me, then yes. If that's what you desire."

"You...you would allow that? You would allow me to...?" She was not sure how to form the thought, let alone the words.

"Allow you?" He laughed. "It's not a sacrifice. I would welcome it. I think I would welcome most things you might want to do with me."

"You've"—she swallowed, aware of how intrusive the question was—"tried it before? That particular form of...of closeness?"

"In a manner of speaking. A lady of the night I visited on some occasions. She preferred to serve clients with a leather phallus."

"Oh, Gracewood." She was not...shocked exactly. Well, she was a little shocked. "What adventures you've had."

He shrugged. "Someone very dear to me taught me not to reject life's experiences. And I had little enough freedom in other areas, so I saw no reason to limit myself when it came to sex."

"And you enjoyed these experiences?"

"Many of them. I don't have much taste for pain."

Her eyes flew wide. "Pain? Why would you seek that?"

"Some people do. For pleasure or catharsis." He brushed his mouth over her shoulder, and the collection of freckles there. "And I think I hoped...after my...my childhood I could make pain mean something different. But I couldn't."

She gazed at him, utterly dismayed at the life he had lived without her. The means by which he'd sought solace. The places he'd looked for peace. "I would never begrudge you any balm you found needful, but—oh, Gracewood, I hate how much hurt you have borne."

"When I am with you, I feel about as far from anything that has ever hurt me as it is possible to be."

It was the most futile of desires—the wish to shield him from his own past. Especially given he had already survived it. And, without it, neither of them would be who they were or where they were. "So," she said instead, "t-tell me. This. Um. Leather phallus. Did you...? Was it pleasurable?"

"Very pleasurable."

"And it did not make you feel any less... I don't know."

"No more than it made the lady who wielded the phallus feel less a lady. Which, in case you're wondering, was not at all."

"I think I could be such a lady." Taking his hand with far more bravado than was probably warranted, she drew it to her.

He was far less hesitant than she had ever been with herself, watching her face for her responses as he closed his palm around her. Somehow, she had not expected it to feel as it did. She had thought, perhaps, it would be like when she did it, or a little better. Instead it was so different as to be its own experience entirely. And, to her relief, less about what he touched than the fact he did—that it was his hand and his eyes upon her, and his body stirring afresh in response to hers. The sensation was sharp and sweet and greedy, awaking certainties in her that made her push him away again.

"I want you naked too," she said.

"Of course. Though in the absence of my valet—"

Dropping to the floor between his legs, she did not even allow him to finish the sentence before yanking his boots and stockings off.

"Good God." Thankfully, he was laughing. "Viola."

She gazed up at him. She had no idea this could be so *fierce*. So freeing. Passion beneath her fingertips, flowing as effortlessly as colour from her sewing needle. "I want to be inside you. I want to know how it feels—to have our bodies joined that way. And I want to see you in pleasure. I want to see you lost in it and undone by it and transformed by it, and know it was me who gave it to you."

"Yes." His look was at once wry and hopelessly loving. "I think you'll discover those are all eminently achievable goals. But please…"

Viola was already at work upon his buttons.

"…please be careful of my leg," he finished, wincing. "And it's…it's not pretty."

Easing his drawers and pantaloons down, she cast them aside. And, still on her knees, looked at what he feared to show her. The grapeshot had caught him mid-thigh, leaving behind a ruin of reddened skin and scar tissue. The rest of the damage—further scars extending in ridges from the original wound—she thought was probably the result of infection. Places where the muscle had been cut away to save his life.

"Oh, Gracewood." She rested her head gently against the edge of his knee. "How close I came to losing you."

"Please"—his voice was a choked off thing—"don't look at it."

"You think I am afraid of scars? I have plenty of my own. See." She pointed to a long one across her ribs. "That was a sabre. Though, thankfully it only grazed me."

He closed his eyes. "It is not the same. You know it is not the same."

"Lie down."

To her surprise, he obliged, pushing himself up the bed with his good leg so that he was settled against the pillows. And, after a slightly skittish moment of her own, she joined him, pressing herself to his side, the edge of her body against his a shivering line of connection that made her head spin. But perhaps the strangest thing was how...effortless it was, to be like this with him. How unself-conscious it was possible to feel. How desired and desiring. All because she trusted him. Trusted herself. Now if she could only convince him he was as safe with her as she was with him.

Propped upon an elbow, she gazed down at him. He turned slightly so he was looking back at her. It was true that life had left its marks upon him. But she did not want some pristine man. She wanted Gracewood—who had shared so many of her days and years. Who knew her as no-one else did. And who, in his own way, had fought to be who he was.

She put her fingers to the tips of his lashes. Felt their soft prickle as he blinked but did not pull away. Then she stroked the length of his straight, patrician nose—shaped, she thought, for sneering down, though Gracewood did very little of that. And finally over the arch of his lips, admiring how a mouth set so sternly could smile so sweetly.

"What are you doing?" he asked.

"Well, I came to the conclusion that there was nothing I could say that would make you believe you're beautiful. So I'm showing you. The way you show me—with your eyes and your touch."

"Viola..." Her name was a sigh. "You don't have to—"

"Oddly enough"—she kissed his throat, where it was rough with the beginnings of his beard—"I'm aware it's not an obligation."

It took gratifyingly little to rouse him to fresh passion. Just her body lowered over his, one knee in the space between his legs to take her weight. Her hands possessive upon his flanks. Her tongue teasing his nipples. Her teeth to the interior of his wrist. She could almost see the moment when he stopped... whatever he was doing. Thinking? Worrying? And slipped gently into bliss with her. Which was enough, too, for her to half forget her purpose. Entranced instead by the sounds he gave her. The little tremors that chased themselves across his skin. The way his muscles tightened beneath a gathering gleam of sweat.

Perhaps it should have surprised her—how far he seemed, in these moments, from the austere duke he'd been raised to be. As he still was, when the occasion merited. But he had always been so willing to be more than that, for her and for himself, that having him like this—soft-eyed and sighing in her arms—felt truly no different. No different to sitting in his library talking the small hours away. No different to dancing their slow and private waltz. Just...more. And the way he opened himself to pleasure was its own lesson. Its own gift. One he offered, she knew, because she had asked for it. Because he understood that she needed this to be as much hers as it was his. Something that—for all his experience and her lack of it—they created together.

"Viola?" he said.

She was almost full length atop him now, his hands digging deliciously into her shoulders, as their bodies moved one-to-the-other in long, rolling motions. "Mmm?"

"If you still want to be inside me... I feel *now* might be a suitable occasion." His voice was so rough, his breath so ragged, it was a wonder he'd been able to get out the sentence.

"How fortunate. I should hate to enter you on an unsuitable occasion."

A stripped-bare laugh. "There's a preparation in the bedside table—for my leg—but it will serve our purpose too."

Easing herself away from him, reluctant to lose the closeness even for a moment, she pulled open the drawer he indicated. Inside she found a glass vial, half-full of an herb-scented oil. "Is there something I should—"

"On you. In me. I can tend to . . . either."

"No, no. I want to."

Her eagerness—the unabashed possessiveness of her tone—made him smile. "All right—just, you first. Let me watch."

It was quite a thing, to kneel between his legs, and stroke herself with slick fingers. Not so very long ago she would have doubted her capacity to do it. She would have doubted her desire to. But now? With Gracewood's eyes all heat upon her? She was conscious only of anticipation, curling through her as bright as ribbons. So she gave herself to the moment, head thrown back, the memory of all his touches, the press of his body to hers, still shimmering under her skin. And there was only pleasure, wrought by her and for her—spiralling from her like stars in the Milky Way.

"God," Gracewood groaned. "The things I want to do with you."

She fumbled the vial open again. "Tell me about them?"

"I want to hold you against me and make you spill across my cock. I want to push your skirts up and take you in my mouth until your knees buckle. I want—"

He lost his words as she pushed his knees apart. Which seemed fair because she would have lost hers too. Something about the audacity of the gesture. And the fact he acquiesced to it without qualm, without shame. For the briefest of flashes, her whole life felt like the most impossible dream. How had she become the sort of woman who got to grace the bed of a duke? Not that it really mattered.

Because, somehow, she was.

And the duke in question was waiting for her, sprawled decadently across his pillows, his eyes grown slumberous in expectation.

"What else?" she asked.

"Would you let me bind you?"

"Bind me?" Her eyes widened. "I'm not here under duress."

He laughed. "That would not be the point of binding you."

"What would be the point?" And this time, the question was as much curiosity as confusion.

"Mutual gratification."

"I'm not sure," she pointed out, "how mutual it would be if I could not move."

"But I would get to have you at my mercy."

"And what would I get?"

"My mercy." He gave a soft gasp, as she breached him with a finger. "Eventually."

He felt...almost unbearably intimate. Heat and softness and strength. "Eventually?"

"Yes. When you were nothing but ferocity and rapture and pure carnal need."

It was a vision of herself she was not yet able to fully encompass. But she loved that it was so clear to him. That, given time, she could be his match in debauchery as in so much else.

"All these years," she said wonderingly, "and I hadn't the slightest inkling you were secretly so—perhaps you are a rake, after all?"

"Rakes are interested in power." Reaching down between

them, he closed his fingers around her wrist and did something with the angle of her hand that made his whole body respond—clench down on her as a shudder like a riptide rolled over him. "I am interested in pleasure. Especially pleasure with you. On the subject of which, I'm not sure I can wait another fucking moment. Let me feel you, Viola."

Her heart lurched with eagerness and apprehension. "Like this?"

"Like this." He eased onto his side. "My leg will appreciate it."

Pressing herself against his back, nestling herself against him, Viola kissed the rise of his shoulder. "I appreciate it also."

He gave a sweet, shivery sigh. "I have dreamed of this—well, not precisely this but something enough like it to make no difference—since the moment I saw you on the north tower."

"You mean, I was breaking my heart for you and you were thinking of sex?"

"I'm afraid so. There you were with your wild hair, and your beloved eyes, and I thought, here is a woman I could be obsessed with until the end of my days. And I am, and I shall be, and oh please just fuck me. You have no notion how I need you."

She had some notion. But she did not have opportunity to tell him because her instincts took over. And it seemed like at once the boldest and most natural thing in the world: a hand upon his waist, her mouth still pressed to his shoulder, a shift of her hips and the slow, slow glorious slide of her body into his. Fingers, she quickly discovered, had not remotely prepared her for the way he would feel around her. How beautifully he would yield, inch by inch, moment by moment, until she was utterly *encompassed* by him. All slick heat and silken pressure. The thudding of her heart against the curve of his spine.

"I...I..." she gasped out. "Oh God. I'm inside you. Gracewood, I'm inside you."

His head fell back against her, sweat-dampened hair clinging to her neck. "I'm aware."

"It's...all right?"

"Better than." He already sounded half-delirious. Reduced to harsh syllables.

"Good," she purred, caught in the strangest paradox of power and humility. "Because I think I...I think I love this."

To that he only groaned, moving upon her in small restless motions she wasn't sure he was even fully conscious of making. She matched him as best she could, rocking into him, their bodies so fully entwined that even the slightest change in position was enough to send a shock of fresh bliss rippling through her. Closing her eyes, she mustered every shred of discipline she possessed. There was part of her that wanted to fling herself into pleasure as she had once jumped from the cliffs of Morgencald, but she feared too swift an abatement. When she needed to keep this. Treasure it. Even if just for a little longer.

So she clung to restraint. Gave herself time to simply luxuriate in this new connection between them. The scent of their skin together. The harmony of breath matched to breath. All the ways they could fit and delight each other, just as Gracewood had promised they would. And, then, when she had learned how to bear the generosity of this deep embrace of selves—how to move in ways that enhanced the satisfaction of it, rather than simply overwhelmed her senses in feral rapture—she recalled how he had adjusted her wrist when she'd had fingers inside him. Mirroring the angle, she was rewarded by a reaction so intense from Gracewood that she felt it in almost every part of her.

"Dear Lord." He twisted slightly, scrabbling a hand back so it landed upon the top of her leg. "I'll spend if—"

"I want you to. I want to make you."

After that, they neither of them had the wherewithal for sustained speech—just fragments of loving nonsense and names exchanged as clumsily as kisses. And then Gracewood turned hot and wild against her, half demanding, half pleading "Touch me" and pulling Viola's hand to his cock. It was mere seconds before he cried out, savage and helpless and abandoned and free, and the heat of him spilled across her fingers. She stilled inside him, soothing him through the aftermath of shudders and moans with soft kisses and idle caresses.

"Now you," he murmured, his voice as lax as his body, all warmth and lazy gratification.

She was achingly close to the edge, the tightness of his clasp about her the sweetest torment she had ever known. "Will I hurt you?"

"Not in any way I won't welcome. Don't desire." He shifted onto his back, and she moved with him, settling carefully between his thighs. "Use me, Viola. Use me for your pleasure. Share it with me."

The change in position brought new intimacies. Deeper heat. His eyes on hers. The leg he raised to embrace her. Pressing her face into his neck, she felt herself begin to fray. Her movements stripped of the last vestiges of control. Breath frantic. Culmination looming like a shadow.

Gracewood's arms closed around her. "Please, my heart. My Viola."

The fear vanished as swiftly as it had bared its fangs. Sweeping away everything but the moment. Then the pleasure claimed that too. And she was lost and found and perfect with Grace-wood, drowned in him, held tight to him, soaring on private wings through the shining forever of her own release.

"Beautiful," Gracewood whispered.

And, for some reason, giddy, satisfied, utterly undone, she began to laugh.

He kissed her temple. "I'm taking that for approval."

"Oh yes," she told him, breathless and bliss-ruined. "Yes. It was . . . it was so, so good. It was . . ."

She was laughing again and it felt like a second release. One of the heart or the soul or the self. As necessary as tears could be sometimes. As powerful as anger. Except this was nothing but love. Love and the triumph of joy.

# CHAPTER 36

Viola left Gracewood's side some time before dawn. She was, she supposed, his mistress now and that came with certain obligations, chief among which was discretion. It was a bittersweet thing. To be with him at last, to have lain with the man she loved and experienced so much that she had assumed she would never—could never—experience was a wonder unto itself. And there was even something strangely affirming in the title of *mistress*. After all, she was in fine company there—many men kept ladies, and those ladies were by and large good, if socially complicated, people.

Still, as she made her way through the house before the servants could catch her, she was conscious of a...a what? A tension perhaps, between what she *wished* to believe—that they had defied the world and chosen love and freedom and happiness beyond its strictures—and the hard truth of her reality. That in spite of all protests she had accepted the ultimatum society laid before her. That she had chosen to live her life in half-worlds and liminal spaces and to be content with an echo of what she wanted, instead of the whole of it.

Back in her room, she returned to bed for an hour or so, largely for appearances' sake. Then she rose and performed her morning rituals—that was another reason to leave early, of course. She was not quite ready for Gracewood to see her without the benefit of her ablutions. When that was done, it was time for her to descend to the drawing room, where she would be required to attend on Miranda, who, doubtless, would be receiving another unending stream of admiring suitors.

As she approached, however, she found the door hanging ajar and heard a familiar voice—Lady Lillimere's voice—coming through it.

"Absolutely not," she was saying.

"Why not?" That was Miranda.

"Because . . . because . . ." Whatever was going on, it was oddly gratifying to think of Lady Lillimere lost for words. "It is not appropriate."

"Do you often do what is appropriate?" Miranda again, and vehement.

"When it comes to green girls," Lady Lillimere replied stridently, "I most certainly do."

There was a pause. And Viola was about to make some noise to indicate she was there when Miranda asked, "Is it my naïveté you find objectionable or the fact I'm . . . well, I rather resent the idea that I'm a girl. I rather think of myself as a woman."

"I'm sure you do." Lady Lillimere sounded dry. "And, as it happens, both."

A definite sort of rap—perhaps Mira stamping her foot on the ground? "I don't believe you. Everyone says you have a preference for ladies."

"And that means I'm duty-bound to oblige any lady who makes a demand of me?"

"Well . . . no. Of course not. But why are you being so contradictory?"

"I am not being contradictory. I know when I am encouraging a lady, and I have never encouraged you in the slightest."

"That is not how I see it. I think your behaviour has been *quite* encouraging." Sometimes Miranda could be terrifyingly earnest. It made Viola want to intervene, and rescue her, except she could think of no gentle way of doing so. "And I assure you I am not half so green as you think. Why, I kissed Viscount Stirling only the other day."

This was news to Viola, though not, she thought, deeply concerning news. They could not have kept Miranda's trust if they allowed her no freedom, and Viscount Stirling seemed a safe enough target for flirtation, being neither a libertine nor a fortune hunter.

"Good for you," said Lady Lillimere, her voice cold.

"Do you think so?" Miranda sounded oddly disappointed.

"I think it's none of my business."

A silence, this time long enough that Viola thought she might be able to breeze into the room with a plausible semblance of ignorance. But then Miranda spoke again. "Why are you being so cruel?"

"This isn't cruelty, you damnable child."

"For the last time"—Miranda's voice rose—"I'm not a child. I know what I want, Stevie, and I have asked for it because I don't know how else I am to get it. And what I don't understand is why…why you're refusing me. Don't you like me? Don't you think I'm beautiful? Everyone says I am. Is it my hair? Would you rather it was red? They say you—"

The clatter of footsteps and a stir of skirts. And Lady Lillimere, unexpectedly gentle: "That's enough. I like you well enough. And you are very beautiful."

"Then…" Something in Miranda's tone Viola could not read, at once imperious and uncertain. "You should kiss me."

Ah. Well, that explained the argument. If argument it truly was. Though it also put Viola in an impossible position. For she had heard both too much to leave and too much to interrupt.

Lady Lillimere sighed. "Miranda, Miranda, admir'd Miranda, I cannot."

"Why not? Just put your mouth on my mine. It's really quite simple."

"The fact you believe kissing to be simple," said Lady Lillimere in tones of restrained exasperation, "only strengthens my argument."

"The fact I might have some mistaken notions about kissing only strengthens mine."

Another pause. It was the sort of pause in which an increasingly uncomfortable guardian of a young lady's virtue might imagine to be filled with kissing.

But all Lady Lillimere said was "Please don't ask me this. I'm not made of stone."

"So"—Miranda's voice trembled with triumph—"you *do* want to kiss me."

"More than there are stars in the sky. But nothing will induce me to do it."

"I don't understand. If you want to kiss me, and I want to be kissed, what is preventing us from kissing?"

"Louise is my best friend. I'm even rather fond of your sharp-tongued companion, and your silly brother, who won't stop staring at her. They would never forgive me. And, on this occasion, they would be right."

"I am not particularly prideful," muttered Mira, making it all too easy for Viola to imagine her pouting, "but I rather feel that kissing me should be about me."

"Then, my little solipsist, when you live in a universe stripped of all context, connection, and consequence, you may seek me out and we shall kiss as much as your heart desires."

"Auntie Lou won't find out. She doesn't know about Viscount Stirl—"

"Do *not* mention me in the same breath as that mewling fopling." Some fresh suggestion of motion. "I am not some quim-struck boy you can play with, Mira."

"I...I'm not. I would never—"

"And yet you think to add me to your lady's commonplace book of kisses."

If Viola had wanted proof that Lady Lillimere could be trusted with Mira, she possessed it now in abundance. And it was bitter knowledge, for neither party would relish her presence on the outskirts of this particular conversation.

"No, no." Miranda seemed close to tears. "Nothing like that. You are gallant to me like a gentleman, but I can talk to you like a friend. And when you touch me, I feel it...I feel it *everywhere* and...and I think about you all the time. And I especially think how lovely it would be if you were to kiss me."

"I'm afraid you have mistaken me for someone I am not. It's a pretty picture you paint, but my kisses are not *lovely*. They are savage and possessive and rapacious. They take. And they burn."

"That's just semantics."

Lady Lillimere made a sound of...frustration? Despair? "Marry your Viscount. Kiss one of your pretty friends if you must. I am not for you."

"I'm not afraid of a little fire," Miranda insisted.

"And I'm sure Prometheus thought the same."

"Oh, that makes no sense at all. I am not bearing the gift of kissing against the will of the gods. Eagles will not come and tear out my liver if you touch me."

Viola had come to the conclusion that the best thing she could do for everyone was slip away and let the scene play out as it would. But, given how tenacious Mira could be, she was starting to wonder if Lady Lillimere would appreciate a distraction.

"They may well come tear out mine," she was saying. "I'm sorry, Mira. Some things should remain precious, and you are one of them. You'll thank me one day."

"I very much doubt it." A crash—breaking china of some kind? "And you should know I am finding this all very patronising."

"Then consider it a mercy you do not know how I am finding it."

"I . . . I think I might hate you."

"As you will, my dear. And now I shall take my leave."

Her exit was so precipitous that it afforded Viola no opportunity to enact a performance of arrival. Instead, Lady Lillimere just subjected her to a long, steady gaze as she flailed unconvincingly in the hallway, tipped an imaginary hat, and departed without another word. At which point there came a second crash from the drawing room, leaving Viola with no choice but to hasten inside.

Miranda was standing by the fireplace, somewhat flushed, and systematically destroying a row of china shepherdesses.

"Oh, good," said Viola. "I've been hoping someone would see to those. They seem disproportionately smug for a collection of ladies tasked with the care of sheep."

"I . . ." The final shepherdess—pink-frocked and pink-cheeked—dangled from Mira's fingers. "I fear I've been the most exquisite idiot."

Dissembling had never come easily to Viola, but she did her best. "Well, you would be living a shabby life indeed if you allowed no space in it for idiocy."

"You would not say that if you...if you..." Mira's eyes filled with tears. "The fact is, I threw myself at Ste—at Lady Lillimere, and she would have none of me. And I'm excruciatingly embarrassed. And now I'm telling you, and I'm sure you think me nothing but a silly girl or...or worse."

"I think no less of you, if that's what you're implying."

"You don't?"

"Of course not. Though"—and here Viola offered the suggestion of a smile—"I slightly question your taste."

"Because," asked Mira, somehow managing to sound both defiant and weepy, "I want to kiss a lady?"

"Because Lady Lillimere is so much older than you. And rather...worldly. And I'm not sure I'd call her handsome exactly."

At this, Mira gave a watery smile. "How would you know? You don't have eyes for anyone but Justin."

There was transparent, and then there was transparent to a seventeen-year-old girl. "I," said Viola, blushing. "I...that is...I..."

"Oh, I didn't mean to make you uncomfortable. Shall we go back to my kissing ladies instead? Or rather, *not* kissing ladies. Which is a very unfortunate state of affairs for me."

Settling herself in her usual place on the sofa, Viola tugged her work basket from behind a cushion and unfolded her latest piece of embroidery—blossom trees in full bloom, riotous in white and pink. "If it's not an impertinent question, do you think you might be, in general, inclined to your own sex?"

"That's just it." Mira cast herself tempestuously into a chair.

"I'm not sure. How is one supposed to discern something like that?"

"Is that why you were trying to kiss Lady Lillimere?"

"Maybe? But I also think I want to kiss Lady Lillimere specifically. If you'll forgive my frankness, dear Viola, I'm quite confused about kissing as a whole."

"I'm afraid," Viola told her dryly, "I am far from expert myself."

Mira sighed. "Lydia is positively wild about it. Mainly as it relates to gentlemen, admittedly. But she says she used to kiss her friends at finishing school all the time."

"You know, you are not *obliged* to kiss anyone. Whatever Lydia feels about it."

"Of course, I know that." Mira's tone was slightly impatient. "It was more that I wanted the experience for myself. So I kissed Viscount Stirling. And it was fine. Should kissing be fine?"

"I suspect, like most things in life, it runs a gamut."

A pause, as Mira considered this. "I will confess, I was quite disappointed. But then I thought perhaps it was not Viscount Stirling's fault."

"Because he is not a lady?"

"Exactly."

Keeping her thread taut beneath her thumb, Viola deftly secured a French knot blossom. "How do you feel about Viscount Stirling?"

"Feel about him?" Mira blinked. "Well…I mean. He's handsome, I think? And…there?"

Viola gave a wry smile. "I'm sure *there* is exactly how a gentleman would wish himself thought of."

"Everyone speaks well of him."

"I'm not persuaded"—Viola snipped her thread and reached for a darker shade of pink—"*exists* and *is broadly considered acceptable* are good selection criteria."

Frowning, Mira plucked at her gown. "Oh."

"And so perhaps your difficulties spring not from the fact that the Viscount is a man, but that you do not particularly like him?"

"Oh," said Mira again. "I had not thought of that." A small, anxious silence followed. Then Miranda went on, "I'm probably being very selfish, but I do wonder sometimes. When am I going to fall in love? I mean, I'm already halfway through my season and—"

"Mira." Casting aside her embroidery, Viola went to kneel by her side. "You are beautiful, rich, and young. Time is your luxury, not your master."

"But what am I doing?" cried Miranda. "I don't know what or who I want. I'm probably supposed to be getting married. And is it even possible, do you think, to like ladies and gentlemen equally? Except how am I to find out, if the only ones who will kiss me are the ones I don't give a damn about?"

Viola felt prepared to address exactly none of this—not least because her concerns at the age of seventeen had been so very different. But she wanted to be as worthy of Mira's trust as Mira had been worthy of hers. "I don't see why it's *not* possible to like ladies and gentlemen equally. It seems no more outlandish to me than only liking one. And as for the rest, I'm afraid there are no simple answers to such questions. But I sincerely believe that to be uncertain and to be at fault are not the same thing."

Miranda slumped dejectedly in her chair. "Everything was a lot simpler at Morgencald."

"You wouldn't wish to go back, though."

After a moment, Mira shook her head. "Only when I'm *especially* uncertain." She made a soft, frustrated sound. "I do wish Lady Lillimere had kissed me."

"I doubt it would have made your life much simpler if she had," offered Viola, as consolingly as she could.

That made Mira laugh. "Possibly not. But I was very sure about it."

"You will become sure of other things. Perhaps not today, or tomorrow, or even this year. When you need to be."

A pause as Miranda contemplated this, the tense line between her brows suggesting she had not been wholly satisfied with Viola's answer. But then she simply smiled and shrugged. "I shall have to take your word for it." Nudging her slippers off, she tucked her feet up and nestled herself cosily into a corner of the sofa. "Would you like me to read to you while you sew?"

Viola could not deny she appreciated the shift to less complicated subject matter. "I would love that. Thank you."

Miranda's eyes brightened with genuine enthusiasm. "Oh, Viola, Justin managed to get me a copy of the most fascinating book."

So much for an afternoon with Austen or Burney. "Is it," asked Viola, accepting her fate, "about a scientist who is able to animate dead tissue?"

"Yes," cried Miranda, brightening still further. "But even more extraordinary is the fact that this gentleman, having gone to all this trouble to infuse his creation with life, runs away in horror. Isn't that so like a man?"

"It does seem an unfortunate way to behave."

Mira nodded. "If I had made a monster, firstly I wouldn't keep saying he was a monster—because monstrosity is very much in the eye of the beholder—and secondly I would give him a name and teach him to read and take him everywhere with me, and tell everyone how terribly proud I was of him. And as a consequence, nobody would have to get murdered or go to the North Pole."

Viola was not *quite* sure what Miranda meant by this, or what the North Pole had to do with a book about a man and a monster. But, as she sat there in the drawing room, working on her embroidery and listening to Gracewood's sister reading an inappropriate novel, some of her restlessness settled. There was, she saw, happiness to be found here. True happiness. Not just with Gracewood himself but with everything that came *with* Gracewood. The opportunity to share his house and his bed. To take care of his sister. Help him—if she could—with his duties and his estates. It was not quite a home of her own or a family of her own. But perhaps it was close enough to make no difference.

# CHAPTER 37

Letters from Morgencald. Reports from Parliament. Updates from various of his investments. Gracewood's day had slid away beneath an avalanche of papers. Tea appeared at regular intervals, as did plates of bread, cheese, and fruit. At some point, the curtains were drawn, candles lit, the fire stoked. And, finally, Viola appeared, dressed prettily but comfortably in a light muslin gown embroidered in tiny roses, trimmed with Pomona-green bows.

Thoughts of disrobing her raced semi-unbidden through his mind. It was something she still preferred to do for herself, for she did not always feel like being naked with him—not that he lacked for enticements in a body half-revealed, half-concealed through a haze of cotton and the slick-smooth rub of her stockings against his flanks as he moved atop her. But he hoped that one day she would let him unfasten all her hooks and buttons. Untie her garters for her. Coax her like Aphrodite from her clothing. Or perhaps just leave her exquisitely disordered amid all the intricacies of her ribbons and silks.

"...Lady Marleigh," she was saying.

He looked up, hoping he wasn't too visibly flustered. "I beg your pardon?"

She laughed, as if she recognised the source of his distraction. "Miranda has gone to a masquerade ball with Lady Marleigh."

"You did not wish to accompany them?" he asked, mainly out of courtesy. Had it been up to him, she would never have left his side or possibly his bed. But that would not have been practical for either of them.

"I was welcome but not needed." Her footfalls were almost silent upon the library rug as she crossed the room. "I thought perhaps I might prefer an evening at home."

That was understandable. Miranda's life was a whirlwind of social engagements, and Gracewood had done more than his fair share of keeping Viola up late. "Yes—you do so much for my sister, for both of us. You must allow yourself to rest."

Now she was on his side of the desk, leaning slightly against it, watching him with an expression he could not quite decipher. "I confess, I wasn't feeling particularly tired."

"Well," he offered, reassuringly, "you still have a right to your own time."

"What if I wished to spend my time with you?"

"Then I'd be delighted, of course." He gave her a slightly quizzical look. "I wasn't aware you were in doubt of that."

An odd little silence. "I mentioned, I think, that Miranda has gone to a masquerade ball with Lady Marleigh."

"I'm sure we could catch up to them, if you wished."

"That…that is not what I meant. I was simply pointing out that we have the house to ourselves. No friends, family, or other obligations to concern us."

"What luxury." Slanting a smile at her, he cast his quill defiantly aside. So many years between them, so much that had changed and not changed, and yet she still came to remind him of a world beyond his estate, his name, his fortune. Like Ariadne's thread, guiding him safely through the labyrinth of duty his father had built for him. "What do you say to a quiet supper and a game of chess?"

Her hand slapped the edge of the desk in frustration. "Gracewood. Are you doing this deliberately?"

He blinked, startled at her sudden passion. "Doing what? We have always played chess."

"Yes, but"—her voice trembled with something close to laughter—"as your mistress, I believe I am entitled to certain compensations."

Oh God. Lost in the pleasure of being with her at last, he'd been abominably selfish, to say nothing of short-sighted. "Viola, of course. I'm so sorry. You will need your own household. An allowance. I will have accounts set up for you with—"

Her fingers covered his lips. "Gracewood. That is a conversation for another time. The only compensation I am interested in at present is the privilege of having the master of the house whenever I so desire. Which is now, by the way."

He gazed at her, feeling a flush upon his cheeks, and the rough embroidery of her gloves against his mouth.

"I know I am no practised coquette," she told him, shaking her head in exasperated amusement, "but you are utterly hopeless. I am trying to seduce you. Can't you tell?"

"You're trying to..." Truthfully, the idea was a little bewildering, for it had never occurred to Gracewood to consider himself an object worthy of seduction. But then the absurdity of the situation caught him and he started to laugh. "I'm beginning to understand your sudden aversion to chess."

"Not unless"—Viola's eyes flashed with familiar audacity and new wickedness—"you care to play it naked. With my mouth on you."

"I think"—God help him, he was half-hard already—"that might diminish my capacity to oppose you."

"Then perhaps for now," she suggested, "you should simply allow yourself to be seduced?"

"I don't need to be seduced. I'm already yours."

Her look turned searching. "Perhaps I want to. Perhaps I want you to feel the way you make me: desired and cherished and overwhelmed in the best possible way."

He swallowed. "You do. Believe me, you do."

"Then"—her expression was half-pleading, half-defiant—"let me show you."

It was not a request...command...invitation he could deny. Reaching for his cane, he pushed himself to his feet. "Shall we go upstairs."

"How many times must I mention this? But Mira has gone to—"

"To a masquerade ball, with Lady Marleigh. Yes"—he tried to smooth the impatience from his voice—"I know."

Her gaze sharpened, the darkness of her eyes gleaming with subtle currents. "Sit."

It took him a second or two—and a nudge—for him to understand what she was asking. And then he settled himself gingerly on the desk, papers crackling beneath him. He had thought himself worldly enough. Not lightly shocked by the things people might do with and to each other for pleasure. And this was certainly no great act of depravity. But it had taken him unawares nonetheless. "This," he said, his voice sticking in his throat, "this is *my father's desk*."

"No, it's *your* desk. And I have...a fancy." There was laughter in her voice, a look in her eye that could almost be called winsome.

It was half pain, half bliss—the yielding of some locked-tight place that had been inside him so long he had forgotten it was there. He took a deep breath. "Tell me of your fancy?"

"Spread your legs."

He did, and she stepped between them. There was always such certainty in her, each movement as precise as the prick of a blade, when since the war he had been nothing but hesitation, stumbles, the ever-present possibility of weakness.

"I have a fancy," she told him, "to have you here. So that when you sit at your desk, you remember how we came together on it. So that when you vanish into the silence, you remember the sounds I made and the ones you gave to me. So that when your work tries to claim you, you remember that you're mine."

Twisting a hand into her hair, he dragged her into a kiss. It was an artless offering, full of rough hungers, but she met him, as she always did—without a moment of doubt, her own appetites as ferocious, as eager, as his own. When they broke away, they were equally breathless. His lips tender, sticky-sweet from the taste of her lip salve. "I promise you, I am in no danger of forgetting."

"Nevertheless." She pressed into the $v$ of his open thighs, all heat and pressure—even the promise of friction enough to make him gasp. "Indulge me."

"Always, my heart."

Leaning back on his elbows, he hooked his good leg across her hip and pulled them both down onto the desk. It was some sixteenth-century monstrosity, built of dark oak as solid as Noah's ark, and took their combined weight with barely a creak. And then they were kissing again, time blurring into shared breath, the press of mouths, the back-and-forth of tongue to tongue. He was a little dazed by how quickly desire swept over him. How easily it was to offer this, or take it, upon something he had believed sacrosanct. Though sacrosanct to *what* he had never allowed himself to wonder. Someone else's priorities. Someone else's sense of integrity. For all that it was his house, he had always come here, much as he had at Morgencald, to be a de Vere.

But, with Viola, he could be Gracewood too. A man who was more than a duke. Because—unlike so many of those who had preceded him—he loved and was loved.

"You look debauched already," Viola said, a world of satisfaction in her voice.

He felt it—his hair disordered from her fingers, his cravat partially undone, the blossom of warmth upon his throat from the most savage of her kisses. "I will debauch you back."

"I should hope so."

"Upon every piece of furniture in the house."

Her eyes widened. "You own a lot of furniture."

"Then it will take me a while. Probably a lifetime."

The play of thoughts across her face reminded him of summers at Morgencald. Almost made him miss them. Down south the sky was a lacquered thing—a smooth blue forever—but up north it was ceaselessly mutable. Restive clouds that, on bright days, shone silver with secret sunlight.

She spanned her palm possessively across his chest. "I love you."

"I love you too." He smiled up at her, his heart beneath her hand. "Now how about we put this desk to a purpose for which it was not intended?"

"Impatient, aren't you?"

"Can you blame me? I've never desported myself in a library before."

She arched against him, arousal to arousal, almost unbearably tantalising through the obstruction of their clothes. Then came rapid footsteps in the corridor. A voice crying out their names. And they just had time to disentangle—put their garments into some semblance of order—when the door crashed open and Lady Marleigh burst into the room.

"What—" began Gracewood, far too conscious of his flushed cheeks and his unravelled cravat.

"It's Mira." Lady Marleigh, who was unmasked but still wrapped in her black silk domino, seemed genuinely distraught. "I can't find Mira. I've... I've lost her, somehow."

Viola's hair was halfway down her back, but she was otherwise composed. "What do you mean, *lost her*? This must be some kind of misunderstanding."

"That's what I thought at first," wailed Lady Marleigh. "But it is not as though she would be easily missed. She is green, for heaven's sake."

"She's green?" repeated Gracewood. He was aware that this was not particularly salient to the story, but since it was highly unlikely that his sister had come to harm at a private masquerade, he allowed curiosity to get the better of him.

"Well, greenish yellow. She insisted on attending in the guise of some kind of monster? From a book she'd read. Oh, I can't remember now."

Viola glanced his way. "Frankenstein's monster."

"For God's sake." That was Lady Marleigh, striking emphatically at the air. "It doesn't matter whose monster she is. She's gone, don't you understand? I thought she might have come home for some reason. But she's not here either. I don't know where she is."

"She will be at the ball," said Viola calmly. "You've just managed to miss each other somehow."

At this juncture, Lady Marleigh made an unladylike sound. Something rather close to a roar. "I *looked*. She's not there, she's not here. I tell you, she's gone."

"Gone? As in run away?" asked Gracewood, still unconvinced that this was half the calamity Lady Marleigh seemed to believe. "While green?"

"Greenish yellow."

"I'm sure she hasn't run away." Taking Lady Marleigh's hand, Viola ushered her into a chair. "Can you tell us exactly what happened, Louise?"

Lady Marleigh managed to remain seated for all of five seconds before she bounced up again and began pacing the room. "We arrived. It was quite the crush. Mira said she had to make some adjustments to her costume. And that was the last time I saw her."

"And there is no possibility you failed to spot each other in the crowd?"

"How many greenish-yellow young ladies do you think were present?" exclaimed Lady Marleigh. "But I waited and waited. Looked everywhere. Asked everyone. Nobody else had seen her either."

Ice was creeping slowly across the surface of Gracewood's heart. "Why would she do this? I...I thought she was happy. That she was beginning to—"

"Gracewood." Viola was by his side in an instant. "I'm sure she hasn't eloped, if that is your fear. Young ladies planning such adventures rarely undertake them while dressed as re-animated corpses."

He turned to her, instinctively. Seeking the safety, and the certainties, he always found in her eyes. "Then what can have happened?"

"I'm sincerely hoping it is nothing more than a logistical mishap."

"Excuse me," put in Lady Marleigh. "But when have I ever been susceptible to logistical mishaps?"

Viola made a conciliatory gesture. "It's so easy, though, to lose each other at a masquerade."

"We had a designated pot plant. We were to meet there."

"Yes, but you're not at the pot plant now, are you?"

"Badger is. Stevie is making further enquiries. And I am here. Believe me"—Lady Marleigh's expression grew very fierce indeed—"I don't want to accept that I've lost Mira *either*. But I have. So can we please stop asking silly questions and do...I don't know...whatever needs to be done?"

Hearing the rising panic in Lady Marleigh's voice, Gracewood put aside his own concerns and strove to be reassuring. "My sister," he said gently, "is her own person. Wherever she has gone, it is not your fault."

Lady Marleigh blinked at him, a few tears caught on her lashes. "She was in my care. And I think someone has taken her."

"Surely not. Such events belong on the stage." His hand tight upon his cane, Gracewood walked slowly round to the other side of the desk. He had no wish to sit at it—certainly no wish to be distracted by what had almost happened upon it—but he needed a moment to master himself. Shock, fear, burgeoning dread, even the love he had never quite found a way to demonstrate: None of these would be any use to Mira now. He had to remain calm. Think. Then act.

"Supposing, for the sake of caution, that she has been taken," he said finally, "who would do such a thing, and for what? Her fortune? Something more personal? Some act of retribution against my family?"

Viola, too, looked grave. "Do you have enemies of such significance?"

"Not that I'm aware of. Is there any chance"—Gracewood knew he was grasping at straws, but he grasped for them anyway—"she has developed a tendre for someone she might believe to be unsuitable? That this could be, in any way, an act of mutual folly?"

Viola bit her lip. "There are the notes."

Had he been forced to speculate, Gracewood would have said it was not in him to feel anger at Viola, but he felt it now. "You assured me that those were harmless."

"I may"—the pained look on Viola's face went some way towards restoring Gracewood's sympathies—"I may have been mistaken."

"What notes are these?" asked Lady Marleigh in the indignant tones of one who considered being kept informed to be something of a birthright.

"Mira has been receiving notes through Miss Avon," explained Gracewood. "But Viola assured me that this was normal behaviour."

Setting aside the deep personal betrayal of a thing existing that she didn't know about, Lady Marleigh thought for a moment. "I suppose it is. I used to pass notes all the time when I was a girl. But this is different. I never got kidnapped."

"We're wasting time," said Viola, heading for the door. "Whatever has become of Miranda, if anything has become of her at all, the notes are our best hope of finding out, and the notes will be in her room."

The three of them hurried upstairs to Miranda's bedchamber, where to everybody's relief they discovered that while she was an original in many respects, Miranda had still kept the secret notes from her admirer in a small box underneath her bed in accordance with tradition.

"Well!" exclaimed Lady Marleigh, leafing through a couple. "These are positively steamy. *I dream of feeling your*—oh I say—*beneath my*—well, I never! If things weren't looking so troubling, I'd have said good on the girl."

Gracewood, who had needed a moment to catch his breath after tackling so many stairs so fast, was waiting at a discreet distance. Besides, it would not have done to read his sister's intimate correspondence when there were ladies to do it for him. "Are they signed?"

"One moment," said Lady Marleigh, "they're quite long and—my God."

*"What?"* demanded Gracewood, who was fast coming to the end of his patience.

"Stevie."

"They're from Lady Lillimere?" asked Viola, although from her tone she seemed more disappointed than surprised.

"That's what it says here." Lady Marleigh thrust a note into Viola's face. "See? Plain as day."

Viola stared at the note for longer than Gracewood was entirely comfortable with. "I don't believe it. I *shan't* believe it unless she confirms it with her own lips."

"She may be doing that already," observed Lady Marleigh.

"And the woman is a notorious seducer," added Gracewood. "Were she a man, I would..." But he wouldn't, of course. The days when he could defend his sister's honour as a brother should were past. Even Lady Lillimere, he suspected, would be able to outmatch him.

Lady Marleigh had been sorting the notes into chronological order; their composer, having been nicely trained in the art of letter-writing, had dated each. "Here's the latest. *I will meet you at the ball where you shall have all you desire. My coach will await you outside, come to me at eight.* Surely she can't have been so impetuous?"

"Ordinarily," said Viola, "you admire impetuosity."

"Yes, but this is very, very impetuous."

Having heard enough, Gracewood was already turning back towards the door. If Lady Lillimere had spirited Miranda away in her carriage, then she would be far away by now. Fortunately there were only a limited number of places they could have gone. Lady Lillimere's own home was likely far too obvious for a clandestine assignation, but at least there he would find servants who he could persuade—force, if necessary—to tell him where she might be.

Back in the library he stopped again, cursing his infirmity for making this harder than it already was. Breathing shallowly, with his eyes closed, he felt Viola come up behind him, felt her place a hand on the small of his back, so warm even through her gloves.

"We'll find her," she said. "Together, we will find her."

At that moment the door flew open and Lady Lillimere, dressed in a gown of patterned lace designed to look like snakeskin, rushed in upon them. "Badger's still waiting. One of the footmen said he *might* have seen a lady who *might* have been green being helped into a carriage. It's not much, I'm afraid. But it's all I've got."

Gracewood glared. "Lady Lillimere, if this is some manner of joke, it is in extremely poor taste."

"I'm sorry?" It was hard for Gracewood to look at her objectively in that moment, but Lady Lillimere seemed genuinely confused. "What is in poor taste?"

"You've been corresponding with Mira." Lady Marleigh, who had pursued them downstairs, brandished one of the notes.

Lady Lillimere looked indignant. "I most certainly have not."

Advancing like a line of angry infantry, Lady Marleigh shoved the offending missive right under Lady Lillimere's nose. "Then what is this?"

"I have no idea." Snatching the letter, Lady Lillimere stared at it in mounting fury. "Louise, this isn't even my writing."

"I'll admit," said Lady Marleigh, "that did strike me as peculiar."

"And if I'd spirited Miranda away in order to do beautiful vulgar things to her, do you not think I would currently *be* away doing beautiful vulgar things to her, not standing around exchanging pointless conversation with you three?"

Lady Marleigh nodded. "Yes, that struck me as peculiar too."

"Then *who*"—Gracewood was doing his best to keep his temper even—"has taken my sister?"

"Miss Avon must know, surely," suggested Viola. "She was the one handing the letters to Mira in the first place."

Gracewood pulled over a chair and sat down. There would be no sense running the length of town looking for Miss Avon— it would be tiring and undignified. Instead, he gave a nod to a passing servant. "There's a masquerade ball currently in progress at Farnsworth House. Go there and fetch Miss Avon to me at once."

It was then just a matter of waiting before Miss Avon arrived. It was high-handed, he had to admit, and the lady would not like it, but she would not ignore a duke's summons. The Miss Avons of this world played the great game of society well, but the de Veres of this world were the ones who wrote the rules and stacked the deck.

And, sure enough, she arrived within the hour.

"Your Grace?" Miss Avon appeared in the doorway, bobbing a curtsey. She looked much as she had at their last meeting: beautiful and poised, and a little defiant.

There was no purpose in circuity. "Where is my sister?"

For a moment Miss Avon's eyes flashed panic, but she controlled herself with a cold confidence that would have made the old duke proud. "I haven't seen her in some while, Your Grace."

"Come here," he commanded, and she obeyed with only a touch of reluctance. He laid out the letters they had found under Miranda's bed and let them make his point.

For a moment, Miss Avon seemed resolute. And that would not do.

Justin de Vere, eleventh Duke of Gracewood, looked up at her and said nothing. He did not have to. Eight centuries of his ancestors spoke for him.

"It was a game," offered Miss Avon, finally. "A foolish game. I—we—it was not my intent that Miranda come to harm. Only that—the Duke of Amberglass said..."

*Amberglass?* "What did he say, exactly?"

The panic was back in Miss Avon's eyes. A dark flush creeping up her throat. "He said that if we were to lure her into a compromising exchange, it would—she would—there would be less competition for eligible gentlemen. And I thought—I thought he might look favourably upon me, as you would not."

It made the worst kind of sense. What young woman could—or should—resist intriguing with a dashing duke, especially having recently been slighted by a significantly less dashing one. "And so you lured her."

Miss Avon hung her head, but not before he caught the slide of a tear down her cheek. She looked young and defeated, and Gracewood felt wretched. More truly his father's son than he had ever been. "We meant only for her to be seen entering a strange carriage," Miss Avon went on, her voice trembling. "His Grace—the Duke of Amberglass, I mean—he said it would be empty. That she would be embarrassed but unharmed."

"That, as I am sure you are aware"—Gracewood kept his tone flat and cold—"is untrue."

A second tear escaped Miss Avon's best attempts to conceal her weeping. "She—she will be all right, won't she?"

Did she really care? Gracewood wondered. Would he have cared, in her position? "You had best hope so. Where has she been taken?"

"I don't know." Taking the handkerchief that Viola had offered her, Miss Avon scrubbed at her face. "Truly I don't. It was never meant to—Amberglass will know only...only he isn't here."

It was all the information they were likely to get. "Go home, Miss Avon," Gracewood told her. "If there comes a time when you are welcome in my presence again, you will know."

For just a moment, it looked almost as though she would break down entirely, but instead straightened her back, nodded her acquiescence, and then, with a final hasty curtsey, she fled.

There was a silence.

"Amberglass" said Gracewood, at once unsurprised and incredulous. "But he has no reason. He is titled, influential, rich on his own account. What could he possibly hope to gain?"

"What Amberglass seeks from his actions is not easily discerned." Lady Lillimere had gone to stand by Lady Marleigh, one arm wound tightly about her waist.

For all he was trying to control himself, Gracewood's mind was a nauseating churn. "I will pay him a visit." His own words served to steady him. And his head cleared once he'd spoken them. Doubt, fear, even fear for Mira, were luxuries he could simply not afford. "If we have wronged him, I can be embarrassed later. For now, it's our last lead."

Truthfully, he wished it were a more substantial one. But wishing would not help Mira either. And having something to do—whatever use it proved to be—also brought with it a certain clarity. He was in the entrance hall, waiting for his coat to be brought and his curricle readied, when Viola joined him.

"You know"—she pulled up the hood of the cloak in which she had wrapped herself—"I'm coming with you."

He ought to have told her she shouldn't or couldn't, to think of her safety and her reputation. His father would have called it weakness that he didn't. For himself, he wondered if it was selfishness. And maybe it was. Or maybe it simply it didn't matter.

Because this was Viola. There was no-one in the world he trusted more. No-one in the world he would rather have had at his side.

"I know" was all he said.

And took her hand in his.

# CHAPTER 38

It turned out that the Duke of Amberglass was not at home. As to where he might be, his cold-eyed, immaculate butler was not at liberty to say. Not even at the behest of the Duke of Gracewood.

"Good God." Back in the curricle, he put his head in his hands. "Good God."

Viola did not quite dare touch him in the middle of Berkeley Square, but she nudged her knee to his. "We will find her. We just have to find Amberglass first."

After a moment, Gracewood looked up. "Well, we know he is not here, nor at the masquerade."

"Could he be at his club?"

"He favours Brooks's, I believe. As with much else, his political leanings can be somewhat contrarian."

"Then let us make some enquiries."

"It will be difficult to do so discreetly. We are hardly intimates." Gracewood's eyes were smudged with despair as he glanced at her. "If I'm not careful, I could do as much damage to Miranda's reputation as this misadventure will."

"Then be careful," Viola said.

Which drew the softest laugh from him. "Thank you. Your advice is always impeccable."

They tried Brooks's. And the theatre. And—with increasing

desperation—Almack's. Viola waited with the curricle, walking the horses if Gracewood was gone for any length of time, feeling far from inconspicuous in her cloak. It had seemed a sensible choice as she had rushed from the house, being both warm and obscuring, but in practice there were few garments more likely to broadcast clandestine business. Although she also suspected that worrying about her outerwear was a trick her mind was playing on her to stop her worrying about Mira. Even so, every time Gracewood returned, her heart would seize and crack afresh, for she could tell from his expression alone that he had no news to impart. He was limping heavily on the third occasion and did not even try to conceal a sound of pain as he climbed into the curricle beside her.

"What now?" she asked.

His jaw tightened. "I have...there is...a place gentlemen of his sort are known to frequent. But I cannot take you with me."

"You can and you will."

"Viola, it's a—it's not somewhere for a lady."

"So"—she gave him a hard stare—"it's a brothel? You have taken me to brothels before."

That left a sour taste in Gracewood's mouth. It was not a fact of which he enjoyed being reminded. "I didn't know, then, that you were a lady."

"For heaven's sake, I may be a woman, but I am no more in need of your protection than I ever was."

He gazed at her, half commanding, half pleading. "I will not leave you unattended on the streets of Soho. It's not safe."

"Then I will come inside with you."

His sigh contained a note of exasperation. "I'm not sure that's safe either."

"For my virtue, or my person?"

"Both?"

"And what," she snapped, "of *your* virtue and person?"

"My virtue is secure by dint of my being a man. And as to my person..." He gave the head of his cane a deft twist, revealing for the barest of seconds the blade concealed within.

Had they not been arguing in the street—had the situation not been so dire—Viola might have smiled. For Gracewood always thought ahead. "That will be more than enough protection for both of us."

"Oh, Viola." His shoulders slumped. "I cannot help Mira and fight with you."

"Good. Because only one of those things is necessary."

He took up the reins again. "I fear we will both regret this."

"I think there are things we would regret far more." She glanced at the sky, where the dirty bronze of a London evening was flaking into an ash-grey night. "But come. Speed is becoming a factor."

Gracewood only nodded, urging his horses into motion.

They travelled, for a while, in silence, wrapped in their individual thoughts. By the time they arrived at Soho Square, a sallow mist was rolling in from the river. It gave the fading light an eerie, saturated quality, as though the world lay half-submerged in silty water.

"Perhaps," said Viola, glancing at the tight rectangular terraces and the wretched ruin of the central fountain, "you could tell me what makes this particular establishment so potentially detrimental to my well-being. Am I to bear witness to...great abuses or illegalities?"

Whatever reverie Gracewood had fallen into was deep enough that it took a second or two for her words to reach him. "Nothing like that. It's just that the Silken Tiger prides itself on its capacity to cater. And Amberglass's tastes are reputed to be singular."

"Disinclined as I am to defend him, I suspect all our tastes would be considered singular were they reported upon."

"Indeed," said Gracewood, as though he did not like to dwell on the matter.

He helped her down from the curricle and offered a youth who was lingering nearby a sovereign—and the promise of another on their return—to watch it. Then led her down a narrow side-street to an unremarkable door. A knock, a murmured conversation, the exchange of further coins, and they were inside. Viola wasn't quite sure what she'd been expecting from somewhere as extravagantly named as the Silken Tiger, but all that lay before them was a shadowy corridor, its rugs well trodden and its wooden-panelled walls ill tended.

It was not the right occasion to think overlong about the fact that Gracewood seemed to know exactly where he was going, his steps swift and certain as he made his way through the gloom. He pushed open a further door and, suddenly, everything was light. The hard glitter of mirrors and chandeliers. Tooth-sharp glints of gold and silver, unsoftened by the tongue-red velvet that drenched the room beyond. Roses, heavy in the air, too sweet and too rich. And the faintest edge of salt: sex and strangers' bodies.

Viola's fingers curled into Gracewood's arm. The memory of other rooms—that same smell—pressing upon her heavy as hands. The sickness of pretending riven into her skin. Watching her loved ones through the bars of a life that felt wrong. Not understanding enough of herself to even dream of escape. The constant dread that someone would truly see her.

"My heart." Gracewood's voice. A bare whisper against her ear. "My Viola. I'm with you. Stay with me."

She drew in a rough breath. The past receded, more slowly than she might have wished, but it receded, dragging the chains of its old, unconquered pains behind it, leaving Viola to her present. Which was…a room. Just a room. Nothing to frighten or hurt her. Unless you counted the decoration, which was gaudy to the point of grotesque.

It was occupied by a selection of what Viola presumed to be the night's offerings, all finely dressed and at their ease, arranged in attitudes of indulgent sensuality. A striking woman, plucking idly at a bunch of grapes, as she reclined upon her chaise, her skirts disordered in such a way as to reveal the softly gleaming smoothness of her leg. A slender gentleman, spectacles perched upon his nose, seated by a side table, giving every impression of being absorbed by his book. Smirking behind an extravagant fan, a larger woman with shrewd eyes and a profusion of silver-blonde curls. And resting idly against her generous thigh, a sylph-like, painted beauty in breeches and a corset.

"My Lord, My Lady. Welcome to the Silken Tiger." An older woman—in a burnt-orange gown that clashed so horrendously with the furnishings it had to be deliberate—rose from a chair sufficiently large and ornately gilded it could easily have warranted the description *throne*. Her accent had that sanded-down, faintly strained quality that suggested she was working hard to refine it. "How can we serve you tonight?"

Gracewood offered a slight bow. "Madam Mercy, I'm looking for someone."

"Aren't we all, sir, aren't we all?" She smiled, showing a flash of a gold tooth. "But if you tell me what you have in mind, I'll warrant you'll find it here."

"I'm looking for someone in particular."

At this, she made a clucking sound. "I'm afraid I don't know anybody *in particular*. What sort of house would we be if I did?"

"And I'm afraid"—Gracewood did not raise his voice, but there was ice in it, ice and steel and certainty—"that I am not in a position where I can take no for an answer."

The madam put her hands on her hips. While she was not tall, she was not slight either, and possessed her own air of implacability. Of having not so much lived as weathered. "Then I'm afraid we can't help you."

"I'm looking," Gracewood told her softly, "for the Duke of Amberglass."

Viola thought she saw something flicker in the other woman's eyes. But it could also have been a trick of light. "Never heard of him. And I think it's about time you were pushing off, don't you? Play your little game of Bow Street Runner somewhere else."

"I know Amberglass is one of your regular visitors," returned Gracewood, "and I know he's here tonight. Which makes things very simple for both of us. Your reputation, as you've previously intimated, is built at least partially upon your discretion. So I'm giving you the choice: Either you protect this single client, or you protect the rest of them. Because unless you take me to Amberglass yourself, I will throw open every door in the building until I find him."

Her eyes widened behind their mask of kohl. "You bloody well will not. Perce?" Her voice lifted into a yell. "Perseverance?"

"Yes mum?" The door opened to admit a young man of pleasant features and hulking aspect. "You need help with something?"

"Do your old finger and thumb a favour and throw this piss-bucket out."

He nodded cheerfully. "Will do."

Sensing that mobility was about to become very important, Viola drew her arm from Gracewood's and stepped clear.

"Now then, sir." Perce was already advancing on them. "Let's have no more trouble, eh?"

The youth—who must have had significant experience throwing unruly gentlemen into the street—loomed over Gracewood. But before he could get close enough to lay a hand on him, Gracewood pivoted his cane into a position that Viola remembered well from bayonet drill and thrust it into his assailant's solar plexus. It was a firm blow, though not as brutal as it could have been, and sent poor Perce staggering back, doubled over, and wheezing. Viola felt almost sorry for him—she had taken hits in that region herself, and recalled all too vividly those interminable, agonising moments without breath. Without even the possibility of breath.

The rest of the carefully staged scene had degenerated into a chaos of over-turned furniture and hastily retreating figures.

"I'm sorry to—" began Gracewood.

At which point, Perce surged forward and made a grab for the cane. Wheeling it in a circular arc, Gracewood rapped the young man sharply across the knuckles and, taking advantage of the few seconds his opponent spent yelping in pain, retreated a few paces.

"Perseverance," he said, "listen to me please. This is my signet. I am the Duke of Gracewood. I won't be able to keep you at bay much longer, but if you strike me, you will surely hang for it."

Still winded, his hand tucked protectively against his chest, Perce glanced from Gracewood to the madam and back. "But mum said—"

The door opened again, this time admitting a tall, hawk-faced woman clad entirely in black. "What's the commotion?" she demanded, in an accent as rarefied as any Viola had heard. "This is a decent house of fuckery. Not a tavern brawl."

The madam jerked a thumb in Gracewood's direction. "This one's asking questions. Causing trouble. Claims he's the Duke of Gracewood."

"Madam Chastity," murmured Gracewood, with another bow.

Her eyes narrowed. "That, my love, is because he *is* the Duke of Gracewood."

There was a long silence. Then Madam Mercy flung herself onto the recently vacated chaise. "Well, fuck me. And fuck all fucking dukes."

"So"—Perce rubbed his knuckles—"I shouldn't throw him out, then?"

Madam Chastity glided over to where Madam Mercy was seated, her hands coming to rest gently—reassuringly almost—on the other woman's shoulders. "What do you want from us, Your Grace?"

"I want," he said softly, "the Duke of Amberglass."

"And what do we get in return?"

"I take it"—his mouth turned up into the suggestion of a smile—"my leaving the premises quietly is not motivation enough?"

To Viola's surprise, Madam Chastity seemed almost amused. "You've struck my son, annoyed my wife, and disrupted a lot of people's evenings."

"My sincerest apologies," said Gracewood with as much sincerity he could muster given the urgency of the situation. "How can I make amends?"

A thoughtful pause.

"I like money," said Madam Chastity eventually. She leaned down and pressed a kiss to Madam Mercy's temple. "What about you, darling?"

She did not hesitate. "I *love* money."

Madam Chastity's attention flicked to the book-reading gentleman, who was now pressed into a corner by the fireplace. "Gwilym?"

He smiled. "Money buys a lot of books."

"Athena?"

"Money is power." The lady popped the final grape into her mouth and dropped the denuded branch onto a nearby platter.

"Delly?"

The blonde peeped round from behind the ornate chair. "After sex, money's my favourite thing in the world."

"Jay?"

"Voting reform," they suggested, sitting on the edge of a nearby table, and draping one leg elegantly over the other. "Better working conditions in factories and coal mines. More humane poor laws. And an end to the exploitation of child labour."

"Well." Gracewood looked slightly taken aback. "I'll see what I can do. But I'm one man, and changes of such magnitude are likely to take an extraordinarily long time."

Jay grinned—though it was a bitter expression on their narrow face. "Then you'd better pay me like the rest."

"I will pay you," Gracewood promised. "I will pay you more than generously."

Madam Mercy fixed him with a sudden glare. "And protect us. Protect this house. Because I don't trust your high-and-mighty sort for spit, and I trust Amberglass even less."

For the first time since they had entered the premises, Viola saw Gracewood waver. "Protect you? I'm not sure—"

"Don't give me that. I know how it goes. Who the law comes down on, who they look past, who gets gaoled and who gets rich."

"You know she's right." That was Madam Chastity. "Though if you want to claim it's beyond your power, you can leave with our blessing."

"It's not beyond my power," Gracewood said slowly. "It's just not a use of it that I'm accustomed to. Nevertheless, I'll do it. You have my word. Now take me to Amberglass."

A long silence, taut as a harp string.

Then Madam Chastity nodded. "Follow me."

# CHAPTER 39

The Duke of Amberglass was engaged, so they were told, in the Elysium Suite. Another anonymous door at the end of a dimly lit corridor, where Madam Chastity led them, then left them. Gracewood cast Viola a look—it was not an occasion for words—and then simply, and without ceremony, pushed inside.

The room within was white upon white upon white—from the furnishings to the walls to the rug-strewn marble of the floor—starkly accented with glass and silver. If this was paradise, its magnificence was cold indeed. Not that the style of decoration was of much concern to Viola in that moment.

Upon the vast, silken bed, which swung from the ceiling on silver ropes entwined with carven vine leaves, a man and a woman were engaged in an act of purchased intimacy. And watching them with an expression of profound disinterest from where he sprawled on another of the ornate chairs the house seemed to favour—this one in shades of white and silver, with lions carved into the arms—was Amberglass himself.

He was visibly intoxicated, his pale eyes bloodshot, their silver blurred to a misty morning, and half-undressed, without coat or cravat, his untucked shirt exposing much of his chest. Between his legs knelt a woman, preserving at least some of his modesty and labouring upon his pleasure with diligence rather than enthusiasm.

It was not so terribly debauched a scene. Viola had excused herself from far worse back in the days when she and Gracewood had first come to London. But what arrested her, shocked her almost, was its joylessness.

Amberglass regarded them with neither surprise nor consternation. "Well, now," he murmured. "I wasn't expecting guests, but never let it be said I am not an accommodating host. Help yourselves, won't you, to wine? And holes or genitals to your preference."

Gracewood met his gaze with equal indifference. "Where is my sister?"

"Who? Oh, your sister. The little blonde morsel who doesn't know when to stop her mouth?" Amberglass slurred out a mirthless laugh. "How should I know?"

"I think," said Gracewood steadily, "you do know."

With a dismissive flick of his fingers, Amberglass indicated their surroundings. "You're welcome to look around. Maybe she's hiding under the…" His attention was briefly, if perhaps unintentionally, captured by the woman at his feet. "Did I say you could stop?" Then, turning to the couple on the bed, "Did I say *you* could stop?" He heaved an exasperated sigh. "Fuck her, for Christ's sake. You're dilly-dallying like a virgin who's never notched his tarse before."

The man obligingly increased his efforts, moving upon—and presumably into—his partner in smooth strokes that made her, either from professionalism or genuine interest, sigh rather sweetly.

Amberglass stifled a yawn. "My grandmother swives with more conviction, and she's been dead since Farmer George was shitting a normal colour. What am I even paying you for?"

Pausing, the man—whose rugged good looks gave him something of the air of Byron's corsair—glanced over his shoulder. "Not for my cruelty, sir. For that is beyond price."

"Everything has a price, lambkin. And in my experience cruelty is usually free."

"I think," returned the piratical gentleman, "that probably says more about your experiences than it does human nature."

This drew an excruciated groan from Amberglass. "God fucking save me. I paid for a prick and I got a philosopher."

"Amberglass." Gracewood's voice was hard as diamond, sharp as fine blade. "You will tell me where my sister is."

"I will," conceded Amberglass, with incongruous ease. He let the silence hang for several long seconds. "After you suck my cock." Pushing the woman roughly away from him, he gestured at his member, spit-slick and barely stirred, exposed through the open fall of his pantaloons. "See if you can do a better job than this one, and I'll sing like a nightingale."

"I'm afraid," Gracewood told him, "I have no intention of sucking your cock."

"Whyever not? It's just flesh. You aren't afraid of a little perdition, are you?"

No doubt Amberglass's intent had been to embarrass, if not shock them. Except he could not have chosen a less effective way to do it. After all, Viola knew for a fact that Gracewood sucked cock with great facility and passion. He simply had no taste for gentlemen. Or blackguards.

Gracewood shrugged. "Not in the slightest. Though I still cannot indulge you. Not least because I sincerely doubt the act you're requesting would bring delight to either of us."

"Oh, I don't know." Tarnished light glinted in the depths of Amberglass's eyes. "I might like to see you on your knees."

"I will beg," said Gracewood softly, "and gladly. If that is what you need to tell me what you know of Mira."

"Why don't you try it and see?"

"Only because I doubt its efficacy. Clearly you would prefer to play with us than help us."

"What do you expect?" Amberglass spread his hands expansively. "Life is long and dull. One must pass the time somehow."

"Is that why you did it?" Gracewood asked him. "Is that why you took my sister?"

Another of Amberglass's world-weary groans. "For the last fucking time, I don't have your fucking sister."

"You're still involved."

"As you said…" A clumsy, drunkard's shrug. "I'm *playful*. I like to play."

"Why Mira, though? What has she ever done to you?"

"Why?" Tapping a finger against his lips, Amberglass repeated the word as though he'd never before considered it. "Because I could? Because I'm bored. Because I despise you and your happiness. And for slights, of course. Old and new."

From the set of his mouth and the lines upon his brow, Viola could tell that Gracewood was beginning to lose his grip on his temper. "How could she possibly have slighted you? She's a seventeen-year-old girl."

"Maybe I mislike her taste in Shakespeare. And maybe I mislike your taste in mistresses. Former mistresses at least. They say you lost your manhood at Waterloo."

Viola reached out a steadying hand, but it was too late.

Gracewood's control snapped with the thoroughness of a bone breaking. "Fuck you, Amberglass."

Amberglass only smirked. "I think not, lambkin."

"Enough of this." And Gracewood, pressed beyond the limits of his patience, advanced upon Amberglass, only for the other man to snatch up a pistol from a pile of empty bottles beside his chair and level it.

"Not so fa—"

Before Amberglass could even finish his sentence, Gracewood shifted his weight to the side, covered the gun with his free hand and wrested it from Amberglass's grip. Stepping back out of reach, Gracewood steadied himself on his cane and trained the weapon squarely at Amberglass's heart.

"Where"—Gracewood was panting slightly—"is my sister, you prating degenerate?"

Amberglass regarded him with far less apprehension than the situation might have warranted. "And if I'm not disposed to tell you?"

"Begging your pardon," said the woman whose oral expertise Amberglass had recently impugned. "But can we leave?"

"Yes," added the corsair, draping one of the bedsheets around his companion. "I'm not being paid enough to fuck through a firefight."

"Oh, sod off the lot of you." Amberglass waved an aggrieved hand. "I've been better entertained by pissing myself."

Needing no further encouragement, the assembled professionals trooped out, leaving Gracewood, Viola, and Amberglass to their confrontation. Though, if she was being honest, Viola feared it might be a stalemate. Amberglass clearly had no intention of telling them what he knew about Mira, if he knew anything at all, and even being so swiftly disarmed didn't seem to have daunted him.

By contrast, Gracewood was very pale, the hand on his cane too tight, and the hand on the pistol too slack. She hated to think of the toll the evening's events had taken upon him, physically as well as emotionally. But she also suspected that going to him would only put her in his way. Or be seen as weakness by Amberglass.

"I do hope," said Amberglass, fastening his pantaloons and rising somewhat unsteadily to his feet, "you'll see your way to shooting me soon. I'm a rather busy man—people to see, lives to ruin, et cetera et cetera."

"What have you done with Mira?" The gun wavered slightly in Gracewood's grip.

Amberglass took a step towards him. Then another. "Why don't you shoot me?"

"I'm growing tired of your games, Amberglass."

"Come on. Right here." Amberglass's mouth curled into a sickly smile as he tapped his chest. "Point-blank. It'll be easy."

"Stay back." Gracewood's hand was trembling on the gun.

Amberglass did not stay back, closing the distance between the two men with the sort of fearlessness that had nothing to do with courage. Had the situation been different, Viola might even have pitied him for it. "Put a bullet in me. None would blame you for it. Some would likely thank you."

"I…" Gracewood faltered into silence.

All that separated them now was a slim length of metal.

"You can't, can you?" asked Amberglass, the grey of his eyes as dull as the pistol.

Gracewood's hand was shaking so badly that Viola doubted any shot he fired would land.

"What's the matter?" Amberglass's lips twisted mockingly. "Scared of the noise?"

No reply from Gracewood. Just the slow slide of sweat from his temples.

Taking the gun by the barrel, Amberglass pressed it against his breastbone. "Bang," he said.

Then threw back his head and laughed as Gracewood flinched.

"Call yourself a man." He twitched the weapon free from Gracewood's grasp. "Was it the war that broke you? Or your own father? The stories one hears."

Gracewood dropped to his good knee, his breath coming in great harsh gusts. And, for a moment, Amberglass just watched him, his expression so shuttered that Viola had no idea what he could be thinking.

"How infuriating," he muttered finally. "You were right. I remain undelighted."

He sauntered back to his chair and reclaimed his seat, flinging a leg over one arm and resting the gun upon the other. "I believe this brings us back to my original offer. Or I suppose you could have your pretty lady friend oblige me instead, if you don't have the stomach for it."

Past caring what Amberglass did, said, or thought, Viola had moved to Gracewood's side. There was, she would always believe, no shame in his suffering, but to see it mocked was unbearable. "I'm afraid," she said to Amberglass, "I don't want to suck your cock either."

His gaze raked her from head to foot, though there was little lust in it. Just an unfocused acquisitiveness. "Then I do hope you'll both be leaving soon. For we have comprehensively run out of things to say to one another. And I believe I may have mentioned how intolerable I find being bored?"

Viola cast him the most withering look she could manage. "My heart bleeds for you."

At this, he laughed, sounding almost surprised. "I think I could enjoy your tongue, madam. Are you sure you won't apply it to my nether regions? Your too-gentle duke does seem rather preoccupied with his sister. Rouse me, and I'll tell you everything I know. I give you my word."

It was a disgusting thought, to let herself be so used, and by such a creature. But would it be worth it? For Mira, for Gracewood. "Your word, Your Grace, isn't worth spit."

"True." Amberglass rose once more and sauntered over to where Gracewood was kneeling. "Still it's worth a deal more than this pile of ruined flesh." He gave Gracewood a sharp kick in the ribs, sending him sprawling. "Tell me, lambkin, would it be worse if your woman *would* suck my cock to save your sister, or that she wouldn't?"

Lying on the floor, Gracewood was laughing. "You're a weak man, Amberglass."

The Duke of Amberglass looked down. "You know, I think I could piss in your mouth from here."

"Weak and cowardly."

"My dear Gracewood, you say that as though it will wound me. I know full well how worthless I am." He kicked Gracewood again, and Viola felt it in her own body. "But I can still hurt you. And I take comfort in that."

"Where is my sister?"

Stooping, Amberglass picked up Gracewood's cane. "Do you think that if you keep asking, I'll eventually drop into a monologue like the villain in some cheap melodrama?" He jabbed the point of the cane into Gracewood's stomach. "I'll admit it *does* sound like me, doesn't it?"

"Get away from him." Viola hadn't been conscious of stepping forward, but step forward she had.

"Or what?"

"Get away from him," she repeated.

"Look at me, Miss . . . I'm sorry, I never asked your name."

"My name is Carroll. Viola Carroll."

"How lovely. Perhaps later this evening I shall make you sing. But for now, Miss Carroll, look at me. Do I seem like the kind of man who would hesitate to strike a woman?"

"You seem like the kind of man who would hesitate to do most things."

"Wrong answer."

And he struck her, hard, with the head of the cane. It was an odd strike—not the playful roughhousing of youths nor the desperate brutality of a soldier who knew that you would kill him if he did not kill you. It was as though Amberglass simply didn't care if he hurt her or not. Still he caught her a sharp enough blow to rattle her, to take her off her feet and, she thought, cut her scalp. He threw Gracewood's cane after her, contemptuously.

"You see," Amberglass said to the still-prone Gracewood, "that's what happens when you try to hide behind your woman."

Blinking the tears from her eyes, Viola noticed that the cane was within reach. She had not fenced in years, but perhaps she could remember enough. She seized the hilt, twisted and drew the sword free.

The Duke of Amberglass had his back to her. He had just spat in Gracewood's face.

Rising, she levelled the blade at Amberglass's neck, holding it dead still in quarte. "I *said* get away from him."

"My dear lady"—Amberglass turned towards her with the curiosity of the viper towards the mouse—"His Grace has been teaching you to handle *quite* the wrong kind of sword. Now put that down before you do yourself an injury."

An odd calm had come over Viola. This was part of a life she had long left behind, this stance, this steel, the weight of the weapon perfectly balanced in her hand, but then so was Gracewood, and he was hers also. "Away. Now."

"Or what?"

The old drills came back without even thinking. Her hand turned smartly to tierce, a slight flexing of the elbow and an opening and closing of the fingers just as her lunge landed to deliver a clean cut from the corner of Amberglass's right eye down the length of his cheek.

Amberglass pressed a hand to his face in disbelief. "You... you *berserk harridan*."

"Away."

Amberglass, his hands raised, backed towards the chair where he had previously been lounging. "All right, all right. You know you could be quite a magnificent creature if you weren't so repulsively prim."

"Mira."

"Yes, yes." As he neared his seat he stooped and took up a walking cane of his own. "Now. You were about to threaten me at swordpoint."

"Tell us where Mira is."

"But of course. No need to be so vexatious. You see, Miss Carroll, there are two things you must understand about me."

In spite of her better judgement, Viola took the bait. "Which are?"

"That I take delight in nothing save the misfortune of others and"—he turned the head of his cane, revealing his own small-sword concealed within—"I always take precautions."

Amberglass's blade came up sharply to cross Viola's, but she slipped down and around in a tight arc, bringing her weapon back to strike his and bear it aside. She thrust at once for his exposed shoulder, not aiming to kill or even to wound but to draw a response.

Still half-drunk, Amberglass just managed to spring back to avoid her point and then lunged forward clumsily. She parried his attack with a neat semicircular parade, but intoxication was making Amberglass erratic, and the cruel truth of swords was that an unskilled fencer was more dangerous than a skilled one. A trained and sober opponent would think first of their own defence, but one who was reckless, or addled, or had no regard for their own life would pursue relentlessly, and it took only a single mistake to be wounded fatally.

So she retreated and hoped that eventually Amberglass would tire or grow bored. Where she could she struck out with harrying thrusts against his forward wrist, which his sloppy guard exposed, or towards his face, hoping that even a man as far gone as Amberglass would naturally fall back to defend his eyes.

But it wasn't working. Amberglass kept pressing her, and she was running out of space to evade him. The room was crowded and messy, and at last, inevitably, she stumbled over a low stool, letting her guard drop for a fraction of a second. Amberglass wouldn't have had the reflexes to seize the opening if he hadn't been attacking already, except he had done nothing but attack. His blade came forward straight and true and then at the last moment veered to one side and down, scoring a line through her skirts, leaving her unharmed.

Looking down, Viola saw that Gracewood, nowhere near recovered from his earlier mistreatment, had crawled along the floor and caught Amberglass by the ankle—a weak grip but enough to make him turn and pull his blade off line.

"What do I have to do," the Duke of Amberglass snarled, "to make you stay down." Crooking his elbow at an awkward angle, he aimed his blade directly at Gracewood's body.

Viola had less than a heartbeat to act. She had a clean, open line to thrust, but if she killed Amberglass, she would be hanged, and Mira would never be found. So she darted forward, raising the blade of her sword to point backwards over her shoulder, and with all of the force she could muster drove the pommel into the bridge of Amberglass's nose.

There was a crunch of cartilage and a spray of blood, and Amberglass let his weapon clatter to the floor.

"My nose," he burbled, hands pressed to his face. "You broke my *fucking nose.*"

"And you"—Viola was almost surprised at her own confidence, at how *right* it felt to be here, now, saying these things— "abducted my friend. You beat the man I love. And you tried to kill me."

"But my *fucking* nose."

Bringing her sword level with Amberglass's breastbone, for she still didn't trust him an inch, Viola crouched down to help Gracewood to his feet. "Where," she said, "is Mira?"

"Leave him be." Gracewood leaned against her, letting her take more of his weight than he ever had before. Unself-consciously vulnerable and, in his own way, stronger than she had ever seen him.

Then he looked up at their enemy. "I had thought you a monster, Amberglass, but you aren't. You are little more than a wounded child. We will find Mira without you."

A splutter of blood and spite came from the direction of the Duke of Amberglass. "You're bluffing."

Slowly, achingly slowly, but with a dignity that belonged entirely to himself and had nothing to do with his name, Gracewood bent, retrieved the other half of his cane, and screwed Viola's sword back into position. Then the two of them turned, and he let Viola lead him towards the door. "Good-bye, Amberglass."

"You will *not* walk away from me," insisted the Duke.

They walked away from him.

"You are a cripple and a coward, Gracewood. A cripple and a coward who hides behind his woman's skirts."

After a few more paces, Gracewood stopped and turned back. "I came here for one thing, Amberglass. Seeing that I will not get it, I am leaving."

"You came here so I could tell you where to find your whore sister who killed your whore mother."

Gracewood nodded. "Yes."

"And you failed."

"Yes. Which is why I am leaving."

"You are..."

Taking a quiet breath, Gracewood inclined his head just fractionally to one side. "Yes?"

"Your sister is..."

"Good-bye, Amberglass." And again, with painstaking slowness they turned to leave.

"I know who has Miranda."

It was hard for Viola to ignore him, but Gracewood seemed determined to go and she trusted him to know what he was doing.

"Aren't you listening. She slighted me, and I arranged to have her taken."

They kept walking.

"For fuck's sake, Gracewood, isn't this what you came here for?"

They stopped one last time in the doorway, and Gracewood turned once more, each step deliberate and more masterful than the last. "I came for a place, or a name, or both. But I cannot make you give them to me."

"Because you are—"

Somehow, Gracewood was smiling. "Yes, yes, because I am weak and a coward and a cripple and less than a man. And I do not deny that when I first learned of your involvement in my sister's disappearance, it pained me that I would not be able to take satisfaction from your hide."

Amberglass, Viola noticed, was swaying a little. Partly the pain, she suspected, partly the drink. "And now?"

"Now I find I have had my fill of a world that judges men by their capacity to hurt. You are not the villain of this story, Amberglass. You are no part of it at all."

"And you?"

"I am no part of it either. It is Miranda's life. Help her, or don't. I have no hold over you, as you have none over me."

Amberglass scowled. "I have a hold over your sister."

"You do." Gracewood was still calm, and this, Viola was sure, was not the reserve that his father had beaten into him; it was something else. "You have it in your power to harm a seventeen-year-old girl, if you choose to. If that is what pleases you."

"It pleases me."

"Then why have you not let us leave?"

For a long while, Amberglass was silent. Then at last he said, "Viscount Stirling has taken her to his estate on the Kentish border. The man owes me money, as he owes everyone money, and I was amused by the thought of his paying me back with your fortune." When this drew no discernable reaction from Gracewood, Amberglass swept an unsteady bow, spattering blood upon the previously pristine floors. "There. You have overcome the wicked duke and made him tell you where to find the fair damsel."

"The wicked duke," observed Gracewood, "should probably see a chirurgeon."

Amberglass's mouth twisted into a wretched sneer. "Oh, fuck off and let me bleed in peace."

So, without another word, Gracewood and Viola turned, and were gone.

# CHAPTER 40

"Do you want me to drive?" Viola asked him, as they returned to his curricle.

His leg was burning, his hands were unsteady, and his heart still felt half-strangled in his chest. Not long ago, he would have told her no regardless. But instead he tossed her the reins. "Please. Can you find your way?"

"Well enough, I think. If I push the horses, we'll be there in three hours, perhaps a little less."

"Three hours," he repeated, clutched by fresh dread. "But Mira—"

"Is not in any immediate danger. If Stirling has debts, as Amberglass implied, then his aim will be to entrap Miranda into marriage. Not..." She swallowed. "Well."

A grim silence descended upon them and did not lift for some time. Viola navigated deftly through the emptying London streets and onto the road to Kent. The night beyond the city was mild and clear, the landscape a silvered forever—mirror-smooth fields, the ribbon-twist of an occasional stream, ash trees, in curly-headed silhouette, cast like images from a magic lantern against the sky.

A sky whose like Gracewood could not remember ever seeing or, at least, having opportunity to dwell upon. Bare of cloud and strewn with stars as thick as dust motes, the edges of the Milky

Way glistening sharply like the interior of a geode. There was at once something taunting in such beauty—and consoling too.

"Viola, I—" he began at the same time she said "Gracewood, I—"

"You first," he said. "I insist."

"I am sorry," she said, "that my first instinct was to take up a sword. I know how you feel about…about what we did in the war."

Gracewood gave a rough laugh. "The war was the war. And that room was that room. I will not think ill of you for drawing steel on my behalf."

"Let us hope I do not have to think ill of myself."

"Whyever should you?"

"I was glad not to be at that man's mercy." One of Viola's shoulders lifted in the barest of shrugs. "But it is hard to forget that I would have been had I not been taught to fence."

"What you know," he told her, "is not who you are."

She offered a tight little nod. "Indeed. And it is a foolish thing to fear, is it not? That I could be so easily stripped from myself, by the trappings of a life I left behind."

"I am the last person to be judging the fears of others." A too-sharp memory of the gun in his hand flashed across his mind and made his stomach churn with fresh nausea. "Especially since it was not a fear you would have had to face if it were not for me."

"Nonsense, Gracewood." The sharpness of her dismissal was familiar. The deep affection in it, though, that was something only recently unbared. "It should not have taken a drunkard with a sword cane to show me that defending the man I love could never make me less a woman."

He turned his head so he could watch the moonlight silver her profile and the dark waves of her hair. "Nevertheless, I wish I had not needed it. A man should not—" But then he stopped himself. Those words also belonged to an old life. "On second thoughts, fuck what a man should not. I'm grateful to you, Viola, for both your protection and your love."

"Those are freely given, and do not require your gratitude. Besides"—her smile was a pale gleam in the uncertain light—"I think we have always loved and protected each other."

It was then he noticed a shadow upon her brow. "My heart, are you bleeding?"

"Oh…" Her fingertips moved almost absently to her head. "It's nothing. A shallow cut."

Taking his handkerchief from his coat, Gracewood did his best to clean the wound, his touch as gentle as he could make it in the jostling curricle. When he was done, the quiet persisted softly between them, as did their closeness, Gracewood letting himself drift in the heat of Viola's body next to his, her strength and her softness, the hands she did not like in their beautifully embroidered gloves as masterful upon the reins as they were with a needle. As they were upon his body. He closed his eyes and listened to the harsh breath of the horses heavy in the air, the rattle of the curricle wheels against the road, the stir of the wind through unseen trees.

"What a fucking prick Amberglass is," he muttered.

Viola made a sound of concurrence. "Indeed. I have rarely encountered someone so determined to be disliked."

"Fortunate for him, then, that his talents and his preferences are in such harmony."

Out of the corner of her eye, Viola cast him a concerned glance. "Did he hurt you very badly?"

Gracewood turned his face to her neck and breathed in the

familiar scent of her skin. The tang of sweat and the sweetness of her cosmetics. "No, or no worse than I can bear. Certainly no worse than he hurt you. He was aiming to wound my pride more than my body, I think, and I find—I find myself no longer so vulnerable in that regard. Why should I care what Amberglass thinks of me? Or any man. Or any woman, for that matter, save those I care for." They rode on a little longer, and then he added, "But I'm afraid for Mira."

"She'll be fine," said Viola with an artificial-sounding certainty that Gracewood suspected was for both of their benefits. "She's resourceful. And green," she added, in an attempt to make him smile. "Which, if nothing else, should discourage any untoward amorousness."

"Greenish yellow," Gracewood reminded her. "But how will she ever trust me again? I was supposed to protect her."

"You didn't kidnap her. Or at least"—Viola's tone was still carefully light—"I hope you didn't, because that's a gothic twist I was certainly not expecting."

At last, in spite of everything, he smiled. "No, I didn't. That would be a little too Matthew Lewis. I just failed her. As I have always failed her."

"We will find her. That is what matters here. And what will matter to Mira."

"He came to see me, you know. Stirling. To ask for her hand. I thought him merely naïve."

"You are not omniscient."

"Should I not have—"

"No." She nudged her leg against his—a gesture as comforting as it was exasperated. "Let us place the blame for this nonsense squarely where it belongs. With the perpetrators."

It was a relief to let his thoughts quiet. To simply believe her. "You're right."

"Louise's two favourite words."

"Oh God." He stirred slightly. "We must send word to her. As soon as we can."

"And we will. But rest for now. We've some ways to go."

"Some rescue party I shall make if I'm asleep."

"On the contrary." She drew him closer. "It will be very impressive. Anyone can effect a rescue while awake. It takes real skill to do the same unconscious."

Laughing, he tucked in against her and closed his eyes again. He did not actually sleep—that would have been impossible. But it felt soothing, somehow, to let time untether itself. Just for a little while.

Which meant he was not, in the end, sure how much later it was when he was roused by the clatter of hoofbeats in the distance. A lone rider by the sounds of it. Coming towards them at some speed.

He sat up abruptly as a horse tore past them. Caught a flash of pale hair in the moonlight. A cloak streaming on the wind. And Viola bringing them to a bone-juddering halt. While behind them now the rider wheeled round.

"Mira?" He was out of the curricle with a swiftness that almost made his leg buckle under him.

Running, as best he could, along an unfamiliar country road.

Towards his sister, who had thrown herself to the ground, and was running towards him in return.

"Justin," she cried. "Oh, Justin."

They came together in something that was more of a collision than a hug, Gracewood with no notion how he kept his footing.

And Mira was half laughing, half crying in his arms. "I knew you would come. I *knew* you would."

He had no words. He was just breath, and a beating heart, and arms that could do nothing but hold her.

"Can you believe," she said into his chest "that I got kidnapped? Actually kidnapped. What a business."

He still could not bring himself to relinquish her. "Are you all right? What happened?"

"I'm absolutely fine." Despite her attempt to reassure him, Gracewood could feel her trembling. "I mean, it was an awful shock at first. And I can't say I enjoyed being incapacitated by some kind of sponge soaked in narcotics."

"But you weren't hurt?" he asked, and where he might once have felt an anger he would have mistaken for strength, now he was only concerned. Only wanted to know she was well.

"Not in the slightest." Mira laughed, or tried to—the sound that emerged was a little shrill, and wavering. "I fear I shall never understand men. After all, if you turn down someone's proposal of marriage when they *haven't* abducted you, *being* abducted does not make you better disposed towards them."

"No," Gracewood agreed, kissing the top of her head. "No, I suppose it wouldn't. But thank...thank anything, thank everything that you're unharmed."

His sister gazed up at him with wide, slightly damp eyes. "I am. I promise I am. And I'm so, so sorry I got kidnapped."

"You have nothing to be sorry for."

"It's hard not to wonder if I've been at fault somehow."

"You have not," Gracewood said firmly. "We tell ladies that their virtue is their shield, when it is no such thing. When the only true protection against the predations of powerful men is—"

"A pistol?" suggested Miranda.

"I was going to say a society of laws, the companionship of loyal friends, and a world that knows better."

Viola had joined them upon the road. "A pistol may prove easier to come by."

And then Miranda let out a sharp gasp, her hands flying to her mouth. "Good heavens. I don't know how I forgot. In all the excitement, I...oh, Justin, I don't quite know how to tell you. But, well...I think I may have murdered Viscount Stirling."

# CHAPTER 41

It was, Viola thought, one of the things—one of the many things—she appreciated about Gracewood that he accepted the news his sister thought she'd killed someone with remarkable equanimity. Merely suggesting she tell him exactly what happened from the beginning.

"It's a bit muddled," Mira admitted, "because of the narcotic sponge. But when I realised I wasn't going to be able to persuade the Viscount to take me back to London, I panicked a little and hit him over the head with a vase." A pause. "It was one of those Chinese ones, you know? With a picture of a sage crossing a river on it. I feel quite bad about it, because it was terribly pretty and now it is smashed to bits." Another pause. "I mean, I also feel bad about murdering Viscount Stirling, but that's such a vastness of wrong-doing my mind can't really encompass it. So I keep thinking about the vase instead. Am I going to be imprisoned? Or transported? Or hanged?" Her hands came to her mouth again, and whatever whimsical bravado had been sustaining her thus far seemed to evaporate. "Oh dear, oh dear, will I be hanged?"

Gracewood drew her into the circle of his free arm. "No, of course not. We will do...whatever it takes to resolve this."

"But what can we do? I suppose we could hide the body and—and concoct some story about—about his leaving for a long journey." Mira's face fell. "Except the servants saw me. And I needed the stableboy's help to steal this horse. And now I'm a horse thief as well as a murderer."

"We will return the horse," Gracewood told her.

"And," Viola added, "if you'll forgive the pragmaticism of my perspective, it's highly unlikely that the Viscount is dead."

Mira turned big hopeful eyes upon her. "Is it?"

"Yes. Killing people is at once far too easy and actually quite difficult."

"I hit him very hard. And he fell facedown on the hearthrug and stopped moving."

"Did you"—had the circumstance been less grave, Gracewood's expression would have been comically awkward—"check his breathing?"

Slowly, Miranda shook her head. "N-no. I ran away. Was that wrong? Can I not even murder a man correctly?"

"Do you *want* to have murdered Viscount Stirling?"

"Of course not," Miranda cried. "I'm so confused. And I haven't even thanked Viola properly for coming to rescue me."

Viola went to embrace her. "You don't have to thank me. I'm just glad you're safe."

"And you have done well in a bad situation," Gracewood said. "You have been brave and resourceful. I'm nothing but proud of you."

"Really?" Miranda relaxed a little in Gracewood's arms. "You are? Oh, Justin."

"Mira, I am *always* proud of you. How could I not be?"

"Because I'm strange. And because I'm silly. And because if it wasn't for me, our mother might—"

"Stop." Gracewood cut across her hoarsely. "You mustn't think like that. You mustn't *ever* think like that. You're my sister, and you can be as silly as you damn well please, but I have always loved you. Always wanted you to be a part of my family."

Miranda stared at him, her mouth perfectly round with surprise. "Oh."

"I just... didn't know how to be a brother. How to show care. I wasn't raised in a way that allowed for such things. Though ever since I understood that life could be different—that I could be different—I have been trying. God knows I've been trying. Please don't tell me it's too late."

"Not too late," she whispered. "Not too late at all."

It seemed a necessary moment for Viola to give them a little space, so she returned to the curricle. And for a while Gracewood and Miranda conversed just out of earshot before coming back to join her.

Gracewood was frowning. "Come. Tonight's adventure is not yet over."

"I'm not convinced I like adventures." Mira's eyes still glistened with tears. "I'd hoped they would make me feel more thrilled and less sick. I think I would very much like to go home."

"I'm sure, but you've been gone long enough that you will have been missed. And there's your reputation to think of."

"My reputation," muttered Mira. "Because of course a lady being kidnapped reflects badly on her."

"It's unfair, I agree. Though I'd prefer to debate the inequities of our society some other time."

"Really?" Catching his eye, Viola offered Gracewood a smile she suspected he might need. "Some of the finest debates happen by roadsides in the middle of the night."

His eyes gleamed with amusement, their colour swallowed by

the moonlight. "We can talk about it on the way back to Viscount Stirling if you wish."

"Back?" wailed Mira. "Justin, I don't think you understand how escaping is supposed to work."

"I'm afraid so." Gracewood's gaze was very steady, his voice very certain. "While I think you *probably* haven't killed the Viscount, I believe it behooves us to…check. And I would also strongly prefer that we haven't stolen his horse."

"Do I have to?" asked Mira, her voice suddenly tremulous.

"No. But it's by the far best thing we can do. So I'm asking you to consider it. And to trust me. Please."

As it turned out, Mira did not need long to consider. "As you wish. But under protest. And only because it's you who's asking. And because, you're right, ideally I won't have murdered anyone."

It didn't take long for them to get under way, Gracewood helping Mira back into the saddle of her *borrowed* mount before taking up the reins of his curricle again. He was exhausted, Viola could tell from his pallor and the lines carved into his face, but there was something unyielding in him too. Not anger, exactly— he rarely indulged in that, perhaps because of his father, perhaps because it was simply not in his nature. Still, she would not have wished to cross him tonight.

There was a strangeness, sometimes, in being able to see all the pieces of him. The wounded man and her laughing friend, her generous lover and the formidable duke. Yet there were also moments, like tonight, where they coalesced, seeming neither flaws, nor weakness, nor contradictions, and she saw only his strength. How it need not, for him, be a cold thing.

And this, this was the man she loved. Who loved her in

return. It was not an occasion to be sentimental. The night had been long and fraught and could have ended badly in so many ways. Could, in fact, end badly regardless. But still. What a marvel it was. What freedom. To be a woman unabashedly in love beneath a multitude of stars.

Auclere—Viscount Stirling's Kentish estate—possessed a long carriageway, winding languorously through shadowy woodlands, before the trees parted like theatre curtains to reveal the house itself. It was too dark to see much of it, but Viola caught a fleeting impression of Tudor charm—timber-framed and many gabled.

The butler who answered their knock had the air of a family retainer and was too well trained to express visible confusion. But his brow creased ominously.

"Your master is expecting us," said Gracewood. "My sister, I believe, you'll be familiar with already. She was kind enough to escort us back when we were delayed on the road."

For a moment the butler hesitated, apparently trying to navigate which of the various possibilities before him was the most outlandish: That the Duke of Gracewood would turn up unannounced in the middle of the night. That the man he served would have brought home a respectable young woman for the express purpose of ruining her reputation. That any of this could possibly be true. And if the truth mattered more or less than the fiction. Eventually he stood aside, with a bow. "His Lordship is in the library. But I fear he is...indisposed."

Gracewood was already handing his coat and hat to a footman. "Which way, please?"

"Here." Mira—who really was very green in the light—darted off down the nearest corridor.

Thankfully the house, though well proportioned, was not sizeable, and Viola was able to pursue her at a more seemly pace, entering what she presumed would be the Viscount's library in time to hear Mira address the gentleman with:

"Well. Now my brother has come. What do you have to say to that?"

Viscount Stirling was looking neither in good shape nor good spirits, slumped in an armchair with a half-empty decanter of brandy at his elbow and blood matted into his hair. "L-Lady Miranda?" He blinked blearily at her. "What are you doing here?"

"You invited us." Gracewood strolled into the room, cane tip-tapping against the floorboards. "I mean, you did invite us, didn't you?"

While Viscount Stirling probably possessed many fine qualities, he was not quick on the uptake. He continued blinking. "Did I?"

"I should sincerely hope so." Gracewood offered him a bland smile. "Since the alternative is that you made a rather committed attempt to abduct my sister, which I would be inclined to view with some displeasure."

"I am certainly very displeased about it," added Mira, who looked indignant but sounded more fragile than Viola would have liked.

Though she might as well not have spoken for all the heed the Viscount paid her. His gaze grew at once sour and speculative. "If that was indeed the case, Lady Miranda would have spent some several hours alone in my company. Such an—"

Miranda gave an outraged little squeak. "Being unconscious does not count as company."

"Such an affair," the Viscount went on doggedly, "would undoubtedly prove detrimental to her reputation."

"How fortunate then"—Gracewood settled himself comfortably into an armchair—"that she spent a night at the home of a family friend in the company of her brother and chaperone."

The Viscount's mouth twisted sulkily. "She hit me with a vase."

"I beg your pardon?" Gracewood betrayed no emotion. Despite the travails of the evening, he was ice again, serene and regal.

"Your sister hit me with a vase."

At this, Gracewood actually laughed. "I'm sure you're mistaken. What possible cause would she have to do something like that? Why, it's almost as ludicrous as suggesting that a decent man would stoop to abduction and coercion."

There was a tense silence, although Gracewood contrived to look entirely at his ease—one booted foot stretched towards the fire as if the faded hearthrug was not scattered with pieces of broken china.

"I think we can all agree," began the Viscount, "that the lady's behaviour has been quite beyond the pale." Another noise of protest from Miranda, which he chose to ignore. "Nevertheless, I remain willing to repair the damage her actions will have done to her future prospects by offering her my hand in marriage."

Up went one of Gracewood's eyebrows. "Your generosity *astonishes* me, sir."

"Then"—the Viscount pulled himself semi-upright—"you will agree to the match."

"Not for the wide world. The fact you feel obliged to prevail upon my sister by force tells you everything you need to know about her wishes."

"She's a seventeen-year-old girl," protested the Viscount. "What can she possibly know about her own wishes?"

Gracewood's gaze was as cold as winter seas. "More than you."

"But you are Lady Miranda's guardian. You must want what is best for her."

And still Gracewood was calm, though Viola was certain that the Viscount's impertinence was irritating him. "Marrying a man with no respect for her choices can in no way be what is best for my sister."

"I will be a good husband, Your Grace." Leaning forward in his chair, the Viscount twisted his hands together almost imploringly. "I am not profligate nor licentious. I am told that women find me comely. She will have no cause to regret me."

Gracewood briefly massaged his temples. "Stirling, you don't even consider it worth your while to talk to her."

"This is men's business."

At last, Gracewood let his voice betray a hint of passion. "It is *Mira's* business."

"Then"—Viscount Stirling's lips tightened—"she may live with the consequences of this evening's *choices*."

"May I hit him with another vase?" asked Mira, into the silence.

Which caused Viscount Stirling to leap to his feet with ill-advised alacrity, almost knocking the decanter from the table as he tried to steady himself. "Stay back, you little—"

"Please do consider," murmured Gracewood, "very carefully what word you might be about to use in my presence. And, once you have completed your considerations, I would strongly recommend that you return to your seat."

"How dare—"

"I dare because I am Justin de Vere, Duke of Gracewood, and it is my *right*, as you well know. Now sit."

It was probably shock, as much as volition, that sent the Viscount reeling backwards into his chair again.

"Thank you." Smiling faintly, Gracewood folded his hands neatly on top of his cane. "Perhaps a little frankness is in order? You may, of course, spread whatever rumours you wish regarding tonight's...misadventure. But I suspect any less than flattering comments you make about Mira will look like little more than pique. Your attentions have been quite marked, and no-one appreciates being rejected."

"You will have her branded a coquette."

Gracewood's eyes narrowed thoughtfully. "Perhaps, but it'll be you the ton are laughing at."

This image seemed to strike the Viscount rather strongly, and he flushed, an unflattering, purple-ish shade better suited to a dowager's turban.

"It really is up to you," Gracewood told him, shrugging. "Although, while you are weighing up your options, I should also mention that if you cross my family again I will dismantle you, piece by piece."

Gracewood had spoken so quietly that it took a moment for the Viscount to respond. And, even then, it was more of a gargle. "I...you...what?"

"I know your debts are substantial. I will buy them all. And then I will take apart everything you have. Sell off every last shred of this life you would threaten my sister to keep. I will own you, Stirling, and you will have nothing. You will be nothing. And"—a pause—"I am increasingly tempted to let Mira hit you with another vase. Perhaps you should think about apologising?"

The Viscount's eyes were wild, flashing their whites like a frightened horse. "B-but...*she* hit *me*."

"Then consider how powerless she must have felt"—it was only because she knew him so well, because she felt for him so keenly, that Viola heard the tremor enter Gracewood's voice— "how frightened and alone, that she would attempt to overcome you, a man both larger and stronger than she, armed only with a type of decorative container famous for its fragility."

"She...she took me by surprise."

"Given the situation, I call that damn good sense."

The Viscount's gaze slid to Mira. "I...I..." His throat bobbed, as if he was literally attempting to swallow his pride. "I apologise, madam. I truly intended you no harm. You would have been safe beneath my roof."

"Oh good." Mira glared. "I'm much reassured to know your purpose was subornment rather than ravishment."

A nerve ticked in the Viscount's jaw. "I have expressed my regret," he said stiffly. "And yet still you cast these unsubstantiated aspersions on my character. I would *never* sully myself by engaging in unwilling congress."

"Gah," exclaimed Mira. "There are creepy crawlies that live under rocks and logs I would rather marry than you."

The Viscount turned back to Gracewood. "There. Are you satisfied? And I would prefer...I would ask..." Another convulsive ripple of his throat. "That you do not make my...my circumstances public knowledge. I am attempting to restore my family's fortune."

"Unpleasant, is it not"—Gracewood's tone was still cool to the point of disinterest—"to find yourself in the power of a relative stranger?"

"Yes, yes" came the ungracious reply. "So what is it you want of me?"

"Mutual agreement as to what occurred this evening. Your hospitality for a couple of days. Public civility. No more threats against my family. Or, now that I come to think of it, anyone else's. If you wish to marry money, I'm afraid you will have to do it consensually."

"But…" A shadow passed across the Viscount's face. Something helpless and despairing and all too human. "What else am I to do? I was raised a gentleman. I have two younger brothers, twins, both still in school."

"You have the strangest definition of gentleman," muttered Mira, "considering it deems allowable your behaviour towards me."

"Necessary." The certainty in the Viscount's voice was, to Viola, more galling than all of Amberglass's spite had been. "I deemed it necessary."

"So," Mira asked, "you don't actually think it was right?"

The Viscount put a hand to his brow, wincing as his fingers explored the edge of the cut. "Amberglass said it wouldn't matter once we were wed."

Mira folded her arms as if to protect herself, or to hold herself together. "It would have mattered to me a great deal."

He sighed. "Won't you marry me, Lady Miranda? I swear upon my honour I will be the best of husbands. And you will come to love my brothers as your own family. They are everything that I am not—clever and lively, like you."

"Do *not* try to make me feel sorry for you. It's not fair. I will not marry you for pity."

"I'm sure"—the Viscount gave an odd, hollow laugh—"there are worse foundations for matrimony. And I don't know what else to do."

Mira was silent for a long moment. Then, "I am sorry. Surprisingly, I am. But I can't help you, My Lord."

"Stirling"—Gracewood's voice was still ice-calm—"please stop proposing to my sister and have guest rooms made up."

"Guest rooms?" Viscount Stirling stared at him blankly.

Gracewood nodded. "Well, it would not do to invite a duke and his sister to stay at your estate and then have them sleep in the stable."

"Whatever you wish." Reaching for the decanter, Viscount Stirling poured himself a glass of whiskey with an unsteady hand. "Make yourself at home. Why the devil not?"

"Thank you." And since the Viscount seemed unlikely to move again any time soon, Gracewood rose and went to ring the bell on his behalf.

# CHAPTER 42

It was strange for Viola to sleep alone, even after a bare few weeks of sharing Gracewood's bed. He did not always rest easily—pursued by pain or nightmares—but her presence would soothe him, as, she now realised, his soothed her in return: the comfort of his body next to hers and the strength of his arms around her, the soft certain business of life, like the rhythm of his breath and the beat of his heart. And the now-familiar scent of their passion caught upon his skin. Without Gracewood the night seemed long and every shadow Amberglass.

Viola had fought before, of course, at Waterloo. But it had been very different. That had been war, a low and bloody matter of survival gilded with lies about glory. The French, despite their ferocity, had only been soldiers doing what soldiers do. When Amberglass had come for her, when he had lashed out and beaten her down, it had been—not cruel exactly, not even personal. He had simply taken for granted he had the right to hurt her. What business, after all, did a lady's companion or a young girl's chaperone or a duke's mistress have standing up to a man like Amberglass? A peer of the realm, even if he was a reprobate.

Indeed, had Gracewood not been there, she would in the end have been powerless. And not because Amberglass was stronger than she, or quicker, not because there was nothing anybody could truly do to fend off a drunken man with a death wish. She would have been powerless because society gave Amberglass and his kind the right to do what they would. Gracewood too, for that matter. Although he was kinder and wiser and was learning to use his power to raise rather than to ruin.

Still, it was a strange world, Viola reflected, that risked so much on the character of titled men. And that was not a thought to calm her mind, nor was the sting of the cut Amberglass had given her—though that, at least, would heal cleanly—or the memory of the desolation in his eyes as he had swung his sword at her, over and over and over again.

But she was safe. And Miranda was safe and Gracewood was safe. They were all safe. Most importantly, she had been at Gracewood's side, where she belonged, and Amberglass—who had only desperation, and hollow spite—had been unable to harm them.

Eventually, Viola drifted into a fitful doze, only to be awoken a mere handful of hours later by a rattling at her window. At first she dismissed it as a tree branch or a bird or a quirk of the house, but the noise persisted: a soft tap-tapping against the glass, too regular to be accidental. Rising, she did her best to make herself presentable and drew back the curtains.

Gracewood was standing in the garden beneath her, holding a handful of pebbles, which he had been casting at her window. He was fully dressed and looked far too awake for the hour, as well as oddly boyish, with mud on his boots and his hair lightly tousled by the wind, his face tilted up to her like that of a hopeful suitor.

"What are you doing?" she called to him.

He smiled—no grinned, his eyes shining like fresh-made sky. "Waking you up."

"Well, you've succeeded." She tried to sound severe, but in that moment, with last night's fears and uncertainties already slipping into the past, it was beyond her.

"Come down." He made a beckoning gesture. "I have something to show you."

"You cannot show me from where you are?"

He shook his head, somewhat exaggeratedly. "No. You can only see it from outside."

"And I suppose it cannot wait?"

Again, he shook his head.

Not that she would have made him wait—his excitement was too infectious, and she was too curious. Too happy, in all honesty, to indulge him, for he was not a man who often indulged himself. Though it also felt a little strange. She had always been the impulsive one, the adventure-seeker, the rule-breaker, and the whim-follower. But then she had also found what she had spent so many years looking for: the simple peace of being herself, and the hard-won freedom of it.

She dressed in haste, eschewing her gloves and adorning her throat only with a simple ribbon, and hurried to join Gracewood downstairs. He stilled her half-formed questions with a sweet, swift kiss. Then took her by the hand and led her almost solemnly through the gardens.

There was, as far as Viola could tell, nothing particularly special about them. They were pretty enough but had been allowed to grow a little rough, tangles of pink and white roses overspilling the geometric beds supposedly meant to contain them, the central fountain left stagnant, and slick with moss.

For a while, they wandered between the yew hedges and herbaceous borders, across emerald lawns and down gravel paths. Viola was still a little bewildered, but content enough to be with Gracewood. And this, too, she realised possessed a certain strangeness, for they were together, and neither at Morgencald nor in London. Of course, they had also spent time in France, and at Cambridge, and visiting the country estates of acquaintances, but this was different somehow. It felt like its own piece of elsewhere. A private world.

At last, they paused.

"What am I meant to be looking at?" asked Viola.

Gracewood, who had taken a moment to rest on his cane, made a sweeping gesture. "Everything."

So she looked at...everything, turning in a slow circle. Away from the roses and the fountain. To the little dell with its stone archways and the promise of cool green secrets. The apple avenue that separated the gardens from the park, a few shreds of blossom still clinging lace-like to the gracefully arching branches. Then the fields and woods beyond, and the dappling of wildflowers that pricked the horizon purple, yellow, and blue. The glassy shimmer of a medieval pond, ivy-shrouded and swept by chestnut trees. And back to the house again, which shone russet in that clear dawn with all the preening splendour of a wild fox.

"It's beautiful," she said. Because it was. The manor had not received the care it needed, but beneath the ivy and the neglect there was something good and strong and entirely itself.

Gracewood nodded. "I intend to buy it."

Whatever Viola had expected from this early-morning outing, this was certainly not it. "Buy it?"

"It will help Stirling clear his debts, and he has other holdings."

To Viola's mind, that was not a particularly compelling reason to do anything. "Might it not look like you are rewarding him for abducting your sister?"

"I did consider that," Gracewood admitted. "But taking an interest in the property will lend further credence to our visit, and protecting my family is more important than punishing my enemies. Besides, a little financial stability should put Stirling out of Amberglass's reach, and that makes all of us safer."

"But what will you *do* with Auclere?"

And now Gracewood turned his gaze upon her, his eyes still full of the day's first brightness. "We are going to live here."

"Live here?" she echoed. *"We?"*

"I begin to think," he said slowly, "we inhabit a world too defined by ideas of *this* or *that*. Morgencald is my duty, but it need not be my prison. And London may be convenient, but frankly it suits neither of us. I think we would do well in the country. In a place like this."

Viola took a sharp breath, and with the cold morning air, a rush of conflicting thoughts and feelings assailed her. In some ways, an offer like this was another step towards something like home. But what would it make her? What would it make them? "It is one thing to be your mistress in London, Gracewood. But to be your kept woman in some—"

"That"—he cut her off gently but surely—"is not what I'm asking, Viola."

Impossible. What he implied was impossible. "Gracewood, I—we can't."

And all at once a change came on him. Eight centuries of undisputed power settled over him like a mantle, but without the stony chill it usually carried with it. "In the last few days," he said, "you, my sister, and I have suffered at the hands of two men who will face no punishment for their actions."

"And you want to get your revenge by marrying me?" It seemed a peculiar and, frankly, unflattering line of reasoning.

"They will face no punishment," Gracewood went on, "because they are rich, and they are powerful, and the rich and powerful may do as they like." He paused for a moment. "Then so be it. I am richer and more powerful than any of them. If Viscount Stirling can abduct innocent debutantes and the Duke of Amberglass can start a fight in a brothel and have nobody say a word about it, then I'll be damned if I can't marry the woman I love."

"But the law," Viola protested.

"Need concern us no more than it concerned those who sought to harm us."

"And the church?"

"Is packed full of spineless old men who will jump at the chance to do a favour for a duke."

Viola's mind was still full of objections and impediments, but Gracewood seemed determined to brush them aside like so many matchsticks. "What of society?"

He shrugged. "What of it? The matrons and masters of the ton have nothing we want, while the things that *they* want—wealth and power and influence and pedigree—I already possess in abundance. It is for *them* to live up to *our* standards. Not the contrary."

This was absurd. It was a fantasy. Surely, that was all it could be. "And what of your line?" asked Viola with the harsh conviction of a judge handing down sentence of death. "Will you be the last de Vere at Morgencald?"

"For you," Gracewood said at once, "I would, and I would not regret it for a heartbeat. It is only habit and fear that made me believe otherwise. Let Miranda's children take it, if she chooses to have them. Let it go to some distant cousin who did no less to earn the place than I did. But I would far rather leave it to our children."

And now absurd was becoming cruel. "Gracewood, there are some things beyond even—"

"There are," he agreed. "And if the only child you would consider yours is one that shares your blood, then...then I am content to leave the estate to Mira. But for myself—well—what good has my father's blood ever done me? England is full of children in dire need of mothers and fathers, and while I do not flatter myself that we would be *ideal* parents, I do not think we would be so very terrible. And wealth, you know, covers a multitude of sins."

For a moment, Viola was silent. That Gracewood could bend the world to his will, she had no doubt. That he would do it for her—for nothing but her—seemed almost beyond imagining. As Viola Carroll she had little, and everything she had, she had fought for, bled for, gone to war for. And here was her oldest friend offering her...everything. Surely it could not be so simple. There had to be a reason to say no. To say that he asked too much, that he moved too fast, that this—all this—could not possibly or rightfully be hers.

"Well?" Gracewood's composure, Viola could see, was cracking just a little. "Have you no answer for me?"

"I..." she began, still not sure how she would end. Then "If I..."

She shut her eyes. Somewhere in the grounds, two birds were singing back and forth to one another and she let her thoughts drift away on the nonsense of their melody. Her memories too, in that moment, were a kind of nonsense. Emotion stripped of meaning. Crossing a classroom to an ice-eyed, stern-mouthed boy: *I hear you're a godawful prig, is it intentional?* A moment of clarity within the haze of convalescence: *perhaps in death, I may find myself at last.* The echo of a gunshot against stone walls. A mouth not quite pressed to hers upon a wind-scoured beach. A private waltz with its own steps. Bodies that learned each other in the dark and in the light. Laid out like this, she could barely distinguish the choice from the happenstance in the tumult of her life. But when it mattered the choices had always been there. And she had always made them. She had dared—in the face of the world itself—to choose Gracewood. To choose herself. And now she would choose again. She would choose both of them.

"If you will forgive me the vanity," she said, "you haven't strictly asked me anything."

He gave her a haughty look. Not a very convincing haughty look, for it was mostly full of love. "You are impossible."

"You have suggested so many impossible things this morning, I thought it only fitting."

"Very well." He frowned. "But I fear my leg will not take kneeling. Viola Carroll, will you do me the honour of marrying me?"

She didn't know why she hesitated. For once, it wasn't to make sport of him. It was just so vast and consuming a question that to answer at once seemed almost disrespectful. More than that, it seemed a waste, to rush past the moment when she could savour it, cling to it, and watch the details of her future come together like a pattern beneath her needle. "And we will live in this house?" she asked, letting herself imagine how Auclere would look in the summer, in the autumn, a year from now or ten.

"Yes," Gracewood told her.

"And at Morgencald?" And what might they make of that dark, foreboding place together if they dared? If they filled its grey halls with light and chased the last ghosts from its chambers.

"Yes."

That alone would have been enough. More than enough. It would have been a wonderful life. "And have children?"

Gracewood did not hesitate. "Yes."

"And this is what you want? With me? For every day and year that comes?"

"Yes." He drew back slightly, but only to kiss her. Close-lipped and tender, soul to soul. "I love you. I have, in some form, for as long as I've known you. You are my joy and my truth and my heart and my dreams. You are the best of me."

At this she could only smile. "You've always been wrong about that, Gracewood."

"Oh?"

"Yes." She nodded. "We are the best of each other."

They stood together then, arms around each other, a chorus of birdsong breaking through the early-morning air. "Viola," Gracewood whispered, "you know you still haven't answered me."

Hadn't she? She'd almost forgotten. She felt like she'd been saying it always. "Yes." It was the only answer that existed for her. "Yes, and yes, and yes forever. You know—of course. Yes."

He kissed her again, the fresh-risen sun casting off the last vestiges of its nightly reticence to paint the world behind her eyes in shades of endless and impossible gold.

# EPILOGUE

He had gone to the Long Gallery, to look at the pictures of the men. Men who looked like each other. Like his father. But not very much like him.

There was only one of his father, which he half recognised, half didn't. Might not have believed *was* his father without the name plaque beneath to prove it.

*Justinian de Vere 1804.*

Because obviously his father had been young once. Had walked without a cane. Had been smooth-faced and golden-haired like a prince from a fairy tale. It just *felt* strange to think about it.

A time when his father hadn't been his father. Had been someone else.

Someone who looked sad, somehow. Even with painted eyes.

"Jack?" His father's voice. The familiar tippity-tap of his cane. And there he was in person, almost like he'd stepped down from one of the portraits.

"Oh, here you are," he said. "What on earth are you doing?"

Jack shrugged. "Just looking."

"Not much to see here. Rather a lot of terrible people, preserved for posterity." His father had a way about him—something to do with his eyes or the shape of his mouth—that made you think he might be laughing or about to laugh. As if the world was full of jokes only he knew were there. Which made no sense, because nobody laughed at his actual jokes except Mother, and Eliza said that was probably out of pity.

"Will I be here?" asked Jack.

"If you want to be, Jackscallion."

"But…" And here he paused, struggling with a thought that seemed both new and to have lived inside him for a long time. As long as the memories. The other memories that came upon him like dreams: dreams of cold and darkness.

His father's hand came down lightly upon his shoulder. "What's the matter?"

"You're not…" began Jack carefully, because even the words made him fearful. Sat heavy in his mouth like marbles. But, somehow, not saying them was worse. "You're not my real father, are you?"

Except now he wished he hadn't spoken at all. Because he didn't know how his father was going to react. He wouldn't get angry—he never got angry, not even when Eliza broke four windows in the orangery at Auclere—but maybe Jack would have disappointed him. Broken something worse than the windows in the orangery.

His father's hand was still on his shoulder. And Jack, risking an upwards glance, found his face much as it ever was. Perhaps a bit more serious. But not shocked or sad. "Do I feel like your real father?"

"How would I know?" It came out slightly stubborn, like when Jack knew he should be doing something that was good for him—eating broccoli, washing behind his ears, or geometry—but didn't want to do it. Not that this was something to be stubborn over. The problem was, he couldn't work out how not to be.

"That's a good question," his father said at last. "Does it make a difference, that you feel like my son?"

"Am I your son, though?"

"Because your mother and I did not make you with our bodies?"

This was something else about his father: He was never afraid to *say* things. Even if they were scary. Or the sort of things other people thought shouldn't be said. "Maybe?"

"I think"—his father had the look on his face that would make Eliza groan and attempt to flee the room in fear of a lecture— "there's something a little presumptive in the notion of *making* another human being. But leaving that aside, and taking as read you are a person in your own right, have we not made you with our hearts? As you have, in turn, made us?"

Jack looked again at the faces of the men in the portraits. Cold and handsome and sure of themselves. When he was smaller than small. And he didn't know if his father was right. If he could have made anything. "I have?"

"All my life, I've longed for family, Jack." His father too was looking at the portraits. "I mean, true family. Not these repro- bates, who cared only for their own power. Well, perhaps not Constantius. He believed he was a duck."

That surprised a giggle from Jack. "Really."

"Really. But he was a duke, so it didn't matter. Or rather, it probably mattered quite a lot, and everyone pretended it didn't."

Jack thought about this for a moment. "Is that why it doesn't matter about me? Because you're a duke?"

"Oh," said his father, with one of his most confusing smiles, "I think that would make it matter quite a lot more to quite a lot of people. Though they are quite, quite spectacularly wrong. It doesn't matter, Jack, because you're my son and I love you."

His father said this a lot. The second part, anyway. Sometimes Jack deliberately didn't say it back, just to prove to himself—to whatever imp needed such things—that his father would keep saying it. He always did. But this was still a not-saying-it-back day.

"I'm terribly aware," his father went on, "that I am, in many ways, the most fortunate of men. To say that when I grew up this"—he gestured around them—"was all I had sounds beyond absurd. Wealth, comfort, a great name, a great house, an assured future. It was, however, all I had. And all I was."

It was hard for Jack to imagine: Morgencald without Mother laughing, without Eliza to argue with, without Rory to cause trouble. Without Aunt Mira and her stories. Without Auntie Lou and Uncle Badger. And Little Bartholomew, who was strange and dreamy and not little at all. Without Father. "What about your father?"

"He was…" His father hesitated. "He was born to power. Which made him who he was."

"So were you."

"Yes, but I had your mother. And now I have you, and Eliza, and Rory as well, and I cannot tell you how happy that makes me. How complete, and replete, my life feels now. Compared to what it was. And what I used to think it had to be."

"What about me?"

"What about you?"

Jack stuffed his hands into his pockets. "Am I to be a duke one day?"

"One day. When you have travelled and danced and fallen in love and done all the things you want to do. For you know I will have to die in order for you to become a duke."

"Father." It was meant to sound stern. But instead came out as a sad little sheep noise.

"I have no intention of dying, Jack."

"Is it up to you?" he asked, scowling.

But his father only smiled, twirled his cane, and said, "Yes." Then he smiled again. "Or more likely, up to your mother. And I don't think she'd stand for me dying."

"You could still die." Jack was feeling stubborn again.

"I'm taking this as concern for my well-being, as opposed to commentary on my decrepitude. I'm not so very old. Nor, for that matter, so very infirm."

He was not. In his way, Father was as strong as Morgencald. Jack just didn't like the idea that there was anything in the world beyond his father's control—or his soothing. "What if I cannot be a duke?" he blurted out. "Look..." He pointed to the portraits in turn. "Justinian. Tiberius. Maximus. Tiberius. Constantius. Justinian." Then at himself. "Jack. I'm not like them."

"No, darling." His father put his free arm about him. "You're better."

"How do you *know*?"

"Because I know you. And"—his father's eyes did their laughing thing—"at the very least, you do not believe you're a duck."

Jack was silent. Then offered a very solemn "Quack."

And his father laughed in such earnest it echoed all through the room.

"Didn't you want me to be an ius or inian?" Jack asked, after a moment or two.

"It didn't come up. You were already a Jack."

"But I could have been?"

"Maybe. It would have been taking something from you,

though." His father gave him a squeeze. "Shall we go find your mother? We had a letter from Louise, and she'll want to read it."

"Auntie Lou? What does she say?"

Already the faces in the Long Gallery were fading. They had felt so important an hour ago. And now they were just pictures again. Pictures of people who didn't matter.

"Well, you mustn't spoil the surprise for everyone else."

Jack tried hard to be trustworthy—not like Rory, who couldn't keep a secret to save his life—but he always loved it when his father confided in him. "I *promise*."

"They're going to visit before Christmas. Louise, and Badger, and Little Bartholomew."

"What about Auntie Mira?"

"The last I heard, she was in Rodosto. I do not think we will see her until the new year."

"Oh."

"She'll be here before you know it, Jackscallion."

Which wasn't, strictly speaking, true. Because Jack kept track of these things. But he also knew it would be worth it when Auntie Mira did turn up—sweeping in like the west wind, full of adventure.

They met Mother coming back from the beach with Eliza and Rory, all of them red-cheeked and tousled. Eliza's skirts were sodden with saltwater because she'd fallen into a rockpool. And Rory had been bitten by a crab, so he was now insisting he was a crab, and trying to pincer Jack. But only because he couldn't pincer Father because Father was too busy kissing Mother. Which all three of them were, for once, united in protesting. Not that it ever did much good. Father *would* persist in kissing Mother. And Mother would persist in kissing Father. And Jack hoped he wasn't going to fall in love someday, because he wasn't sure he wanted to spend that much time on kissing. It would have to get boring at some point, wouldn't it? On top of which Eliza had told him some other things that people did when they were married. And he definitely didn't want to do those.

"Mother said," Rory began, having successfully pulled her—laughing and complaining—away from Father, "that when she and Father were young they once jumped off the cliffs here."

"Which you absolutely must not emulate." It was Mother's stern voice. And she was rarely stern, so you knew you had to listen when she was. "At least, not until you're older. But for now I will have no dead children in my household."

"What does *emulate* mean?" asked Eliza, without much interest. In Jack's opinion, she liked asking why more than she liked knowing the answer.

"Copy," he told her. "From the Latin, aem—"

"I could be dead now," said Rory. "I could be a ghost."

Father gave him the look that Jack thought of as his Rory Look. "Aren't you a crab?"

"I could be a ghost crab."

Eliza, her hair un-ribboned and horrendously snarled, was already roving towards the edge of the cliff. "How old were you?"

"Oh God." Mother pressed her face against Father's shoulder. "About Jack's age, I think?"

"So Jack can jump, then?"

"Jack cannot jump." Mother's stern voice was back. "What did I say about dead children?"

"I must agree with your mother," said Father. Which was not surprising. He agreed with Mother about almost everything. "I am strongly opposed to dead children."

"You're not dead," pointed out Eliza.

Mother's brows had gone all arched and teasing. "Your powers of observation are second to none."

Eliza was staring out across the sea, which looked very big and very grey. "What was it like?"

"Cold," offered Father. "It was cold."

Mother smiled. "And boring."

"That's a lie." Eliza plonked her hands on her hips. "You're telling lies so we won't do it."

"You shouldn't do it"—Father's stern voice, though it was way less stern than Mother's—"because we've told you not to."

"Can I do it when I'm Jack's age? Please? Pleeeeeease? Please-please-please."

Mother and Father exchanged a series of swift glances, which they probably thought their children hadn't noticed. Which was very silly because they did it all the time. Talking without words.

"All right." Mother made a gesture of surrender. As people often did around Eliza. "When you're Jack's age. And only on a clear day. And only when I'm with you. Actually, only when we're all with you. Do we have a deal?"

They had a deal and shook on it, making it the most important kind of deal. The kind you could never break or try to bypass. That not even Rory would go back on.

"Shall we go inside?" suggested Father. "I have news from—"

But Eliza had been thinking. "Jack's Jack's age. Jack, you should jump off the cliff."

Jack did not want to jump off the cliff. "I don't want to jump off the cliff."

"Why not?" Eliza seemed genuinely confused.

"Well, because I'll fall into the sea from high up."

"But"—Eliza's eyes got big—"that's why it's fun."

Mother beckoned her over. "That's enough. Jack gets to decide when, or if, he jumps off cliffs."

"Did you jump as well?" Jack turned to Father.

"Yes. But it was a long time ago. And I couldn't do it now." He tapped his boot with his cane. His leg had been hurt in the war, Jack knew, but he moved so effortlessly, his cane seemed so much a part of him, it was easy to forget. "And, to be honest, I probably only did it at the time to impress your mother."

Mother blushed. "Really?"

"Did it work?"

They were gazing at each other.

Rory glared at them. "You'd better not start kissing again."

"I did marry you," said Mother. "So yes? On a very long timescale."

"Why did you think jumping off a cliff would impress Mother?" asked Eliza.

"Well"—his father had that laughing look—"because I was very young and very foolish and didn't have any idea what I was doing. But I think I also wanted to feel free as she was."

"I'll do it," said Jack, out of nowhere. "I'll jump."

His mother's eyes were too knowing. "Jack, you don't have to. And you shouldn't feel you have to. And Eliza will probably have forgotten all about it in, oh, I would bet three days?"

Eliza made an outraged noise. "I bet I will not."

"Nobody," his mother went on, "needs to jump off any cliffs for me. I'm impressed with all of you, just as you are."

Rory, hopping in order to pour sand from his boot, looked up and then fell over. "You're not impressed with me. Yesterday you said I was a giddy kipper."

"To an impressive degree," returned Mother calmly, "of giddy kipperness."

Father was nodding. "Also, Rory, you *are* a giddy kipper."

Now Jack was standing where Eliza had stood, although perhaps not as close to the edge of the cliff. Because getting too close made his stomach swoop like a seagull. The wind felt stronger and colder here, and got its fingers into his hair, and he could taste the salt on it. There was nothing to see except the sea and the sky and the long drop at his feet.

Then his mother's arms were around him. "That cliff isn't going anywhere, Jack. If you really want to jump off it, we can come back any day, any time."

The strangest thing was that, while he didn't, he also did. Because he knew he wanted to be like Father. To think as much as he did and always know what to say somehow. But he also wanted to feel like Mother did. To be less afraid of things that he didn't have to be afraid of. And to believe more easily that he didn't have to be afraid of them. Of course, now he knew for sure he wasn't *really* like either of them. Except in the ways he chose to be.

"Will you jump with me?" he asked.

His mother glanced at the sky, then the sea, then at her dress, which had big puffy sleeves and lots of strawberries printed on it. Jack didn't know much about dresses, but he knew Mother liked them a lot and wouldn't want to ruin this one by jumping in the sea. And he was about to tell her it didn't matter, he'd changed his mind, when she nodded. "On three?"

His ears roared as if he'd already jumped. He nodded back.

"One," said Mother.

His lips were dry. The waves rose up into little curls below, the crests frothy and white like someone had poured milk over them. "Two."

"Jump if you want. Remember, you don't have to." Mother hugged him tight. "Three."

Then she ran. And leapt. Arms spread wide like a bird. Her hair spreading black and silver over the empty air. And her laughter caught up on the wind like one of her embroidery threads in a colour that was just her.

And then Jack, too, had run. Jumped. Let the nothing of the horizon catch him.

Until everything was sea and sky, and the falling was flying, and he realised he was laughing too.

# ACKNOWLEDGMENTS

My sincere gratitude to the Forever team, especially my ever-patient editor, Amy Pierpont. No book I've written would be possible without the dedication and support of my agent, Courtney Miller-Callihan. And without my assistant, Mary, I would be a wreck. So, thank you both.

# READING GROUP GUIDE

# A Letter from the Author

Dear Reader,

Thank you so much for taking the time to read *A Lady for a Duke*. I hope you enjoyed it, especially if you're reading it as part of a book club and somebody else picked it for you. Or perhaps even more especially, if you're the one who picked it. If you did, I really hope you think you made a good choice, and that you aren't going to have to go back to your friends next week and say, "Sorry, he's usually better than this."

Something I always say in these reading group introductions is that after this letter, you're going to read some questions-for-discussion that I've been asked to provide. Which makes me uncomfortable, because I'm a huge proponent of the Death of the Author and so I really don't, on a fundamental level, think it's my place to be telling people what they should be thinking about when they read my books, or what questions they should be asking themselves.

There's an added layer of complexity here because one of my goals in writing *A Lady for a Duke* was to write a historical romance with a transgender heroine in which the fact that the heroine is transgender is not the main source of conflict or narrative tension. And I feel I'd rather undermine that if I wrote a lot of discussion questions about the fact that the book has a transgender heroine, but on the other hand it would be disingenuous to pretend it's not something people are going to want to discuss at all.

So, please see below for a set of discussion questions in which I will try and fail to square that particular circle while also permitting readers the freedom to interpret the text however they wish. And, as ever, please feel free to ignore me. I've been dead since 1967.

*Lots of love,*
*Alexis Hall*

# QUESTIONS FOR DISCUSSION

1. Let's start with the question I flirted with in the introductory letter (if you've not read it, flip back, it should just be on the last page). My intent for this book was for the fact that Viola is transgender not to be the main source of conflict. Was that intent successful? If not, why? If so, what *is* the main source of conflict?

2. Coming back from the grave to discuss my own question: you could reasonably answer question one (and as ever, that answer would only be one possible interpretation) with the suggestion that a lot of the conflict is grounded in *gender roles and gendered expectations*. And while the fact that Viola lives in a highly gendered society reflects on her trans identity, it is also ultimately independent of it. What ways do *other* characters in the book interact with gender in their society?

3. How do you think the Cascade at Vauxhall Gardens actually worked?

4. What is historical fiction even for? And I appreciate that's a broad question, so here's some context. Both Viola and Gracewood are dealing with issues that the society in which

they lived would have had no language to discuss or, arguably, way of thinking about. Viola is transgender at a time when "transgender" isn't a term anybody would use or understand. Gracewood has PTSD at a time when PTSD was just called "cowardice." Why is there value in exploring those ideas through characters who wouldn't have understood them? *Is* there value in it?

5.  What is historical fiction even for (part 2)? There's often resistance among fans of historical fiction (including historical romances and in some cases even including fantasy) to writing stories about LGBTQ+ people that don't just consist of wall-to-wall bigotry and misery, on the basis that it's "historically inaccurate." So, two questions here, really: Firstly, *is it*, in fact, historically inaccurate? Secondly, *does it matter*? Is the purpose of historical fiction only ever to imagine historical societies as they were (or as we are in the habit of imagining that they were)?

6.  How obvious is it that Amberglass is sequel-bait? How okay with that were you?

7.  Sequel-bait question part 2: You might have noticed that Viola is named after the heroine of a Shakespeare play about identity and falling in love with a man who thinks you're a boy when you're really a girl. You might also have noticed that several other characters are named after Shakespeare heroines as well. If these characters *were* to get their own books (as ever, I can make no promises), what would they be about, and which would you be most interested in reading?

8. Many of the characters in *A Lady for a Duke* speak in an idiom that reads slightly more "modern" than some readers may be used to. Which characters in particular? What effect does this have on the way those characters come across? Relatedly, are phrases that read as "modern" to us always actually "modern" at all?

9. If you were going to go to a Regency costume party, which monster would you be dressed as? Why?

10. Although much of Gracewood's baggage comes from Waterloo, much more of it comes from his father. How is Gracewood's personality shaped by his father? If part of it is that he has reacted *against* his father's teachings, does that, paradoxically, mean that the old duke's cruelties actually did make Gracewood a better person? Does this justify them?

11. Miss Avon betrays Miranda in a way that is not only hurtful but puts her in real danger and at risk of an actual forced marriage (which, let us be clear, is a form of sexual assault). Is she entirely to blame for her role in it? Or is it all on Amberglass? Or is she, or are they both, just living out the only roles they can in an unjust society? Or does blaming society deny Miss Avon her own agency and ignore the other young ladies who *don't* stoop to having their rivals abducted?

12. As a strong proponent of the Death of the Author, I sincerely believe that any interpretation of a text is valid, as long as it can be justified by reference to that text. So, what's

the wackiest, most out-there reading of the book you can reasonably support? Are there indications that it's all taking place in a holographic simulation in the future? Is it all really an allegory for the journey of Osiris through the underworld? You have as much authority here as I do: go wild.

# About the Author

**Alexis Hall** lives in a crumbling gothic manor that he inherited in mysterious circumstances. He is a genial host provided you swear that you will under no circumstances venture into the west wing.